THE SOCORRO BLAST

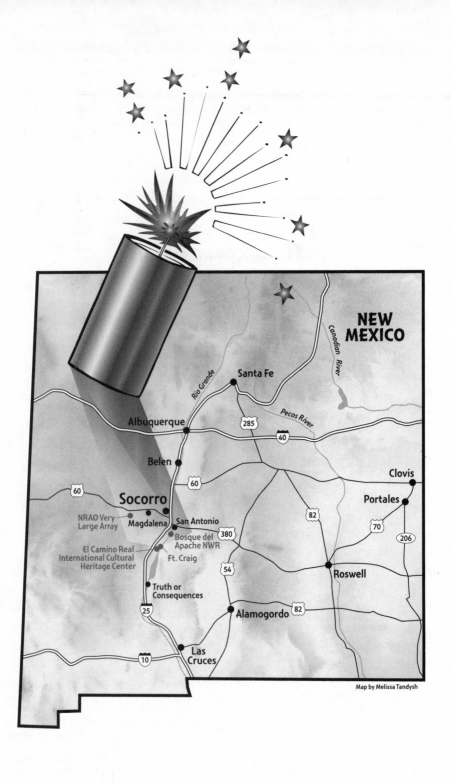

NEW MEXICO

Canadian River

Rio Grande

Santa Fe

Pecos River

285

40

Albuquerque

Belen

Clovis

60

60

Portales

Socorro

82

NRAO Very
Large Array

Magdalena

San Antonio

380

70

206

Bosque del
Apache NWR

El Camino Real
International Cultural
Heritage Center

Ft. Craig

54

Roswell

Truth or
Consequences

25

Alamogordo

82

Las
Cruces

10

The Socorro

A
Sasha Solomon
Mystery

Blast

To Marie

Pari Noskin Taichert

Pari N. Taichert

UNIVERSITY OF NEW MEXICO PRESS   ALBUQUERQUE

This is a work of fiction.

The events described herein are imaginary; the characters are entirely fictitious and are not intended to represent actual living persons. While many of the locales are real, they too are used fictitiously.

---

13 12 11 10 09 08   1 2 3 4 5 6

Library of Congress Cataloging-in-Publication Data

Taichert, Pari Noskin, 1958–

The Socorro blast : a Sasha Solomon mystery / Pari Noskin Taichert.

    p. cm.

ISBN 978-0-8263-4384-0 (cloth : alk. paper)

1. Women public relations personnel—Fiction. 2. Murder—Investigation—Fiction.
3. Socorro (N.M.)—Fiction. 4. Religious tolerance—New Mexico—Fiction.
5. New Mexico—Ethnic relations—Fiction. I. Title.

PS3620.A35S63 2008

813'.6—dc22

                    2007036547

Book design and type composition by Melissa Tandysh

Composed in 11.25/14.5 Minion Pro   ⸴   Display type is Montara Bold Gothic

Printed on 50# Natures Natural

To everyone who works against ethnic and religious prejudice.
To everyone who works toward *Tikkun Olam*.

Thank you.

"Bada-bing . . . bada-boom."
—Darnda Jones

1

If **hell exists,** it's filled with old boyfriends . . . and a cat.

I added another bandage to the three bloody lines of mismatched adhesives now adorning my right forearm. Shocked from a sound sleep, Leo da Cat had inflicted the scratches in retaliation for my abrupt waking from yet another nightmare about hitherto heartthrobs including unremembered heroes like the guy with the baking-soda white hair and new-grass green eyes, or the one with the banana-soft face and lips the size of plump tomato worms.

For the past two weeks, every bad relationship—from high school through yesterday—had shimmied into position, vying for the privilege of torturing me the minute my eyelids kissed. Alas, though too experienced in the game of love, I'd never won or learned how to lose with grace.

Failed liaisons littered my life like spring pollen on a windy day. My anaphylactic reactions of anger didn't help. Slammed doors, defaced conference tables, anonymous phone calls to police stations in the middle of the night—well, let's just say love hath no fury greater than a girlfriend wronged. Or one who perceives she's been wronged. Or one who gets tired of somebody's whining. . . .

Though Hades charred my blameworthy subconscious with visions of Herbies, Sams, and Mikes past, the true instigator of this current inferno was a certain Peter O'Neill, director of New Mexico's Poison Control Center. Peter O'Neill. He of the Baikal-blue eyes and *mole-brown* hair. He who'd informed me a fortnight ago about his impending move to Maryland to take a new job. The premonition our relationship wouldn't last must've nibbled on some level because I'd never given him a key to my place. Still, this was the first decent lovership in my life and it would end before I could even ruin it.

A glance in the bathroom mirror made me sigh. Puffy bags under my eyes smudged charcoal dull. Minute capillaries around my nose had begun to pop, leaving maps in my skin of places usually accessible only to mountain climbers. It didn't help that I'd gained five pounds eating chocolate since Peter's revelation.

Exasperated, demoralized, and feeling yucky, I went back to sleep, dreaming of hands, my hands, clasping a screwdriver and stabbing thirteen holes in an ex-boyfriend's waterbed.

The phone rang, robbing me of the remembered satisfaction of his surprise. Without turning on the light, I mumbled an annoyed greeting.

"Sasha, what's happened?" Darnda's concern slid under my skin. She'd been my closest friend for years and had a knack for sensing disaster. That, combined with the fact that she'd recently become a major client, kept me from hanging up.

"It's two a.m. That's what happened." Sure, my response could have been a tad more cordial, but she'd disturbed the first good dream in days.

"No. I mean it. *What's* happened?"

"How the hell do I know, Darnda? It's still dark out." Leo dug his claws into my thigh. They made a ripping sound when yanked from the flannel. Dumped on the floor with an unceremonious thud, he flicked his tail at me and walked out of the room. "Maybe you're picking up on someone else."

"No, it's definitely you." She cleared her throat two times, ending with a small cough. That sound meant trouble. It ferried a black shiver from the untreated roots on my head to my unclipped toenails. "It's bad, Sasha, really bad."

Did I mention that Darnda is psychic? Her hunches and visions twanged with bull's-eye accuracy. Mine, on the other hand, shot past every target like malfunctioning missiles.

Well, upcoming doom wouldn't fit into my schedule today. An eighteen-wheeler full of work was parked in my office, demanding attention before I hit the road for tomorrow's public relations consulting job in Socorro. If the weathermen were wrong, and it *didn't* snow, first thing Tuesday morning I'd grin-and-skin with a passel of tourist industry bigwigs at a super-planning meeting. Hundreds of miles awaited my analysis and masterminding to bring beaucoup bucks to one of New Mexico's most interesting counties.

On top of work, my youngest niece, Gabriela, aka *Gabi*, had invited me to spend the weekend with her. It'd be fun to hang out with a twenty-one-year-old grad student for a couple of days, to see the world through fresh eyes again. And maybe I'd shed the dusty remorse that clung to my everyday life. If guilt about former boyfriends etched creeks into my subconscious, the gunk flowed in wide corrosive rivers through my waking hours when it came to family. The vestiges of Mom's numerous strokes and acidic demeanor served as potent repellents, though she lived only miles from my house. My sister's latest phone calls had gone unanswered and I'd rationalized missed birthday presents to her four children in terms of my busy, busy schedule and flimsy, floppy budget.

Accepting Gabi's invitation would assuage my shame at being such a lousy daughter, sister, and aunt. Plus, I liked Gabi. Of all of my nieces, she showed the most gumption and independent spirit. Want to know my favorite story about her? At seven, she'd blown up her oldest sister's birthday cake with a junior chemistry set she'd gotten for Chanukah. Eva, *my* sister, screamed; I couldn't stop laughing when she told me.

"Sasha? Are you still there?" Darnda's voice glided on Indian flute music, but the calming strains only served to jar my sleep-deprived nerves.

"Yes, but I don't want to be."

"Promise you'll call later this morning."

"Right," I said, already flirting with the next dream cycle. An image of Jim, the chipmunk-faced boy who took me to the prom, squiggled through my REM stage. The class bell rang in the middle of the dance. He tried to kiss me and . . . Why did the bell keep ringing?

I emerged from the dream and answered the phone, all of my irritation sluicing out in a single word. "What?"

"Ms. Solomon?" The man's New Mexican accent had been suckled on the smooth undulations of Spanish before cutting its teeth on the rough edges of English.

"Yes?" Monosyllabic responses prevented longer rants and wasted energy.

"This is Detective Sanchez from the Socorro Police Department. I'm sorry to disturb you so early."

I turned on the light, moved out of the bed. "It's no problem."

Policemen never called me for fun. With dread replacing my warm blankets, I walked into the kitchen. Wafts of winter air scurried under the uncaulked wooden door and my feet protested on the freezing brick floor. I cinched the fraying belt on my ratty robe tighter and opened the fridge to examine a half-eaten cinnamon roll. Heated, to melt the frosting, and topped with a coat of whipped cream, it might provide comfort. I had the pastry in the microwave before the person on the other end spoke again.

"Gabriela Shofet asked me to call you."

"Gabi? What's happened to Gabi?" I nearly stepped on Leo. He hissed and swatted at my leg. Feeling for a chair, I sat down. My finger pressed the whipped cream nozzle, dousing the roll in yards of sweetness. Leo leapt up to inspect my breakfast and stuck a paw in all that white. I batted him away. He didn't get the message until an elbow shoved him off the table.

"There's been an accident."

Gabi hurt? I didn't know she even owned a car. "Oh my God. Where is she?"

"At the hospital. They're still checking her out, but she's conscious now." He paused. I heard voices in the background but couldn't make out the words. "Your niece asked if you could come down today. Apparently her mother is unavailable?"

"Eva's in Europe." Darnda had been spot-on! *Ohmigod.* "Tell me what happened." My imagination flared with a vivid picture of my lovely niece smashed up in a twisted, bent mass of metal and glass. "Never mind. You can explain later. I'm on my way."

4

2

The bite of sweet roll fought back, lumping in my throat. A second gulp of water forced it down again. *Poor Gabi.* She'd only been in New Mexico for four months.

Auto accidents always reminded me of my impermanence, an empty-stomach feeling of lonely helplessness. Everything could change with an unheeded stop sign or a faulty brake. To have an accident when you're alone, your parents and siblings far away, that was the pits. Gabi needed family. Even so, even though I might regret it, I opted not to call Eva until after seeing her daughter in the hospital myself. Mom's frequent strokes, along with my professional experience, had trained me to be cautious. A transatlantic phone conversation with meager information could worsen a bad situation. My sister would grill me for details; without seeing my niece, the answers wouldn't satisfy.

The sigh that singed my lips held resignation. I'd have to pack, get everything together for my trip to Socorro a day early. No problem there. Could we cancel the meeting? Impossible. It included too many people who'd stylused the appointment into their Blackberries. Well, I'd deal with that tomorrow.

Oh, Gabi. I pictured her towering over me, tall, strong, and cocky with the arrogant intelligence of someone who knows she owns the world. The last time we'd seen each other, she'd exuded invincibility, an adolescent about to soar off a high mesa with the absolute confidence that she'd rise on the thermals. The idea of her injured, lying in a hospital bed with tubes coming out of her arms and gauze coating her injuries, made me want to cry.

I sank to the floor, and did.

Minutes later, I mopped myself up and went into the bathroom. A quick shower was nonnegotiable. Dirt from four indulgent days of sulking needed to be rapidly bullied from under arms and behind knees. When Peter had told me about his upcoming move, I'd reacted with typical maturity by banishing him from my sight. He'd called several times since and had finally sledgehammered through my wall of hurt. Tonight, we'd planned a big reconciliation abetted by sushi, dancing, and sex. Lots of sex. I sighed again.

Steam clouded the curtain and I stepped in to face the showerhead. Lack of sleep, coupled with the fact that my forty-first birthday loomed at the end of the week, befouled my mood further. Minutes later, I struggled into velour burgundy pants that had become tighter somehow. A black chenille sweater over a white blouse would spar the season's iciness. Then, on to the makeup. My fingers messed with the foundation, my haste lobbing drops of it everywhere including the sink, the mirror, my clothes. I'd always spurned the stuff until, at forty, my skin sprang new spots each day. The greasy concealment buoyed my denial.

Gabi didn't need makeup. High cheekbones set under almond-shaped eyes, flawless skin the color of warm sand. Ah, damn it. My fingers slipped again, and a slash of oily brown now adorned my collar. Efforts to clean the blouse made everything worse. I almost gave up right then but forced myself to go back into the bedroom to switch tops.

With the skill of a retired NBA pro, I threw the bottles and containers of my newfound age-spackle into an overnight bag along with a wad of clothes. In the office, also known as the living room, clutter reflected my peripatetic mind. Leo provided a moment's welcome distraction when he regarded me from atop the refurbished armoire that served as my bar and entertainment center. I popped my tongue three times against the roof of my mouth, called his name, and held out my hands. He blinked once and then with an act of faith that still astounded me, he leapt into my arms.

"Good kitty. Smart kitty." I retrieved a small handful of raisins from a pocket.

Leo adored dried fruit. Peter's good influence had brought trail mix into the house. One morning, after leaving out a bowl of the stuff the night before, I caught the cat red-pawed, digging past the oats and flax to get at the mangos, cranberries, and raisins.

Right now, my feline purred with each sweet morsel held to his mouth and I looked for a sign that he might talk once again to me. This wasn't the cutesy fantasy of a feline fanatic. We actually had conversations. Fortunately, a good doctor of oriental medicine had squashed the visions with tarry black pills, repugnant herbal teas, and acupuncture treatments. Our former tête-à-têtes, the unpredictable byproducts of a stress-induced mental imbalance, hadn't hurt anyone, though. Darnda even claimed they heralded my psychic development. To tell the truth, I missed them.

When the reward was gone, Leo pushed himself out of my embrace, leaving enough fur to make a pillow. With several clumsy swats at the fluff and a last attempt to straighten my coat, I filled his water and food bowls and then commanded him to guard the house. The door's creak could've awakened Rip Van Winkle.

Outside, a single star battled the yellow haze from my porch light. To the east, dawn was merely a wish. My navy blue Subaru gloated in the driveway; I'd traded in my Tercel for this beauty, a roadworthy partner in my travels around the state. Though cold in this early morning moment, it started with the first turn of the key. My tires crunched on the driveway's graveled surface. I turned right at the end of my block and onto Fourth Street. Its traffic lights blinked with only my car to obey their orders.

On the freeway, billboards flashed by, their messages too cheery to register in my flustered heart. Skid marks from past accidents formed an odd asphalt calligraphy that looked wild in the manufactured light of the tall, lifeless, steel lamps. Just beyond the city limits, night clung to the land with the fervor of a frightened child. I zipped by a notice saying "Speed monitored by aircraft."

"Oh, I'm *so* scared," I said, taunting the universe. It'd be easy to see planes in this vacant sky. My foot sunk heavier on the gas pedal, pushing me ever more quickly south to Socorro.

What would I find at the hospital? Would Gabi be conscious? In surgery? The last of four daughters, Gabi had inherited both of her parents' brainpower. That wasn't always such a good thing. From the moment she'd emerged into the world, she'd been a gutsy fighter who questioned every authority figure, from father to rabbi, who dared assert dominance. You can just imagine how well this went over in my sister's rule-bound, conservative Jewish household. I mean, Eva even wore a wig in public and insisted her daughters dress like they belonged in a different era, circa 1917, when our grandmothers wrapped their meager shawls around their shoulders and kissed American soil for the first time.

I just didn't get it. Well, maybe Gabi had decided to shed those fetters now that she was on her own. I'd see soon enough.

My lack of coffee now asserted itself with a floating sort of drowsiness. I opened the car window. The frigid blast entered my full-mouthed, loose-jawed yawn and made my fillings ache. This recent insomnia couldn't go on. Boyfriends be damned; I needed sleep.

Damn Peter, too. A few months of real pleasure, and now this. He hadn't mentioned that he'd applied for the job at NIH until he laid the fait accompli on me. I felt betrayed and couldn't understand his choice. I mean, what would you go for: hot sex or well-paying bureaucracy?

Screw the government.

For a wild moment, we'd talked about me moving to Maryland with him. But that road promised ruts of depression, sinkholes of conflict. I couldn't live on the East Coast. In my twenties, I'd tried D.C. Without sharp mountains and azure skies I'd turned into a troll, miserable and sick. I even got chilblain, red sores on my fingers, from lack of vitamin D. Face it, this kid couldn't live without sunlight, endless vistas, and chile.

I rubbed my eyes, closed the window, and cranked up the heat. KANW, my favorite radio station, pumped that good ol' New Mexico music into the ether. I wailed along with the song and made up my own words when the Spanish confused me.

The police patrolled other roads tonight. A maternal urge to protect Gabi knocked the speedometer over ninety. The faster I drove, the more my niece's accident felt like a beginning rather than a culmination.

Taking the second exit into town too fast, I screeched onto California Street, Socorro's misnamed main drag, and hung a right onto Highway 60. In these wee, somber hours, the city lay suspended in filmy numbness. Even the hospital parking lot, illuminated by unhealthy lamps, glistened with flabby slumber. The single-story buildings of the small medical center huddled in unimpressive silence. I left the car, the air cuffing my cheeks with cold. Above, stars, so many stars, reminded me of how small we humans are.

Mounted beside the locked emergency room door, a grungy plaque instructed visitors to use the phone, presumably right there, to request admission. The instrument, however, had been vandalized. There was no receiver. Obviously, the ER didn't get many late-night walk-ins. My pounding fists against the metal produced an incurious woman. A fingertip of lettuce clung to her bottom lip like a green leech. A mole sprouted black hair on her cheek.

"The police called me. My niece is in here. Her name is Gabriela Shofet," I yelled through the glass window, wondering if she'd move from her fixed position, arms crossed over her thick chest. Finally, she extended a lackadaisical hand to let me in.

"She's asleep right now," said the woman without emotion. The scent of deli mustard hung on her breath. The hospital's heat thawed my inefficient coat and made my nose run. I followed her, sniffling and hunting for a tissue in my purse.

Soft lighting rendered the world dingy, but the man standing to greet me brought it back into crisp definition. He wore denim jeans, his waist encircled in a leather belt with a fist of a buckle, turquoise and silver, that accentuated his paunch. Tooled boots ending in sharp points covered his feet and a cowboy hat tilted forward on his head. Without an introduction, I knew he was a cop.

"Ms. Solomon?" His semi-visible, smooth-skinned face mirrored the color of exposed pine bark and his dark eyes rebuffed lies. If it weren't for his mouth's downturn and the two half-moon creases on either side of his lips, he'd pass for thirty-something. To earn those wrinkles, he must've frowned from the moment of birth. For that reason alone, I put his age comparable to mine.

"Yes," I said, searching for Gabi.

He removed his hat to reveal thinning black hair and held out his hand to shake mine. "I'm Detective Sanchez." A glance at his watch, and the left side of his mouth rose into a lopsided smile. I liked the mirth in it. "Thank you for coming down so *quickly*."

"Traffic was light." My witticism slunk to the floor.

"Your niece has already been X-rayed." He put his hat back on. "Her hand and forearm are in pretty bad shape."

"What about the other person?" I blew my nose, wadded the tissue in my hand, and threw it at a garbage can.

"What other person?"

"You mean it was a hit-and-run?"

"Why don't we sit down?" The detective pointed to a scrawny set of chairs. I noticed his wedding ring, one of those popular Celtic designs with interlocking bands of gold and copper. "I think I need to explain something." We sat in the drab, gray-green seats. "Your niece wasn't in a car accident." He leaned forward to look in my eyes. "Someone rigged her mailbox with an explosive device."

"What?" I yelled it, getting to my feet with disbelief. "A pipe bomb?"

"I didn't say that it was a pipe bomb." Sanchez held out his hand, inviting me to sit again. "We've had a rash of these during the last month, a bunch of firecrackers bundled together, but none have detonated until now. We think a group of high schoolers are taking their chemistry lessons a little too far."

"Some prank." I held on to the chair, discomfort nagging at my back.

"I know this must be a shock." He pushed his hat up so that I could see his face more easily. "We'll do everything we can to catch them."

Unable to voice the hundreds of half-formed thoughts crowding my mind, I couldn't stop shaking my head.

"Other than her hand and arm, her injuries aren't too bad. Well, except for a possible concussion," he said.

Sitting again, I hunted in my purse for a second tissue. The bag had grown too big, too full of everything but what I sought. The back of my sleeve worked just as well. A line of makeup remained on my coat after I'd finished wiping eyes and nose. None of this made sense. My legs moved back and forth with an urge to bolt out of the hospital, to run as far away as possible.

The detective straightened. "I'm sorry to ask you this, but do you know anyone who might want to harm your niece?"

"No. No one." I gripped the arms of the chair again, my taut fingers hurting. "She's a great kid. She hasn't been here long enough to make enemies." Nausea clenched at my stomach. Nearby, a vending machine hummed. "Do you mind?"

The bubbly soda pop gave me something new to do with my hands and its coolness soothed palms now tingling with worry. "You said there've been others. So, you don't think this was directed specifically at her? Right?"

"We're not sure." Sanchez frowned and produced a vibrating cell phone from a pocket in his pants. He answered with a curt "yes" and listened, watching me. The person on the other end stopped talking. The detective stood to the accompaniment of cracking joints. "Something's come up. I have to go." He handed me a business card. "I'll be in touch later. If you need anything in the meantime, call me."

I murmured a shell-shocked thank-you.

Sanchez loomed over me. "I'm not sure you'll thank me when you see her."

3

A **soft tap on** my shoulder carried me out of an ashen sleep. The wall left indentations where my face had lain against it long enough to puff. Light seeped through the waiting room's blinds. Dust frosted each slat.

"Miss?" A woman, whom I presumed to be a nurse, peered into my face. Her zombie eyes held the dullness of someone who had long ago abandoned whimsy. Frizzy, doe-colored hair framed her face in merciless lines.

Cricks in my neck snapped with each movement side to side. My legs protested from having been bent under my butt for so long. The pain sharpened my other senses. I smelled coffee and wanted some.

"Your niece is asking for you," she said.

"Thank you." My eyelids stuck together, coated with the kind of paste we used to eat in kindergarten. I rubbed them apart and shook more kinks out of my neck. Seven thirty a.m. I stood, put on my shoes, and wobbled with feet lacking circulation. "I can't believe I fell asleep."

"There's not much else to do when you're waiting," said the nurse, turning her head to address me before leading me through the ER's double doors.

Once in the room, dizziness overcame me, along with a lack of oxygen. Sensing my distress, the nurse came to my side and placed her hand under my elbow. The kind action made me feel feeble, as if a piece of my youth had guttered away.

The hush in the ER shattered with the sound of thrashing against a metal bed railing, a queer clanging. Elsewhere, a child moaned and then cried. We walked past a private area where two adults struggled to keep someone down. All I could see was the movement in the white sheet straining against their grasp. One of the women cooed, "It's okay. It's all right."

A few steps more and the nurse pulled back a faded pale green curtain to reveal Gabi, her face bandaged in two places. Blood and yellow ooze clung to her gauze dressings. Purple and red bruises screamed against her strangely firm, shiny skin, the bulge of which gave her the air of an unsuccessful boxer.

Gabi's right arm lay at her side, an IV dosing her with fluids. I hoped most of them were painkillers. Someone had propped her left arm, a bandaged tree trunk with new glistening blood, on a small pillow. Eyes opened to mere slits rested in blackened circles. She regarded me with a hazy lack of recognition.

My niece's rust-colored hair lay in strands, stylized sunrays, across the white sheet. They provided the only warmth in this appalling scene. Her mermaid eyes, blue-green and watery, opened a half inch more, their corneas splotched with scarlet. Fighting back tears, I negotiated past the IV line and took her uninjured, frigid hand in mine.

"Gabriela," I said, silently swearing to do everything possible to nail the idiot who'd done this to her. Within two breaths, my resolve disintegrated into doubt. Had I made the wrong decision? Should I have called Eva sooner? Panic scalded my fingertips, compelling me to pull my hand away.

"Aunt Sasha?" Gabi's voice, no louder than a gnat's wing, stilled my movement. She squeezed my hand in her meager hold.

"I'm here." I tightened the muscles in my butt to prevent total collapse.

"I hurt." The simple sentence reminded me of my own pain, less than two months ago, when an angry man had socked me square in the face.

"I know, honey." The memory of those contusions and swelling, the constant wish to exchange my head with anything else, accelerated my heart rate and brought on a stronger impulse to flee. Hospitals sucked. I hated them.

"Aunt Sasha?" A new drop of blood formed from a crack on her dried lips. I wanted to find her ice chips, to apply lip balm, to do something to staunch her pain.

"Yes, sweetheart." This was too wrong. The world was off its axis when a young woman lay in a hospital bed and the psychos who did it to her were running free. My face flamed with the heat of tragedy.

"What time is it?" Gabi swallowed hard.

I gulped as much air as I could, took it down to the bottom of my lungs before saying, "A little before eight."

"Morning or evening?"

"Morning."

"I guess I won't make it to class," she said, her lips moving ever-so, the drop of red rolling toward her chin. At first, I thought she was about to cry. That's what I would have done. "I bet my students are dancing in the streets."

"How can you joke?" I used a corner of the sheet to wipe the blood away.

"What else am I going to do?" She became silent, eyes focused inward, brows nearly joining in concentration at the top of her nose. With the voice of a child one-tenth her age, she said, "Do I . . . do I still have my hand?"

"Yes. You've got both of them."

"Are my fingers wiggling?"

I stared at the bandages, watching hard, willing them to move. My disappointment echoed in the sole word. "No."

"I can't feel them. I can't feel anything there. Nothing. Oh, God." Tears wetted the bandage on her cheek. "What am I going to do if I lose my hand?"

"Listen to me. You're young. You're healthy." I had to keep her spirits up, to make sure she marshaled all her strength to heal rather than to worry. "They've got your arm and hand bandaged and elevated, probably to keep them immobile. Believe me; they wouldn't bother doing that if you were going to lose them." It sounded like B.S. to me, but maybe she'd buy it.

"God, I hurt."

"It's going to get better, Gabi. The pain will go down each day. I promise." I coughed once, suddenly thirsty. A resolution solidified in my brain and struggled into consciousness. "Do you remember anything about what happened?"

"I got home really, really late." She closed her eyes.

"What happened when you got home, Gabi?" I squeezed her healthy hand to encourage her to think it through, to remember, to stay awake long enough to give me even the smallest slice of information to begin to hunt for those stupid teens.

"Mom always sends me postcards when she's out of the country, so I checked the box. And, then . . . and then I was here, screaming. That's it. That's all I remember." She shifted her position and groaned. "My tailbone feels like it's broken."

"It might be. You probably fell straight backward with the blast."

Next to us, beyond the curtain, a doctor introduced himself to someone. The person on the other side whimpered, then shrieked, and an overwhelming stench permeated our space. Gabi gasped. I plugged my nose and breathed through my mouth. Footsteps ran past.

I saw Gabi's lips move and bent closer to hear the words. "A blast?"

"They think it was a bunch of firecrackers in your mailbox, rigged to explode."

A loud sucking sound from the area next to us overpowered her response at first. When it subsided, she said, "You're sure?"

"That's what the police said."

Gabi relaxed, took a deep breath, and nodded. "Okay."

"What does that mean?" I stepped back, concern torquing my face into a scowl. The non sequitur worried me. Was this evidence of the concussion?

"There've been a couple of those around town. I read about it online. But no one's been hurt." She attempted a smile. "So, it was random."

I liked that idea. "Well, that's good in a way, isn't it?"

Gabi didn't say anything more, but a sense of relief brought a springtime lift into the room. I hadn't acknowledged the internal terror of thinking someone might want to hurt my niece in particular.

Moronic high school punks playing a prank seemed safer.

Almost.

4

Detective Sanchez cleaved the curtain with an icy calm. Hat in hand, face purposeful, he positioned himself to obstruct Gabi's view of me and mine of her.

"Can't this wait?" Peeved at the downpour of negativity, I sought to shove him out of our lightened space with my words.

"No." He stepped closer to her. "If you don't mind, I'd like a few minutes alone with your niece."

"I'd prefer to stay."

"Please let her stay," said Gabi.

The policeman's shoulders rose. "All right. This shouldn't take long anyway."

"Thank you," I said, bracing against the danger cowling his presence. In order to get a better view of his face, I crossed to the other side of the bed and parked myself catlike, toes twitching, ready to pounce.

"Ms. Shofet, what do you remember about last night?"

"Nothing." The response came quicker than an anxious heartbeat. Playing with this fire, antagonizing the man, would char her chances for sympathy. A rumpling sound made me look at her good hand. She drummed her fingers. Perhaps with their motion, she realized how uncooperative she'd sounded. "Nothing at all, sir."

"Not a thing? How about where you ate dinner or what you watched on TV?" Why had he said it with such disdain?

Someone must've turned up the thermostat in the room; I'd begun to sweat again. Had I hit early menopause?

Gabi stared hard at him, her face a Grecian mask of impenetrability.

"I'm waiting, Ms. Shofet."

"I don't remember." Gabi amplified his tone with an even snottier reverb. Couldn't she see me shaking my head? Irritating a policeman yielded only trouble. This I knew from unpleasant experience.

An unfriendly pause bobbed between them. Sanchez regarded the two of us with arctic eyes, his phone humming again. "I'll be back in a minute."

Near my niece's head, a mechanized bell pinged. A nurse peeked her head through the opening in the curtain, glanced at the IV, and left.

"What was that about?" I changed my perch in order to hold Gabi's healthy hand. It had warmed a bit, thank goodness. The bell continued its dinging.

Before Gabi could answer, the woman returned. "I bet you're both starting to feel a little claustrophobic in here," she said, walking past me with a bag filled with clear liquid in her hand. I smelled a sweet lily odor about her. She pulled the curtain aside so that we could see the activity in the room. With brisk ease, she checked Gabi's vital signs.

Uniformed heath care workers scurried past. People wearing thick coats and crumpled hats spoke in low tones and wiped red-rimmed eyes. Directly in front of us stood Detective Sanchez, his broad back hunched forward, an elbow resting on the counter of the ER's administrative hub. He turned and saw us scrutinizing him. With a flick, he closed his phone and approached us.

"I owe you both an apology." Rather than try to get me to move, he took my former place on Gabi's other side. "I'm sorry."

"It's okay," said my magnanimous niece.

"I'd like to ask a few more questions, Ms. Shofet."

"Sure." She'd believed him too readily. I waited for the snare.

"Try to think back. What do you remember last? Nothing is too small, too insignificant right now."

Gabi looked at me. I couldn't imagine that she awaited my permission, but I nodded. My eyes conveyed a warning. She blinked an unreadable response.

"I went to the library to do some research and get a quiz ready for Chem 101." She tried to roll onto her side and moaned. Mouth open, she started to talk, took a shallow breath, and began again. "At about eleven or so, I went over to the El Camino to get dinner."

Sanchez wrote as she spoke. I strained to see his notes. He must have sensed my efforts because he slanted the notepad farther from my view. (I guess not all was sugar and honeyed candies between us yet.)

"Did you meet anyone there?" he said.

"Sure. I saw some friends, ran into my advisor. Standard stuff."

"Can you give me their names?"

"Heather Apodaca and Marcel Garcia, her boyfriend."

Sanchez nodded. "And your advisor's name?"

"I didn't really talk to him," said Gabi with a speed that made me think she was lying. Why bother with something so innocuous? "I'm not even sure he saw me."

"May I have his name anyway?"

"Aaron Wahl."

"Do you remember what time you left?"

"I think it was about two. I don't remember exactly." My niece's mood plunged into an unknown place; I couldn't put my finger on it. Darnda could've helped me figure out what was going on if she were here. *Oh, hell, I forgot to call her.*

Gabi's fingers began their drumming again. The noise resembled a tiny galloping horse.

"Who was the last person you saw when you left?" said the officer.

"I don't know." The high-pitched response startled me. Gabi's throat had constricted as if air no longer flowed through it freely.

"Are you all right?" Sanchez stopped writing.

Gabi nodded.

"Are you sure?"

My niece avoided our eyes, a motion filled with deception. The policeman's body stiffened. With a slow regard, he studied her. Though under pressure to respond, she remained silent. Sanchez closed his notebook, shook his head. I sensed that he wanted Gabi to make things right, to stop the game-playing before it hurt her. She continued to rebuff our nonverbal entreaties. It was an elephant-in-the-room moment, the kind where all of the important action happens in the breaks between scratching a nose or rubbing an eye.

The detective's hyperbolic sigh filled the room with disappointment. "I understand they'll be keeping you through tomorrow morning for observation."

Gabi's brittle rigidity concerned me. Was she holding her breath, refusing to let her blood travel through her veins?

"I'll check in later to see how you're doing." He prepared to leave and then fixed my niece with a final stare, frustration creasing his face into a corduroy patch of straight wrinkles. "Perhaps you'll remember more."

How could Gabi be so stupid? I reigned my panting back into semi-natural respiration. What on earth was she thinking? To withhold information from Sanchez, to be so defensive, she'd turned an ally into an antagonist. Bad move. Who knew how many of her future answers he'd dismiss now that he couldn't believe the ones she'd just given?

"How could you do that?" I said as soon as the detective was out of earshot. My thumbs ached from holding the bedrail with such force.

"What?"

"You lied. How are any of us going to help you if you lie?"

"I didn't."

"Of course you did." I bent close to her face, giving her the full benefit of my undoubtedly sour breath. "Don't you want him to find out who did this to you? Don't you want to know the truth?"

"I didn't lie."

"You certainly did. Withholding information is the same as lying in a police investigation. That man knows you're not telling him everything."

The panic in her eyes gagged my recriminations.

"What is it, Gabi? What do you know?"

5

Gabi's mental retreat staggered me with its force. Silence shot from my niece like ink from an injured octopus, black and foreboding. She'd shut down, her eyes closed against it all, against me. Soon, her breathing normalized; she'd found refuge in sleep. I turned around. Beyond us, phones chirped and buzzed. Voices mumbled. The astringent scent of medicinal chemicals and cloying disinfectants intruded.

Our privacy stolen by the open curtain, I stood there, visible to the bustling ER, feeling unprotected and, suddenly, bone-tired. A portion of my exhaustion stemmed from the anticipated phone call to my sister. How do you tell someone you love that her daughter is in the hospital, that she might lose a limb? There's just no easy way.

With cell phone in hand, I headed toward the anonymity of the waiting room and resolved to do my task before it became an albatross on my conscience. There it was again, a scent of coffee determined to turn my head. I searched for the blessed smell. A man, whose forlorn face made me recoil, walked past with two large Styrofoam cups. Despair glazed his eyes and blunted his features. I didn't dare stop him to ask for directions to the cafeteria.

A second before pushing the button to leave the ER, I halted, transfixed by memories of similar incidents. Each of my mother's strokes remained as vivid as if they'd happened moments ago. It had always been difficult to regain admittance once I'd abdicated my position on this side of the double doors. Lesson learned. Careful not to block entry or egress, I dialed Eva's number from where I stood.

When was the last time I'd talked with her? Two months? Three?

Ah, now I remembered. We'd gotten into a fight about cremation. The subject had been difficult enough when Mom had brought it up, but I didn't expect Eva's volcanic response. Maybe I should have waited to broach it in person, but when would we see each other? She traveled extensively. I didn't.

Plus, ever since Eva had moved to Maryland, she'd become even more Jewish somehow, her zeal flowering ever wider, citing this rule and that. The change provided a real disincentive for me to visit. Even on the phone, I felt she judged me. Mom's request had evoked my sister's outright rejection. She'd rebuffed every one of my rationales and Mom's reasons. I'd hung up on her then.

"Excuse me. You're not supposed—"

I held up a finger, listening to the phone's intermittent clicks.

"Ma'am." The speaker, a lanky, long-haired young woman, hovered near me. Her thick eyebrows evinced discontent and an imperious frown tugged at her lips. She resembled an angry wood nymph—a dark tree though, deep in the forest—the kind who'd be waging battle in Narnia with a trident or magic wand. In one hand, this medical dryad held a handled plastic tub filled with clear tubes and colored stoppers, the tools of her blood-drawing trade. Her cheery uniform had small, bright flowers crowding a turquoise cotton shirt, which increased her aura of dourness.

The phone clicked one more time.

"Allo?" said my brother-in-law, his voice puny with the crappy connection. Even though he'd been in this country for more than forty years, he retained his Iranian accent.

"Zach, it's Sasha." I didn't want to launch into the bad news, but I didn't have a choice.

"What's happened?" Zach's concern corseted the thousands of miles separating us.

The young woman held her ground opposite me, eyes laden with blatant disrespect. Her irritation smelled of old citrus. Or, maybe, she needed a bath.

"What's happened?" This time the speaker was Eva.

"I don't know how to say—"

"Just tell me."

"Gabi's in the hospital."

The young woman stepped back, offering me space, finally. I'd been standing, stork-balanced, on one foot and now switched to the other. The girl had left.

"I don't have all the details yet, but something exploded in her mail-box," I said.

An animal yowl burst from the other end of the line, devolving into a sob.

"Eva? It's not as bad as it sounds." A soft mewing began and my knees faltered. I pushed my back harder against the wall. "She's going to be all right. They're taking really good care of her." The acidic remains of my crummy breakfast rose to the front of my mouth, melting a layer of esophagus on its way.

The young woman, who'd admonished me moments before, returned with two cups of coffee and held one out to me. I nodded a thank-you.

"We'll call you back in a couple of minutes," said Zach.

"Where's Eva?" Why had he come back on the line?

"We'll call you back."

Still relying on the wall to hold me up, I drank the coffee and looked at my phone.

"Were you talking about Gabi Shofet?" said the young woman.

"I'm Sasha Solomon." I extended my hand. "You are?"

"Forget that," she said. "What happened to Gabi?"

"I said, 'I'm Sasha Solomon.' And now, you're supposed to be polite and introduce yourself." My stare pinned her in place, a reluctant moth on a display board.

"I'm Heather. Gabi and I are friends." Her hand came forward an inch, as if she were ready to shake mine, but the impulse passed. "What happened to her?"

"Heather Apodaca?"

"How do you know my name?"

"She mentioned you."

Heather jumped out of the way of the ER doors. Two paramedics rolled a gurney past us. She watched their progress, her expression neutral. "What happened to her?"

"They think her mailbox was rigged with firecrackers."

"No." She surveyed the ER, presumably looking for my niece. "I saw her last night and she was fine."

"Well, she's not now." That sounded too harsh, as if I blamed Heather for Gabi's misfortune. "Do you know anyone who'd want to do something like this to her?"

"Why would you ask me that?" The grimace contracting her young face hinted at a sour middle age.

"You're her friend."

"I need to see her. Where is she?"

I pointed in Gabi's general direction. Heather's head moved forward on her long neck in a position that must have hurt.

My cell phone rang. I pushed the button to answer, watching Heather stride to the side of Gabi's bed.

"Firecrackers?" said Zach.

"That's what they think."

"Tell me about her injuries."

I told him what I'd seen.

"They're lying. It was a pipe bomb. I know it was," he said. In the background, I heard Eva demand, "Give it to me."

"The police didn't say that." My protestation dissipated within seconds. Zach, a chemist who worked on top-secret projects for the government, knew about explosives; I'd trust his read of the situation more than filtered information from a reluctant cop.

"Who did this to my daughter?" Eva's shrillness made me hold the phone away from my ear. The hospital's overhead announcements couldn't diminish her volume.

"They don't know yet."

"'They'? Who?"

"The police."

"Sasha, I want you to find out who did this to her."

I closed my eyes and brought a hand to my forehead. "The thought has already occurred to me. I'm just not sure how to do it."

"You ask around . . . a little here, a little there. You find the person who did this to her."

"It's not that easy, Eva. I can't just jump in. It's not really my business." My legs buckled. I sat on the floor, blocking out everything but my sister's voice.

"Not your business?" She shrieked something in Hebrew. I was glad I didn't understand. "She's your niece. Your flesh and blood."

"That's not what I meant." I took a breath, held it for three counts, and exhaled. "I don't know how to do it or where to begin. This is for the police, not for an amateur like me. I'd get in their way."

"You didn't let that stop you with Mom and that blasphemer in Belen. What about that murder you solved in Clovis?"

The coffee tasted like liquid rubber, but I drank it anyway. "If I can find anything out, you know I will."

"Do the police know Gabi's Jewish?"

"What does that have to do with anything?" How could she exasperate me so easily? I tried to cap my responses to give her time to adjust to the news. My sister had every right to be insane at the moment.

"You'd be surprised how it affects people," she said, each syllable enunciated with anger. "Believe me, I know."

Great. That's just what we needed to endear us to the Socorro police department, a nice dose of paranoia. I'd deal with that later. Right now, I needed to calm my sister down and get her here in one piece.

"I believe you, Eva," I said. The world spun, making me more nauseated. "I'll do what I can, what's reasonable."

"This is no time to be reasonable," she whispered. "I'll be there as soon as I can."

I tried to hold on to the floor before the room went black.

6

My pants were wet. The cup of coffee had emptied on my legs when I'd passed out. Lovely. I'd smell like a dirty café for the rest of the day. Other personnel had gathered around, ready to plop me onto a gurney and stick needles into my unwilling veins. "I've got low blood sugar," I told them. "It'll be okay in a minute."

"You should eat," Heather said, kneeling at my side. "Let me help you."

I didn't want to move, but her insistence forced me to show the others I wasn't going to disintegrate into blubbering goo. With effort, I got up, my joints squawking with unforgiving reminders of my squandered youth.

Heather escorted me to Gabi's bedside where a nurse already stood. Ruby studs pricked the woman's ears, rose glossed her lips, and her cropped hair shone the color of a wet cinnamon stick. With the sureness of a longtime professional, she turned knobs, shot medicine into the shunt on the IV line, and fiddled with this and that.

Then she said to Gabi, "Do you know your name?"

The sleep must have done Gabi good because her eyes flashed with a suppressed smart aleck retort. I recognized the glint and thanked heaven for it. Humor. A healthy sign.

"Yes," said Gabi.

I squinted in warning, my head tilted to the right. If my niece came out with an imaginary name, the nurse would probably call in a neurologist. Gabi caught the caution and blinked her acknowledgment.

"So, tell me," said the nurse.

"Gabriela Chagall Parvaneh Shofet."

"Great name," said the nurse. She walked around the bed, visually assessing Gabi's arm and hand, careful not to touch them. "How do you feel?"

"Like hell."

"I bet you do." She tucked in a corner of the sheet. "How about we get you into someplace nicer?"

"That'd be great."

After the woman left and Heather excused herself to go back to work, Gabi whispered, "Yippee."

"Hey, at least you'll have a better view," I said.

"Well, there's that."

Within minutes, the nurse returned with a male orderly, or whatever we call them nowadays. While she turned off and detached monitors, she mumbled instructions to him. He nodded glumly, his eyes as alert as a mud puddle. I watched him uneasily. The guy could've played defense on a professional football team. He weighed at least 350 pounds before breakfast. Rather than greet Gabi and me, he stared at his hairy bratwurst fingers. They dwarfed the gurney railing, straining against an internal pressure. This boy held on to stress like a fly strip. I recognized the symptoms. I'd been dancing the tango with them for nearly two years.

I thought about asking for someone else to help us. In response to my unarticulated request, the uniform slipped a little on his chest. A black tattoo outlined in red scowled an inch under his left clavicle. A swastika. Intersecting it, a gold cross dangled on a thin chain around his neck. How incongruous. He saw me gawking, pulled the shirt back into place, tucked in the chain, and then regarded Gabi with curiosity.

I had a very, very bad feeling.

"Don't I know you?" He punched the big metal button to open the ER doors so hard it gonged.

"I doubt it," said Gabi, oblivious to the hostility that abscessed from his pores. I wanted to warn her to be careful, to watch out for this guy.

He stopped rolling the gurney and moved to the side so that both of them could get a better view. "Chem 101."

"Ralph? What are you doing here?"

The monster shrugged and blushed.

"What on earth did you do to your hair?" Her pleased tone made me stumble over my own foot.

"Job interview." He nodded to himself several times, a massive bobble-head toy. "Dang. I thought that was you."

"Well, it looks great." Gabi turned to me. Delight pinked her swollen face with patches of health. "Last week, he had the most beautiful long, black hair. The color of a raven and so thick. And his beard was just this big full thing." She raised her good hand and winced. Her other hand remained immobile on the pillow.

"What happened to you, anyway?" Ralph eyed her, toenail to topknot.

"My mailbox and I had a fight."

"Really?"

The little reunion had gone on long enough. I didn't trust him, not with that Nazi symbol just beyond view, not with those Neanderthal brows overarching reptilian eyes. Perhaps it was the spot on his chin where he'd missed shaving. Or maybe it was because I thought I saw a hint of pleasure in his smile—a grudge satisfied—when he realized who she was.

"My niece needs her rest. Can you please get her to her room?" I sounded like a bad version of a spinster aunt. It came natural to me, I guess, seeing as how I was.

Ralph resumed wheeling Gabi toward a semiprivate room. "Why do they have you in a double? Why do you have to share?"

"Student health insurance," she said.

"We're not *that* busy. Let me park you here for a second." He rolled her next to the room's entrance and straightened the gurney so that it was flush with the wall. "I'll be right back."

When he left, I asked Gabi for the headlines of Ralph's story.

She smoothed down a wild eyebrow before speaking. "He's in his last term and thought my class would be a slam dunk. His brother Marcel is in my department." Gabi tried to bite a nail on her thumb, but her jaw must have hurt. "Anyway, Ralph could've gotten help if he wanted to. But he didn't and I flunked him on the first test."

"I bet he didn't like that." Did Ralph have any little brothers who liked experimenting with fireworks? Crimes had been committed for excuses flimsier than bad grades.

"College is about life skills, Aunt Sasha. Slacking isn't going to help Ralph once he graduates. He needs to learn to work." She reached for her bandaged cheek, felt the gauze, then let her hand fall to her side again. "Actually, I think he kind of likes the attention—"

"Did you see that swastika tattoo?" Had Eva been right? Ralph didn't seem too bright to me. If he subscribed to the beliefs of that abhorrent symbol, he might've decided to do a little ethnic cleansing of his own.

"From what I heard, he used to be in a gang."

"Do you think your buddy here knows enough to bundle a bunch of firecrackers together?" He lumbered toward us. "Watch out, he's coming."

"Everyone makes mistakes."

"You were talking about my tattoo, weren't you?" Ralph began pushing the gurney again. Okay, so maybe he wasn't so dense.

"I've never seen one quite like it before," I said.

"Look, I was a dumb kid." His slow pace gave me time to notice a crack in the wall, the smallest amount of grime nestled in a corner, the typical talismans of an older facility. "When I get enough money, I'm going to have it taken off, even if they have to cut it out."

"See?" said Gabi, as if Ralph's comments could calm my suspicions.

Not quite. Anyone who'd go through the pain of having such a tattoo pinpricked into his skin merited distrust. Gabi could be as innocent as she wanted, buying his story, but I didn't have to give it undying belief. Plus, how would Eva react if she knew her daughter had befriended a neo-Nazi?

"Here we are." Ralph stopped. "I got you a private room."

"Isn't that sweet, Aunt Sasha?" Gabi's eyes brightened. "That's so sweet. Thank you."

"Hey, you need anything, you want anything, you ask me and I'll do it."

Why hadn't I brought Darnda with me? Ralph's actions pleaded for reconsideration. If she'd been here, she could have deciphered him. Yet again, I felt like a psychic moron.

Without warning, Ralph lifted my niece onto the clean bed. She wailed in pain.

"¡Dios mío! I'm sorry," he said. "I thought it was okay."

"What the hell were you thinking?" I rushed to her side.

Tears forming in her eyes, Gabi said, "It's all right, Ralph. You didn't know that would hurt so much."

"Aw, jeez," he said, regret tingeing his features.

"Just leave her alone." I pulled a wetted strand of hair from her cheek.

"Aunt Sasha, it's not his fault. He was trying to help."

A priggish headmistress of a nurse swept into the room and ordered Ralph to stop bothering the patients. He complied, but not before sending a thumbs-up sign to Gabi. Alas, the nurse stayed. With a ventriloquist's ability to project her voice through nearly closed lips, she doled out all the dos and don'ts hospital lawyers pretend will staunch litigation.

My attention wandered in and out of her diatribe about visiting hours and washing hands, about when to press this button and that one. The information, though delivered with the enthusiasm of a sea slug, might be important.

With a final warning to limit the number of visitors, get plenty of rest, and keep the noise down, Gabi's officious caretaker left.

My niece immediately pushed the television's power button and said, "Oh my God. I'm breaking news."

On the screen, crime scene tape squared off an area in front of a drab little house, made even plainer by the man now speaking. Teeth agleam, eyes atwinkle, pecs aburstin' out of his dark uniform with *APD Bomb Squad* emblazoned on the front, he smiled. Bailey Hayes, a reporter who'd become more than a professional associate, but not quite a full-fledged friend of mine, beamed at him. Her face, the envy of any goddess, showed sheer enthrallment. He returned her adoration and anted it up to lust. But I knew Bailey well enough to understand the pyrotechnics on her side sparkled less due to his chiseled physique than his potential for a great story.

Gabi turned up the volume.

" . . . it's still too early to speculate," the man said.

"Doesn't 'APD' mean the 'Albuquerque Police Department'? Why'd they bring in someone from there?" Gabi straightened her blanket.

"I doubt Socorro has a bomb squad of its own." I sat down and watched with her.

The program switched back to an inane talk show. Soon, my niece's eyes blinked slowly, then closed. The television droned, giving me plenty of time to marvel at the vapidity of our culture. An actor spoke about his love life. A woman complained about a plastic surgery gone bad. Who the hell cared?

Sure, some of my current prickliness could be attributed to weeks of lousy sleep and my niece's broken body. Most of it, however, emerged from self-loathing due to my upcoming birthday and the sense that I hadn't done much with my life. No marriage, no children. No great accomplishments. A rancid balance in my checking account.

My stomach rebelled again, overburdened with negative thoughts. Nothing prevented me from turning off the television and getting a jump on work. A short trip to the parking lot and I could get the laptop. Food would be good. Was the cafeteria close by? Commercial after commercial, I sat, hoping that something would axe the monotony or inspire me to take action. For once, when my cell phone chirped, I felt grateful for its electronic salvation.

"Aunt Sasha?"

"Davielle?" This couldn't be a coincidence. My oldest niece lived in Scottsdale, and right now she sounded like she was in the next room. "Where are you?"

"At the airport. They're going to be boarding in a few minutes. I should be there late this afternoon."

"Honey, I know you're worried, but I've got things under control." I also didn't want to have to deal with even more family.

"Well, I can't just sit here and do nothing."

Oh, but I hoped she would. Davielle was—and I'm being generous here—the kind of person you'd like to shove out of a plane. In particular, my eldest niece reeked of religiosity, as if she bathed in nothing else.

"Who is it?" Gabi's eyes fluttered with new awareness.

"Davielle," I mouthed, turning in the hard plastic chair.

Gabi said, "No."

I shrugged. "How are the children?"

"How can you talk about children when my sister is lying near death in that hellhole?"

"Davielle, calm down. Gabi's not dying."

"I will be, if *she* comes." Gabi kept her voice low.

I put a finger in front of my mouth to shush her. Voices and banging in the hallway, along with the scent of bacon, proclaimed lunch was on its way. Boy, a BLT sounded good. My mouth watered. What a lousy

Jew I was. I didn't even observe the most fundamental proscription against eating pork. Talking to Davielle made me feel even scummier. She expanded my sister's conservative Judaism into an art form perfected with canvases of full-out, opinionated, holier-than-thou observance.

"I've got to go. I'll see you in a few hours." Davielle disconnected.

An image of her labored its way into my mind, her hands clutching bags filled with kosher foodstuffs, her short legs running to the ticket counter, and her loud mouth complaining about weight restrictions. Actually, she probably wouldn't run.

"Well?" said Gabi.

"She's coming." I folded the phone and put it back in my purse.

"Crap. Just what I need."

"There's nothing we can do."

"I'm in hell."

"No, you're in Socorro." I'd said it to get a laugh, but the attempt failed.

"Mom's going to flip out and Davi's going to start bawling the minute she sees me." My niece reached for a lidded water cup, then gave up. "The worst of it is that my dear sister can't help herself from harping on every single one of my shortcomings."

"Just let her try," I said, holding the cup so that she could drink. "As far as I'm concerned, you don't have a single flaw."

"If you only knew," Gabi said.

7

"**D**on't change the subject." I picked up the uneaten sandwich on Gabi's tray. The food tasted slightly off with its old mayo and soggy bacon. My sights set on the limp lettuce and dill pickle garnishing her plate. A minute later, a green cigar jutted between my lips.

"Please don't take this the wrong way, Aunt Sasha, but . . . this is, like, the last opportunity I'll have to be alone before everyone descends on me." The discomfort in her eyes had nothing to do with pain. "Do you know what I mean?"

"Don't say any more." My selfish urge to nurture, and my inquisitiveness, had overshadowed her need for solitude. I fumbled with my coat.

"Please don't be mad," Gabi said.

"Honey, I'm only angry at myself." The chair grated on the floor. "You need quiet time and I haven't given it to you. Point taken." Stretching my arms over my head, I yawned. "Plus, I wouldn't mind getting out of here for a couple of hours." Perhaps I could grill Ralph about his whereabouts last night. Or maybe make a visit to the high school to ask about kids who liked playing really mean pranks.

"Do you want to take a nap?" said Gabi. "My house is messy, but you're welcome to it."

That held even more appeal than amateur sleuthing. Tired down to my molecules, I'd have to find extra layers of strength and kindness to face Davielle, steamrolling ever closer, and to protect Gabi from her sister. A nap might restore a few ounces of self-control. "Sure. That sounds good."

"I don't know where my backpack is." She moved her hand in front of her mouth. "Isn't that weird? It's like my mind is coated with some kind of oil or something, just really thick and slow." Gabi scrunched her eyes closed, concentrating. "God, my backpack could be anywhere. It has my wallet and everything. For all I know it could be lying in my front yard just waiting for someone to steal it."

"I'm sure the police recovered it."

"Do you think so?"

"Yes." How had lying become so easy? What if the person who'd hurt her now had the backpack? Was he or she using her credit cards, draining my niece's life savings while she lay here?

"Will they give it back?"

"Of course they will." There had to be a way to find out who'd done this to Gabi and why. One foot already in the hall, I stopped. "So, do I break a window to get in?"

Gabi rubbed her nose with the uninjured hand. "I keep an extra key under the pot by the back door." With a wave of the same hand, she said, "*Mi casa es tu casa.*"

"*Gracias.*" I hoisted my purse onto my shoulder. "I'll be back in plenty of time to shield you from Davielle's fireworks." Ouch. Had I really said that? Thank goodness my ill-chosen words hadn't registered.

My good-bye kiss hadn't made it across the room before Gabi's faint voice called me back. "Aunt Sasha?"

"Yes?"

"Could you do me a favor?"

"Anything."

"Would you mind looking around the front yard a little bit?"

"For what?" I moved farther into the room. Did she really think her backpack might still be there?

"Just observe. When you come back, you can tell me what you saw."

"It'd help to know what I'm looking for."

"I don't know exactly." She pushed the button on her bed to make it rise. "Just notice stuff, like if any pieces of the mailbox landed on the other side of the street or . . . if the blast made an indentation on the sidewalk. That kind of thing."

"It sounds very CSI." I laughed. "Sasha Solomon, forensic expert."

"Never mind." Gabi snapped shut again, air-tight and hurricane-ready.

"I'll look."

"It doesn't matter. Just go," she said, exhaustion overcoming her social etiquette.

I paused at the doorway, waiting, hoping she'd let me in once more, but her potent self-protection rebuffed my wishes.

A few minutes later, my car radio blared and the heater struggled to overcome its own chill. Though my Spanish wasn't perfect, I knew enough to belt out choruses at the top of my lungs even if the words didn't match the artists'. My pent-up energy found release through improvised drumming on the steering wheel.

Keeping up the salsa beat required focus. So did driving. The music won; I missed a turn and then took a wrong one, ending up at Socorro's diminutive plaza. Oh well, maybe I was supposed to get a little work done on the way to Gabi's house.

Around the square, rundown buildings housed businesses that had the cohesion of a mangy herd of camels, with about as much appeal. Their wares weren't bad in themselves; people needed insurance policies, computer repairs, and clothes. But the plaza was one of the town's main marketing assets and, right now, nothing about it tempted anyone to stop.

My new employer, the San-Socorro Foundation, had made the unpopular decision to evict said shops, raze several of the buildings, and create the most ambitious tourism project Socorro County had ever seen.

Led by Pablo "Papi" Sanchez, the foundation expected to fund the construction of a huge visitors' center spanning three sides of the plaza. The buildings would be modules with an overarching design element to tie them together. Only the Capitol Bar, a local hangout with enough Old West history to intrigue, and the large post office on the west side of the square would be recognizable once the project had been completed.

The center's goal was to lure sightseers into spending their time and money throughout the county, to pique their interest enough that they'd visit places like Magdalena, the Very Large Array (VLA), San Antonio, Ft. Craig, and Socorro itself.

Papi Sanchez's grand vision included hiring an outsider—me—to help figure out which sites to show off and which ones didn't merit as much consideration. This was, by far, the most fascinating, political, and controversial consulting job in my career; it was bound to be a gas. And I'd better be rested up for the work ahead.

Gabi's house called, its promise of a bed as alluring as any resort. My car edged around another corner and reality slapped that fantasy upside the head, replacing it with muddy disenchantment. Gabi's home possessed the charisma of a neglected dump.

A metal stump in front bore witness to the early morning's violence. Parking, courtesy of the police and that yellow plastic tape, had to be across the street. So, I got a broader view. Dirt and gravel surrounded the structure with grays and light browns. The closed-in porch promised to fall down if a mosquito sneezed on it. Typical student housing.

I bet the entire building swam below code, the architectural equivalent of a lantern fish. Well, some of the places I'd lived during college and grad school didn't even measure up to this. The price of privacy, no roommates, often meant substandard wiring, peeling paint, and plumbing that evoked the wrong kinds of adventure each time you flushed a sluggish toilet or turned on a sputtering showerhead.

With a wan hope that my expectations would be wrong, I circled the house. A stench emanated from it, presaging filth within. Next door, to the left, a lace curtain moved. I thought about sticking out my tongue at the spy, but decided Gabi had enough trouble without my assistance.

A large clay pot, hand-painted with geometric shapes, fronted Gabi's back door. I lifted it, found the key, and let myself in. Stuffiness permeated the house with traces of roasted chicken, stale pizza, and sandalwood incense. A stink hovered above it all and increased with each step forward. Plants drooped in the darkness. I opened the blinds to get a better look.

No dishes sat in the kitchen sink, no food left out on the counters. Cabinets lacked handles and most of the drawers didn't close all the way. A cockroach skittered across the chipped linoleum floor. This wasn't a comment on Gabi's housecleaning; it was the result of the fist-sized hole gaping where the room's heater met the wall. I opened the grungy fridge and saw a half-eaten cheeseburger. Well, that answered the question about my niece keeping kosher; she didn't.

Gabi's dinette set had only three chairs, one of which looked rusted. In the center of the table, a multicolored Israeli ceramic bowl with a jaunty flower and bird design held apples, oranges, and other fruit. I grabbed the least ripe of the bananas. Peeling it, I walked through a doorway into a second area that served as an office and bedroom. The futon, much rattier than the one I used for my couch, had been folded back on the floor. A plank of wood atop cinderblocks held a modern computer with a monitor as large as a big-screen television. Papers, notebooks, and an elegant menorah also resided there. Gabi's few dresses and shirts hung from a rope across one end of the room. Cardboard boxes held the remainder of her garments. My niece's priorities shouted her indifference to comfort; she was a student through and through.

The bathroom stank, though Gabi had one of those wall deodorizers in the only visible electrical outlet. Bowls of dried lavender and rosemary rested on the floor, toilet top, and on the freestanding bookcase she used for towels and toiletries. They struggled to overcome the smell with paltry results.

Returning to the living room, I sniffled with memories, felt more than seen, of my own years before graduation. Had I lived this cheaply, this unpleasantly? Now, the thought of laying on that futon, so close to the grimy floor, repelled me like a queen faced with eating straight off a clump of dirt. When had I become such a snob? It's not as if my own house was four-star.

Though I shivered, outside air could only improve this dismal living space and get rid of that smell. I unbolted the front door and the barely eaten banana dropped from my hand. In the distance, a car horn honked, brakes screeched. A scream froze between my clamped teeth.

Who could have done this? Gallons of dark red paint, the color of dried blood, covered Gabi's porch. I stood on the threshold, my hand searching the air for something to hold, my breathing strained from the stink. The vandal had gone to the bathroom right in the middle of the mess. Quickly turning to shut out the odor and sight of this atrocity, I saw something worse painted in the same red on Gabi's faded wooden door: ARAB WHORE.

8

My disbelief multiplied with each exclamation of disgust while I waited for the police to show up. Had Eva been right? Was the exploded mailbox a hate crime rather than a random act? If so, she was only half correct. Whoever had done this didn't object to Gabi's Jewish heritage; it was the Iranian genes that rankled. Anyone who'd bothered to know my niece understood her father's family had come to the United States to escape repression. They stood with our country against religious fanaticism.

Oh, hell.

Within minutes, a knock sounded at the back door. Uneasy, I peered out of the kitchen window—a cowering animal—before opening it to Detective Sanchez.

"Are you the only policeman on the force?"

"We're a small department." He noticed the table. "Let's sit down."

"Aren't you going to look at the porch?"

"I already did. That's why I came in this way." He pulled out his notebook. "Tell me exactly what you saw, what you did, from the moment you left your car."

"There's not much to tell. I walked around the house, got the key, and came in." I pointed to the wall. "One of Gabi's neighbors watched me do it." The detective wrote while I talked. "I looked at the kitchen, went into the living room and bathroom, and then opened the door and saw, well, what I saw. Then I called you. That's it."

"Did you go out onto the porch?"

"Absolutely not."

He put down his pen. "Ms. Solomon, has your niece given you any clue about who might do this?"

"I haven't talked to her about it yet. She's got enough on her plate. Don't you think?" I let myself calm down before continuing. "It has to be someone who doesn't know her well. Anyone else would know she's not Arab. Iranians aren't Arabs."

The policeman watched me, eyes weary but alert. Stubble had begun to darken his chin and upper lip since we'd spoken at the hospital.

I rolled my shoulders in backward circles to release tension and pulled back a strand of hair that had escaped my braid. "My sister Eva thinks that the mailbox might have been a hate crime, not just a prank. I'm beginning to believe she's onto something."

"What makes you say that?" The question, uttered slowly, implied I might be overreacting.

"You saw the front door. What else could it be?"

"These could be two distinct crimes, Ms. Solomon. We don't know yet." His dispassion infuriated me with its patronization.

"Right. And Gabi could be playing for the major leagues this afternoon." I picked up an apple, considered biting it, then returned it to the bowl. "I know a hate crime when I see it, and this is a hate crime."

Sanchez pushed back from the table and folded his arms over his chest, a typical demonstration of close-mindedness. "I'll grant that the porch looks like it might be a hate crime."

"Oh, that's generous of you." What if his guarded responses belied a latent anti-Semitism? Would I have to investigate this myself? "I happen to know the two crimes are related as sure as I know my niece doesn't deserve either one."

"How can you be so sure?"

"I'm a Jew, Detective. We've been dealing with hate crimes for thousands of years. We've got a sixth sense about these things." No need to disclose how lax a Jew sat across from him. Until that moment, I hadn't realized how fully my heritage informed my worldview, deep down, on an atomic level. I picked up an orange and rolled it on the table, back and forth between my hands. Oranges grew in Israel. Jaffa, right?

Outside, men's voices droned in mumbles, probably police. Inside, the motion of the orange comforted me and provided a better option than screaming. I broke the unhappy silence. "Sanchez. Are you related to Papi Sanchez?"

The policeman's eyes batted twice, as if the question surprised him. Of course, it really had nothing to do with anything. "If you go back far enough, most of us Sanchezes are related. How do you know him?"

"I'm working on a project for his foundation." I lobbed the orange harder than intended. It skipped over my hand, landed with a thud on the floor, and rolled to a stop under the detective's chair.

"I don't know what to tell you," he said, handing me the fruit. "We've never had anything quite like this before." Then he did that cop thing—the stern look in the eyes, the serious tone, the assertion of authority—a puffer fish puffing up. "Don't even think of taking the law into your own hands, Ms. Solomon."

"I wouldn't dare." My head bent with the burden of this lie.

"You do your job and we'll do ours the best we can."

I wanted to believe him, but doubt had already found several toeholds. My cell phone's chirrup upped the tension between us. Sanchez jutted his chin at the second ring, indicating that he wanted me to answer it. He waited, silent.

"Hello?" I said.

"Sasha, this is Michaela Jones. I've got great news," said the executive director of the San-Socorro Foundation. "Papi surprised us this morning. He's in town and would like to meet you."

"Really?" I'd never expected to glimpse the wealthy patriarch who'd founded the charitable organization. His travel schedule resembled a commercial pilot's. "It just so happens that I'm in Socorro right now. I came down a day early and plan to stay through tomorrow night. Do you think he could fit me in?"

Sanchez cleaned his fingernails with a credit card while he waited for me to finish.

"Let me see," Michaela said. Sounds of shuffling paper and a clicking keyboard met my ear. "He can make time for you in about thirty minutes. Would that work?"

"Great."

The policeman's phone now rang. Lips pressed into a plane of discontent, he answered it.

"It'll be great," I said, watching the detective's expression deteriorate into a full-out scowl before the conversation ended.

"You'll be staying in Socorro?" The detective frowned again.

"I'll be at the hospital until they kick me out and in town until my sister arrives and can take over."

"Good." Sanchez got up and walked into the front room. "Ms. Solomon, given what your niece has gone through, I'd suggest you don't mention this to her until I give you the go-ahead."

"Who's going to clean it up?" I stepped toward the back door, ready to catapult out of the house, to leave the stench and hatred of the sickos who'd done this to Gabi's place.

"I'll give you the name of a service."

"Detective, have you figured out about the explosive in the mailbox? Was it really just fireworks?"

"Why wouldn't it be?"

He'd answered my question with a question. Suddenly, he found his boots far more interesting than my face. His jowls hardened into jerky.

Gabi wasn't the only liar today.

9

A ragged behemoth stood in front of the well-kept house across from Gabi's. Her elephantine feet made ruts in the asphalt, a broad shoulder width apart. Each hand could have palmed the round part of a tennis racket. Gray hair, in those curlers with pink foam that women from Mom's era wore, rippled around a moon face. Scowling eyes the color of kelp squinted. Her tucked-in plaid shirt covered an ample belly straining at gray blue jeans. If she was younger than sixty, I'd have to go to an ophthalmologist.

"Hello," I said, amiably enough.

"What's that kid gotten herself into now?" Her scratchy intonation befitted a poltergeist, one with a head that did that nifty 360-degree revolution.

I glanced over my shoulder. In less than an hour, my niece's property had lost more value. Two police cars, the men in uniform, and Detective Sanchez spelled the kind of trouble homeowners wanted in other neighborhoods. Talk about lousy curb appeal.

"I'm sure I don't know what you're talking about." I shook my purse hard to dislodge the keys from a hairbrush.

"Judy, close that door!" Another woman's equally discordant voice lashed out from behind my interrogator.

"You were just in there. I saw you," said Judy, coming forward to take position in front of my car. The only way to escape would be to back up or run her over. Given the aggression exuding from her balloon face, option number two seemed pretty good.

"It's police business," I said.

"You're no policeman."

I considered pointing out my gender, but this woman wasn't in the mood for humor.

"Judy! What the hell's the matter with you, woman?" The voice boomed through the megaphone of the house. "Close that door!"

The minx who appeared a split second later had to have been born in Lilliput. If she met my chin, and I wasn't taller than five feet four inches, she'd be in high-heeled elevator shoes. Her brazen black hair, in sweetsie curlers, too, gleamed with gel. New wrinkles would've had a difficult time finding purchase on her face. She had to be eighty, though I began to reassess when she stomped to the car to stand by her Judy. "What's going on here?"

"Nothing," I said.

"She knows something about that kid across the street."

"Stop calling her a kid. She's my niece and she's lying in the hospital right now. Some idiot nearly blew her arm off." I'd started crying. What a marvelous way to assert control.

"Oh, that's just terrible," said the older lady, coming to my side and reaching up to put an arm around my shoulder. "How would you like a nice cup of tea?"

"I can't. I have to be somewhere."

"How about something stronger?" She let go and regarded my face. "Whiskey?"

"Harriet," said Judy, a hand to her chest in apparent mortification.

"She looks like a whiskey drinker to me."

"No, thank you." If only I could take her up on her offer, could postpone the meeting with Papi Sanchez.

"Well, at least come in and wipe that face off. You don't want people to know you've been crying. It'll just make them pity you and make you look namby-pamby." She'd transformed into everyone's favorite grandma, but the glint in her eyes said she drank acid for breakfast.

Though reluctant to cross their threshold, I didn't want my boss's first impression to be that he'd hired a clown, or an angelfish, since the mascara most certainly now trailed down my cheeks. I moved toward the door.

Harriet led the way, her light body almost floating into an open room with twin teak desks and matching chairs. Black computers purred and manila folders teetered. Hundreds of rock specimens covered bookcases and any other available flat surface. Seismographic paper with spiked patterns in black and red served as paintings, taped to all the walls within view. Speakers as tall as filing cabinets chortled polkas into the air. In the center of it all, a large wooden table held open containers of—I moved closer to see—goopy creams and mud masks.

"Monday is our beauty day," said Harriet, noticing my interest. "The rest of the week, we don't give a damn about what we look like."

"Don't you have to be somewhere soon?" Judy's lips pouted into a perfect O. She motioned for me to follow her farther to the bathroom. With an abrupt clap that made me jump, she turned on the light and pointed to a rack of jade green towels. "Use these."

I closed the door. Amethyst and quart crystals shone in cracked geodes on the counter. Two bumper stickers had been affixed above the toilet. One read, "Everyone digs geologists." The other said, "Geologists Rock!"

By the sink, one of those free-standing magnifying mirrors that show every zit and pore tilted upward. I regarded my overblown reflection and quickly backed away from the horror show of greasy makeup creases. On the wall, someone had mounted reflective tiles; though my face looked disjointed in their mismatched cracks, they offered consolation rather than condolence. I smoothed the oily base and added layers of powder and rouge. A new brush of mascara might liven up my eyes. No. I'd been crying too much. With Davielle on her way, the flood would only increase.

I emerged from the room to raucous voices. I followed them down a hallway.

" . . . no one's business," said Judy. At least I thought it was Judy.

"It's her niece, for heaven's sake. Show a bit of compassion." Something clattered with a loud ringing sound and then bounced a couple of times before settling.

"Don't start that again. We don't want to get involved." Something thumped. "Here, let me get that; you'll burn yourself."

"Involved in what?" I said, entering a cluttered kitchen with wooden cabinets the color of pecan shells. On the tiled floor lay a large stainless steel bowl, facedown. Water boiled in a big pot, its steam rising to the ceiling and clouding the two double-paned, curtainless windows. The old-fashioned stove had lion's feet, like a turn-of-the-century bathtub.

"Nothing." Judy whisked cream and grated white cheese into a large pan.

"For crying out loud, we *have* to give it to her. Gabi's in the hospital." Harriet took the whisk from Judy. "If you beat it any more we'll have a soufflé." She turned down the heat under the pan and began stirring its contents with a wooden spoon.

Judy huffed out of the room. Harriet looked from the doorway to me and then back again. "Come here," she said. When I was at her side, she handed me the spoon. "Stir this."

"I have to go."

"Just hold your horses. I'll be right back."

The doorbell rang and Judy called, "I'll get it."

I stood there, spoon in hand, stirring the Alfredo sauce and cursing my decision to come into their house.

"The police are here," said Harriet, returning. "They want to ask us more questions."

"You've already spoken to them?"

"We're the ones who called after the explosion." She opened a drawer and pulled out a bent piece of metal. "Here. Give this to Gabi."

"What is it?"

"Gabi will know."

"Tell me."

"What do you *think* it is?" Harriet's booming voice had lost all of its volume, but her disillusionment showed; I'd become a failing student. She turned off the stove.

"It looks like a piece of charred pipe."

"Good girl." Her next question was even quieter. "Where do you think we found it?"

"I have no idea."

"Use your noggin!" She peered out of the kitchen, then came to me and took the pipe. "It was embedded three inches into the front of our house."

"Damn," I said with wonder. "Those must've been giant firecrackers."

"What in heaven's name are you talking about?" Harriet's incredulity showed in a hundred ways, back-tilted head, wide eyes, mouth unable to settle on a single expression.

44

"The police told me that someone bundled a bunch of firecrackers together to blow up Gabi's mailbox."

"They said that?" Harriet leaned against the counter, her hands balanced on either side of her spaghetti body. "Honey, trust me, Judy and I know about explosives." She took the piece of metal and held it up. "This isn't from firecrackers."

"Harriet! The police want to talk to you," Judy yelled with too much gusto.

"That explosion felt like a damn earthquake and I'm a geologist. I know from earthquakes. It had to be a pipe bomb."

I grabbed the handle on the oven to steady myself. Harriet gave the artifact back to me. I put it in my purse and nodded. "I'll give it to Gabi. Thank you."

Together, slowly, we returned to the front room and those smelly unguents.

"Ms. Solomon, I thought you didn't know anyone in Socorro," said Detective Sanchez, studying me hard.

"We just met."

"And?"

"It's been lovely." If I'd had a hat, I would have tipped it for emphasis. Instead, I made a big show of looking at my watch. "Wow. I've got to go."

Sanchez's stare singed the top of my head as I searched for my car keys once more.

"Detective, have a seat, won't you? How about a nice cup of tea?" Out of the corner of my eye, I saw Harriet pull out a chair from one of the desks.

The diversionary tactic worked. Judy, observing the scene, nodded to her . . . partner? . . . mother? "Here, let me get the door for you, Ms. Solomon," she said, pushing me toward the front and unbolting it in the same motion.

I nearly flew outside with her shove.

On the way back to my car, I looked across the street at the stump that had been my niece's mailbox and the wounded porch beyond. A pipe bomb. That didn't sound like a prank. Not one iota.

The piece of contorted metal in my purse might give Gabi a clue about who had done this. For once, I didn't feel dishonest, like I was keeping anything from the police. Surely, Judy and Harriet had given them the other chunks that must have landed in their yard when they'd spoken with the officers or detectives earlier in the morning.

Sanchez must have known about the pipe bomb when he came to interview Gabi. He had to have known by the time we'd talked in her kitchen.

Omission can equal deceit.

10

When you have an interesting conversation, always take the time to rewind it in your mind. I did now, and curiosity flourished in the analytical aftermath. Harriet had used Gabi's name twice without a cue from me. Why had Judy pretended not to know her? Had they seen more than they'd let on? Damn these questions! My life had become a modern Perils of Pauline. But who was Snidely Whiplash?

And where the hell was I going anyway? Driving down Bullock back to California Street, I realized Michaela hadn't told me where to meet the great Papi Sanchez. My already-stale clothes exhorted me to detour to the dress shop on the plaza, to abandon them in a dumpster so that they could feel the sun on their synthetic fibers and the wind cleansing their Plasticine threads. Their pleas went unanswered; it wouldn't do to keep the boss waiting.

A phone call to Michaela yielded specific but convoluted instructions to the Sanchez compound near the Rio Grande. The subtle turnoff dared me to miss it. Down, down, down the bumpy dirt road I bounced, catching a glimpse of why people bought Hummers and SUVs. Then, among the barren winter trees, a gleaming white wrought-iron fence appeared. Purple signs posted at regular intervals warned of prosecution for trespassing and, if that wasn't scary enough, electrocution. Another five minutes of jouncing and I arrived at an occupied booth.

A gargantuan man-child with an angry dark scar above his right eyebrow, and baby fat snuggling his cheeks, stepped out to inquire about my business.

I told him.

"This is Papi's siesta time."

How civilized. I could use a nap, too. "Michaela Jones told me to come right now."

My interrogator asked for ID, his expression impassive. The entire interaction had a military feel, but even the guys at Kirtland Air Force Base in Albuquerque smiled occasionally. Here, the guard scrutinized my driver's license before making a call and then thrusting a clipboard through my window.

With a flourish, I signed my name and added a little heart with an arrow going though it at the end. Don't ask me why I took the time to do it.

He looked at my signature and rolled his eyes, shaking his head slightly.

Okay, that's why I took the time.

"You'll need to sign out when you leave," he said, returning my license and resuming his seat. The gate rolled back just enough to allow my car's entry.

Twenty feet farther and the road became a smooth ribbon of paved bliss. Four single-story adobe houses, thrice the size of my casita, kneeled in awe of a double-decker building with a purple and white tiled circular drive. This dwelling dwarfed its children both in square footage and outward elegance. In the center of the astounding driveway, a Gaudi-like fountain awaited spring and the re-greening of its surroundings.

Someone must've spent serious money on feng shui. Tranquility filled the area with a calm hitherto unknown to my scattered soul. Oh, how I longed to stand here, to grow roots in this rich soil, to breathe the clean, cool air forever. Gawking, I stumbled up the first of the five steps to the oversized, intricately carved wooden doors with their brilliant stained glass and two purple interlocked Ss, the logo of the San-Socorro Foundation.

The bell sounded, carillon clear, and I glanced upward searching for the tower. A man dressed in a white butler's suit, as perfect as on any movie screen, greeted me by name and ushered me into a library. On the way, exquisite mosaics of flowers, their blossoms vermilion and aquamarine, curlicued beneath my feet and above my head. I dawdled to look at their beauty. With a come-hither wave of his hand, my escort urged me past filigreed plaster tentacling in the round edges of arched entrances to doors and hallways creating this New Mexican version of the famous Alhambra. Even more impressive and incongruous in this hidden gem, dozens of diamond-clear, full-length glass windows stretched twenty to thirty feet, floor to ceiling, and opened onto a private patio as big as a golf course.

Though plush chairs invited, their comfort obvious, I couldn't sit down. Never had I been in a dwelling so opulent, so graceful. It would be easy to forget the world had any ugliness here, to be wombed from it forever. If only for a few minutes, I tried to push Gabi's attacks from my mind.

Here lay paradise. I pretended to be the owner of this modern castle, indulging in the stuff of fairy tales with handsome princes and blessed lives. An inharmonious burst of shrill laughter seared my fantasy with the precision of a laser cut.

On the opposite side of the house, a miniature poodle of a woman with the body of a twig cricketed past. A man skipped after her. She giggled. They disappeared behind a veil of hibiscus bushes blossoming with scarlet-centered white blooms. A second tee-hee and the couple scurried beyond the protection of lush-leafed indoor trees bearing orange, waxy berries.

Another movement, this one slow and commanding even in the distance, made me pull back into the library. I sat down, my hands primly on my lap, waiting. Books, so many leather-bound books smelling of erudition, birthed quick fantasies of me as a lady awaiting my servant's call to dinner. "Thank you, Smithers," I'd say, donning my elbow-length satin gloves and allowing my stunning, handsome husband to conduct me to an expansive marble table adorned with silver-domed delicacies. *Ah, wealth.* What a wonder it must be to have every whim met, every desire someone else's duty.

"Sasha?" Michaela stood in the doorway, her strong hand lightly supporting the arm of a wisp of a gentleman, his hair the color of a used quarter. The blue silk of his suit caught the sunlight and improved it. Under the jacket, a klieg-light white shirt and thin royal purple tie showed more pride of presence than I'd ever seen. A lavender handkerchief triangulated from a single breast pocket. Wonder dancing in her voice, Michaela said, "I'd like you to meet Pablo Sanchez."

"Papi." Though he'd been born in New Mexico, this man belonged to the Spain of a bygone era, when my state was no more than hoof-kicked dust and hardened rock, a time when no one in the Old World knew that people already lived in the new one. He held out a hand, the fingers long and manicured. I responded, expecting to shake, but he kissed the top of mine with supple, warm lips. Thoroughly enchanted, I followed the two of them along the bright interior to a sitting room dominated by a table laden with pastries on custom white and purple china, and those ever-present Ss. "I'm pleased you could make time for me," he said, his accent cultured. "I trust you had no trouble finding us?"

"None at all. Thank you." I doubted we would discuss business today. This was a kindness, a courtesy bestowed by a curious courtier on a skilled craftsman. If it had been with anyone else, I would have called it "whiff-reading," the kind of sniffing dogs do when they're checking each other out. In this context, the momentary image felt vulgar.

"I'm glad you're taking a few extra days to familiarize yourself with our county, Ms. Solomon. I trust your sightseeing today has been fruitful?"

"Actually, I've spent most of the day at the hospital."

"Nothing serious, I hope."

Should I ruin the splendor of this place with Gabi's troubles? "My niece was injured in a pipe bomb blast."

Michaela's startled eyes brought me condolence.

"How terrible," Papi said. "If there's anything I can do to help, please tell me."

I tried to smile, but my face crystallized. Any emotion might shard it into jagged pieces.

"Please," said Papi, handing me his embroidered handkerchief. "My nephew is a detective here. Would you like me to call him?"

"We've already met." My teeth ground with the effort not to bad-mouth Sanchez. He'd done nothing wrong, just not enough right. "He's been very kind."

"You're distressed." Papi leaned toward me, his cologne spicy but subtle, and put a hand on mine. "Please, I insist. Let me help. Would you like a private investigator? Private care for your niece?"

"I appreciate the offer, but I think we're all right." I paused a second too long. "And, I'm sure the police will do everything possible."

"Pardon me, Ms. Solomon, but you sound quite unsure."

Damn. Was I that obvious?

Michaela held out a plate, offering small Mexican wedding cookies, sugar blizzarding them in white powder. Trembling, I took two and kept my peace.

With eyes constricted to straight, piercing lines, Papi studied me. "Ms. Solomon, I'm going to be eighty-six in four months. You don't live as long as I do without learning a thing or two about people. I think, perhaps, you're worried that this crime is more than it seems."

"I am. I really am." My words exploded in pops, their fluency stymied by the ugliness of their meaning. I hid my face with one hand and continued eating the cookie with the other.

High heels ticked past the room. Their crispness conjured falling mahjong tiles on brick. They stopped and then returned to pause at the room's entrance. The three of us swiveled to greet the noise.

"Oh. When did you get here?" The woman I'd seen on the other side of the house now stood at the doorway, her eyes trained on Papi. Her innocent words reeked of contempt.

"I arrived this morning," he said with the restrained tolerance of an observed parent speaking to a juvenile delinquent.

"Where arrrrrre you?" sang an unseen man.

"Who is that?" Papi's gaze hadn't left the woman's tight face.

"If I'd known you were going to be here, we wouldn't have come," she said.

"Then I'd urge you to leave." He turned away from her with a small, apologetic shrug to me. "I'm so sorry you had to witness that, Ms. Solomon. My other children have more manners."

I snuck a look at the woman still standing there. She regarded her father, mouth open, ready to say something more.

"Sweeeeeetie, I've got something for you," sang the mystery man's voice again.

The woman's head turned quickly toward the sound, and a second later her high heels clacked in the opposite direction.

"Please, you were telling me about your niece," prompted my host.

But before I could speak, the man who'd chased Papi's daughter peered into the room, his face full of naked anticipation. Within a wink, he'd suppressed all that sexuality into a bland mask. The masterful transition had a practiced ease to it.

"I'm sorry to bother you all," he said. "Have you seen Cecilia?" He looked familiar and for a wanton moment, I wondered if he'd ever been my boyfriend. No. If he had been, I'd robbed a cradle. Plus, he was too movie-star handsome and those kind of good looks made me suspicious. Still, I knew him from somewhere.

"That way." Michaela pointed in the wrong direction.

"Thank you." The man nodded and left us in an uncomfortable silence.

Papi put a thin-skinned hand to his forehead. "Cecilia should know better than to bring her trash here."

What could I say to that?

A phone rang. Its jingling further unraveled the mood in the room. Michaela answered it, and handed the receiver, on a lengthy cord, to Papi.

He listened for a few long minutes, then said, "You're sure?"

My hostess proffered more food, but some people just take your appetite away. Papi's daughter embodied every sticky, snooty stereotype I'd ever had about a rich, rude bitch. My dislike of her had been instantaneous and her behavior toward her father had deepened it. Good thing we'd never have to meet in a dark alley. I might scratch her eyes out for fun.

"I'll be there as soon as I can," Papi said. He stood and Michaela moved to his side once again, an elegant nursemaid. "It seems that I'm having a family emergency of my own."

"Oh, no," I said stupidly.

"It can't be helped." He smiled and patted my hand, just as Detective Sanchez had done in the hospital when we'd first met, and stepped noiselessly to the door. "Please consider my offer of help. Call Michaela if you need anything at all for your niece."

With that, the audience ended. I almost curtseyed.

11

Here's my advice: if your lover isn't available, satisfy those cravings with food. The choices proved difficult. Should I opt for seven pounds of fresh lemon gelato at the Manazares Street Coffeehouse or more substantial fare? I chose the latter in order to prepare for the upcoming tidal wave of Davielle's hostility. Heavy food, pungent pastas, and salads the size of hubcaps would bolster my ability to keep my head above her fluid insults. Thank goodness the Socorro Springs Brew Pub perked nearby. Originally, the restaurant/bar had been located just off the plaza. Frankly, I wished it had stayed there as an additional draw once we got the visitors' center up and running.

But wishes weren't reality. The new building stood modern and large on California Street, better to catch people driving in from the freeway. During the day, the pub's lounge area served as a coffee bar. The other side served the meal I needed: a roasted garlic, red pepper, and goat cheese pizza. If Davielle got really obnoxious, my breath could knock her out.

The dinner salad was a nod to my handsome, almost-gone boyfriend's yammering about the lack of veggies in my diet. Peter didn't even think that dill pickles counted as greens. He'd scoffed when I'd justified a second candy bar with the fact that chocolate came from beans. Well, he wasn't here and I liked my own logic. I ordered the largest latte the restaurant offered, with a triple shot of espresso. See? More healthy beans.

"There was work to do this morning and he chose to go home. Yes, that's right. He went home." Wrapped in her own tattletale world, a woman sitting next to me talked on her cell phone, her side of the conversation broadcast with an indignant, too-loud voice. Rather than listen, I committed a similar sin as soon as the main dining room had emptied.

First, I called Gabi.

"Please give me another hour . . . or two," she pleaded. "I appreciate everything you're doing for me, really. I just want to be alone for as long as I can before Davielle gets here."

She didn't need to persuade me. Telling Gabi about her front porch held as much allure as ripping off a large scab. I glowered.

"Is everything all right?" My server stopped on her way to another table.

"Fine, thanks." I dipped a finger in the coffee to get at the foam. How could anyone ever get Gabi's place clean? It'd be better if she moved to a bigger, nicer house, one with a real closet, for example. Maybe Mom could kick in money to help.

I munched the pizza and made the next call. As usual, Darnda's answering machine picked up. Small mercies. It didn't take a psychic to know I felt flattened by today's events. My friend would have pressed me further, eliciting tears for the umpteenth time in hours.

Peter's service asked if this was an emergency. *Nah. I'm just missing you.* Over at Mom's house, my timing sparkled; she was in the middle of an occupational therapy session. I got virtue points for calling without any of the discomfort of conversation. Instead, I chatted with her saintly boyfriend Paul and told him Eva and Davielle would probably be in touch.

"I'm not surprised," he said.

"Really?"

"I saw it on the news."

"Does Mom know?"

"No, and I plan to keep it that way." Paul whispered now, his hurt pinning me to the chair. "You should have called. It was quite a shock."

"I'm sorry."

"It's water under the bridge now." His voice became an upbeat smile.

"Mom's in the room?"

"Yes." He cupped his hand over the receiver, saying something to her. I waited, smooshing the pizza crust into the remnants of the balsamic vinegar dressing. "If we're interested, we'll be sure to call back."

During the last couple of years, Paul and I had had to move to subterfuge. While it didn't bother me much, it upset Paul terribly. I was used to keeping confidences and doling out information for best effect. He said he felt like a liar, though he never questioned the need to protect Mom from too much worry. Every time we had a problem like this, I wondered if he'd have the patience to stay with our baggage-laden, emotionally askew family. . . .

Rather than travel down *that* road, I made more phone calls. Josie, my landlady, agreed to watch Leo. A couple of freelance jobs—writing an op-ed, planning a book launch for a self-published author—progressed beyond the initial stages. I picked up a chunk of roasted garlic and chewed on it while listening to messages. Three hang-ups and one request for my rates from a potential client in Carlsbad. *No way.* That was too far to drive. *No. Well, maybe.*

To prolong the virtuous feeling of work accomplished, I decided to visit one or two of the landmarks on my list of potential tourist attractions in Socorro itself. A short diagonal across from the brew pub, the roof of the Garcia Opera House pitched skyward, its tin sides shining in the wan light of a cloud-heavy winter sky. Built in the early 1800s, the renovated building now served as a venue for theater performances and other events. I would have liked to have seen the inside, but no cars rested in its lot and I wasn't in the mood to try locked doors.

Killing time sure could be boring. I drove to a convenience store. One can of whipped cream and a few candy bars later, I debated my next move. Bailey Hayes, my reporter buddy, had told me about the town's public library. We'd talked about it when we'd last gone out for drinks. Turns out she'd been born in Socorro and felt tremendous pride for her hamlet. I had the time now. Why not?

Thoughts of Bailey brought the memory of today's breaking news broadcast, the one I'd watched with Gabi. That bomb squad guy had to be the man I'd seen at the Sanchez compound. He just looked so much better in the flesh. Amazing. How could anyone be so handsome? I sighed. Attraction only lead to heartbreak, or worse.

I'd wager Bailey had never had nightmares about former boyfriends. I waited at a red light, remembering the time she'd set me up with an older weatherman on a double date. Her hunk had a PhD. My guy had the intelligence of a summer windstorm, swirling hot air and a lot of dirt. Too bad he couldn't muster a breeze of interest out of me. At least one sunny spot had come of that debacle; Bailey and I had grown closer, especially with the good guffaw we'd had afterward. Our age difference gave us an interesting dynamic. I almost thought of her as a younger sister or cousin.

Gabi's story appeared to be Bailey's purview and that could be a good thing. Since Detective Sanchez didn't seem too forthcoming with details, my acquaintance with the reporter might be a win-win asset. She'd be inclined to help if she could. I'd rather give her the inside scoop on our family than talk with an unknown reporter. Right now, I'd bet Bailey and her ratings-hungry station would love the hate-crime angle.

At least that gave me a possible way to flush out Gabi's attackers. I had a first step rather than feeling totally at a loss for direction. With a lighter heart, I parked the car in front of the library and entered the adobe building.

A fireplace warmed the front room, comforting me with a scent as cherished as the finest perfume in New Mexico. Piñon wood. Its smoke evoked family, good health, and well-being. No matter how large or small the collection, no matter whether the card catalog was automated or antiquated, this library had already won me over.

Velvety sunlight through thick glass haloed a woman in her mid-fifties with dust-colored hair. Dark eyeglass frames dominated her face, reaching up to the middle of her forehead and down to the middle of her cheeks. They reminded me of safety goggles. She sat behind a wide countertop, working.

Her magnified eyes met mine with insect curiosity. "May I help you?"

I introduced myself and told her about the San-Socorro project.

"Oh, I've heard about that," she said. "You're not thinking of including us, are you?"

"Why not?"

"Well, for one thing, we're a library, not some place to pop in for the sights."

"True enough. But wouldn't it be nice to attract more patrons or funding?"

She held up her finger to silence me, the stereotypic librarian. "Just let me just finish this thought and we can continue our conversation."

Her attitude annoyed me. Even if she didn't want her precious little turf to be mentioned in the visitors' center, she could use a lesson in public relations. Public awareness, especially for organizations that depended on government funding, was better than being ignored. Small-mindedness and a lack of vision tolled the twin death knells of most nonprofit organizations.

"There." Dressed in a wooly brown sweater and fuzzy black slacks, the woman emerged from her protective space to shake my hand. "I'm Beth Grable, director of the library."

"Pleased to meet you." My ruffled feathers hadn't settled yet.

"If you've got time, I'd be glad to show you around."

It couldn't take more than ten minutes. "That'd be great."

"This room is where it all started in 1929," she said with a broad sweep of her right hand. Her palm looked as dry as matzo. I chucked my ungenerous thoughts way down and tried to pay attention to her spiel.

The thick, original adobe walls lent a bomb-shelter security to the place, only prettier. Vigas—natural, rounded wooden beams that are often no more than bark-stripped tree trunks—held up the ceiling and the lattice-worked smaller branches that formed an intricate zigzag pattern above our heads. I felt like I'd walked into an ancient home or kiva, authentic and exuding tradition, truly wonderful, magical. In the corner near the fireplace, women talked quietly, smoothing curly hair on sleeping toddlers' foreheads.

"Our founders wanted to preserve the original building," Grable said. "When they reroofed the place, they made sure to keep everything just as it should be, including the six inches of mud used for insulation."

We toured room to room, this one built in the '50s, that one added in the '70s, and so forth. Each space had something special, something that a tourist would appreciate. The collection itself, with its southwestern specialties and friendly presentation, would entice even the most reluctant reader.

"I'm impressed," I said. "Are you sure you don't want to be included? It could raise your visibility and increase use."

"Is Cecilia Sanchez involved?" Grable impaled the name with distaste.

"I don't think so. Why?"

"Never mind." She led me down a step into a much newer room with exposed metal beams replacing, but still evoking, vigas. Neon carpeting and dangling mobiles signaled a different target audience. Teens sat at computers. Littler kids sprawled on beanbag chairs in not-so-hidden nooks. "In case you couldn't tell, this is our children's room."

"I like it," I said, watching an adolescent, long hair covering the acne on his face. He bent over a binder, writing with all the intensity of pubescent passion in which everything vibrates to perceived life-or-death consequences.

At twenty-one, Gabi hadn't left high school *that* long ago. She must be feeling the same way now, wondering if she'd have an arm, a hand to use. I felt angry that she had to experience such emotions, to even ponder such questions.

"Ms. Solomon?"

With a shake of the head, I refocused on the present. "I'm sorry. I didn't catch your last comment."

"Since we can't grow out, we're planning to grow up," said the librarian, each word deliberate and rude. She forgot her displeasure, though. "We hope to gut the upstairs and create a meeting area for civic groups. Your employer, the San-Socorro Foundation, is supposed to help us out."

"Really? I just met Papi Sanchez." The full interview came back to me, including that weird cat-and-mouse between the blonde and her handsome pursuer.

Grable's face lit with pure love. "He's been so good to this community, so supportive."

"Mr. Sanchez—"

"Papi," she said.

I nodded at the correction. "It's difficult to think of him that way; he seems so formidable."

Grable led me back to the front room. "Yes, he is impressive. It's astounding to think of how much he's accomplished, growing up dirt poor, getting to college, earning a scholarship to Harvard Business School when minorities weren't the flavor *du jour*. I can understand why you might be a bit intimidated." She'd returned to her seat, a sour smile coming to her lips.

"What?" I hoped she'd dish.

"I just wish his children shared the same noble attributes."

"Really?" I should have waited two breaths before saying it.

"Oh, don't mind me. It's been a long day," she said with irrevocable finality. A line had been crossed. Grable had retreated to the Ice Age.

12

My overly observant niece Davielle galumphed ever closer to town. I could almost hear her telltale heart of discontent, thumping, thumping down the freeway. Louder, louder.

Plagued by the looming vision, I drove around the plaza yet again. The Socorro Chamber of Commerce perched on its eastern edge. Tomorrow, I'd meet the director. Why not go make nice-nice now?

Outside, the chamber didn't have much curb appeal. Inside, the first impression said *blah squared*. Old office resale outlets had furnished the main room with flaccid, heavy pieces. I recognized the brand names; they'd been my mainstays in the past. A new paint job, modern accoutrements and, maybe, some interesting artwork could remedy the cosmetics in a nanosecond. Yeah, and I could lose ten pounds, too. Right.

"Hi there," said an elderly woman, her smile ready. She wore a white turtleneck and one of those seasonal knitted vests with holiday themes. This one sported a turkey and a horn o' plenty. She had to be a volunteer.

"Is Olivia Okino here?" I said, asking for the director.

"Oh-*kee*-no. You say it like, 'Oh-*kee*-no.'"

I tried a second time.

She nodded her head in approval, leaned back, and said, "She's not."

"Oh, well. It was worth a shot." A surge of relief swept through me. The San-Socorro project might not be welcomed here. Some county employees saw the grandiose visitors' center as a threat, usurping their territory and power to promote.

A noisy heater ka-chunked before emitting its prize. The warm air wafted around the room, nestling under the hair at the back of my neck and cuddling my upper arms.

"Nothing ventured, nothing gained," said the woman. She sealed an envelope from a large stack in front of her and placed it in another one. "Although, when you think about it, that expression leaves a lot to be desired."

"What do you mean?" She reminded me of a sensible aunt, the kind I'd never be. Her accent intrigued me, too. I couldn't place it and wanted to hear her say more.

"It's just asking for trouble, isn't it? 'Nothing ventured, nothing gained.'" She stopped to look at me over her half-moon reading glasses. "That *something* might just be a whole kettle of worms."

"Good for a fisherman."

She laughed and the amiability of it made me yearn to hug her. The depth of my response thrust me into a chair. Was I really feeling so fragile?

The woman picked up a piece of colored paper, goldenrod, I think, and did a masterful three-way fold, then stuffed it into an envelope.

"Do you need help?" I sat at a round table topped with fake wood. Colorful brochures broke its monotony.

"How nice of you. Don't mind if I do." She rose with a cup in her hand. "I've got a fresh pot of coffee. Would you like some?"

After serving me, she returned to her desk. "My name's Sallie Bourgeois."

"I'm pleased to meet you." I smiled. "I'm Sasha Solomon."

"I thought so." She sipped her drink. "You look exactly like your mother."

Not again. Though New Mexico was the fifth largest state in land mass in the United States, it often proved too small. Everywhere I went, someone knew someone who knew someone I knew.

"Oh, don't get that look on your face." Sallie's rich, smoky laugh could become addictive. "Your mother was a beautiful woman in her day."

"Are you an artist?"

"Heavens, no." Sallie handed me a pile of paper. "Would you work on these?" With a deft press-press, she showed me how to do the three-way fold and left an example in case I got confused.

The chamber's door flew open.

"Sallie, we've got a few—" Swaddled in a thick brown parka, Heather Apodaca walked to the table. "Oh, hi. How's Gabi?"

"She's hanging in there."

Sallie looked at us both. "Well, I won't bother asking if you know each other." She picked up a stack of envelopes. "Do you want to help us get these out, Heather?"

The young woman shook her head. "It looks like you two've got it under control. I just stopped by to say hello." She moved toward the door.

"Don't feel like you've got to go," I said.

"Actually, I'm on my way to meet some friends." She blew Sallie a kiss and waved to me. "Tell Gabi I'll stop by later. Nice seeing you again." With that, she let another blast of cold air in and left.

The volunteer watched Heather's retreating form until she disappeared around the corner, probably heading to the Manzanares Street Coffeehouse. "How do you know Heather?"

"She's a friend of my niece's."

"Well, then, your niece is a lucky girl. I've known Heather, and her mom, for years. They're very good people."

"That's nice to know." I lifted a sheet of paper and began my task. "Speaking of moms, how do you know mine?"

Sallie's laugh warmed my toes. "Before your time, my husband and I used to own the Route 66 Trading Post in Old Town, up in Albuquerque. Your mother's gallery was next door. When I saw your name on a letter from the San-Socorro Foundation, I put two and two together. There aren't *that* many Solomons in New Mexico. Not spelled that way, anyway." She settled into her chair. "I heard she's been having health problems?"

"She's had a few strokes but she's holding her own now." No need to give details about Mom's Swiss cheese short-term memory or her increasing frailty. I pressed a seam, trying to get it a bit more even this time.

"Old age is the pits." Sallie shook her head.

"I'm beginning to see that."

Mindless office work soothed when it was someone else's responsibility. In my twenties, I'd volunteered for a literacy program and did this kind of stuff all the time. Once Peter moved, it might be good to do again, a regular mitzvah, a good deed. At the rate I was going, earning good karma might buffer me against the truckloads of blunders committed in my daily life. At the very least, it'd keep me off the streets. Maybe I'd volunteer for a domestic violence shelter; that might put me off men for a while.

"Have you lived in Socorro long?" I said. Sallie might be a good source about the town. Maybe she knew some nasty high schoolers, too.

"I've lived here at least twice as long as you've been alive."

"You're a hundred and fifty?"

She laughed again and I wanted more. "At least."

I grinned at the jest. "So what do you think about the visitors' center? Will it work?"

Sallie's hands stopped their mission. "Overall? I think it'll be great for the county. But, you're in for trouble with everyone trying to get their piece of this pie."

"I was afraid of that."

"Well, forewarned is forearmed."

"Can you tell me who to watch out for?" I wasn't sure if she would take the bait so soon after meeting me.

She licked an envelope. "You're asking me to gossip."

"Kind of."

"That's ungodly."

"You can tell me good things." I pushed the mound of papers forward. "Maybe you've got an opinion about which projects might deserve a bit more attention?"

"Now you're just parsing gossip into hearsay." No vexation accompanied her words. "I've got a question for you."

"Anything."

"I know you're going to have a meeting with everyone tomorrow, but why are you here today? At the chamber, I mean." She retrieved my work. "Don't get me wrong. It's nice to have the company, but I'd imagine a high-powered consultant like you has better things to do."

No one had ever referred to me as "high-powered," except in my dreams . . . the good kind, the kind my subconscious had currently misplaced.

"Did you hear about that explosion in the neighborhood near Tech this morning?" I watched for acknowledgment. "My niece was the victim."

"Oh, the poor thing!" Sallie's hands danced in a complicated self-massage, making sounds like carbonation squirting from a plastic bottle. A high red color splotched her loose cheeks. Could she know something about the incident?

"Have there been hate crimes in Socorro before?" I studied her, wondering why anxiety nibbled at her features.

Her once-open face acquired a shutter.

"This isn't common knowledge yet, but in addition to the pipe bomb, someone vandalized my niece's porch with a horrible racial epitaph." It was risky mentioning this, but I wanted Sallie to trust me, to tell me what she knew. "That's a hate crime to me."

The older woman's internal debate rendered her motionless as a telephone pole.

"I was just hoping you might've heard something," I said, glancing at my watch. An hour had passed in a minute. "I'd better go. My niece is expecting me back before dinner."

Sallie scooted her chair out and walked me to the door. "I just despise gossip."

Frankly, I loved it. In this case, gossip would give me ideas about how to help Gabi. My hand touched the brass knob. Outside, the sky flamed with bright pink clouds against a solemn blue. Lines of jet exhaust crisscrossed, creating a giant X on the western horizon.

"You'll find this out sooner or later," said Sallie. "So, I might as well tell you the truth as I know it." Could she see I was holding my breath? "You're working for Papi Sanchez, but you might not know that he has five children. Three are from a first marriage. His wife died young." She bent in to whisper. "His second wife gave him two rotten children and so many headaches he threw her out of his life."

"Thank you for telling me." Cecilia must be from wedding number two. But who was the other child? "Do you think one of them could commit a hate crime?"

Sallie opened the door. "The police think one of them already did, a long time ago." I wanted to follow up on her response. She shook her head. "I've already said too much."

Stalled by her obstinate expression, I put her zinger in my mental file and thanked God for a bucketful of new avenues to explore.

13

True happiness is born of lowered expectations.

A superhero I wouldn't be today, but I could undertake mundane tasks. The local grocery store had whipped cream. The Holiday Inn Express had two available rooms. Eva and Davielle could share one of them. My king-sized bed ensured that neither one would sleep with me.

A tanker of dread slammed into my stomach when I got back into the car, my hands clammy when they placed the magnetic keys in my wallet. How had Davielle gained such power over me? Though we hadn't seen each other in a few years, I still smarted from her unending, unuttered reprimands. That I even claimed to be Jewish insulted all she stood for. From the moment we'd met she judged me, a strange sensation to experience with a preverbal baby.

Unlike Eva, whose life became richer with her professional kudos, Davielle realized her dreams through pregnancy. She'd never worked outside the home and only left that refuge to ferry mini-Davielles hither and yon. Her pompous husband reminded me of a giant grub, pale, slimy, and full of himself. Their wealth came from inheritances on his side. I doubted they donated much to charity.

Their extremism offended my nerves and made me watch my back. It wouldn't surprise any of us if Davielle and her husband opted to recolonize the West Bank themselves, birthing squadrons of little Israeli children to take up arms against their Palestinian counterparts and to foil any attempts for peace. While I was all for Israel's continued and healthy existence, Davielle's cries for war, issued from a comfortable home with every amenity, rang as false as a polygamist's protests of undying love.

I turned on the radio, opened the can of whipped cream, and took a hit while waiting for the light to change. How had this happened to our family? Why had Eva gone off the deep end with Judaism? Blame it on New York. My sister met her future husband at Columbia University. He was a chemist and she was a doctoral candidate in cross-cultural education. They'd spotted each other over the roasted egg at a Passover seder.

The man in the car behind me honked his horn. I turned onto Highway 60.

Before that fateful Pesach, Eva had more than everything going for her. She possessed beauty, intellect, and an untamable spirit that electrified everyone around her. When she'd earned her PhD at twenty, unsolicited job offers jammed her apartment's mailbox. That was in May. By the end of June, she'd decided to marry Zachariah Shofet.

My sister embraced her new family's orthodoxy and appalled those of us she'd left behind. For a decade, the only things Mom and I could agree on were that Eva had gone mad and she was wasting her potential marrying this stout, surly man who rarely spoke and never smiled. We consoled ourselves with the thought that their union would never last. Boy, were we wrong. They'd celebrated their thirtieth anniversary this year.

Other than her zeal, Eva had an additional flaw. She panicked any time her children got sick. This reaction had its base in the horrible death to SIDS of her only son. Though she'd had four daughters after the tragedy, the memory of that first extinguished life had never healed. I hoped Gabi's injuries wouldn't send my sister overboard.

The hospital's small parking lot lounged semi-full. Emerging from the car like some kind of hibernating animal, I pulled the edges of my coat together to protect my chest from the wind. The lobby's heat overpowered its square footage and the smell of despair emanated from each chair. A harried receptionist answered the phone and tried to console a man whose attention lanced from her to his three young, active children. I left their ping-pong ballet in search of Gabi. At her door, I heard voices and paused to listen before entering.

"If you know anything, now's the time to tell me," said the man I'd seen just hours ago.

"She's lying," said Gabi.

"So are you."

Without waiting for more, I went in. Detective Sanchez stood at the base of Gabi's bed, his lips succumbing to a gravitational pull far stronger than earth's. He looked from my niece to me. "Should I tell her or do you want to?"

I had no context. What were they talking about? The vandalism? The pipe bomb we weren't supposed to know about?

"Ms. Shofet's boyfriend is missing," said the detective.

Gabi winced before her mouth flattened into a straight edge.

"Oh," I said.

"You don't seem concerned."

"Did he get mangled by a pipe bomb, too?" The slip reinforced my conviction that I should have brushed my teeth with superglue. To staunch further leakage, I put my purse on the windowsill and attempted an air of detachment.

Sanchez regarded me with an archer's eyes, ready to shoot. "Who said anything about a pipe bomb?"

"You can quit the charade, Detective." I pulled out the piece of metal and handed it to Gabi, but my words were for the policeman. "I'm sure you've seen more of these. This one made a three-inch crater in the house across the street."

"Oh my God," Gabi said.

"We're still not sure it was a pipe bomb." Did detectives take courses in how to act as clueless as pigeons?

"It's a piece of pipe, for God's sake," said Gabi. "Someone tried to kill me and you're dicking around with a grown man's choice not to go home to his shrew of a wife? How dare you." She couldn't have mustered this much indignation earlier today. The solitude had brought her strength. *Good for you, Gabi.*

Waitaminute. "Wife?" I said.

"That's one of the interesting things about all of this," said the detective, his gaze frozen on my niece's every blink. He bent forward so that his elbows rested on the metal edge of her bed. "Ms. Solomon, has your niece ever mentioned Aaron Wahl?"

"He's her advisor, right?"

Gabi's face icicled.

"Do you really think his disappearance has anything to do with my niece?"

"I doubt it's a coincidence." When Sanchez frowned, his doughy jowls created a valley, his mouth a lake of disgruntlement. "Ms. Shofet here is almost killed and her lover's wife calls the station in a panic. No. It's not a coincidence."

"That's bullshit. The only reason they still live together, and he goes home every single night, is to keep her rich daddy happy," said Gabi. "Panic? I don't think so. The only thing she cares about are her Manolos."

The color left my overheated face. I sat down hard, the chair moving an inch backward with the force. "And you know these details how?"

"It's a long story," said my niece.

"Hey, I've got a whole lifetime, at least until Davielle gets here. Perhaps you'd rather tell it to her, too." I'd been snared, trapped into sympathy by the same kind of need-to-know information flow used by armies, and PR pros, for decades. No wonder Gabi had closed up so thoroughly this morning. A creepy sense of betrayal tensed my jaws. I wanted to throw up my hands, to walk away. But familial obligation planted my feet in the cement of duty.

Gabi turned her head away from me.

"The good professor has quite a reputation for seducing his brightest students," said the policeman. "You should be honored, I suppose."

His tone skinned my pride. How dare he be nasty to *my* niece? Sure, I was mad at her, but that didn't give him to right to be. With a cornered badger's readiness, I slashed out. "Are you certain, Detective? Isn't it the wife's word against Gabriela's?"

"There's the rub." He made a melodramatic show of shaking his head. "Your niece isn't talking. Mrs. Wahl, on the other hand, has a lot to say. She called us, frantic with worry and accusations." When he tapped Gabi's bed for emphasis, his wedding ring clinked against the metal. "And yet, rather than defend herself or tell me her side of the story, Ms. Shofet here chooses to impersonate a rock."

"Don't the police wait for twenty-four hours before investigating adult disappearances?" Though I felt twice his irritation, his pique evoked mama-bear instincts in me. "How can you be so sure Gabriela was his lover? Maybe he's having an affair with someone else. Maybe his wife is just making it all up."

"It's fascinating the pictures people carry in their backpacks," said the detective.

"You had no right." Gabi's stare would have intimidated most people.

Sanchez's voice descended to the earth's molten center. "Believe me, Ms. Solomon, we're absolutely certain about this. The question is, why is your niece stonewalling us if she has nothing to hide?"

"I don't understand why you're attacking the victim here." I crossed my legs. "So what if she's having an affair? Even if the story is true, a moral lapse doesn't justify the crimes committed against her."

"You're absolutely right." Sanchez glanced at Gabi, whose blanket moved up and down with her breathing. "But I continue to be disturbed by her unwillingness to talk. In police circles, that's a red flag." He shrugged. "Well, maybe you can talk some sense into her. You know where to reach me if you do."

"Bye," I mumbled after he left.

How could Gabi throw her life away on an oversexed, indiscreet old man? She had to be smarter than that. I sighed.

"What?" she said.

She'd lied to the police at least once that I knew about. What else was she keeping from all of us? With cold fingers, I rubbed my temples and tried to delete my overreactions.

"Don't just sit there judging me." Gabi's voice cut through my efforts. "Aaron is the most brilliant man I've ever known. He speaks ten languages, has twelve patents, has been at the center of some of the most important chemical discoveries ever made. I'm honored to work with him, to love him, Aunt Sasha."

No man could be that good. I already mourned the upcoming destruction of her idealism.

"Say something."

My deep breath calmed fizzled nerves and frazzled thoughts. I'd been blaming the victim just like Detective Sanchez. Gabi didn't deserve to be lying here in the hospital, her hand unmoving, her arm pulverized, her life in turmoil. Youth included the entitlement to make mistakes. Adulthood didn't.

I moved the chair closer to her bed and took her healthy hand in mine. "Does your mom know?"

14

Davielle Cohen swooped into the room, a Semitic blur of dark skin, dark hair (even though it was a wig), dark almond eyes. Her father's daughter. She'd fit into a nomadic tribe from the Old Testament, wearing a flowing caftan, her plump arm extended with a finger pointing, ordering some poor slob to move his camel.

Within two breaths, she'd managed to suck up all our air and arouse tornado-gusts of tension. She'd always had that talent.

"Oh, Gabi! Gabi! Baby! What's happened to you?" Tears rivered from her eyes and coursed down canyons on her cheeks; she must have started crying when her plane landed in Albuquerque. How she'd managed the seventy-mile drive through such moisture testified to her sheer force of will.

Gabi sighed. "Hi, Davielle."

"Hi? You say 'hi' when you're lying here covered in bandages and looking like you're one step away from death? 'Hi'? That's all you can say?"

I didn't bother pointing out all the inconsistencies in that little missive.

Gabi rolled her eyes and looked at me.

"Hi, Davielle," I said.

"What? Oh, Aunt Sasha. You can go now." Pulling a white leather book from her purse, Davielle began mumbling in Hebrew and swaying at Gabi's side. I half expected her to lay her hands on her sister's head and say, "Be healed!"

"I think not." I tugged at my sweater, pulling it down over my thighs in a customary and self-conscious effort to hide my stomach's little roll of fat. On second thought, Davielle made me feel thin. Remembering the can of whipped cream in my purse, I fetched it and took a hit.

Gabi's miniscule smile was an added bonus.

"What's that?" Davielle's imperiousness bugged me—from the brown corduroy jumper with long-sleeved blouse to the shoes that tied, from the greasy wig to the wide lips and heavy brows. How had my sister issued such a creature? Could her love for Zach ignore the monster they'd created?

"Surely you've seen whipped cream before," I said.

"Why do you have it in your purse? What's wrong with you?"

Yep. Davielle *was* as bad as I remembered. "I carry it in my purse because it has fewer calories than booze, dear."

Gabi laughed. What a glorious sound in the flurry of the day's horror. I coveted it, plotting more ways to coax glee from her. I took another, much longer toke on the can.

"You're disgusting," said Davielle.

"No, I'm your aunt. Show some respect."

"You must be tired," said Gabi to her sister. "Why don't you go to the hotel and relax for a while?"

"What? You want to get rid of me already? If I'd known you'd do this, I wouldn't have come all the way from Scottsdale. Brigid volunteered to watch the children so that I could be here. And me, pregnant, barely able to walk." She eyed the chair in which I sat. Another one was positioned near the bathroom door. "Could you get that for me, Aunt Sasha?"

None of the responses that came to mind resembled anything gracious, so I stood and carried the chair to the other side of Gabi's bed. At least that way I wouldn't be sitting next to Davielle. Gabi could make faces at me if she wanted.

A dietary services worker brought dinner in, covered with an aluminum top. She unveiled it with the panache of a waitperson at a fine restaurant. The spaghetti sauce smelled good, sweet.

"Can you help me with this?" said Gabi, and the race was on. Davielle heaved to a stand. I inched closer, too. We vied for position as chief caretaker.

"Do you want me to cut it into bites, so that you can feed yourself?" I said while Davielle unwrapped the plastic cutlery.

Gabi nodded.

I lifted the packet of Parmesan cheese and wiggled it. "You want?"

"Sure." Gabi took the piece of garlic bread in her good hand and dipped it in the meat sauce while I sprinkled the spaghetti with cheese.

"What are you doing? That's not kashrut!" Davielle reached for the plate and headed toward the garbage can. I hadn't seen her step so fast in years. "What's wrong with this place? Don't they know you're Jewish?"

"Don't you know you're in Socorro?" said Gabi.

"Could you turn the decibels down by, say, fifty percent, Davielle?" I took the plate from her pudgy hand and returned it to Gabi's bed tray. "At least they didn't give her pork chops."

"I'm hungry and a heathen," said Gabi, biting the bread. "You would be, too, if someone nearly blew off your arm with a pipe bomb."

I cut the pasta into baby bites and then returned to my seat so that Gabi would have room to eat.

"How could you?" Davielle's sails had gone limp. Her skin became muck. I thought she might pass out. Her question, addressed to no one in particular, hung above us all, a deflated recrimination.

Into this lovely scene bleated my cell phone.

"You don't even say a prayer. No gratitude?" Davielle recoiled from her sister with candid incomprehension. "Can you really have forgotten all Mama and Daddy taught you? Can you really care so little?"

I watched her despair grow with each word and understood a part of her shock. She'd rearranged her life, dropped everything to fly to Gabi's side, only to find that her sister had become irreligious. It must have jolted her as much as Eva's total immersion had me. The phone continued its plaint and I answered before the person had to leave a message.

"How's your niece?" said Peter, his voice tickling me just below the belly button and radiating in both directions. *Damn him.*

The contrast between my reality and what was happening in Gabi's room proved to be too much. My niece could deflect Davielle's disillusionment for a few minutes; I had to get out of there before my body turned into a ball of lust.

Ducking out into the hall, I said, "She's got some fight in her now but, boy, this whole thing is just going from bad to worse." The wall felt cool against my back. "I miss you."

"Want me to come down? We could have dinner and hit the bosque early tomorrow."

"You'd do that for me?" Even though I had that big meeting in the morning, we might be able to swing a trip to the bird refuge for the dawn fly-out.

"I would."

Then why won't you stay in Albuquerque? Why do you have to go all the way to Maryland? Empty food carts lined the corridor, ready to receive their remnants of dinner. An old man, using a wooden cane, passed me. He nodded. I reciprocated.

"Sasha?" Peter's voice cut through my self-pity.

"Sure, come on down." Even small doses of my lover were better than none at all. If we couldn't make up at my place, why not here? "I'll be at the hospital until I get kicked out. After that, I'll be at the Holiday Inn."

Clicking off the phone, I returned to hear Gabi say, "You just don't get it, do you? You're always saying I like to blow things up as if I'm some kind of terrorist. Do you talk this way to Dad?"

"It's not the same."

"Like hell it's not. He's a good guy. I'm a good guy. We both blow things up to save lives. Can't you get that through your thick skull?" Gabi's hair hung in strings around her newly wet face. "The work I'm doing right now, even more than Dad's, will help defend our country, the entire world, from terrorists. God! You're such a fucking, self-righteous idiot."

Davielle gasped, her face a shattering frame, the world unsteady beneath her swollen ankles. She found the chair, dejection anvilling her body further onto its unforgiving surface. Her wig rested slightly askance on her broad forehead.

"Why don't you head over to the hotel?" I said to my oldest niece. If Eva depended on me to keep things together until she came, I'd done a rotten job. The gray in Davielle's cheeks worried me. This anguish couldn't be for show. "You can freshen up, take a shower, and then come back."

"I never should have come," she said, rising. "What was I thinking?"

"That you love your sister." I stood in front of her. "You haven't even told us when you're due."

"Who cares?" She reached down to gather her coat and a purse the size of a forty-gallon garbage bag.

"Hey, you," said Gabi, who'd morphed into a sunny day full of cotton candy clouds and cavorting bunnies. I turned, ready to lambaste her for the cruelty with which she'd just doused her sister. How could she now sound so full of delight?

"Hi," said Ralph, waiting at the door. He stood, accompanied by a painfully thin man. This new person had to be his brother; he resembled Ralph, only chopped up and pressed through a sieve. His bony elbows poked against his navy blue sweater and his eyes had the vacant look of someone who did too much speed or was dying of some kind of wasting disease. A cross, similar to the one Ralph wore, glistened on its chain for all to see.

Gabi's grin extended her permission for them to enter. Both men had bouquets, bright things wrapped in plastic, probably bought at Gene's Flowers & Gifts near the plaza.

"You ditching school again?" said the man I didn't know.

"Yeah, Marcel. Fighting with a mailbox was easier than giving that quiz." Light came into Gabi's eyes; her visitors had displaced Davielle and me in the room and in her consciousness. "Who took my class?"

A minute later, Heather showed up with a big plastic cup and a bunch of multicolored balloons. "No one said you couldn't have a milkshake."

"Chocolate?"

"Double chocolate." Heather handed the balloons to me, then noticed Davielle. They turned away from each other as if burned, their instinctive dislike so pronounced it sizzled. Gabi's friend pretended to pummel the men. "Get out of my way, you lummoxes. Can't you see I've got the medicine she really needs?"

"God, I'm glad to see you," said Gabi, her relief so hearty I felt stung.

"You ready for some gossip?" Heather unzipped her backpack and pointed at Ralph's brother. "Marcel here pissed off Narayan with his latest equation."

"Serves him right," said Marcel. "Someone had to take that ego down a notch."

"Yeah, but why you, Brainiac?" Heather put the straw in the drink, bent it to a convenient angle, and held it up to Gabi's mouth.

My niece closed her eyes, savoring the flavor. "Perfect."

"Sweetie, I think we'll leave you to your friends for a while," I said. "How about you call when they've gone?"

"Visiting hours end at eight. We can stay until then. Can't we, guys?" Heather still held the shake.

Davielle pushed herself up with a groan and walked to the door. I watched the four of them and their comfortable familiarity, feeling as ignored as an old woman in an understaffed nursing home. The sense of having been dropkicked into another generation dried the inside of my mouth.

It hurt to be supplanted so easily.

15

"Sasha! Is that you?"

Deep in our private miseries, neither Davielle nor I noticed the television camera or pretty woman dressed in a trench coat and schmoozing with a volunteer at a desk in the hospital lobby.

"Bailey. Imagine meeting you here." I couldn't remember what information had been released to the media, but I knew that my friend would be angling to get the best story about the explosion. Then a rancid thought curdled my pleasure at seeing her. How would this kind of attention affect Gabi's career? Right now she was a victim, but as soon as the possible liaison with her advisor came out, everything would change. It'd be a juicy tidbit for a few nights' viewing but could desiccate her employment prospects for years.

"There's been a bombing, just like the ones last week in Albuquerque, in the Northeast Heights. You know, those firecrackers?" Bailey excused herself from the first conversation to join us. Her face flushed through expertly applied makeup. "Only this time, somebody got hurt."

Okay. She didn't know about the pipe bomb. I might trade that info down the line. It might be useful if my niece's rep started to tank because of the affair. Oh, who was I kidding? Sex always trumped everything else.

Bailey's reference to the pranks in Albuquerque brought back vague memories. I should've paid more attention. Were any of those mailboxes in *my* hometown in front of Jewish homes? Or Arab ones? Were the Albuquerque police hiding similar pipe bombings, too? The man Bailey had interviewed this morning would know. And I knew where he was, or at least where he'd been playing hide-the-salami with a spoiled brat of a woman earlier today.

Sex, again. How long would we be able to keep the affair quiet? I glanced at Davielle. Modesty may be a virtue, but a brush with fame had pinked her cheeks with girlish blushing. *Oh, Lord, not this.*

"Since I'm from Socorro, I got the story." Bailey turned to see what her cameraman was doing. "Pretty cool, huh?"

"That's great. We should have drinks again soon and you can tell me all about it." I tried to nudge Davielle toward the door. She'd gained weight in the last couple of minutes.

How could I have ignored the potential media attraction to this kind of story? It would be a bear to convince Gabi she needed PR prepping, talking points, interviewing rehearsals. Hell, if Gabi had been a client, I would have had an entire media plan in place by now. The headache tap-dancing at my temples jitterbugged down the back of my skull.

When Gabi's identity came out, there'd be a rush. I could hear the whistle of excitement now. Everyone would forget my niece was as American as a corn dog; they'd focus on that Iranian angle. It was just too damn scrumptious, too tempting for any self-respecting, ambitious reporter.

My job was to protect her privacy as long as possible and to manage the goodwill that would flow toward her for these few precious hours, or days, before her affair hit the ether.

It would help if I knew more about Aaron Wahl. Was the man really missing? I'd had enough bad experiences with boyfriends to suspect he might have skipped town just as things were, um, blowing up. *Sorry.*

" . . . yeah, I've interviewed the policeman on the case and know that the girl who was hurt is still in Socorro, but that's about all they'd tell me." Bailey flicked a piece of hair back into place. "We decided to stop by here and see if we could get any more information."

Smooth move. If this hospital had a public relations director, he or she would have already gone home for the day. This was the perfect time to get details you shouldn't have. I bet Bailey had dangled flattery and an interview in front of that volunteer's eyes before we'd interrupted her.

"So, what are you doing here?" Bailey said.

"Taking care of my sister," boomed Davielle.

The only muscles to move in my body silenced outward sound while screaming cosmic entreaties to smite my oldest niece with lightning. With the keen observance of an eagle, Bailey saw me tighten. She reached out to shake Davielle's hand and motioned to the cameraman at the same time. "Hi, I'm Bailey Hayes with KBRK, New Mexico's most-watched news station."

Shit.

"My sister's the one who was hurt." Davielle wiped her forehead and licked her lips. She wanted to be on television. What happened to humility? Her eyes widened as her voice went into a conspiratorial hush. "Her arm almost came off with that pipe bomb."

The cameraman made it over and prepared to film.

"Can we have a minute?" I said to Bailey. Without waiting, I tugged Davielle far enough away to spit, "What do you think you're doing? Do you want Gabi to be national news?" My eyes closed, I took a breath and held her with fingers turned to talons. "Follow my lead and keep your mouth shut."

"You're hurting me," whined Davielle. Her arm hadn't gone blue yet. Why the complaining?

"Well?" said Bailey, walking over to us.

"Well, Davielle is right, her sister *is* in this hospital. However, she's not up to being interviewed."

"You're sounding like a PR flack, Sasha. What gives?"

"Your niece." Davielle's stage mumble flew on the wings of spite.

"What did she say?" The reporter grabbed my wrist. We made a human chain now and I could feel those links squeezing every good thing out of my reach.

"It's true—" began Davielle. "Ow!"

"Bailey, we've known each other a long time."

"Long enough for me to recognize bullshit, Sasha," said my friend, her chin sinking with skepticism, her feet shoulder-width apart in anticipation of a hurricane of excuses. "Here it comes."

"My sister, the girl's mother, is coming in tomorrow. How about you give them a little time to deal with this before you run with it?" I met her stare. "I promise I'll call when she's willing to talk. An exclusive, Bailey. *You* and no one else."

"How old is she?" Bailey shackled my gaze; I didn't dare glance elsewhere.

"Early twenties."

"So I don't really need to wait for you, do I?"

"No. But you will, because it's the right thing to do." Even as the voiced hope met the air, we both knew it'd be trammeled. Still, I persevered. With my pointer finger, I made a cross over my heart. "I promise you'll be the only one to interview her."

"Why not let her tell her story now? What's she got to hide?"

Oh, great. Her suspicion grew stronger with each second.

"She's drugged, Bailey. Even if she wasn't, her public comments might mess up the investigation." I feigned nonchalance. "*I* wouldn't want to be responsible for screwing up their work. Would *you*?"

"Was it really a pipe bomb?" Bailey wanted a scrap, something to entice viewers, something no other station would have.

"The detective says he doesn't know, but I don't buy it." I let go of Davielle and moved to whisper in my friend's ear. "I bet that guy you interviewed this morning would be able to tell you for sure. The one from the bomb squad."

"I don't know why I didn't think of that myself." Bailey's eyes became mascara-lashed half-moons. She yawned, a flawless hand before her mouth. The action reminded me of high school boys with girls at the movies. Yawn and an arm drapes a shoulder. Yawn again, and a hand touches, as if by accident, a breast. Fake, fake, fake.

Davielle shuffled beside me. When I looked back at Bailey, her assessing glance rested on the volunteer at the info desk. Weighing options, strategizing leads. Were I her, I'd be doing the same thing. With a little more sugar and flattery, Bailey might be able to get Gabi's room number from the woman.

"You do for me and I'll do for you," I said. "You know you can trust me. I can trust you."

"Why don't you give me a comment?"

"I can't." This was as bad as saying "no comment." It begged the reporter to dig, to find dirt for herself. "Not yet."

"I've got to do my job, Sasha. I can't wait for you for very long."

"I'll make sure you don't have to."

Bailey relaxed her high shoulders, reached into her coat pocket, and pulled out two business cards. She handed one to Davielle and then one to me, saying, "Here. Just in case you don't have one on you."

"Thanks," I said.

"You'll call as soon as she's willing to talk?"

"I promise."

"Great. And let me know if you find out anything else?"

"You'll do me the same courtesy?"

Surprise opened her mouth before she spoke. "I bet you wouldn't say that to any other reporter."

"I don't consider any of the others my friend." I hoisted my purse back onto my shoulder. "My niece has been hurt, Bailey. I love her. She's very important to me."

"I'll think about it," she said.

Davielle cleared her throat with the gusto and volume of a hacking smoker.

In an instant, I could tell Bailey had finally snapped to Davielle's wig. That up-down look, a mix of inquisitiveness and typecasting. With scorpion-tail swiftness, she'd misjudged, and dismissed, Davielle's orthodoxy. "It was nice to meet you."

"Likewise," said my niece, unaware of her downgraded status.

"You call me, Sasha."

"I will." We'd made it to the door.

Outside, the cold air tipped my worries with frosty thoughts. Davielle got into her car and headed to the hotel. On a disagreeable hunch, I swung by the front of the hospital to look through those double glass doors once more. Sure enough, Bailey inclined gracefully against the information desk. The volunteer's wide smile felt as dangerous as a hailstorm.

My protests would yield only more curiosity. Instead, I pulled out the cell phone.

"Hello?" said Gabi.

"Listen."

"Aunt Sasha?"

"Yes. Listen to me. We don't have much time. Ask one of your friends to close the door to your room."

"But—"

"Just do it!" A second later, I heard her make the request. "Now, if anyone knocks, ask Ralph or his brother to answer. If it's a reporter with a cameraman, don't let them in. Got it?"

"What are you talking about?"

"Just do it. This is important." I'd arrived at the hotel. "I've got to go. Promise me you'll do it."

"All right, already," she said. "I promise."

I disconnected without a good-bye. The sun had sunk as low as my mood, but with more flamboyance. While the flame fought with the horizon, apprehension dug into my veins. What a mess this could be.

At the front desk, Davielle negotiated with the clerk about getting a fridge for her room. (How inconsiderate; I'd forgotten.) Suddenly, my enthusiasm for Peter's upcoming arrival plopped to the ground with a rotten splat. I hit the autodial, hoping against all odds that he was still in Albuquerque. Three rings and his perky answering service bid me hello. I hung up, dismay coating my tongue. This wasn't how I wanted to feel when we made up.

"No vegetarian restaurants?" Davielle pivoted at my touch, then resumed her rant. "How can a college town have no vegetarian restaurants?"

From what I understood, people who kept kosher often ate in strict vegetarian restaurants because there'd be no chance of combining meat and dairy in the kitchen. Those of us who loved green chile cheeseburgers thought they were insane.

"Let it be, Davielle. We'll go shopping," I said, weary to the bone.

"This is madness." Davielle clucked like the chicken she roasted every Friday afternoon before sundown.

"A lot of places have salad bars and cheese pizzas," said the clerk, trying to be helpful.

"Come on. I'll walk you to your room." I put my hand at her elbow and led her away. Before we'd taken three steps, the clerk had started to serve the elderly couple behind us.

Out front, a large motorcycle tilted into its kickstand. Two helmets decorated with American flags hung from the handlebars. Its white side bags had been stitched with the ubiquitous "Support our troops."

The good news: we were in the newer part of the hotel. The bad news: we had to get back in our cars and cross a small street to get to the annex.

"Who ever heard of having to drive to another building?" Davielle stomped dangerously near an emotional minefield. It took all my energy not to lash out. I bit my thumb. "What kind of hotel does such a thing?"

"This one," I said.

16

Even the apples didn't meet Davielle's standards. Muzak syruped overhead, cash registers beeped, children screamed. The grocery store's bright lights made me squint. Meanwhile, my niece's running diatribe about the insufficiencies of Socorro's biggest produce department elicited thoughts of muzzles and duct tape gleaming platinum across a certain wide yaw. How many rolls would it take?

"These bananas look like they're a year old." Davielle's commentary had gained volume.

"Just hurry and get what you need. I have an appointment in a few minutes." We'd managed to circumnavigate a bin of avocados twice. It abutted the dairy section.

For all her complaining, my niece's cart held enough food to feed a city of pregnant vegetarians. She'd heaped cans of beans, tomatoes, fresh tangerines, oranges, and carrots willy-nilly on top of each other and threw in two boxes of multigrain breakfast cereals. She sighed and then lugged a carton of milk to her cart before bending over the yogurts. Was she planning to stay through Chanukah?

I spotted the whipped cream and decided a new can could help me cope with everything a bit better.

"What do you need that for?" Davielle stared at me. "Don't you already have one?"

"Don't you already have a year's worth of food?"

"I'm pregnant, Aunt Sasha. I keep kosher." She put eight organic fruit yogurts into her cart and eyed the cottage cheese. "What's your excuse?"

"I'm not." I turned from her, the pressure behind my eyes unbearable. Where had these sudden tears come from?

"Aunt Sasha?"

"Don't mind me. Let's just get to the hotel. I'm exhausted."

"I thought you said you had an appointment."

I headed to the cashier, my face still burning. Davielle waddled behind, her unwanted concern rocketing me through the line and out the automatic doors. It had been a stupid idea to come in one car. If we hadn't, I'd be free of her now, at least until tomorrow morning. Instead, I put her bags into the trunk and drove the short distance back to the hotel. Then I unloaded most of her things and carried them to the second floor. Davielle made grunting sounds when she climbed the steps.

"You could've taken the elevator," I said when we got to the top.

"I need the exercise."

We unlocked our adjacent doors. The longed-for privacy inside my room brought a new quart of tears. I threw the whipped cream can onto the bed and wiped at my face, angry swats smearing my cheeks with saltiness, upset to be so easily downed and knowing I couldn't give in. Not yet. I had to get some kind of plan in place for Gabi. Just in case.

In the bathroom, the day's makeup left an oily beige ring around the white sink and on the washcloth. Not liking the stripped-down version reflected in the mirror, I put on the cold water and cupped handfuls onto my sad face. If only it'd be so easy to cleanse away the worries shimmying below the surface of my uncontrollable thoughts.

Davielle, loud and pregnant Davielle, banged around in the room next to mine, each thud a reminder of how much we'd all continue to disappoint her. And my sister, poor Eva, headed into this calamity.

The inevitable knock on the door caused a fresh fountain of sorrow. I didn't want Peter to see me like this, not when we had so little time left together. I thought about not answering and lay on the bed, whipped cream can poised above my open mouth.

"Sasha?" A woman's voice, not Davielle's.

My elbows became crutches to push myself into a sitting position. "Who is it?"

"Bailey." When I didn't respond, she said, "Do you have a minute?"

No. I sucked on the can again before getting up and opening the door. How had she found me? I guess after Davielle's display, the front desk clerk didn't have any incentive to protect our privacy. Plus, Bailey could be persuasive. She'd had to learn how in order to succeed at her craft.

"Can we talk?" My friend's eyes rested immediately on my puffy, red ones. "Are you all right?"

"This isn't a good time."

Eyebrows raised, her lips slivers, she shook her head. "Okay, then let me do the talking and you listen. This is important."

"I've got someone coming over in a couple of minutes," I said, shifting my stance to let her in.

"This won't take long." She took off her coat and sat in the lounge chair by the window, her feet resting on the ottoman. "I met your niece, Sasha. Why didn't you tell me she's Arab?"

"You just couldn't leave it alone, could you?" I wanted to throw her out right then; she couldn't be trusted. Of course, I couldn't either. "She's not Arab. She's Iranian. She's *American*. Her father is a naturalized U.S. citizen. He came to this country from Iran when he was eight." I sat on the edge of the bed. "They're Jewish, by the way."

"Your anger's misplaced." She kicked the ottoman out of the way and sat straight in the chair. "I was going to find out anyway. People are talking. You know that volunteer at the information desk? She told me she'd heard that your niece is studying explosives."

"What is this? The Inquisition?" Yeah, my comment didn't quite follow. "Gabi is getting her master's degree in explosives technology . . . or something like that. She's studying ways to protect our country. She should be getting medals, not injuries."

That would make a great sound bite. I hoped to remember it if I ever did any interviews about this. In the meantime, I went into the bathroom to pour a cup of water. "Why are you making such a big deal out of this?"

"You can't be that naïve. An Iranian studying explosives in little ol' New Mexico? After everything that's happened? Have you forgotten those terrorists who blew up the Trade Towers went to flight school in Arizona? And we all know what's happening in Iran right now."

Why was Bailey here? Out of friendship? To get me to slip up? I sat on the edge of the bed and plunked one of those super-charged instant vitamin packets into my drink (another concession to Peter's efforts to make me healthier). It fizzed noisily while we both watched it. After a minute, I sipped the orange-flavored, tepid liquid. "What do you want, Bailey?"

"I want you to be honest with me, Sasha. When I ask a question, I want an answer."

How dare she make demands?

"You know that this pipe bomb thing, mixed with your niece's ethnicity, has the potential to jump to national news." She catalogued the items in my room with her eyes. They stopped at the can of whipped cream. I ignored the unspoken question.

"Yeah, and you'll do everything in your power to make it happen, too."

"Everyone knows I want to get to a bigger market. I've never made a secret about that." Without a change in her voice, Bailey said, "So, how do you want the story told?"

Fractals of possibility, most of them bad, tessellated in my mind. I blinked. "Aren't you compromising a source by having this conversation, Bailey?"

"Don't worry. I'm only using you for background."

"Gee, thanks."

An assertive knock with a playful rhythm made Bailey jerk into wary alertness. She glanced at the door and then at me, discomfort contracting her body like a daylily encountering sudden night.

"Sasha? I've got something for you." Peter's timing couldn't have been worse. The last time he'd sung that, he'd come to my house wearing cellophane shorts.

Bailey stood up. "I've got to go anyway."

"No. You came here for a reason. Tell me what it is." I stood, too, blocking her retreat.

"I wanted to give you a heads-up. You know, a quid pro quo. I tell you, you tell me. Some of the things I'm hearing about your niece aren't good." She put on her coat. "The term 'terrorist' has already come up. I thought you should know."

"She's American, Bailey. Born in Maryland. One of the original colonies." *I think.*

"I understand that." She walked around me, her hand on the doorknob. "And I'll try to make a point of it. But, as you know, the public isn't into detail."

"It is if the media plays it right, if certain details become the meat of the story."

"We don't have as much control as you think." She opened the door. "Let me know if you want to talk. I'll try to help if I can."

I needed a diversion, something to cause her to sniff elsewhere. "Hey, I've got a question for you. I heard that one of Papi Sanchez's kids got in trouble for a hate crime. Can you check that out for me?"

"A hate crime? Does this have something to do with your niece?"

"It might."

Bailey twisted the knob without agreeing or disagreeing and opened the door to my lover.

"Happy early birthday, baby!" Peter's smile could have driven an ice factory out of business. Sure enough, he wore a long coat. It was buttoned, thank goodness, but no socks warmed his feet. In his hand, a bunch of roses pointed toward the ceiling and an overnight bag at the floor. When neither one of us responded to his good humor, his luscious lips closed. He kissed me on the cheek, awaiting an introduction.

"I've got to get back," said Bailey. "You know how to reach me."

"'Kay." The floor shifted. Socorro was known for its small earthquakes. Could this be one? No, it was only the vibrations of everything that could, and would, go wrong.

Peter walked past me into the room. "What was that all about?"

"Just hold me, please."

Opening his coat, Peter did much more than that.

Then I remembered the whipped cream.

17

We passed a small pond flecked with hundreds of snow geese, their forms no more than blotches of white in the pre-dawn. The turnoff to San Antonio had been clearly marked and we now zipped down the two-lane Highway 1. The heat in Peter's car fondled my face and legs. I smiled. Last night, we'd discussed how to keep our relationship from dying despite the upcoming distance. Peter's resolve had amazed and pleased me. Maybe, just maybe, we could pull it off. No matter what, I felt warmer and happier than I had in days.

The decision to catch the fly-out this morning seemed better when we'd snuggled together, two content spoons under someone else's covers. Fueled by the exuberance of recent lovemaking, all plans had seemed far away and possible. This one lost its luster when the alarm clock rang at 6:30. We made it into the car well before the stars relinquished their sparkle.

Bumps jostled me closer to Peter and I quietly thanked the lousy paving job. What a magnificent moment. Nothing could intrude, not even getting up so damn early. I reached for his leg and he slowed the car, a grin on his face. Then a cursed pickup truck passed us and Peter's testosterone kicked in. He sped up again, unwilling to be outdone by another man.

Ghostly forms of light-colored cars stopped at watering holes along the way, choosing to watch the resident flocks take to the sky. We continued ten minutes more until the turnoff into the Bosque del Apache. Our headlights now dimmed, we pulled into a large dirt parking lot.

Built near the Rio Grande, the bosque (Spanish for "woods") is winter home to thousands of sandhill cranes and tens of thousands of geese. Depending on the time of year, you can see other animals there, too. Over the years, I'd spied jackrabbits, coyotes, deer, muskrats, bluebirds, grackles, and wild turkeys. My love affair with this place had begun while on vacation from grad school and I had pledged to make an annual pilgrimage from then on. Now, with the project in Socorro, I'd be paid to tout its wonders to the rest of the world.

In the twenty years since I'd been coming here, I'd never managed to see a dawn fly-out. I'd also missed every annual Festival of the Cranes. The latter tied directly to the San-Socorro visitors' center. Papi Sanchez wanted construction to begin on the buildings by the middle of spring. He expected the entire center to be open and serving the public by the time the next festival rolled around. As a result, the coming two or three months would be hectic.

Thoughts of Papi brought questions about his children, especially the one who'd been involved in a hate crime. Unless he had the power to silence the media, there had to be an article or two about his way-ward child. Too many unknowns lingered from my conversation with Sallie Bourgeois. I'd already made too many assumptions: the kid had to be from Papi's second marriage; it had to be a boy; given Papi's local power, his child had probably gotten off with a mere hand slap. Sallie hadn't given any time frame for the crime or any idea what it had been. Why couldn't Cecilia have committed a nasty crime? Or a child from the first marriage? I had to find out more without attracting attention.

Peter pulled the key out of the ignition. Frigid air, smelling of unflung snow, rosed our cheeks and snacked on our noses. We put on knit hats, thick gloves, and scarves. Peter zipped my coat for me, finding several places to stop along the way. It earned him a kiss.

Had I really gotten this sappy?

Hand in hand, we crossed the bridge to the large flight deck and found our spot among grizzled birders and showy photographers. The latter interested me because of their giant equipment, including lenses the size of Mercedes coupes and tripods of titanium. I could spot the amateurs in the group by their envious looks at cameras they'd never earn the right to use. They slinked up to the more experienced guys with questions about f-stops and digital technology. It reminded me of a male bonding exercise, like talking sports in a controlled environment.

The birds groused, gibble-gabbling about standing in cold water before sunup. Imagine how happy you'd be if your feet squashed freezing mud. Plus, it'd be no kick to wake up to a bunch of people gawking at your every move. I once had a boyfriend who liked to watch me sleep. It gave me the willies.

Peter wrapped a muscular arm around me and against the breeze. The sun snuck its outer rays onto the backside of the mountains to our left, causing a slight orange glow. Soon, soon. Black lumps came into definition with the increasing light. The earthy smell of the marsh increased.

Someone whispered, "Look!"

Another person said, "Is that what I think it is?"

The professional photographers snapped rapid pictures. Wannabes zeroed their cameras in the same direction. Click, click, whirr. Hands adjusted binoculars, eyes squinted to see better. Breaths stuttered with hope.

In the distance, straight in front of us, a tall white bird spread his black-tipped wings. People murmured, afraid to frighten the whooping crane, but too excited to hold back their awe. What an incredible privilege to see a bird so rare on this perfect morning. He settled, looking at us, rigid-backed, proud, aware of the joy he inspired.

The sun continued its ascent and additional treasures became visible. Two eagles sat in the leafless tree on one side of the sizeable marsh. The variety of ducks multiplied while we blew warm breath into our cold hands.

Then, as if a work whistle had blared, geese began to honk. The cacophony swelled from group to group until the entire world became sound. Flock after flock took to the air, flying over us, their plump stomachs dipping close enough to touch. Peter and I clenched each other in the rushing wind of thousands of rising birds in wave after wave of white, gray, and brown. Webbed feet waddled from side to side as they gained height. The whoosh of wings pumping hard, up-down, up-down, made me want to hop on a bicycle, get exercise. Luckily, the urge passed.

The holiness of the fly-out, the sheer power of it, robbed us of speech until we'd pulled onto the interstate. I don't know what was in Peter's mind, but mine reveled, yet again, in how miniscule humans seemed in the grand scheme of life.

Too quickly, Peter dropped me off at the hotel. Our anticlimactic kiss, a hurried peck on each other's cheeks, barely registered. By the time my fingers touched the moist memory of where his lips had brushed my skin, he'd tooted his horn and had turned north onto California Street. I climbed the stairs with heavy legs. While Peter had been with me, it had been easy to think our relationship could vanquish any number of miles between us whether in Maryland or on Alpha Centauri.

Now, seconds after separating, doubt punctured my confidence.

18

South of the Holiday Inn, the El Camino Real Family Restaurant's holiday-decorated windows fogged with heat and the moisture from exhaled breaths. Noisy and smoke-filled, it reminded me of the restaurants of my youth, when I'd eat breakfast with my dad on the way to Sunday School.

The hostess looked like she'd worked in diners all her life and hadn't regretted a minute of it. She led me back to a big semicircled booth topped with a Stonehenge of those old-time brown mugs that resemble upside-down bells.

"It's just me," I said, assuming she'd made a mistake. "I'm not waiting for anyone else."

"Do you like the table?"

"Well, yes."

"Are you gonna eat?"

"Yes."

"There you go," she said.

Content in the permitted luxury of taking too much space, I smiled and scooted down on the slippery seat to observe this townie world. At least 50 percent of the customers were Native American. Wizened Hispanic men with their strong-faced wives smoked, talked, and joked. A few college-age students huddled over open books, drinking coffee, totally absorbed in their studies. I searched for ones who might look like chemists, whatever that meant.

I ordered my breakfast and put Gabi's predicament in a PR context. First things first. She shouldn't go in front of a television camera yet;

she was too unpredictable. Maybe Eva would be willing to front for her daughter. It was worth a shot. Eva lectured around the world; she could handle a couple of questions from local reporters. Also, she didn't look even slightly Semitic. No one would associate her with the Middle East, terrorists, or any of the hot buttons used as shorthand to evoke fear. Could I coax my sister into wearing a blonde wig to further diminish the Iranian connection in people's hearts and minds?

Another plus was that Eva had played enough political games in the cutthroat world of academe to understand the need for discretion. If I came up with good, honest talking points, she would honor their purpose. Had Eva made it onto American soil yet? I sure hoped so.

The waitress brought my steaming meal. Smothered in cheese and fresh-roasted green chile, the egg yolks ran onto hard whites. Perfect. The spiciness did wonders for my outlook. Orange marmalade and pats of real butter brought life to the toast and my addled brain. After eating most of the breakfast, I reached for the cell phone. Davielle's number was way down in my directory and it took a minute to find.

"Hello?" My niece chewed on something.

"Hi there. I wanted to touch base before going into my first meeting." I nodded at the waitress when she stopped by with the coffeepot.

"I thought we were going to the hospital together." She crunched her disapproval. "You can't expect me to stay all by myself."

"I know it'll be a sacrifice, dear."

"What do I say to Gabi?"

A chunk of food got caught between my tooth and gum. With a relatively clean finger, I scraped it out and thought about how to conclude my courtesy call. A scratch at the cusp of my awareness pushed through. Davielle could be a major problem in anyone's PR planning. "Hey, I have a question about the Torah."

She stopped chewing.

"Is there anything in there about modesty? Or privacy? About not airing your dirty laundry for other people to see?"

"What dirty laundry are you talking about?"

"Our family's, Davielle. I know you don't think we have any, but some reporters have a way of digging through other people's lives until they find garbage."

Across from me, a group of students sat down. Heather was among them. She noticed me, smiled, and nodded before opening a thick textbook. One of the others asked her a question and she spoke to him, her head turned away from me. In profile, she reminded me of Cecilia Sanchez. Could they be related? Sisters? Hey! Maybe Heather was Papi's errant child. That'd be a kicker, wouldn't it? She could've befriended Gabi to lure her into complacency before committing another hate crime.

"Aunt Sasha, you're not making any sense." Davielle had started eating again, my words no longer meriting her full attention.

"Keep the door to Gabi's room closed. Don't let her talk to any reporters. And don't talk to them yourself."

"Why would you ask such a thing?"

"Because I know more about how news works than you do." I sipped hot coffee as penance for my next remark. "Plus, I spoke to your mom. She's hoping we can keep things private for everyone's sake." That did the trick. I secured Davielle's promise. Though she could be a pain, my eldest niece wasn't a liar.

A burst of laughter popped with a cloud of cigarette smoke from a table nearby. I took a shallow breath, trying to filter in only good air and to center enough to be "on" for all the people in my fast-approaching meeting at the foundation. Might as well practice diplomacy right now. I dialed again.

"Go to hell." Mother's indiscriminant venom squirted through the optic fibers, burning holes in their fragile sheaths. Her words were probably directed at an anticipated telemarketer.

"Gee, thanks, Mom." I headed toward the cashier. She took my check and the twenty-dollar bill with a hand topped with sharp, red-tipped fingernails. A waitress passed us with a tray loaded with plates of pancakes, bacon, and hash browns. My stomach tried to follow her.

"It'll never work. He'll find out," Mom said, apropos of nothing. She'd begun skating in and out of an increasingly odd reality lately, as if all of those strokes, those insidious brain injuries, had merged into a megamush of dementia. Still, she might be coherent at the moment.

"What? Who?" I dumped the change and receipt into my purse. No wonder it was always so difficult to find anything in there. "Let me talk to Paul."

The Siberian air outside assaulted my nose, causing me to search for a tissue while I walked to the car. Meanwhile, Mom fumbled with the receiver.

"Sashala." Paul sounded droopy. "Where are you?"

"I'm in Socorro."

"Your mother is having a bad day," he said. "May I call you back?" A bad day and it wasn't even 8:30. The puzzle of how Paul managed to stay with—and love—my mother fascinated me.

In the car, my heater blowing frigid air, I sat watching a family huddle together by the restaurant's front door. My phone rang.

"Paul, what's going on?"

The pause that answered my question filled me with more fear than words ever could. "I don't know how much longer we'll be able to keep her home, Sasha. She's getting worse every day."

"Is she on any new medications?"

"Just one. I'll call the gerontologist." Click. Silence. Nothing.

Add worries about Mom to my tomes of trouble today. We might dodge the bullet this time, but we'd have to decide what to do if Mom got worse. Still, hope sparkled in the melting drops of ice on my windshield. Maybe she would rally again. It happened when we'd removed her from the last rehab hospital. *Please let her get better.* I wasn't ready to put her in an old people's home. Not yet.

My foot pressed the gas pedal, revving the car from its choking attempts to stall. Little putt-putts of smelly exhaust hung in the air. Accordions bounced out a *ranchera* on the radio. Any other time, they would have set my feet tap-tapping. Instead, I rubbed the back of my neck. If Paul couldn't care for Mom anymore, my life, my work would have to be put on hold.

Sisyphus might have had a corner on carrying a heavy load up a steep hill, but, this morning, the burden on my shoulders surpassed his.

19

The Val Verde Hotel flaunted so much potential it hurt. Located on Manzanares Street, the old building's fountained patio, generous portals, evocative arches, and graceful wooden extras entreated for buckets of imagination and banks of money. Across the road, the Monzanari Hotel had already reaped the benefits of entrepreneurial vision. The red brick building had been transformed into modern offices but retained the decades-old advertisement for White Owl cigars painted on its west side. The combo worked.

Papi Sanchez had tried to buy the Val Verde for years, but politics, or bad blood, had prevented the owners from selling. However, they gladly rented half of the bottom floor to the San-Socorro Foundation and permitted Papi's organization to spend hundreds of thousands of dollars to repair bathrooms, redo walls, upgrade electricity, and resand floors.

At 8:45, I tried the door. Though the sign in front said *Open*, the door rejected pushing, cussing, and kicking.

"That never works for me," said a well-dressed man, his eyes amused, his mouth as ungenerous as a discarded Popsicle stick.

"You're probably right, but it's therapeutic."

"Still, it's a shame to scuff up a nice pair of shoes." He reached in his pants pocket and produced a tissue for me to wipe off the dirt. His hand remained extended. "Sam Turin."

"Sasha Solomon," I said after standing straight again. His grip felt too sure through leather gloves. Crumpling the tissue, I pressed my nose against the glass. A small circle of makeup remained when I moved away.

"You're the woman who's going to whip us in shape for the visitors' center?"

"Don't sound so amazed." I wiped the glass, elongating the dot into the top of an exclamation mark. My tap on the door made a muffled, ineffective sound.

"Amazed?" he said. "I'm enchanted. Michaela didn't tell us you'd be so lovely." His silkiness had the quality of a crappy factory knockoff.

"I'm not." I leaned against the door, allowing those first tremors of excitement, the thrills of doing a new job, to run up and down my resting spine.

"I wonder where our fearless leader is." Sam's teeth sparkled in a symmetrical smile that belonged in toothpaste commercials or on a mannequin.

He may have said more, but I'd stopped listening when a faded blue van parked across the street. Dark eyes behind rimless glasses reflected in the side mirror and met mine. Odd, that. Why keep the window open on such a chilly day? The blatant voyeurism tainted my eagerness with the oily sensation of being in a peep show. Eva's paranoia must've rubbed off on me.

Michaela Jones ran up, bundled in apologies and excuses. "I just stepped out for a minute to get some cream. I told the others to listen for you."

A car door slammed. A woman in a peacoat emerged from the hybrid. She wore a long plaid kilt with black boots peeking from under its woolen beauty. Her hair, half-pinioned in a forest green tam, mocked its captor with flares of store-bought red.

"This gets stuck sometimes," said Michaela, fiddling with the knob and pushing hard with her shoulder and knee until the lock released and we entered. Inside, lights glowed gold, transporting us to a cozy contentment rather than an austere workplace. Laughter tendrilled toward us.

Sam, the redhead, and I followed the executive director into a conference room already filled with people positioned around a polished rosewood table. Box-lit santos and other Spanish religious art graced the walls, making a statement about New Mexico's heritage and Papi's pride in counting his family among the original European settlers in the region. While I'd always found this kind of display fascinating, my sister and Davielle would have balked.

The next few minutes passed in grinning and skinning, glad-handing, and introductions. I nodded, smiled, and added cream to perked coffee before picking up a coaster and unpacking the laptop.

"Pleased to meet you, Ms. Solomon," said Olivia Okino, she of the brilliant crimson hair, pulling out the chair next to mine. Her proximity felt like an assertion of power. "Sallie told me about your niece. I'm so sorry."

I nodded while searching for an electrical outlet so that I wouldn't have to depend on the computer's battery.

"We're glad you could make it."

"We all are," said Sam with the sincerity of a hyena. He assessed his clean fingernails, wrinkled his nose with the haughtiness of old money, and approached the free chair on my other side, making a Broadway debut of it all. I suppose he expected me to crumble or everyone to genuflect with oohs and aahs.

Michaela put a proprietary hand on the chair and said, "Sam, if you don't mind, I'd like to sit next to Sasha. She'll need help keeping names straight."

Bless her.

A roly-poly woman with a mop of silver hair pounded into the room with elephant strides. With nods to the group, she opened an expensive briefcase and removed a leather-backed pad of paper, ready for business. Her pen glided across the paper like an ice skater while she made notes, presumably in preparation for our meeting.

"That's Isabel Apodaca," said Michaela, under her breath. "She's director of the El Camino Real International Cultural Heritage Center." She waved across the table. "You have to go there. It's fabulous. She is, too."

Three more people came in. One wore a park ranger's uniform. His cohorts had the burnished shine from long years of serving the government. Brochures fronted them in neat stacks.

"I understand you met my daughter, Heather," said Isabel Apodaca. "She told me about your niece. What a horrible thing to have happen."

My theory about Heather being related to Cecilia evaporated. I absolutely couldn't picture this woman in bed with Papi. Isabel couldn't have produced either one of the women. Oh, well. Something about

Heather made me uneasy. At the moment, questioning her mother would be impossible, but I keyed in a note to myself to follow up after the meeting.

Michaela clapped her hands loud enough to drown out side conversations. "Let's get started." She then introduced me with enough praise to fertilize Central Park.

"It would help if I knew all of your names and what organization or town you're with," I said.

Olivia Okino started the ball rolling, talking about the chamber of commerce and its goals for the center. Laptop plugged in, I worked on a map of the participants, annotating it with the physical attributes and professional affiliations of everyone who spoke. At first count, fourteen people had come. Another four couldn't make it. The sheer number of vested interests daunted me. When the intros had concluded, and every thank-you had been said, I stopped typing. "Michaela alluded to our tight deadline. I don't know if you realize that I have to make my initial recommendations by early next week."

"What?" Sam Turin chafed. "I thought you were going to visit each one of our communities and that we'd do formal presentations there." He pushed back from the table. "I have everything scheduled for a week from Friday. You'll just have to accommodate me."

"Shut up, Sam," said Isabel.

"They've been divorced for years," whispered Michaela. The heat of her breath warmed my ear.

"No, you shut up," he said.

Lovely. I'd have the competition between towns, and the pleasure of a disintegrated marriage, to make my job even easier.

"It's the foundation's deadline, not mine," I said. "If you're unable to meet it, then I'll just have to make do." I sipped coffee until he stopped mumbling. "I'll try to visit as many of your sites as I can before the weekend."

"Thank you."

My heart raced with doubts. This project was too damn big. "What I need from all of you henceforth is as much information as you want to give, and I'll need it by Monday afternoon." Around the table, eyes blinked with the ludicrous deadline. The woman from Magdalena scratched notes with an expensive pen on a legal pad. Others looked as stunned as I felt. "Flood me with details about the interests you represent. I promise to consider it all."

"Sounds good to me," said Michaela, usurping any disagreement. Almost.

"That's all fine and dandy, Ms. Solomon, but there's just one problem," Sam said. "You need to remember that *you're* working for *us*. Not the other way around."

"Stop being an ass," said Isabel. "Sasha is just doing her job. We're not paying her. The foundation is. Everyone else here is willing to play by the rules." Her smile could have corroded metal. "Can you? Or do you want to take your marbles and go home?"

"You know she's going to include your place no matter what." Sam's studied cool had lost its lessons. "If she didn't, half the state would have a hissy fit. But no one ever thinks of including Lemitar. Well, I'm here to change that right now. No big city consultant is going to ruin my chances for tourism."

Oh, this was going to be so much fun.

"Sam, your town's the size of a peanut," said the lady from San Antonio. Hers was only a little bigger.

"We've got a great music scene, a nature park by the river, a charming church, and you know we're opening that factory for food packaging. We're poised for tremendous growth."

"I'm sorry," the woman said to me. "One restaurant and a couple of mailboxes don't make a tourist destination."

"And you think San Antonio does?"

"At least we're on the way to somewhere, big boy. We've got internationally renowned hamburgers, great fudge, art galleries, a coffeeshop. All you've got is dirt and dreams."

"I resent that," said Sam.

When quiet graced the room again, I said, "Well, that was interesting."

"It was embarrassing," said Olivia Okino.

"No, I found it illuminating." I stood up and put a *bizcochito* on my plate. You've got to love New Mexico. How many other places have a state cookie? "With this tough deadline, we need to hit the ground running. If anyone else has a concern about being overlooked, misrepresented, or misunderstood, tell me now."

I forced eye contact with each of them. This wasn't an attempt to intimidate. Not really. But they had to understand that they couldn't push me around. Pissing matches would take too much time from the work we needed to do.

"Besides getting to know us, what do you want to accomplish today?" said Isabel.

I scooted the chair in. "I want to hear your wildest dreams and goals, without censorship, for what this center can be. From these, I hope to define the big elements of the project, the special somethings that will lure tourists to each of your communities and attractions. Now's your time to shine."

"Like hell," said Sam.

"I'll start," said a man in a faded jacket and jeans. His sun-parched skin and rough hands hinted at a life spent farming or riding the range. "Did you know that the first vineyard in the entire country was planted north of San Antonio around 1629? Spanish monks wanted grapes for sacramental wine. . . ."

By the end of the meeting, I was ready to clean out my life savings and head to Mexico. This job couldn't be done within Michaela's time-line. Hell, it couldn't be done well, period. My self-confidence hit a sink-hole. Discouragement led to worry. Worry led to thoughts of Gabi. How could I help her, especially with this project starting up? How could I control the media, prevent leaks, hush up the affair, keep family peace?

Lunchtime approached. People fidgeted. I'd gotten three good hours out of them. That would have to do. On the way to my car, a voice called out, "Ms. Solomon, do you have a minute?"

"Sure, Olivia, what can I do for you?"

"That Sam is a real pain, isn't he?" The wind shoved strands of red hair across her forehead. She tried to control them with an ungloved hand, her fingernails painted a frosty pink.

Professionalism prohibited me agreeing. "Everyone just wants a big piece of the pie."

"I'm paid to be tactful in my work, but Sam strains my efforts. Too bad *you* have to be nice to all of us." Her smile revised my initial impression of her age downward ten years to the nearside of thirty.

We stood in front of the Val Verde. To my relief, the van across the street had gone. With its absence, my paranoia found no purchase.

"I just wanted to reiterate how so sorry I am about what happened to your niece. Please don't think I'm crass when I say that I hope it won't cloud your impressions of Socorro." Real concern laced her comments.

"No, no. I don't begrudge the town for the actions of an individual or two." I rested against the Subaru's door, thinking about Gabi. "Have you ever met my niece?"

"No. But my uncle is her advisor."

"Aaron Wahl?" I unlocked the car. "Is he still missing?"

She nodded.

"I hope he's all right." I knew how she must feel. A few months ago my mom had twice disappeared, unobserved, from a rehab hospital. It had been terrifying.

"I still can't believe it." Olivia's eyes clouded. "In spite of what you may have heard about his colossal arrogance, he's always been wonderful to me." She stepped away, ready to leave, but hung back a moment more. "It's strange. About the only person who *doesn't* seem upset is my aunt. She's acting like she couldn't care less."

20

I believe that hell will be catered by angry hospital chefs.

The red chile–swaddled, cheese-engorged enchiladas swam in an orange pond of yesterday's grease. Who knows? Maybe the institution needed more patients. A translucent green salad and prune-based soda pop completed the ideal repast to clog my arteries and clear my mind.

In spite of the visible fat, or perhaps because of it, the food tasted pretty good. After the third mouthful, my hitherto questionable motivation for eating this particular meal, in this particular place, became evident. Proximity to Gabi allowed me a calmer conscience, while refuge in the nonkosher cafeteria prevented a run-in with Davielle.

To balance my conflicted psyche, I pretended to work. The laptop alternated between windows with talking points for my niece, or sister, and reams of notes from the foundation meeting. Mostly, though, I worked on the plan to disappear somewhere in Mexico. Dollars lasted longer there, and I liked the beach.

My phone rang. Maybe it was the travel agent.

"Aunt Sasha," said Davielle. "Do you ever plan to get here?"

Ah, the dulcet tones of accusation.

"I can be there in seconds. Why?"

"I need a nap. I'm going." Poof. End of conversation. Well, who wanted to chat anyway?

A person sat at the table behind mine, his or her presence strong and emanating that anxiousness, that desire to unload all of one's emotional baggage on a stranger. No, thank you. I didn't want to interact with anyone yet. I felt all peopled-out, especially after this morning's meeting. The person's chair moved. I looked down, avoiding contact, and thought about Gabi's unpredictability. It hung above my head like an emotional sword of Damocles. Contemplating knives, I cut into the biggest piece of chocolate cake known to man and took a disappointing bite. Too dry, flavorless. I glanced up, wondering if I could trade the dessert for another, when Bailey walked over to me.

Oh, great.

"You look like you're attacking your food instead of enjoying it, Sasha," she said as she sat down across from me.

"You know, normally, I'd be happy to see you, but today..." I shook my head a couple of times and ate the cake anyway.

"Maybe it's remorse?" Her hungry eyes searched for rips in my shabby armor. "Really, Sasha, you look miserable."

"I've got a lot of work to do, Bailey. You have no idea how much work I've got to do." Had I really stooped to whining? Mewling voices in restaurants, begging for candy or French fries, brought out a misanthropic side of me that threatened to turn into violence. Could I use my newfound pout to drive her away?

The reporter picked at her fruit salad. "Why don't you tell me your troubles?"

"Well, then I wouldn't be working, would I?" My stellar impression of a four-year-old had no more effect on her than if I'd sneezed. "And speaking of work, you're not going to tell me Gabi's such big news you have to stay down here. Are you?"

"I'm on it full-time, Sasha. You and me, baby." She popped a red grape into her mouth. "You've got to admit it's sexy. A pipe bomb, an Iranian who works with explosives, and her world-renowned advisor missing? It's got legs."

"You gunning for a Pulitzer?"

"They don't give Pulitzers for television. You know that. But I wouldn't mind a Peabody." She pushed a piece of canned pineapple to the side of her bowl. "I'd like you to give me the truth even more."

Each bite of my sawdust cake laughed at the promise of indulgence. That was the problem with so much of life: it let you down hard. I almost gave up on the sweet but decided to give it one last chance. With a flourish, I dumped coffee on top to create a mocha thingy. It worked, sort of.

If Bailey thought it strange, she didn't acknowledge it beyond an amused stare and another piece of fruit into her own mouth. When she'd finished chewing, she said, "So, how's your niece today?"

"Nifty."

Exasperation added a sweet flush to her porcelain face. "Sasha, why are you being so hostile?"

"Did you talk to the bomb squad guy?"

"Not yet."

"Well, I'll be nicer when you do. Okay?"

"You said you'd get me an on-camera interview with your niece. Is that still going to happen?" She'd stopped eating.

Bailey's phone rang. She looked at the caller's number, made a face, and answered it. I finished my cake and half listened to her talk to her boss. The conversation didn't go her way; irritation and protests flew from her mouth with equal emphasis. I lifted the dessert plate to my mouth and drank up the rest of the coffee.

When Bailey disconnected, I said, "What's wrong?"

"Breaking news, Sasha. Only I don't get to cover the drunk idiot who forced an emergency landing at the Sunport. No, I get to go back to Albuquerque and interview someone about tofu turkey."

"Gee, that's too bad." I finished drinking my water.

"I can see you're heartbroken. Don't think I won't follow up on your niece."

"I hope you do, Bailey."

"That's the first blatant lie you've told me today."

"I'm not lying. You're one of the few reporters who'll give Gabi a fair interview. The only thing you have to get through that gorgeous head of yours is that she's American." I played air guitar and imitated Bruce Springsteen. "Born in the USA."

"Cute." Bailey gathered her purse and buttoned her coat. "Her father's from Iran, Sasha. You can't get around that."

"Your dad's from Georgia. Does that make you a redneck?" I closed my eyes, ready to apologize again.

"Touché." Her phone sang again and she sighed, letting the air build behind her lips first. We hugged good-bye while she said, "Hello?"

Though my speed imitated a slow sloth, eventually I made it to Gabi's room. Inside, she slept with the television on low. Her face had lost two pounds of fluid and her cheekbones had gained a tad of definition. Beyond the ugly scrapes, bruises, and scratches, her sallow skin contained healthier islands of color. Progress.

My niece's slumber kicked at consciousness, her uninjured hand repeatedly clutching her stomach as if it hurt. The fingers on her other hand twitched. Another good sign. I sought not to disturb her while sitting down, but the chair grazed the floor with a loud screech.

"Aunt Sasha?" Gabi's eyes opened.

"What's the matter, sweetie?"

"I hurt." Her breathing changed to a pant.

"I know." I took her hand. "You're going to feel better every day. I promise."

"No, it's not that. I've got cramps, like I'm getting my period . . . only worse."

"Do you need me to call the nurse?"

She shook her head in refusal, tears falling without sound. Her hold on my hand tightened. I couldn't blame her for crying, not after everything that had happened. Then her breathing shortened even more and she arched her pelvis up. It was a quick action, as if someone had elbowed her violently in the lower back.

"Gabi, what's happening? Talk to me." Her heightened pain and chilling distress convinced me there was nothing normal about this period.

Without her permission, I lifted the blanket to see what we were dealing with. Blood, bright and copious, girdled her and pooled on the sheet. Oh, hell. Had an internal injury gone undetected? I should have insisted they transfer her to a bigger hospital, to the University of New Mexico Hospital with its specialists and high-level trauma center.

She moaned.

"Honey, I've got to call the nurse." I feigned calm but pressed the nurse's button at least fifteen times.

"No." Gabi pulled my arm hard. "Don't."

"Something's really wrong here. It can't wait."

She pulled on my arm until I bent my head close to her lips. "Please don't tell anyone. Promise me."

"What, sweetie?"

"About the baby."

21

The nurse's face blanched. People ran. Consigned to the hallway, I paced its sterile length, feeling smaller than a gnat and less powerful. When minutes passed into nearly an hour, my feet found their way to the hospital's little chapel, but its intentional calm provided no balm for my soul. Desperation clung to the backs of the metal chairs forming two semicircles focused on the freestanding, ecumenical, stained-glass sculpture with its prominent cross, crescent, and Star of David. Pleading dripped off the ceiling. Had God answered any of the uttered or silent heartfelt prayers with more than indifference?

At the nursery, red-faced babies cried. Others slept with the innocence of ignorance. Beside me, a man goo-gooed at one of them. What had it been like for Eva and Zach? Two seconds after they'd married, my sister got pregnant. She'd had five children in seven years of marriage. How had they survived after Nathan's death at only four months? How had they had the strength and courage to try for more? Through the Plexiglas window, my eyes settled on a squirming creature of need wrapped like a fat, pastel-striped grub. Five times? How had Eva endured the spitting up, the poop, all the effluvia?

Out of the corner of my eye, I watched the man next to me make a fool of himself and regret dusted my heart. At nearly forty-one, with no permanent boyfriend, no husband material in sight, having a child was an option slipping away. Eva claimed that childless people forever remained selfish, out of touch.

Yeah, but I could hop on a plane right now and go to Tibet if I wanted with no worries beyond the weather and prevailing political climate in China. I had freedom. Without dependents other than Leo, I could be my own boss, work just enough to pay bills, and organize my time for my own pleasure. Eva and Zach had never had that option.

And yet . . . yearning wormed a thin tunnel through my smugness.

With that sense of lack, I returned to Gabi's room. A caustic odor lingered as pungent as smoke from an unwanted fire. Blood loss from the miscarriage and an emergency D and C rendered her cadaver-skinned, an eerie bluish gray. She refused even an ice chip.

Self-protective mountains earthquaked skyward, cutting her off from the world and imperiling her sanity. This was the grief of a mother. She must have planned to keep the baby. My questions bounced off her body like super balls, banging against the hush in the room. Only the *drip-drip* of the leaky bathroom faucet offered relief.

"Gabi, your mom's going to be here soon. Please. Talk to me." I forced eye contact. "I can intercede, smooth things over. For God's sake, if you don't want your mom to know about the baby, you need to tell me what to do."

Outside, the sky spat snowflakes that wouldn't make it to the ground. I prayed that Eva would run into a blizzard. Maybe she'd have to pull off the road for, say, three days. A terrible wish, but Gabi needed time to pull herself together.

Would Eva's mother-love be able to transcend her daughter's transgressions? So much depended upon her reactions. She'd be the mediator, the apologist. Without her support, Zach and Davielle's rigid righteousness could cleave this family apart.

Gabi's open eyes were fixed as a frozen fish's. Was this what shock looked like?

"Honey, I'm going to take a little walk. I'll be back in a few minutes." I rushed into the hall, furious with the conflicted emotions—the urge to help, the desire to flee—overtaking me. Into this turmoil blundered the oblivious Heather.

"Hi," she said with searing brightness. "I was just coming to visit."

I closed my eyes so that she couldn't see the sorrow lodged in them. Too late. Her happy anticipation fell from the updraft of hopefulness, the plunge sharp.

"I don't think Gabi's up to visitors right now," I said quietly. "She's had a setback."

"It's the baby, isn't it?"

My silence answered too thoroughly. In the awkward moment, Heather put a sympathetic hand on my shoulder. "My mom had two miscarriages and they hurt her so deeply none of us thought she'd survive. But she did. Give Gabi some time to grieve."

"I met your mom today. She seems like a great person." I should've asked Heather if she was related somehow to Cecilia Sanchez, but my mind couldn't shake the image of Gabi's lost hopes. That, and the fact that she knew more about my niece than I did.

Heather patted me. "Tell Gabi I'll come by later. You take care."

The curtains refused to let even the weakest joy of sunlight through the room's window. Amorphous mourning darkened it further. Resisting capitulation, I opted for tough love, though it felt cruel. "Gabi, you either talk to me or I'll let you deal with Davielle and your mom alone."

"I lost my baby. Can't you understand?"

"Honey, your mother is going to be here soon. Do you think *she's* going to understand?" I wanted to cry, to embrace her and protect her, but that couldn't penetrate her sad stupor.

"You were going to drive out to Magdalena for your job, right?"

What a non sequitur. My mom's battles, and my own, with shape-shifting realities had trained me to humor Gabi, to get more information rather than immediately reject the comment. "Yes, sweetie. I was going to go there and to the Very Large Array. But I'll cancel. It's no problem."

"No. Don't cancel. Go. Now."

The command to leave hurt me to my core.

"Please, don't cancel anything," Gabi said with effort. "I need you to go to Aaron's . . . to his place, to see if he's there." She pushed the button to raise the top half of her bed until she was almost sitting.

"I thought you said he lived with his wife here in town."

Salt lines from tears had left trails of white on her cheeks. "He's got a little retreat, a place she doesn't know about. It's close to Magdalena, in Hop Canyon. He keeps a key for me under the doormat in front."

"What do you want me to say if he's there?"

"Just tell him to call me. I need him."

22

A shredded white cloud gripped the ground between two hills near what looked like a mini–strip mine. The contrast of its purity against the dark hills and the grimy sky created a strange, sublime splendor. The smoke made a statement, unwilling to rise or dissipate, the remnant of a probable explosion.

Why had Gabi chosen such a violent specialty? Though she insisted explosives jived with birthing world peace, I couldn't imagine how. Serenity rarely cuddled up with things that went boom.

Sunlight knifed the dense dome above with the precision of a diamond scalpel. Outcroppings, hills, and masses of black rock stood out in crystalline definition against the browns and lighter beiges of the snow-moist soil. I opened the car window and let the air hit my face. It smelled of rain, a too-rare scent in this desert of mine.

Within minutes, Highway 60 became a lonely ribbon. To my left, mountains called, free and open. On the right, warnings dotted flimsy fences with imperial claims for New Mexico Tech and its ownership of the horizon. The school filled this particular possession with testing ranges and hidden labs.

Magdalena popped into view. Five minutes more and I'd driven through it. Given the time of day, I decided to head to the VLA first and then double back to see the town and honor Gabi's wishes.

Rugged desert, alpine forest, and rolling hills flecked with juniper bushes whipped by. My car apexed above a vast flat bowl cradled by distant blue mountains, the Plains of San Augustin. Though nearly 7,000 feet above sea level, the oxygen content had halved. The lapping waters of the ancient lake that formed this giant moonscape could almost be heard in the land's memory.

The Very Large Array stood in the basin's center, its otherworldly radio telescopes pointed to the furthermost regions of space. Wind buffeted my light car, forcing me to hold on hard to the steering wheel. The feeling of nothingness here, of magnificent desolation, increased with each yard traveled.

Signs posted at the entrance to the laboratory exhorted visitors and workers alike to turn off radios and cell phones. At the tiny visitors' center, the yowling wind bullied me back into the car. I succeeded the second time. Cold penetrated thick clothing. The building's unassuming metal door required both hands before it relinquished its inner warmth. Inside, the quiet rang in my ears.

Photographs of the telescopes by moonlight, from airplanes, lined a hallway with text about the facility's ownership and management. More red tape, bureaucracy, vested interests—governmental and private— that might want a say in the foundation's efforts to bring tourists to this out-of-the-way attraction.

Here, a small theater area, its tiered seating doubling as steps, played a well-made video. There, a sign invited visitors to take a self-guided tour outside. Though my face froze, I made the circuit past parabolic dishes, operations buildings with anonymous cars parked beside them, and a close view of one of the radio telescopes. Weighing hundreds of tons, the machine had an unexpected gracefulness. I wanted to climb those white stairs zigzagging up its exterior and slide down its interior dish.

After another fight with another door, I continued the tour inside. Explanatory plaques informed about the lab and plans for improvement. I liked this one: "If the telescopes were expanded to the farthest ends of their tracks, they'd cover about as much area as the Washington, D.C. metro area." See what I mean? New Mexico is big.

More walking, more learning. Multihued images of comets, pulsars, and stars reminded me of the unwelcome auras I sometimes saw emanating from people's heads and hands. Maybe I'd finally found the explanation for my erratic visions. They stemmed from a strange and acute sensibility to radio waves. I laughed at the thought and my mirth found its mate in a plaintive sigh. Its source came from a wink-sized gift shop. An older woman sat behind the counter, her expression intent on a computer screen. I coughed to get her attention. She jerked at the noise.

"You startled me." She turned the screen away from my view with a definite huff.

"I'm sorry," I said, unrepentant. If the store wanted to turn a profit, she'd need to replace that prissy attitude with a friendly smile, especially if no one else was here to do it.

A stand of merchandise boasted rainbow disks, ultraviolet ray warning beads, cards with photos and facts about Saturn and tempted me to open my wallet. However, the clerk's unpleasant demeanor cancelled that impulse. She refocused on the monitor, clicking her mouse at quick intervals. Curious, I walked behind her to stacked bins filled with rolled-up posters. She didn't notice my spying. Computer solitaire. *How appropriate.* I left her to her game and vowed to talk to the rep from the VLA about improving customer service.

In the bathroom, custom ceramic tiles, decorated with little radio telescopes and galaxy designs, cheered the otherwise blasé wall. What a great touch. I washed my hands before going to the car. This little center deserved more than one visitor a day. The challenge would be to find ways to lure tourists to take the trip, to leave the comfort of Socorro, for a place that would open their minds to worlds beyond.

Outside, the struggle with the wind seemed less intense now that I knew what to expect. My car bounced down the long access road to the blue highway. I waved farewell to the telescope dishes once more before losing sight of them.

My cell phone rang the minute I hit the power button. "Eva?"

"Wrong-o." Darnda's voice cracked with the bad reception. Pretty funny considering where I'd just been. "Why didn't you call me back?"

"I forgot." Without police in sight, ninety miles an hour felt almost legal. "What's up?"

"Are you all right?"

"You sound like a broken record, my friend." I swerved to miss a flattened skunk. "Everything's fine. We're all fine. Life is good." Well, it would be as soon as Eva arrived and I extricated myself from hospital duty and could begin to work and to nose into who'd hurt Gabi.

"Methinks thou dost protest too much." She grunted. "I know damn well that things aren't fine. I'm telling you for your own good, you should come home now, even if it means leaving the Socorro job."

"I can't afford that, Darnda." Bills. Those little envelopes with the plastic windows, the ones that lined my living room coffee table and squabbled for my meager earnings.

"You can borrow money from your mom."

"That's never an option."

"Sasha, I mean it. I'm getting a really bad vibe off of this."

"Do people still say that, *vibe*?"

"Stop the editorializing, dear heart. I keep seeing this guy," she said. "He's maybe fifty years old, good-looking, head full of white hair. He's not talking, but, boy, he's bad news."

"You're just picking up on one of my nightmares. I dreamed about him the other night." I wasn't going to let her spook me.

"No, I don't think so." She grunted once again.

"What are you doing?" I dug in my purse for oral solace. My fingers surrounded a promising blob and extracted it from the morass of pens and crumpled receipts. Though the foil had pulled away in places, and a couple of hairs dangled from it, the chocolate looked okay. I popped it into my mouth, working the wrapping off with my tongue.

"What?"

"Right now. What are you doing?" I sucked the candy, enjoying its last-year flavor and watching a dried tumbleweed roll across the road.

"Yoga."

"While talking on the phone?" I didn't want to picture her lumpy body in a leotard, but the image took root and grounded itself with ferocity.

"It's good for the soul anytime," she said. "Look, I called about something else, too. Karen Kilgore wants us to come out a week from next Friday. Can you do it?"

"Both of us?" The paranormal reporter and Darnda had become fast friends. She planned to feature my client on her television show. Great PR for all concerned.

"Yeah. All expenses paid." She puffed. "Just think, L.A. at the holidays. It'll be a hoot."

"I'm so there." Holding the steering wheel with one hand, I spit the wrapper into the other and dumped it into a plastic trash bag.

"Are you sure you don't need some help down there?"

"I'm fine," I said. "Everything's groovy." On the outskirts of Magdalena, adherence to the speed limit kicked in. "Tell the guy with the white hair to mind his own business."

23

A fan circulating the risen heat downward twirled from the high, tinned ceiling at Evett's. The eatery had been my second choice, but the Magdalena Café's door rebuffed my efforts at entry. Evett's boasted an ice cream parlor ambiance rather than a full-service, sit-down venue. However, I needed to do research for my job, and that ancient piece of candy needed company.

Chromed black-top barstools mushroomed before a pink counter. Slapdash tables and chairs, an odd assortment of nearly antique mercantile equipment including crank cash registers, musty mason jars, and farm implements, all lent an old-time feel to the establishment. Posters touted the joys of drinking Nesbitt's Orange and Coca-Cola in their original curvy bottles.

People talked in gruff voices, laughing over cups of coffee at four of the eight tables. The ethnic mix was tricultural: Hispanic, Anglo, and Native American. Blue jeans were de rigueur and coats hung on arm-length pegs in the wall.

I put the laptop on the table and began writing. My round-faced, dark-haired waitress, probably from the Alamo Navajo Reservation nearby, didn't wait for me to study the menu. She suggested the special, a beef tostada heaped with cheese and red chile. Who could resist? After making the rounds at the other tables, she returned with a jar filled with water. Though conversations never surrendered their rhythms, eyes observed me. I tapped out my notes about the VLA and sights seen in Magdalena so far. The boxcar museum, the fairgrounds, the library, and old buildings such as the Charles Ilfeld Co. structure with its painted advertisement bragging, "Wholesalers of Everything," would please a variety of visitors. Above all, I wrote about the art galleries and knick-knack shops lining Highway 60, the slow-moving main street in the town. Tourism thrived here.

"You a writer?" The man who'd asked was probably Mom's age. He sat at the table next to mine with other grizzled gentlemen, all in faded plaid shirts.

"Not really. I'm thinking about how Magdalena fits in a tourist project I'm working on."

"Tourist stuff, huh? Well, then you should talk to Marta Correo. She owns that B & B Silver Dreams. She's the big tourist person here."

"No, she should talk to Skip. He could tell her more than Marta," said a tablemate. He held up a mug and wiggled it. Without saying anything, the waitress refilled all of their cups.

"Thanks, Hon'," the new speaker said before addressing the restaurant in general. "Hey, this lady wants to know about Magdalena. Anyone here got any ideas?"

Someone at another table pointed past my head and said, "Turn that thing off."

A person by the radio hit the power button and diminished the background noise to a purr. Suggestions flew my way. Aged and adolescent, they told me about the town's history, its cattle shipping and mining, and the proud days when the trains used to go from here to Socorro. What impressed me most was that everyone seemed to be on the same page about Magdalena's growth. Most places lacked such cohesion.

My fingers cricketed on the keyboard, a happy sound, the sound of work being done, money earned. Hop Canyon was only minutes away, so I decided to detour to Marta Correo's B & B before visiting Aaron Wahl's place.

My stomach pooched with the extra meal. I angled the car off the highway onto a semipaved street. Silver Dreams stood out among the mix of electricity-challenged shacks, remodeled school buildings that now served as homes, and more typical dwellings. A pristine turquoise stucco wall surrounded a neat patio, its garden turned down for the winter. Ahead, a carved door with a stained-glass pane invited visitors into a piñon-scented room furnished with Victorian chairs, love seats, and too many frills for my taste.

A standard poodle, evincing patrician nobility, trotted in and sniffed my hand. He left me standing there, his toenails clicking on the brick floor, to convey a message to his owner. Soon, a lean, mahogany-skinned woman greeted me. Her beauty evoked a Mayan with an aquiline nose, sky-high cheekbones, and straight back. She wore old jeans and a denim work shirt covered in part by a well-used apron. A spot of flour dotted her broad forehead. "I see you've met Lincoln," she said, signaling with a snap for the dog to come to her side. "May I help you?"

I introduced myself and mentioned my business.

"I've heard all about it," she said, proffering her hand with the kindness of a new friend. "I'm Marta Correo, chief chef, handyman, and owner of Silver Dreams." A bell rang. It sounded like a timer, and Lincoln's ears perked up. "Come on back. I've got to get something out of the oven."

Marta led me into a barracks of a kitchen smelling of yeast and happy memories. The vigas in this ceiling were as thick as dodgeballs. Pots hung from hooks grasping the black cylinders. Pizza ovens lined one wall.

"You look like you're set up for industrial baking here," I said, watching her dislodge cookie sheets topped with steaming baguettes. She put them in multishelved carts to cool.

"I am." Marta faced me. "I sell to restaurants in town and a couple of stores down in Socorro and Los Lunas. I'd like to get into the Albuquerque market, but I'm a one-person operation."

"And you run the B & B, too?"

"My husband used to help, but he got tired of it and left."

That stopped the conversation. I walked over to the edge of a table with several maple-colored loaves now freed from their pans. "What kind are these?"

"War bread."

I must've given her an odd look.

"They're from a recipe that was developed during World War II, at least I think that's the right war. Anyway, the bread developed in a time of want and now it's helping me in my time of need." Her smile faded, the effort of good humor testing her too much. Lincoln nudged her hand and she absentmindedly petted the top of his head. "If it weren't for Papi . . . I know he's the brains behind your project . . . I'd've lost this place long ago." Marta pointed to two stools.

"Do you mind telling me what he did for you?" I sat, elbow on the table, head resting on my hands.

"After I realized my husband was really gone, things were bad. I didn't have enough money to pay the mortgage on this place. One day, I bumped into his daughter, CiCi, in Socorro." Marta brought over two mugs and a blue ceramic pitcher of cream. Lincoln settled underneath the table near her feet. "I learned long ago not to confide in her, but I was upset. So, I told her what had happened. Good thing, too. The next thing I knew, Papi called." She smelled the coffee and smiled. "When I told him about that rat bastard Roberto, Papi said he'd take care of everything." She snapped her fingers. "He did. No loan, no IOU. He just paid it all off."

"Amazing." I needed a guardian angel like that, someone unlike my mother, someone who gave with no strings attached. Perhaps I *should* take Papi up on the offer to help Gabi. Why not? A private investigator might find her attacker faster than the local police, or me.

"I lost you," said Marta, pulling my zigzagging thoughts back to the present moment.

"How do you know CiCi? He's got only one daughter, right? I think I met her yesterday."

"Blonde hair? Skinny? Snooty?"

I nodded.

"Yeah, that's her." Marta shrugged. "We went to school together until Papi sent her back East. That finishing school and her bigwig husband just added mayo to a rotten egg." Another bell dinged.

"What's her mom like?"

"Oh, she's a real piece of work. A nosy, money-grubbing bitch, pardon my language. Thank God CiCi had herself fixed, if you know what I mean." Marta retrieved more trays of bread and shelved them, too. "Papi must've known something was up with her because he had a prenup. Her second husband's a creep. They deserve each other." With a swift corking of that vintage bottle of discontent, Marta escorted me out of the kitchen. "Let's talk about nicer things. What would you like to know about Magdalena?"

So much for gossip, for the information I needed to help Gabi. Oh, well. For the next twenty minutes, Marta regaled me with stories about the people who'd stayed at her B & B and showed off new beds, a tiled hot tub, and the hole where a swimming pool would go next summer. With the right positioning, Silver Dreams could be a must-stop on the road to the VLA. Did I dare include individual businesses in my suggestions for the visitors' center? Hey, advertising revenue could help the center sustain itself. Why not propose it?

After our interview, I sat in the car and thought about the woman with whom I'd just spoken. Tough, strong, and independent, she could serve as my unofficial role model. She was doing it, living the life she wanted. Nothing stood in her way.

What was my excuse?

24

As small as Magdalena was, it had a suburb.

Marta Correo's instructions had been simple: drive south on Kelly Road until it forks. Turn left.

The street wound high into rocky, alpine terrain pocked with old tires, faded beer cans, and cigarette butts. When the sign told me to turn right, I did the opposite, impulsively choosing to check out the now-abandoned Kelly Mine. No one representing the place had been at this morning's meeting, but I was curious. Perhaps it had tourist potential. I was here anyway.

The road turned into a mud brickle of ruts and boulders. My car's underbody shrieked. Nothing merited being stranded here in the cold. Still, I forged on, determined to get a glimpse.

A forlorn church, its windows broken, marked the location where further driving became impossible. Slowly, I backed up and parked next to the building. The malicious wind blew, penetrating miniscule holes in my coat and making me shiver. This couldn't be worth the effort. I walked farther, careful of my footing in smooth-soled shoes, and strained to see the neglected hulk of wood.

A few steps more and there it was, still yards away, a weathered, desolate thing reminding me of every sad news story of a cave-in ever written. Just a couple steps more and I spotted a car to my right, one of those old clunkers with sun-bleached paint jobs and uneven fenders, but the tires looked new and the windows had survived better than the church's. Something about the vehicle, sitting in the middle of nowhere, zinged my intuition. I'd learned to pay attention to those signals. The abandoned mine could remain so.

Rather than continue my trek, I backtracked to my own car feeling grateful for its sleek exterior and the heater that hadn't yet had time to cool. Even so, the wretchedness of the mine loitered in my bones; no amount of giddy music or blowing air could shoo it away.

Ah, here it was, the turnoff to Hop Canyon, a world of secluded wealth. Winding my way up this junipered road, I spotted a two-story home, at least 5,000 square feet, teetering on a hill. Next, a well-graded, graveled route lined with pines and chain-link fences bedecked with No Trespassing signs.

Mountains shouldn't be owned by anyone. It wasn't right.

I stopped the car for a moment to dig out Gabi's more precise directions, then revved the motor once again. Up for one mile and then past the orange mailbox with the red flag. The chassis protested the bumpy four-tenths-of-a-mile ride on the rutty road through trees, rocks, more trees.

"Hang on, baby," I said aloud. How could I not have seen it minutes ago? Aaron Wahl's "little retreat" scoffed at wood in favor of round adobe lines. My car chortled with delight onto the doublewide, smooth driveway. No tiny weekend getaway, this. The building reached up to the clouds in sweeping supplication, maybe three stories high at its center. The good professor had money. Lots of it.

But who'd ever heard of painting your garage windows black? How tasteless. How could anyone see the Maseratis, or Escalades, residing there? For shame. Knock, knock at the front door. No response, of course.

Eschewing the front door, I ascended the woodpile on the left side of the house and peeked over the top to see if Mr. Moneybucks might be doing a little yard work . . . in the winter . . . under a hostile sky. Never mind that the only noise I heard came from the swooshing of wind through the trees. I was determined not to go in unless I had to.

Aaron Wahl mustn't have been too outdoorsy. No one could sit in that rusty lawn chair. Other than that, he'd cultivated rocks, weeds, and a whole lot of wasted space. The white tanks, decorated with red flames warning of fire hazards, did little for the landscaping.

Resigned to my fate, I stooped to pick up the key from under the mat. Damn Gabi! It wasn't there. I'd driven all the way out here for nothing. I banged on the door in frustration. What the hell should I do?

After walking back and forth in front of the house a few times and weighing my choices, I climbed the woodpile and heaved myself onto the wall. It was only a five-foot drop to the other side and I could use the frame of the lawn chair to hoist myself up later on the way back. At least this way Gabi would know I'd tried everything.

The seat of my pants ripped on a nail. Even worse, the back door opened with a simple twist of the knob.

"Hello?" My yell flew, a sonar-challenged bat, banging on the walls of this too-quiet home. It felt like a bomb shelter. Ha-ha. *Bombs*, get it?

The man had the esthetic sensibility of a piece of soggy toast. The place resembled a dank warehouse on the wrong side of town. I'd entered through the kitchen, its Formica counters a drab cream color with avocado green accents. Just lovely. The stainless steel fridge intimidated the other appliances. The dinette set's table, while in good repair, didn't deserve to be. Could Gabi really love someone with so little panache? A half cup of cold coffee kept a solidified egg yolk company. The used napkin lay on the blah-coated concrete floor.

I wondered how often Aaron came up here for a midday fling with Gabi. She claimed he always went home to his wife at night, but that didn't jive with the abandoned breakfast before me.

"Hello?" I called again, moving into, well, a giant room within the room. What on earth? Here, the door was most certainly locked. I knocked on it, wondering if it was some kind of soundproofed space, maybe a recording studio or a camera darkroom. Talk about a lousy layout. No stairs to a second story. No other rooms. Nada. Downright weird.

"You need a better interior designer," I hollered into the hollowness, heading down a hall to a bedroom that exuded testosterone. Evocative of a contemporary Neanderthal's cave, it contained an unmade emperor-size bed with sheets the color of sludge. The blankets matched. Piles of books stood on the floor and covered the cheap metal table that also held a lamp and an alarm clock.

At least the bathroom showed evidence of human life with its cologne, a shaving kit, snippets of dark hair in the sink. The black Jacuzzi had a lime collar around its once-sleek interior. Gingerly, I lifted back the dirty shower curtain. Dollar-store shampoo, a grungy chunk of once-white soap.

"Oh, Aaron, Aaron, I hardly knew thee," I said. "I'd hardly want to."

If Gabi considered this place a lovers' nest, she'd obviously inherited the idea from Zach's side of the family. Mom would have a heart attack if she saw it. A building like this? The location gorgeous, privacy guaranteed. Oh, the things I could do here. The art I could buy, the whipped cream I could store, the love I could make.

Finding the front door proved challenging. The room within a room overtook most of the space. If I'd eaten another bite of food, I wouldn't have been able to squeeze through to the narrow hallway. This led to an anteroom where shoes had been shed and coats hung. A variety of different-sized slippers, the kind you'd find at a crime scene, lined one side of the entry. Odd and odder.

I turned and looked back. Could that monstrosity be a safe room? If so, it'd been built for a dinosaur. An unobtrusive door slit its otherwise smooth exterior. Hand outstretched, I pulled at the notch Wahl must have used in place of a knob. Locked tight. I pressed my ear to the wall and heard a thump. Had that come from within? Breath held, I counted a long minute before pounding on the door, my knuckles beginning to ache quickly on the hard surface. No one answered, and I couldn't guess what lay beyond my view. In spite of the secrets therein, Aaron Wahl's lair couldn't compel me to linger. With an effortless twist of my wrist, I opened his front door and emerged once more into the cold afternoon.

A few minutes later, winding my way down the curvy road in Hop Canyon, I looked closer at the few trailer homes that dared impose their slovenly ways in this moneyed area. Kids' broken swing sets, deflated rubber balls, and junk despoiled the yards. Parked here and there, unkempt cars resembled beached whales. One looked like the vehicle I'd seen at the mine, same broken fender, same good tires. But it was more a type than a replica. And there were vans, too, with their unremarkable exteriors similar to the one that had been parked opposite the foundation. Boy, I could get really paranoid if I wanted to.

Nah. Leave that to Eva.

25

Detective Sanchez bent over Gabi, resembling a chuffy bear in cowboy boots, a very nasty-tempered bear. "Ms. Solomon."

"Detective." I scootched up a chair.

"Ms. Shofet and I will be done in a few minutes."

"I'd rather stay." The air crackled. I'd walked into the middle of a Superfund site of tension. "Gabi, do you want me here as an informal witness?"

"I'd like that very much."

"That's not necessary," said the detective. "She's not in trouble ... yet."

"*Yet.* What a worrisome word." I edged closer to the bed. "Does she need a lawyer?"

"Why would she?"

Oh, great. I was making things worse. "What's this about, Detective?"

"Your niece is an adult," he said.

"Ah, but she's not herself right now. Drugs, you know, and she had a setback this morning." I placed my hands on her blanketed toes in a show of support. "Plus, I promised her mother I'd take care of her."

From where he stood, Sanchez couldn't focus on both of us. He gave me a nifty view of his back. His irritation manifested in a muscle spasm twitching in his neck.

"Would you like a chair, Detective?" I said, offering mine.

"No, thank you." He paused before settling into a different tone, a gentle, dangerous one. "Ms. Shofet, what were you working on with Dr. Wahl?"

"Aaron should be the one to tell you." She inclined her head forward to explain to me. "Aaron says that scientific collaboration is a myth. He's told me about all the times he's been screwed by students stealing his ideas, putting their names on papers that belonged to him. He's had colleagues steal ideas for patents. It's horrible what they've done to him."

"You're both chemists, right?" said the detective, ignoring the lesson about cutthroat competition.

"Yes. But you know that."

My unvoiced mantra became: *Keep calm, Gabi. Keep calm.*

"With a specialty in explosives, right?" He must be making a point. "Yes."

"Did this new discovery have something to do with explosives?"

"Yes, but not like you think."

"What do I think, Ms. Shofet?"

"I don't know. You just make it sound so dirty, like we're doing something illegal." Gabi's increasing agitation could be misinterpreted in thousands of ways. If she didn't watch it, Sanchez would assume more guilt than he'd already implied.

With hands forming an inclined T, I signaled a time-out, like you see in football games. But no one noticed. What could I do to caution her against impulsive answers?

"Why does your advisor have a secret lab off campus?" Sanchez persisted.

"You mean his office?"

"You know what I mean." The minute he said it, I knew something had turned sour here. "His lab in Hop Canyon. The place even his own wife didn't know about."

"I don't know what you're talking about."

"Ms. Shofet. May I remind you that lying won't get you anywhere? We have witnesses who've seen you and your advisor driving up to the place. And now it's caught the serious attention of a lot of people." He paused for effect. "If your advisor has nothing to hide, then why was he working in secret?"

"The military works in secret all the time," my brilliant niece said.

Oh, my kingdom for a muzzle.

She smoothed her blanket. "Everyone knows the government keeps secrets far worse than what we were doing."

"Do tell me more," said the detective.

"Gabi, you shouldn't answer any questions. Not until your mom gets here." I went to the door. "I think it's time for you to leave, Detective."

"Why? Aaron and I haven't done anything wrong," blurted my niece. "And if we're right, Homeland Security will be giving us awards. We're working on the Holy Grail, Aunt Sasha. We're creating an entirely revolutionary product."

Revolutionary. *Bad choice of words.*

The detective nodded a thank-you my way.

"Be quiet, Gabi." I opened the door wider. "Detective Sanchez, it's time for you to go."

"Why? I'm not scared to talk to him." Gabi raised herself to a full sitting position. "Our work is Nobel Prize material. It's that big. Just ask Aaron."

"He's still unavailable." Perhaps the detective's legs had grown tired, perhaps he was being obnoxious. Whatever the reason, he sat in the chair I'd given up. "So, you're working on creating a new kind of explosive."

"That's right." He'd hit her passion. Gabi's flushed face erased the pale trauma of miscarriage. She held her thumb and first finger an inch apart. "We're this close to getting it right." She looked at me. "I can't go into the details—you wouldn't understand them anyway—but here's the gist of it. Up until now, no one has been able to make an explosive that's extremely powerful, quick to ignite, *and* stable enough to transport safely."

"You have?" Sanchez wrote in his notebook.

"We're close. And if we succeed, we'll be able to help our government protect our country, to detect what terrorists might be developing on their own, to preempt attacks."

I hadn't seen Gabi this animated since she was a teenager. In a tiny wash of self-pity, I wondered what it would be like to feel so strongly about something.

"Okay," said Sanchez. "That's great. But why do it in secret?"

"I thought I explained that." She turned her head from him.

"So you can get a nice patent? Make a lot of money?"

"No. Well, yes. That's part of it. Why's it such a bad thing to want to avoid all the red tape?" She shook her head. "If you've got something this big, you want to make sure there are no holes."

"If it's so noble, why are you worried about red tape?"

Call me mistrustful, but the scene fast-forwarding before me didn't sit well. "Gabi, I really think you should stop and think about what you're saying."

"This is ridiculous!" Gabi slammed her bed with her good fist. "Aaron has told me a million times how stupid people are. 'Most people are idiots,' he says, and I always tell him he's wrong. But this . . ."

"Really?" said the detective.

"Sometimes you have to break rules a little in order to get stuff done." She adjusted the bed down a few inches. "The amount of bureaucratic crap Aaron would have to go through could take years. Add the fact that I've got an Iranian surname . . . Don't look at me like that. I know about prejudice because my dad has had to deal with all kinds of inane questioning ever since 9/11." She took a breath. "If we did everything by the book, Aaron would be an old man and I'd be working at a mine in some godforsaken part of the world."

I couldn't keep quiet any longer. "Gabi, remember you're talking to a policeman. Even if you've got nothing to hide, you need to can it."

"I can't believe you, Aunt Sasha. I thought at least you'd understand. I mean, what are you afraid of? That I'm doing something dangerous? Illegal?"

Why did she have to keep bringing up that word "illegal"?

"I just have more experience with law enforcement than you do, Gabi." I spoke to the detective. "Pardon me for saying this, but I've had my words and actions misconstrued on more than one occasion. From that, I have a healthy and *guarded* respect for the fine men and women who work in your profession."

"If it were respect, Ms. Solomon, you would have let me interview your niece alone."

"Let me clarify, Detective. It's the same kind of respect I'd show a rattlesnake." I needed immediate antivenom for that comment. "I'd avoid provoking it and would keep my distance."

"A rattlesnake, Ms. Solomon? Have your experiences really been that bad?" His amusement irked me.

"Only when I was stupid enough to answer without thinking," I said, staring at Gabi.

"I don't get why you're asking me all these questions, anyway," she said. "Haven't you found Aaron yet?"

Sanchez shook his head.

Gabi turned to look at me. Her voice made me want to protect her from every bad thing in this world. "Did you?"

The detective stared at me, the interest in his eyes shading into suspicion, and I prepared to be questioned, too. Instead, his cell phone rang, he looked at the number, held up a finger, answered the call. Without excusing himself, he left the room and spoke quietly in the hallway.

"No one was home, Gabi," I whispered. "I walked through the entire place and couldn't find him. Is that giant room his lab?"

"Yeah. Didn't you go in?"

"It was locked."

"That's weird. He never locks it. I—"

Detective Sanchez folded his cell phone when he re-entered. His brown skin had drained to tan. "I need to go. We'll talk again later."

"What's happened?"

His face a montage of indecision, he regarded both of us until we squirmed. "This will come out anyway. There've been explosions in Hop Canyon. Guess where?"

26

Eva arrived in a flurry of fuss and fury, a mother badger ready to protect her kit. Enveloped in a dowdy, thick coat, she entered the room and stomped water off her sensible shoes. One look at Gabi, and Eva crossed the hospital room in three steps. Before any of us knew it, she had Gabi in her arms and cooed with love. Her hat fell off in the action. I watched what little I could see of Gabi's alabaster face crushed by her mother's overzealous hug. Eva's black bun bounced slightly as she tightened her grip, loosened it, and then tightened it again.

It was the bun that always came to mind now when I thought of my older sister. A bun, made of a wigged braid, twirled into a compact circle, and fastened with countless bobby pins. It had been the first of many shocks when Mom and I realized just how fully Eva embraced her newfound religious identity. Seconds after she met Zach, her lustrous chestnut hair had been concealed in that shoe-polish black, lifeless wig.

Eva's ever-present humility and absence of vanity showed in a million little ways. She hadn't bought a new outfit for herself in decades, choosing instead to sew her own dresses or to accept hand-me-downs from friends. The money she and her husband earned went toward family upkeep, educational funds for all the grandchildren, and mega-philanthropy to Jewish charities in Israel.

"Mom, let go." Gabi's ambivalent plea brought instantaneous release. Her eyes held a little girl's hunger for safety.

Eva stepped back, realized I was in the room, and embraced me with the same fervor.

"You're choking me, sweetheart," I said, pulling away to see if she'd changed in the months since we'd seen each other last. Her hazel eyes sat too close in a bed of wrinkles earned from intense scholarship and profound thought. She looked thinner to me, as if worry had eaten away a layer of happiness, making her more vulnerable. Her nose, with its bump from an adolescent soccer injury, parsed her face evenly. Though puckered a bit with age and lack of makeup, her full lips retained their pink.

"Sashala. What's that you have on your face?" Without letting go of my hand, she squinted. "You use makeup now? How can I tell if you're healthy?" My sister had acquired a way of speaking that reminded me of my grandma from Kiev, very Old World.

"I'll use more blush next time." I beamed, grateful for her arrival and my upcoming freedom.

"Where's Dad?" said Gabi.

One of the things I liked about my sister was her lack of subterfuge. Here was a person who didn't lie, who didn't keep secrets. Now, Eva's jaw clenched, transmitting an unspoken problem.

I mouthed the words, "What's wrong?"

She shook her head once at me and then faced her daughter. In the same tone she'd used to tell me that there was no such thing as magic, she said, "Dad's going straight home. He has work to do. I'll stay as long as you need me."

"What about *your* job?" Gabi said.

"We were supposed to be gone for two more weeks, so that's no problem. If you need me longer than that, a graduate assistant can take over." Eva's voice gained authority. "We made some calls. Cal Tech has a graduate opening and so does Columbia. We've sent them your transcripts."

Her attempts at reassurance had the opposite effect. You could almost hear the sucking sound, the vacuum of former goodwill, as both women's bodies contracted into defensiveness.

"You can't stay here, Gabriela," said her mother. "Someone tried to kill you."

"We're not sure about that," I said.

"Of course we're sure. It's because she's Jewish or her father's Iranian. Either way, someone tried to kill her."

"Mom, I'm not leaving. That would be giving in to fear. You always tell me not to give in to fear. Plus, I want to do my PhD here." Gabi had reverted to adolescent pouting in her mother's presence.

"Without an advisor?" I said, oh so unhelpfully.

"What's this? No advisor?"

"He may be unavailable," I said.

"What's this? Unavailable for how long?" My sister removed her coat, folded it, and sat. "I thought he was the reason you came here."

"He's missing, Eva." Why bother hiding it? "He's been missing for about a day."

"And this has something to do with my Gabi, doesn't it?" She crossed her fingers into a tent of concentration. "He's Jewish, too?"

"Mom, not everyone in the world hates Jews." Gabi trembled, about to cry.

Eva watched her daughter with unblinking eyes. "These tears you're fighting, they're for an advisor?"

"Don't your students feel passionate about you?" I hoped to appeal to her sense of herself as a fine educator.

"They may feel strongly, Sasha, but they don't show this kind of emotion. Not from so deep in the heart."

Crap. Eva knew.

"Gabi's been through so much," I said, trying to salvage the situation. "She's weak and in pain. You can't judge her responses by normal standards."

A lab tech came in with a bucket of tubes. She nodded to us all before rubbing Gabi's forearm, looking for a good vein. The girl then tied a rubber tourniquet to my niece's arm, pressed, and found her mark. She stuck the needle in. Though it made me queasy, I couldn't help watching the deep red blood flow into the tube.

"What aren't you telling me?" Eva rose to sit on the other side of her daughter's bed.

Gabi looked to me for help but I couldn't think of anything to brighten the musty corners of this saga.

"Tell me," said Eva. "You know I love you no matter what. Tell me the truth."

"I think I'd better get going," I said, standing. "You two probably want to be alone."

"No." Eva extended a hand backward, her finger pointing down in a command to sit. "You stay."

Was this how dogs felt? Compelled beyond their own desires to fetch a ball, to roll over on the itchy grass? I couldn't move. My big sister's order had me stuck to the floor with psychic epoxy. She'd been able to do this all of our lives. I hated it.

"Mama, I loved him."

"I see." Eva turned around to me. "He was a married man?"

My eyes couldn't lie, though my mind rushed to find a way to obscure the truth. My sister's lips closed so hard, I thought she might be having a sharp pain in her head.

"Say something," said Gabi.

"What is there to say?"

The tech attached another tube, capped the first container, and prepared the stopper for the second one. I thought Gabi looked paler, like the tech had drained too much of her blood.

"Oh, Mama. Can you ever forgive me?"

"It's not up to me to forgive, Gabela. You must ask forgiveness from his family, his wife and children. And you must ask forgiveness from God."

The tears Gabi fought, won.

For a moment, Eva comforted her daughter with murmurs in Hebrew. Abruptly, she stopped. "There's more, isn't there?"

When the tech left, a nurse came in. "I need to ask you to leave the room for a few minutes. This won't take long."

"I'm her mother," said Eva.

"You'll still need to leave for just a minute."

Standing in the hallway, my sister's weary face crumbled in worry. "I ask myself who is this child that I raised. Why is she closing herself from me, from her mother?"

Was that a guilt trip? If so, it was an entirely different brand than the kind Mom used on us. It was crafty and rabbinical. Thank God I hadn't grown up in Eva's home. I'd be in even worse shape.

The nurse came out, leaving the door open for us to re-enter.

"Why did you need to be alone? What was so private?"

No one would have the strength to resist Eva's questioning for long.

"I . . . I lost our baby this morning," Gabi said, hiding her face with the good hand.

Eva began to sink slowly at the side of the bed, then caught herself. "It was God's will, my love." She took her daughter's hand. "You'll see. You'll marry and have children someday, but this wasn't meant to be." How could she say such a thing to her grieving child? It was like telling a kid that Peanut the puppy was better off in heaven. Gabi turned away from her mother. "You'll see. It was for the best."

Eva, have you no compassion? If only I could have screamed it. But my immobility came with muteness.

"I'm so tired." My sister rose on knees that cracked. Her next words came in a chitchat. "Where's Davielle?"

The heartlessness of it had a galvanizing effect on me. I wiggled a toe, then a foot. "Probably at the hotel. The last time we spoke, she was going to take a nap."

"Maybe I should do the same." Eva closed her eyes. "Actually, I think I'll go to Gabi's house and get her some fresh clothes, maybe a nice nightgown? Being clean always makes me feel better."

"Don't go out of your way on my account, Mom."

To me, Eva said, "Have they found the bomber?"

"Not yet," I said. "It's a very small police department."

"What about you?" Eva came over to me and touched my cheek with the back of her hand. "Have you had any luck?"

I crooked a finger. Lost in her sorrow, my niece didn't notice the exchange. My sister followed me out the door. I told her about the vandalism at Gabi's house.

"Such small minds." Eva sighed. "Well, this isn't the first time we've dealt with this kind of hatred."

"People have targeted you before? Because of your last name?" I was appalled.

"Even among our own, Sasha." The same nurse who'd asked us to leave now passed us with a medicine cup in her hand. "If someone is looking to hate, he can always find a reason."

"I had no idea."

"It's gotten so much worse since September eleventh." She shrugged and headed back into Gabi's room. "We're thinking of moving."

"I thought you liked Pikesville."

"We like Israel even better."

"What?" Gabi's raised voice caught us both off guard.

"I was going to tell you when we got back from our trip."

"That's safer? Are you kidding?" This from me, the ever-supportive sister.

Eva frowned. "You're double-teaming me."

"If we can't knock sense into you, I'll enlist Mom." I grabbed my purse. "I can't believe you're talking about doing something so dangerous."

"You're going to tell me that living in Socorro is safer?"

"As a matter of fact I am." I waved toward the window. "This is a great town. Whoever hurt Gabi is an aberration."

"You're deliberately ignoring the facts, Sasha." Eva helped me with my coat. "The world is a violent place. Anti-Semitism is on the rise. In France, they're destroying Jewish cemeteries, assaulting rabbis, and I see no sense of outrage from people I considered my friends. In Germany, young people have turned the Holocaust into an intellectual idea with no semblance of a sense of responsibility." Eva's arm rested at my lower back while she guided me to the door. "It could happen again, Sasha. All those deaths, like the abominations happening in Darfur and Rwanda in the name of ethnic cleansing. All it takes is complicity. Or laziness."

My sister's monologue echoed the threats that had paved my journey to adulthood, the ones voiced by my mother, grandmothers and grandfathers, aunts and uncles. "If there's another Holocaust, they'll know you're a Jew whether you act like one or not."

Eva's lower lip jutted a quarter of an inch, her jaw hard again. "If I'm going to die because of my faith, I want to be in Israel. Here, even the simplest things—keeping Shabbat, observing kashrut—become big tasks. People notice. You have to explain to everyone, over and over. I'm tired of it. I want to be invisible, Sasha. I want to spend the rest of my life doing mitzvot, not explaining like a Sunday School teacher."

"What about Mom?" I could brandish my own machete of guilt when I had to.

27

Anti-Semitism may have been on the rise, but *I* didn't have to give in to the fear of it. And, in New Mexico at least, there was always somewhere to hide. Not the most joyous solution, but if necessary, it'd work.

At the hotel, the can of whipped cream by the bed rouged me with memories of last night's fun, of Peter. Had we really risen to see the cranes at dawn? No wonder I felt so spacey, out of sorts. What was Bailey up to right now? I didn't have the heart to turn on the television yet, even though I needed to find out what had happened in Hop Canyon. Had my friend's boss taken her off the fluff piece about tofu turkey? Or would she be stuck doing similarly silly fare for the remainder of the holiday season? I could only hope.

I set up the laptop at the pseudo-desk. Eva might need to be in front of television cameras soon. On the wall before me, drops of dried brown liquid, probably pop, made a chaotic pattern, a pretty good metaphor for my thoughts. Eva's speech patterns, the light Yiddish accent and syntax, might work against us. Ah, back to anti-Semitism again.

Objectivity whizzed out of my mind on a skateboard of emotion. Eva was my sister. I loved her but couldn't be certain about her effect on our target audiences. The only other option would be me, and that sucked.

Usually, I loved the adrenaline of crisis communications, the strategizing and stretching my mind with dozens of what-ifs. With Gabi as my client, the inclination to go fetal held a distressingly powerful allure.

No, not now, Sasha.

Information flow was the key. What? How much? To whom? When? I'd have to reframe the bad juju already affecting my niece's reputation and minimize further damage. We needed a counteroffensive to detract from potential negative angles and to change the public conversation. Because of my personal and professional code of ethics, we'd have to do all of this honestly.

But newsrooms didn't have to adhere to the same rules. A double standard now reigned nationwide. The people's "right to know," that oft-invoked refrain, disintegrated into a scary white powder at the slightest official whisper of "an ongoing investigation" or "national security." Those phrases transformed reporters and news directors into plastic-eyed and flaccid-brained dupes. You think I'm kidding? Forget objectivity. Government-generated video press releases run on nightly news programs without any fact-checking at all.

Whatever scrutiny newshounds once focused on the government now lands with gusto on corporations and individuals. These poor slobs must appear forthright from the onset or the media will pursue them to Jupiter. Lord help them if their story is sexy.

There were too many damn pundits on both sides of the aisle. Red or blue, it didn't matter. They all made me see purple.

That's how piddly tidbits made their strange voyage into mass consciousness. Considered from the outside, Gabi's drama was too luscious to remain local. With reporters like Bailey Hayes on the trail, and my friend was better than most, Gabi's reputation would be slimed if we didn't take action soon. A frontal defense wouldn't work since Gabi had too much too hide, especially with that damn affair.

We'd have to divert attention with even juicier stories. I preferred the hate-crime angle. With our country's uneasy relationship to Iran, the Iraq war, and the latest attacks on Israel, it had real potential to expand in a way that would attract the most eager journalists. Another approach would be to get dirt on Gabi's advisor, the student-seducing Professor Aaron Wahl. If I could find skeletons in *his* closet, and there surely existed a stinking pile of them, that might be enough to send the hounds down other paths.

Too many unknowns. The Socorro *El Defensor Chieftain*'s Internet site had a search function. I keyed in "Pablo Sanchez" and got scads of hits, but the online archive only went back two years. Then I tried my boss's name and added "children" to the query. This yielded fewer articles, all of them recent. Since I had no timeline for the alleged hate crime, a microfiche search at the library could take weeks. If it proved necessary, I'd do it, or sic Eva on it. The best way would be to find someone who'd gossip.

After my eyes crossed for the second time, I took a break. The grocery store still had whipped cream. A pack of Little Debbies, those chocolate cupcakes with white cream filling, would provide even more sustenance. A few bites of a fresh apple made it all healthy.

For the next hour, I worked on the San-Socorro project. Ideas had been percolating since this morning's meeting. One would be to give every tourist destination a set amount of square footage based on a precise formula that someone else could figure out. That way, each one could create its own exhibit. This state fair method would be the least political and most egalitarian, the easier choice by far. I favored something less banal. What if we had each of the three visitor center buildings embody an overarching theme: science and technology, arts and culture, history and recreation? We could stick the bosque, Sevilleta National Wildlife Refuge, the VLA, and New Mexico Tech together. Behind door number two could be a kids' arts and crafts area, info about galleries and local artists including the Alamo Navajo contingent and, if Lemitar really boasted a music scene, we could include it there. The final piece would have info about places like the Hammel Museum in Socorro, the Garcia Opera House, the El Camino Real Cultural Heritage Center, Ft. Craig, various Indian ruins, camping areas, and New Mexico Tech's golf course.

While I wrote, someone knocked next door. I opened mine a millimeter to see who it was. Eva stared straight ahead, unaware of my peeking. Her key in hand, she waited for Davielle to answer. She knocked again, harder this time, before letting herself in. A few minutes after that, I heard a slam and tensed in case one of them wanted to be let into my room. Instead, carpeted footsteps sounded in the hallway. My sister must have gone to get her luggage.

I stretched, hands reaching to the ceiling and then, almost, to my toes. The expenditure of that massive amount of calories called for a couple of cupcakes. Davielle's door ka-bammed. Women's voices, though not the contents of the conversation, could be heard through the hotel's thin walls. What dirt were those two arguing about now?

Speaking of dirt, even though it was late, I contacted the cleaning places Detective Sanchez had recommended for Gabi's porch. Surely, the crime scene tape was long gone by now. Answering machines delivered their prerecorded hellos and accepted mine. I'd hire the first company that returned my call.

My phone rang five minutes later. A man from Spot Off offered to meet me at the house early tomorrow morning. At least I'd accomplished something tonight.

The swoosh of cars on California Street provided an angry river's white noise. Given the nightmares plaguing me, the din—along with the battle blaring in Davielle's room—might save me the effort of even attempting sleep.

In a fit of American chauvinism, I decided to make an impromptu apple pie, with dollops of whipped cream on each bite of the fruit. It might not sell on the Food Network, but I liked it. Dessert in bed. Ah, what an indulgence. Maybe there'd be a rerun of an old '60s sitcom on the tube.

The remote didn't comply. There, in all her careerist splendor, stood Bailey. Hey, I'd asked her about Papi's hate-crime-committing kid. Had she turned anything up? I cranked the volume to listen to the five-second teaser designed to ratchet up market share. Funny how she'd still managed to put a story together about Gabi. I guess she wanted more meat than the tofu turkey provided. Tonight's appetizer presaged disaster; Bailey alluded to "disturbing new information."

Channel surfing amused me until I landed on another teaser broadcasting a picture of Gabi. At least the flattering photo didn't make her look like a convict. The commentator spoke about "possible terrorist connections." *Marvy.* Push, zap, and on to the last of the local English-language stations. Same snooze story, different particulars.

With an ungenerous plea heavenward for a major tragedy to pull the media's attention from Gabi's life and limb, I left messages for both Peter and Darnda, asking them to watch the ten o'clock news on different channels and report to me.

Desperate to improve the odds in Gabi's trial by television, I decided to try the outrageous. At a little before 9:00, it would be chancy but worth a shot.

Bailey answered in her most foreboding and businesslike voice. "Hayes."

"Hi, this is Sasha. Did you find out anything about the hate crime that happened here?"

"I can't talk right now. I'll call you back tomorrow."

"How'd you like a little exclusive? Something to pump up your report tonight?"

"Now?" I imagined her lips soft with lupine craving, a wild flicker in her eyes. "Why?" Her skepticism displayed a heartening integrity, but I wanted her to use it on someone else.

"It's the quid pro quo factor, Bailey. You help me, I help you. Remember?" She'd be assessing the pros and cons of cultivating a media-savvy—hence, too strategic—inside source.

"What do you have?"

"You know how everyone is making such a big deal about Gabi's ethnicity?"

"I don't think we're doing that," she said, insulted.

"Bailey, if Gabi didn't have an Iranian last name, and if you hadn't seen her very Middle-Eastern-looking sister, I doubt you'd be lumping her in with terrorists." With the solid backbone of a professional, I dropped the pissiness and pulled myself back on course. "Did you know her house was vandalized the day the pipe bomb went off?"

"How do *you* know this?"

"Honey, I saw it. And if you need corroboration, that nice Detective Sanchez, whom you've spoken with before, can do it himself." I sprayed whipped cream into my hand and licked it. A commercial came on for a toilet bowl cleaner. The manically joyous woman twirled and cleaned, as if the sparkling potty would give her an orgasm. Wouldn't that be convenient? I'd never need a man again.

"What am I supposed to do with this right now?" She sounded distressed. My hook had notched into her cheek of ambition.

"I'd be willing to be interviewed."

"I'd rather talk to your niece."

"The detective recommended not telling her about the vandalism until she recovers a bit more."

"Oh, great. Some exclusive."

"Take it or leave it, Bailey. I can always call another station." I would, too. Family superceded friendship any night.

Bailey sighed. "You're lucky I trust you, Sasha. Give me fifteen minutes to talk with my news director."

"I'll give you ten." I hung up, sniggering. The interaction shouldn't have pleased me so much. Power. It was addictive. Of course I didn't really have much capital in this situation at all. I was leaning heavily on my own good reputation with the media and with Bailey in particular.

Would I be able to reel this one in? I didn't know what I'd do if Bailey didn't call back. My rapport with other reporters didn't have the longevity I'd had with her. I'd been shortsighted. If anyone else dug up the affair, my ploy wouldn't have much effect.

God give us World War III. Something, anything, to get the media off our backs.

Right now, I needed talking points. What to emphasize? Ah, yes. The victim-being-victimized angle. That had a good ring. Would a rape analogy work? No. An enterprising reporter might dig into Gabi's sex life, especially after I brought up the "Arab whore" insult. Gabi's red, white, and blue blood could stir a positive response if used correctly. The hate-crime angle would work, too. I'd need to emphasize the ethnic slur, New Mexico's self-perceived tolerance, and the indignity of politically incorrect stereotypes.

Pacing assisted my thought process. Back and forth from bathroom to window I went, an overweight hamster running to nowhere on its spinning wheel. Each step brought forth words considered and rejected until the best ones could be selected. When I settled on the right combo, I created a script to prevent straying.

The phone rang at 9:55. Bailey sure didn't leave much time for negotiation. She played her own game well.

"Solomon."

"My butt's on the line here, Sasha. You'd better be telling the truth," said Bailey. "We'll cut to you in eleven minutes."

28

Walter Cronkite, where art thou? Used to be, people watched the nightly news with a genuine desire to glean important information, to figure out how to navigate this complicated world. Now, it was all about "infotainment." Predictability and formulas ruled. Every local broadcast began with *breaking news*, be it a car accident, fire, or murder. The rest of the stories devolved from sensationalism to the piffling pieces right before the weather segment. And who cared which movie star had filed for divorce, anyway?

My television's volume almost conquered the heated discussion chez Davielle. Gabi hadn't merited the lead on Bailey's station, thank goodness. That honor went to a police-assisted suicide. The deceased, a grandma, had been arrested the week before for running a meth lab in her home. The segment's visuals included baby bottles lying on a dirty carpet and cuddly toys in a crib. Her tragedy benefited Gabi, though. Talk about a story with legs. With enough of these grandmas, my niece might disappear from public perception. I picked up my plastic cup filled with water and toasted the poor woman's spirit wherever it may be, praying that she'd finally found peace.

"We'll be on in just a second," said Bailey, her voice louder than the television.

"I'm ready."

A nervous gulp later, Bailey's perfect face came on-screen. "Startling new developments . . . pipe bomb . . ." My heart thudded too loudly. The screen flashed with a graphic of a telephone against an orange-ish background, my name in black along with "Victim's Aunt."

"Sasha, hello?"

"Yes, I'm here." I worked on sounding competent but not abrasive; it was a stretch.

Bailey didn't speak.

Nothing to do but talk. "The day the bomb landed my niece in the hospital, someone also vandalized her home and painted 'Arab whore' on her front door." I paused a millisecond before hurrying to my other talking points. The producer might cut me off at any moment. "My niece was born in the U.S. and has lived in this country her whole life. She's about as Arab as our president." I'd practiced to achieve the best note of indignation.

My strategy worked. Bailey's question completely ignored the word "whore." "And you think the pipe bombing was related?"

"Absolutely." There, I'd done it. The next few seconds would be crucial.

"Thank you, Ms. Solomon."

"Thank *you*, Ms. Hayes."

I held the line, waiting to see if Bailey would come back on-screen. Nope. They'd gone back to the anchors again. One of them, a well-loved and respected man, practically tsked, his grim expression implying *what a shame*. That look would influence viewers in Gabi's favor far more than any of *my* words.

"Sasha?"

"Yeah, Bailey."

"Let me know when your niece is willing to talk."

"I'll do it," I said, hoping the story would die tonight.

The knock at my door came before I'd hung up the phone. Eva stood there, her wig off, her salt and pepper hair wavy from its braided binding. Half-moon glasses magnified her eyes. In her hand she held two yogurts. In spite of that, I let her in. She hugged me.

"Thank you, sweetheart." Her voice caught on thick emotion.

"For what?"

"For taking care of my baby, Sasha. For trying to protect us all."

"That's what family is for," I said, surprised at her passion. "You saw the news?"

"Of course I did."

I hoped Gabi hadn't. It'd be horrible to learn about the vandalism that way, but it had been a worthwhile risk.

Eva occupied the chair next to the window and put her feet on the ottoman, more comfortable than Bailey had been last night, and opened the yogurts. "You think I don't watch TV?"

"I guess I figured it was against your religion." I smiled, but the jest held a glimmer of truth.

"You're speaking of Judaism?" She handed me a container. "The religion I thought you claimed as well?"

I peeled the spoon out of its plastic packaging. It would have been nicer to dive into chocolate ice cream. "Well, you've got to admit my Judaism and yours are worlds apart."

"They're closer than you think."

She savored each bite as if it were fine cuisine. Me? I wondered if all this healthy food would give me indigestion. You know, too much of a good thing. The apple could've lasted me a month.

"You don't like the yogurt? We have other flavors in the room."

"It's great. Really." *In a sour milk and chalky sort of way.*

"Is there something you're not telling me?" she said.

"I prefer pudding?"

"Stop with the joking. You're not telling me something about Gabi." She got a lot of mileage out of variations on the same comment. It probably served her well in college, drawing out knowledge from her students. I bet it'd grow mighty old at home.

I put down the half-eaten glop and gathered three pillows on my bed into a nice pile. Satisfied, I leaned against them. "I hate to say it, but Gabi's problems have national news potential, especially if her advisor comes more to the foreground."

"You mean if he's dead."

"Yeah. I guess that's exactly what I mean." I flexed my toes. "She's in for such a rough ride." Without thinking, I opened the whipped cream can and took a hit. My sister used to do it, too, before she'd succumbed to every rule in the world. "Please, Eva. She needs you so much right now."

My sister finished her yogurt before responding. "She's my flesh and blood. I'll always love her, but she's done such terrible things. Think of that man's family, of his wife and children."

"They don't have any children."

"Good."

"Eva, Gabi's young. You made mistakes too."

"I was married by her age." She moved her head right and left, an attempt to relax. "You don't have to plead my daughter's case. I know from affairs."

"What?" Had Zach been unfaithful?

"It's not important." She threw her spoon into the garbage can by the desk. "I'm worried about Davielle, though. If she finds out, she'll probably sit shiva." Humor touched not a pore of her tired face. Sitting shiva was a custom when someone died.

"Oh, hell."

"Tell me why you feel such a need to defend my Gabi." Eva untied her shoes and took them off. She removed her socks, too. A mildewy smell wafted my way. "Since when are you so close to her?"

"Maybe I identify with her impetuousness. Maybe it's just because I like her. I do like her." I wanted to go to a bar, have a heart-to-heart with my sister over something stronger than sweet kosher wine.

"You think it's a good thing to deny your upbringing? To defy it?"

"What's happening with you and Zach?"

"Answer me first. I'll tell you about Zach later."

Honesty is rarely the best medicine in families. Knowing Eva, though, she'd deconstruct any lie I took the time to assemble.

"I think it's good to question authority every chance you can." I scratched my nose. "There, I answered. Your turn."

"Not quite yet." Eva went into the bathroom. I heard the water running and snuck another bit of the white stuff. When she returned, my sister's face glowed from where she'd splashed it. "Lately, every time I've seen you, I get the sense that you're ill at ease, and that it has to do with the way I observe Judaism."

Not this conversation. Not with everything else that's going on.

"What is it? The wig?" She sat on the bed, a hand on my foot. "That I keep kosher? That I go to the mikvah [ritual baths]? Why do I feel so judged by you?" Eva wasn't going to let me off tonight.

I pulled away from her touch, my legs in a crisscross. "It just feels so foreign."

"How can my worship possibly impact you? Why does it make you so uncomfortable?"

How do you tell someone you feel betrayed by their life choices? "You know I love you."

"Stop with the prevaricating. Tell me," she said. "What is it?"

"I miss my big sister, Eva." I bit a fingernail off, then another. "I don't get how you can be so totally, oh . . . I don't know how to say it. How can you ignore your intelligence and freedom and be so damn subservient and docile? How can you submit to reams of rules and never have to think for yourself?"

She smiled. "It seems you *do* know how to say it."

"I'm sorry. I didn't mean to offend you."

"Who said anything about offense?" She moved farther up on the bed and took off her glasses. "Do you think you're the first person who has said this? When I first met Zach's family, I was astounded by the same things that upset you now."

I thought I'd scoffed silently.

"No, really," Eva said. "I couldn't believe his sisters would dress as they did. I thought their clothes and wigs were the equivalents of burkhas." Eva reached behind her back and braided her hair. "But then, I talked to them, asked them questions. In time I came to realize that they were far freer than most of the other girls I knew in college."

"Oh, come on, Eva."

She held my face between her hands, so that I couldn't turn away. "I look at you and see confusion, my love. Your mind runs nonstop with questions. Am I beautiful? Will a man love me? What's the meaning of my life? All these worries prevent you from becoming the best person you can be."

I yanked away from her. She'd gotten too close and I didn't like it. "Yeah, and you spend your life in your husband's shadow, on the other side of a wall if you go to temple, no more important than a baby machine, mother, grandmother, maid, or cook. What for? So that Zach can be a man of God? What's that about?"

Eva's guileless face, open and forgiving, chastened me. "I know we can't agree in a single conversation, but let me leave you with this: Where you see constriction in tradition, I see the freedom to breathe. Where you see subservience, I see definition and clarity and a life more fully my own than any you can possibly imagine." With that, she kissed me on the forehead. "It's late. I'm tired. You need to work tomorrow and I need to get Gabi to Albuquerque."

"Why?"

"I want a specialist to look at her hand." She picked up her shoes and socks. "And, I'd like her to be somewhere that reporters might not think to look."

"Good idea."

"Plus, she needs rest." Eva put her hand on the knob. "I'd like to get Davielle home to Scottsdale, too. Those babies need their mama."

"And Gabi needs Davielle far away from here," I whispered.

"That, too," said Eva, closing the door.

29

A **black chenille sky,** smocked with stars, added to the pleasure of my mission. The bottle of Glenlivet ensconced in a brown paper bag made it perfect. Though the Capitol Bar could afford conversation, my new vow to abstain from drinking and driving proved stronger than the desire to socialize.

The Princess Bride on the television, a plastic glass filled with ice, wide lemon twist, and two shots of scotch. Life couldn't get much better than this. I sipped and marveled at my sister's ability to avoid talking about her problems with Zach. She'd done it as masterfully as the best PR pro. Duck and dodge. I dipped the last cupcake in the alcohol and ate the off-kilter chocolate mousse.

The second drink went down easier than the first. Only the piercing voices from Davielle's room marred this moment of bliss. Yiddish flew, impossible for me to understand. I dipped my thumb and index finger in the liquid to get the last chunk of soggy pastry before it disintegrated completely. One word needed no translation. Gabi's name lobbed back and forth between them. *Tatteh*, which I thought meant "Dad," came up a lot, too. A bang. Someone shrieked. The door slammed. I braced myself, breath held.

Pound! Pound! Through the peephole, Davielle stood red-faced and heaving. I didn't want to answer, but she'd only make more noise.

With drink in hand, I opened it, ready to belt her. "Do you need the entire world to hear your fights, Davielle?"

She pushed past me. "I need to use your phone."

"Don't you have a cell?"

My niece didn't bother to respond. Instead, she opened my drawers, searching for something.

"If you tell me what you're looking for, I can help."

Her non-response grew old fast. I went to her side and grabbed one of her wrists. "You have no right to come in here and look through my things. Either you tell me what this is about or you get out. I don't have time for your histrionics."

"I need a phone book."

"What for?"

"It's none of your business."

"You're in my room. It *is* my business."

Davielle stopped. The absence of noise popped. Her red face relinquished its color as if it had been flushed out in a single tug. "You're absolutely right."

Now we were making progress. I sat back on the bed, sipped the drink, expecting her to take a seat and open up to me. Hey, I could listen. I could be sympathetic, especially in my semi-mellowed state.

My niece had other plans. Without another word, she left. I waited to hear her go back into her room, but her heavy footsteps clunked down the stairs. Eleven thirty wasn't the best time for a pregnant woman to be alone outside. I thought about running after her but nixed that idea. Davielle had always been a drama queen. Why encourage her tantrums in adulthood?

I considered going to Eva's room, offering consolation and satisfying my curiosity, but unsteady legs and a nice buzz kept me close to the bed. My laptop's screen saver fashioned colored pipes that made complicated knots and then dissolved, a lot like life, only my knots just kept getting tighter. Maybe I could work for a few more hours. The result might be useless, but it'd be fun to tap into the shimmering pool of creativity born of disabled internal censors. That'd take getting up. I'd already burned enough calories today. Snuggling the blankets, I made woozy plans for the next day. Meetings, trips, and family. At least my nieces and sister would be ensconced in the big city. That meant I might be able to meet my deadline for the project.

Sleep came but proffered no rest. Dreams churned, none alighting in the roiling morass of ex-boyfriends slugging at my guilty soul. At about four, I sat up in bed, heart pinging with the vigor of bells in a video arcade. Something was near. I could feel it searching the darkness, wanting me. No noise, not even from outside, as if all sound had been siphoned from the room. My stomach bubbled with the rancid remnants of the ad-lib *mousse au chocolat*. Eyes squeezed shut, I listened, thinking perhaps I slept after all.

A charred smell permeated the room—burning wood, perhaps—lifting me into memories of discovered warmth in cold places. Air flitted past my face and an almost imperceptible weight pressed my foot at the edge of my bed.

"Who are you?" I said, turning on the light.

A blurry, green human shape sat before me. Its long hair, on the top of the ill-defined head, stood straight up, white and thick. Its arms, if you could call them that, crossed and uncrossed in front of its chest, repeating the motion until I knew it was trying to communicate.

"Who are you?" I whispered it this time, scared the apparition might answer.

It moved its arms. Nothing more.

Not knowing what else to do, I reached for my cell phone on the bedside table and dialed Darnda's number. She woke me up all the time. I could return the favor.

"Hello?" My friend's voice sounded groggy, lower than usual, and not at all surprised.

"Darnda, it's Sasha. I've got a ghost or something sitting on my bed here, just sitting here, and I don't know what the hell to do. It's like this mass of pale colors with some kind of living awareness." I tried to push back the sob, but it exploded from the rubble of my horror. "I don't like this, Darnda. Not one bit. I shouldn't be seeing things anymore. This shouldn't be happening."

"Calm down. It's not going to hurt you."

"I don't care."

"What's it doing?"

"I think it's trying to tell me something."

"Of course it is, Sasha. That's why it's there," Darnda said as if instructing a child. "Let me think a minute."

Our conversation, the light, nothing inhibited the movement of its arms. It didn't even look toward me, not that I could tell. I thought about getting up and finding my purse. The Chinese herbs might cut this vision down to nothing. But I was too frightened to get up. It could follow me or do something even weirder.

"Ask it if it has something to say," she said.

"You've got to be kidding."

"Just do it, Sasha." My friend's chiding encouragement and her practical manner emboldened me.

When I said her question out loud, the apparition moved one of its hands up and down from the wrist.

"What's it doing?" said Darnda.

I told her and she laughed. "I bet it's sign language, Sasha. It's speaking to you in sign language. That motion means 'yes.' How cool is that?"

"It's crossing its arms again. Do you know what that means?"

"No, but I can find out in a couple of hours. Liz teaches kindergarten and they do all kinds of sign language in there." Liz belonged to Darnda's horde.

"What do I do in the meantime?"

"If I were you, I'd ask if it has anything else to say. If it doesn't, then go back to sleep."

"You can't mean that."

She laughed.

"It's not funny."

"Well, it is in a way, Sasha. I mean, you fight these visions so hard and they keep finding the holes in your efforts. Have you ever thought about embracing them instead?"

"Save the therapy until I can show you what I think of it in person."

Her guffaw endangered our friendship. "Okay, ask it nicely to go away and see what happens."

She disconnected and I felt the tether of her sanity floating away.

The ghost or spirit or whatever it was ignored me. It seemed caught in its own single-minded reality of opening and closing those arms in the crisscross pattern.

"Um, hello," I squeaked. "This is nothing personal, but would you mind just going away?"

With a small sizzling sound, it vanished, leaving me far more alone than I'd been before.

30

An archaeologist would have needed a durable pick to excavate my face from the sedimentary layers of makeup.

"You look terrible," said Eva when I knocked on the door at seven. The hotel phone in her room had rung twenty minutes earlier, serving as my unwanted alarm clock, too.

"I didn't get much sleep." Suitcases lined the tiny hall leading to the beds, making entry difficult. I steered past two overgrown, flowery bits of luggage bulging against a set of sleek black bags. "Are all of these yours?"

"Guess." My sister, already wearing a high-collared, frumpy dress, went to the minifridge and held the door wide open. "We've got yogurt, fruit. Does any of this look good to you?"

None of it did. I wanted bacon, eggs, and cereal, orange juice, coffee, and milk. All of which would be waiting for me, free, in the other building. "Where's Davielle?"

"At Mom's."

I found a chair. "She drove all the way to Albuquerque last night?"

Eva shrugged. "She was angry . . . still is."

"About what?"

"It's too long of a story, and I don't have the energy for it right now." Eva opened a foiled wedge of cheese. "At least she's not here to upset any of us further."

"Thank God for small blessings," I said.

She felt her braid for symmetry and then pulled the end over her shoulder to fasten it with a thick rubber band. With a twist and a twirl, she wound it into a bun and put her wig on. "Maybe you can help me load up the car before we go to the hospital? I'd like to get Gabi out of there this morning if possible."

"Oh." I hadn't counted on her wanting to leave Socorro quite so soon. "Why don't you call me when you're done with breakfast? I'll go to the lobby and get something a little more substantial."

"You don't even try to keep kosher, do you?"

"Nope."

The winter sun shone bright with promise for a clear, crisp day. I walked across the parking lot to the hotel's lobby and found amiable camaraderie among the diners there. Sure, a micron of remorse twinged after the third piece of bacon, but I'd never assumed spirituality hinged on the food a person consumed. Well, that was pretty obvious, I guess.

A little later we lugged the bags down the stairs and into the car. Eva followed me to the hospital. It was just past 8:00; visiting hours had started less than ten minutes before. The two of us walked arm in arm down the hallway, ready to shed the troubles we'd recently encountered, ready to move on.

"Kidnapped?" Gabi's wail collapsed upon itself into a muffled sob. My sister ran to her room. I came in a split second later, in time to see Eva push Detective Sanchez out of the way. Gabi heaved. I grabbed her empty water pitcher, ripped off its lid, and pushed the container under her mouth as she retched.

Sanchez left the room.

With one hand around her shoulder for support, Eva tried to keep her daughter's hair clear while I held the pitcher. Tremors shook my niece. I thought she might go into a seizure.

The detective returned with a nurse. She brought a plum-colored plastic container and helped Eva hold Gabi until she'd stopped throwing up.

My niece lay back in the bed, trembling still, her good hand sheltering her eyes from our view. Tears mingled with blood from a reopened wound. I could only imagine how much the salt stung. Gabi wouldn't be aware of the physical pain until much later.

The nurse cleared away the mess while Sanchez, Eva, and I remained frozen in an anguished tableau. We heard the water run in the bathroom, watched the nurse place a wet washcloth on Gabi's forehead. Then, *click*, we resumed living.

"There're too many of you in here," the nurse said.

We refused to move.

"One of you will have to leave."

I expected Detective Sanchez to volunteer. Instead, he said, "I'll be done in a few minutes." He showed her his badge. "If you've got other duties, I think we can handle things in here."

The nurse bit the inside of her lip and looked at Gabi. She left with an admonishment: "Don't upset her again."

My niece whimpered, a broken puppy. Her grief-filled stare focused on nothing and compelled me to grab the bed for support. Eva hugged her daughter fiercely, trying to absorb the sorrow, to engulf her child in a field of protection. The upswell of Gabi's tears crested into sheer quiet. The seismic shaking ceased. This new calm alarmed me, as if a giant sloop had lost its wind on the high seas.

Eva confronted Detective Sanchez, her face warped with fury, hands on hips. "Who do you think you are to come in here and upset my daughter like this? You should be ashamed of yourself."

"This is Detective Sanchez, Eva. He's been working on Gabi's case," I said. "Detective Sanchez, this is my sister, Eva Shofet."

Detective Sanchez took off his hat.

"You're the one who's been ignoring the anti-Semitism?" The gale of Eva's anger made the detective step back. "Is that right?"

"Contrary to what Ms. Solomon might tell you or imply on the nightly news, we've taken everything in this case very seriously."

"How big is Socorro, Detective?"

"About nine thousand—"

"Then I don't think you've taken this crime very seriously at all," she said, brittle as an old maple leaf. "Otherwise you'd've found out something by now."

"That's hardly fair."

"You've hardly been successful, by any standard."

I could see the television show now, *Socorro Knockdown: Fight to the*

Finish. No matter how extensive the policeman's self-defense training, my money would be on Eva to win.

"Let me see the note." Gabi's request cut through their head-butting, leaving us all with the stark fact that she'd been wounded yet again.

"This is a photocopy. His wife found the original on their dining room table this morning." Sanchez unfolded a piece of paper and handed it to her. "You remember yesterday, I told you about the fire in Hop Canyon?" Sanchez sank into a chair by her bed, his head drooped an inch.

"What happened?" I said.

"Why don't you tell *me*? A car matching yours was seen turning into Dr. Wahl's driveway a few hours before the fire."

I looked him in the eye. "Everything was fine when I left."

"We'll talk about that later."

"But what happened?"

"We're putting it together. The fire, the explosions, and the response to both, left the scene a total mess."

"What explosions?" said Gabi, handing the paper to her mother.

"People in the area reported hearing three blasts. We don't know which came first, the fire or the explosions. The firefighters noticed the equipment in the lab and called the Albuquerque Police Bomb Squad. The FBI's involved, too." He paused. "It'd help to know exactly what you were working on out there."

"I've already told you. And, we didn't have enough material to cause any explosion," said Gabi. "It had to be the propane tanks. The fire must've started in the kitchen."

"Ms. Shofet, I know you've had quite a shock, but more than one witness says there were *three* explosions. The propane would only account for two." The detective put his hat back on. "And, about the only thing we know for certain is that the fire started in the lab."

I went to Eva's side and peered over her shoulder at the note. Written in what looked like Arabic, I could only decipher the number: $4,000,000. A ransom note?

"No way. Aaron is very careful about safety. He's always talking about how we need to watch out, to clean up absolutely everything in the lab. He's obsessive about static and spends a lot of time making sure that we're safe. He's almost paranoid about it." At least the protest had brought some color to Gabi's face. She pointed to the piece of paper. "Who do you think did this?"

"You tell me."

"I wouldn't put it past CiCi to make the whole thing up," she said.

"CiCi? Cecilia Sanchez?" I sat on the windowsill. Pieces snapped into place, shattered, and then reassembled in different patterns. "CiCi Sanchez is married to your advisor? To Aaron?"

"If you've met her, you know what I mean," Gabi said. "She's totally self-centered. A royal bitch. The only reason Aaron puts up with her is because she won't give him a divorce."

"CiCi Sanchez." I shook my head in disbelief. "Holy crap."

Sanchez truncated my astonishment with a mundane question, directed to Gabi, about the note. "What does it say?"

"You know I can't read it."

"Do I?" The policeman prepared to leave. "Ms. Solomon, a word, please." Still stunned by the whole CiCi-Aaron thing, I followed him out. "In the future, I'd prefer if you left the media relations to us."

"Detective, I don't know what you mean."

"You called Bailey Hayes and offered her the hate-crime angle as a tidbit to further your own agenda. You've worked in public relations for years." His basso profundo voice could've made a hole in the floor on its way down to the other side of the earth. "You know what I mean."

When in doubt, act dumb. The look came naturally.

A greenish sheen colored the detective's skin. His chin had sprouted a new crop of silvering hair since yesterday. He crowded into me, close enough that I could smell his coffee breath. He pushed in farther, so that I could connect the lines in his bloodshot, yellowed eyes. "You've got quite a reputation for playing detective, but I'd urge you leave this investigation alone. Do you understand?"

"Isn't Hop Canyon out of your jurisdiction?"

"Your niece's case is ongoing. As to Hop Canyon and the other concerns, my job is to support my coworkers."

"Doesn't that bug you?"

"Not at all." He held his hands a foot apart. "I've got a pile this high of cases I'm working on. I don't need any more."

"Well, bully for you, then." Oh, why couldn't I just keep my mouth shut?

Sanchez freed me, hitching his pants and tugging at his shirt where it had pulled out from the belt. "Can I give you some advice?"

I shrugged.

"Yesterday you mentioned respecting the police. Well, I don't know if you've had experience with federal law enforcement, but the people who work to protect our country in those agencies don't tolerate interference, and they're not known for their sense of humor."

"And your advice is?"

"Steer clear. If your niece was involved in anything illegal, don't implicate yourself, too." He turned to go.

"What do you think Gabi is involved in, anyway?"

"I want to see you down at the station today, for a statement about what you saw at Wahl's cabin."

"You didn't answer my question."

"I don't have to." He tipped his hat and turned away from me.

Back in Gabi's room, Eva held the note, her mouth working to sound out the text. "This is Farsi. Is your professor working with any Iranians?"

"Duh," said Gabi. My sister shook her head.

"How do you know Farsi?" I reached for the paper.

"Duh," said Eva.

Gabi smiled.

"Zach's family has taught me a bit over the years. I recognize some of these words, enough to know that the person who wrote them isn't fluent." She wiped her nose on a tissue. "And, he or she wants money."

The squiggly script threatened with its indecipherability. I had a horrid thought. "Listen. I need you to do something." Both women waited. "Don't answer your phones . . . any phones, unless you know for sure who's on the other end."

Eva's eyebrows formed a sharp V, the question obvious.

In the hush, I said, "If it's not a friend or family, it'll definitely be a foe."

31

CiCi poodled through my mind, a whiny puff of nasty possibilities. Did she know Farsi? CiCi equaled Cecilia. Aaron Wahl was her husband, but she'd kept her maiden name. I wanted to scream with the frustration of so many missed clues, missed opportunities to question people. How had I been so dense, not seeing the connection? Most small towns have only one or two truly prominent families. Papi Sanchez's left the others in Socorro way back in the twilight zone. Papi had referred to a family emergency after that phone call the day I met him. Had it been about Aaron? At least I now understood his disdainful comments about his daughter.

What did the bomb squad guy see in that piece of string cheese? She had all the allure and personality of white flour. Boy, she'd have to be damn good in bed to keep such a handsome man in tow. Did he know she was married? Ohmigod! Was he the investigator on Wahl's case? How incestuous.

I left the hospital, cell phone in hand, dialing Bailey. This would be major currency in my interactions with her. Talk about a great scoop. Plus, Detective Sanchez's warning to leave the driving to the Feds left a lousy taste in my mouth. The only upside to this development would be that they'd probably want to kibosh the media attention even more than I did. The downside was that they'd make our lives hell.

The trick would be to do my, um, research, in a roundabout way. Believe me, if anything useful came up, I'd go to the good detective and present it, wrapped in a pretty package, complete with an edible bow.

Bailey's recorded voice came on the line. I left a message emphasizing the importance of this particular call. For now, I had an hour to kill before driving to Gabi's house to meet the cleaners. Might as well go to the police station and get the statement out of the way. It wouldn't hurt to massage Sanchez's ego with a show of compliance.

Of course, he wasn't available. My generous deed unrequited, I ripped two sheets of paper out of a notebook and wrote down everything, including what the cabin looked like, the locked lab door, the lousy aesthetic sense, and gave them to the receptionist.

At Gabi's house, a canary yellow cleaning van splotched with blue polka dots stood in front. Bright green letters on its side proclaimed: Spot Off! Emergency Cleaning & Repair. It was a bit too cheery, if you ask me, for this forlorn scene. The yard's abused dead grass and trampled gravel appeared more disheveled than before. The home itself had darkened with the crimes inflicted against it. The phantom mailbox remained an amputated stump.

I parked across the street, mindful of the curtain that triangled back to watch me from Harriet and Judy's home. A venetian blind, next to Gabi's house, flipped downward at my glance. With the slam of my car door, a group of cleaners emerged from the van, reminding me of circus clowns—or a human version of the Three Bears—very tall, very small, and one right in between.

The one man in the group said, "You're the lady who called about the porch?"

"That's me." I watched the women assemble an assortment of sponges, mops, buckets, and two large boxes filled with jars and cans of unidentifiable goops and powders. "Did you have any trouble finding the house?"

"We know the neighborhood." He accompanied me, side by side, while the women trailed four steps behind us. Did every culture insist on this sexist hierarchy with women, the workhorses, destined forever to follow hen-cock men? We arrived at the door. "Let's see what you've got."

The man waited for me to open it. "Pee-U! That stinks." He stepped in to look at the damage then said something to the women in Spanish. With the furor about immigration lately, I wondered if they knew English, if they were legal. It didn't matter to me. Few people would be willing to do the job they did. Plus, the company had to be legit if Detective Sanchez recommended it.

"Do you think this is going to be a problem?" I couldn't imagine the place ever getting clean enough again.

"We've seen worse." He took off his logo-emblazoned cap and scratched his scrunchy black hair. "Is this it?"

"Isn't it enough?"

He smiled. "I know it seems like a lot, but we've cleaned after suicides, shootings, fires, break-ins. This is a piece of cake."

We discussed the price and I gave him my contact info so that he could invoice me directly. Gabi might never need to know. Once that was settled, I removed the key from its predictable residence under the flower pot and went in the house to get my niece a change of clothes for the trip to Albuquerque. Same meager kitchen chair, same lovely Israeli bowl, fruit flies now buzzing around its rotting contents. Given Gabi's interior design, she might actually think Aaron's place was a step up.

I lifted the bowl and looked for a garbage can. Nothing under the sink. Maybe she kept her plastic bags in the bathroom. Preoccupied, I entered the front room and stepped on a dress. "Not again!"

An internal tornado had collapsed bookshelves and strewn papers. Shoes lay in haphazard clumps on the floor, on the futon bed. Clothes islanded in layers, their hangers and boxes emptied. Faced with the bedlam, I searched for a buoy in this ocean of chaos, and tiptoed in, my arms extended for balance. What the hell was going on? Had the police done this? The Feds? The only clear surface in the room was the plank of wood that served as Gabi's desk. Her computer—the monitor, hard drive, everything—had been taken.

"Damn them!" I retrieved my phone, punching in the numbers to the police department with too much vigor.

"Detective Sanchez isn't available right now," the placid receptionist said.

"Well, he'd better be soon," I said.

"Would you like to leave a message?"

"Believe me. This is an emergency."

"Your name and number, please."

Grudgingly, I gave them. "Look. I know he has a cell phone; I've seen him use it." I opened the back door to air out Gabi's kitchen. "If I don't hear from him in the next few minutes, I'm going straight to the media."

Bailey'd love this. So would a bunch of other reporters. I hung up on someone for a change.

How dare they just let themselves in? Didn't the police, the Feds need a search warrant? My phone's ring cut through escalating antagonism, and a headache pushed away the little decorum I had left. "Solomon."

"You were rude to our receptionist."

"Spare me the lecture, Detective. I'm here at my niece's house and what do I find? World War III. Someone took her computer, too. You're the only other person who knew her key was under the pot." I heard him breathing. "Detective Sanchez? I'm in no mood for games." Anger flamed my audacity. If he so much as hemmed or hawed, I'd explode. Had the cleaners working out front ever dealt with spontaneous combustion?

Fortunately for all of us, the detective said, "I'll be right there."

I locked Gabi's door and went to inspect Spot Off's magic. The caustic but welcome smell of cleansers had already replaced the stench. The man came up to chat. It seemed to me he did a lot of that, the public relations guy. Or maybe he was just lazy.

"So, what do you think?" he said, his chest puffed for the anticipated praise.

"It's starting to look much better." In less than twenty minutes, about half the paint had been removed. They still needed to hit the door and a bit more of the porch, but the undeniable improvement impressed me.

"Thanks."

"Do you ever come up to Albuquerque?" I said.

"We could. What do you have in mind?"

"My house. Every two weeks."

He laughed.

"Actually, I wanted to ask you to send the policeman to the back door when he gets here."

The man retreated from me and said something to the ladies. They stopped their scrubbing. The mood deteriorated with his wariness. "We haven't done anything wrong. Why did you call the police?"

"It's got nothing to do with you." I held up my open hands in denial. "Someone broke into my niece's house."

"Oh, well, that's okay then." He translated my message to the women. The relief warmed their faces and released the ambient tension.

"Hey, I've got a question for you." Ah, here's where Sasha, Baby-Boomer Detective, could ply her trade. I pointed to the porch. "Have you ever seen anything like this before?"

"Sure."

"Like where?" Had I been nonchalant enough?

"Well, across the street, for example." He pointed toward my car. "Every once in a while some kid gets a stick up his butt and decides to go a little crazy. No biggie."

Maybe when you made your living cleaning up the remnants of human lives, vandalism and hate messages didn't faze you. But his answer flew in the face of Detective Sanchez's denials.

And guess who had just pulled up to the curb?

32

A helicopter couldn't have ascended the canyons bracketing Detective Sanchez's lips. The best course for me remained silence. I watched him bend to lift the pot and wondered if his pants would cover all that flesh during the voyage. He stood, his frown transforming into a scowl, his eyes bulleting irritation.

"No one else is going to touch this key but my niece," I said, holding up his quarry and then unlocking the door.

"You found it like this?" He pushed past me. "Did you touch anything?"

"A bowl. I was going to clean up a little, pack some clothes for her."

"She going somewhere?" Sanchez pivoted with the question, his interest sparking caution.

"Maybe."

"Where?"

I looked down, trying to think through the response and its implications. "I'm not sure."

"Don't lie to me, Ms. Solomon."

"You've been lying to *me* since day one." *Oh, smooth move, Sasha.*

He took off his hat, the brim ensnarled between fingers too anxious for a lighter grip. "I left this place in good shape. Who else knows about that key?"

"You do. Other than that, I have no idea."

The detective halted his assessment of the front room and squinted at me. "Let me make one thing very clear, Ms. Solomon. Your attitude isn't helping anyone."

My tongue swelled with indignant ire. If he'd been doing his job, he would have arrested Gabi's tormentors by now. Teeth gritted, lips clasped, I stood there, breathing hard.

"That's better," he said. "Now, just give me a straight answer. Is your niece still in Socorro?"

"I hope not."

The detective sat at her kitchen table and rested his head against his large hand. "I guess you'll have to ask about the key when you see her."

I took the chair across from him. "I guess I will."

A loud knock on the front door provided an excuse to diffuse the impasse. I opened it to a porch that hadn't even looked that good brand-new. It smelled of sunshine and lemons, the scatological remnants obliterated with elbow grease and citrus cleansers.

I had the good sense to use the opportunity for détente. "Detective, come see this."

He picked a path through the littered floor and came to my side. "Didn't I tell you they'd do a good job?"

I let him have his victory. "Yes, you did."

The women, seeing our approval, grinned with crooked teeth. The man rested against the door frame, inclined to chat. From his position, he could see into the house. "Wow. Do you need us to stick around?"

"I think we can handle it," I said.

"I'd like you to keep this under your hat, Carlos. We don't want to scare the neighbors," said Sanchez with a conspiratorial wink. Though why he bothered, I didn't know. Carlos's loquaciousness meant that he might intend confidentiality but wouldn't be able to follow through.

I closed the door and locked it before returning to the kitchen. "What do we do now?"

"What kind of computer did your niece have?" The detective remained standing this time. "I'm sure she'd like to file a report, if for nothing else than to collect on the insurance."

Insurance? I doubted she had any. "Can I call you later with that? I've got to figure out a way to break this to her. She still doesn't know about the porch." I rose to leave. "Do you swear the police didn't do this?"

"No one in my department did. Beyond that, I just don't know."

He replaced his hat, tipped it in my direction, and walked out the back door.

Oh, for my digital camera. I'd have to fix this scene, to remember it to explain to Gabi. As my vision crossed the space one last time, outside light slit the dinginess. A ray landed on a shard of glass and a glossy sliver of paper. Buried underneath several sheets of handwritten notes lay the pieces of a broken frame and what once had been a photograph. I could feel the vandal's ecstasy in destruction, a sensual pleasure in the sound of tearing, of slamming the frame against a hard surface. The jagged remnants radiated a lusty wrath. I gently moved my hand over the jumble, hoping to salvage part of it.

A slender strip showed tanned arms and a hand with a wedding ring. A piece that stuck to my shoe revealed Gabi staring directly at the camera, happy, secure, insulated in love. Another bit contained a man's face and neck. His blue eyes made bluer by the white hair, so bright and healthy. He wore a gold chain that complemented the curly snow of hair on his chest. I'd been dreaming about him the night Detective Sanchez had called to tell me about Gabi in the first place. This had to be Aaron Wahl. Who else could elicit such unabashed joy from my lovely niece? A chill ran through my body.

I opened my phone and dialed, the question bursting before my friend had a chance to greet me. "Darnda, does a person have to be dead to do what the thing in my room did last night?"

"Not necessarily. I've seen it happen when a person has some kind of psychic split."

"You're getting too esoteric here, my friend." The strips of picture in my hand made me incredibly sad. I wanted to sit but couldn't find a clear surface to plop down on.

"Let's say that someone has gone through a major trauma. Maybe she's so flipped out that she simply closes off a side of herself. This could be her ability to love or trust. If it gets bad enough, the neglected side might manifest in an apparition to someone who's sensitive enough to see it."

"But could that happen without her being in the room herself?"

"Anything can happen, Sasha. Hold on." Her phone clunked on a hard surface. When Darnda came back on the line, she breathed a little harder than before. "Why are you asking me about this?"

"I'm pretty sure I know who that thing was from last night. Now, I want to know if he's alive or dead."

The pause lasted too long. I heard a crisp rippling sound, then a few snaps on her line, and then four more clicking noises.

"For God's sake, Darnda, answer me."

"He's not dead, but I'm getting a really weird vibe. You know what I was just talking about? Well, it's like he's killed part of himself. But he's absolutely not dead."

"Well, that doesn't help a bit."

"Sorry, sweetie. It's all I can give you."

"It's okay."

"The cards aren't cooperating, Sasha. I'm just getting impressions." She flipped another one. "Be careful."

She had said those words so many times before in our friendship that I had my automatic reassurances at hand. Today, I doubted she'd been truly appeased.

Before leaving Gabi's place, I found an intact manila folder and put the pieces of photograph in it. I made certain I locked the door and took the key. The phone rang on my way to the car. Expecting a new volley of doom and gloom from Darnda, I said, "Believe me, I'll be fine."

"Ms. Solomon?" said Detective Sanchez. "Do you have time to come to the station to clarify a few things in your statement?"

"I'll try to stop by soon." A prickly sensation itched the back of my neck, the kind when you're being observed. Turning my head slowly, I caught a malformed hand releasing the curtain in Harriet and Judy's living room window.

33

"**I know you're in** there." I banged on the door again. Voices whispered and hissed on the other side of the wood.

A gnarled woman emerged from the house next to Gabi's. She wore a fluffy, flowered bathrobe cinched with a thick leather belt. Her hair was that over-buffed penny color that has never occurred naturally on this planet, though it might exist on Mars. The clumps of the crimson didn't manage to cover the sheen from the scalp below, refracting anything brighter than a penlight. She tucked in on herself to pick up a newspaper, her head looking in my direction with eyes that dared. I turned away from her gaze and heard her door click closed less than a minute later.

"A little bird told me vandals messed up your house, too," I yelled. That did it.

"Hush! You'll wake up the neighborhood with all that yammering," said Harriet.

"At 10:30 in the morning?" I stepped inside.

If she noticed my impertinence, she didn't let on. Dressed in gray sweatpants and a long-sleeve T-shirt that said, "Go to hell, I'm reading," she walked barefoot through the front room into the kitchen. No curlers graced her hair today, but she wore it in a brown net, guarding the coiffeur from the elements or the zephyr of questions about to blow her way.

"Now, why were you making such a ruckus?" Without asking, she put a cup of coffee in front of me.

"I heard you've been the victims of a hate crime, too. I want to know about it."

Harriet opened her mouth but Judy answered. "I don't think that's any of your concern."

"My niece's home was attacked, not once, but twice. I heard something happened to your house, too. If it did, I want to know." My purse clomped to the floor in emphasis. "Have you considered that there's some kind of maniac out there targeting your neighborhood?"

Judy's chair scuffed the clean floor with that chalkboard sound that makes people wince. Arms folded, she prepared to defend their piece of privacy. "This isn't your business."

"Now, Judy," said Harriet. "That's no tone to take. She's just being nosy." She faced me. "Aren't you, dear?"

"Never mind." I'd have better luck getting the specifics out of Carlos. "I don't need you to find out the answer. Someone at the newspaper or, maybe, the police, will be willing to help me out."

"Why is this so important to you?" said Judy.

"The police have moved on to bigger things and I still need to find out who did this to Gabi. I plan to push and push until I figure out who did it and why. Then I'm going to hand that person over to the police and suggest they throw away the key."

Harriet and Judy exchanged a glance laden with deep meanings and secret handshakes. It bespoke years of shorthanded conversations, the finishing of each other's sentences.

"Oh, go ahead and tell her," said Judy, her hands using the table for balance when she stood. "I know you want to."

"Well . . ."

Judy left us. She hadn't gone far, though. We heard her banging around in the front room, her hostility evident in the occasional string of curses.

"What's she doing in there?" I said.

"Moving furniture." Harriet's grin lifted half of her mouth. "She always redecorates when she's upset. Sometimes I pick a fight with her just to liven things up. It keeps things interesting." The older woman helped herself to another cup of coffee and went to the cupboard, her arthritic bones bulging through thin skin. She pulled out a box of gingersnaps and put several on a plate, never speaking. She seemed to be stalling, so I waited. The trip to Lemitar and, in the other direction, to the Camino Real Cultural Heritage Center, could be postponed. Hell, if she didn't move faster in a minute, I'd put on jammies and ask for the spare bedroom.

Through the clean kitchen window, I looked into a backyard that held a riot of rocks, rainbows of boulders, and mountains of stone. Turquoise abutted malachite. Volcanic glass nuzzled bright yellow lumps. Could they be uranium? The conglomerate effect rivaled a flower garden.

Harriet came to the table with the snack and her drink. "It'd be good if people showed some of the attributes of rocks, don't you think?"

"Really?"

"Well, think about it. Rocks are useful. They're beautiful." She uttered her next words with intent. Bundles of new wrinkles formed around her taut mouth. "They don't butt into your life and they don't judge."

Rocks also stayed still, a skill I practiced now.

"Do I really have to spell it out for you?" she said.

What was I missing? Her expectant stare embarrassed me with the same sense of insufficiency that teachers once wrought, believing I'd studied my lesson or was smarter than I thought myself.

"Oh, for Pete's sake!" She shook her head in dismay. "Judy and I are lesbians. Sapphites. Queer as seven-leaf clovers."

"So what?" I didn't care about their lifestyle. It had nothing to do with me.

"Oh, honey, I'm sorry." Harriet's laugh made me feel even more stupid. "Your reaction was so blessedly sincere." She held out the plate of cookies and I took one despite their lack of chocolate. "I wish more people felt the way you do."

"This is a college town. There's got to be more tolerance here."

"We thought so. But a few months ago, we came home to find obscenities spray-painted all over the front of our house. Whoever did it took great satisfaction in announcing our orientation to the world."

"How awful." No wonder they hadn't wanted to tell me. "Did the police ever find the idiot who did it?"

"They didn't even try," said Judy, who'd re-entered the kitchen as noiselessly as a dream.

"Be fair. That Detective Sanchez asked the neighbors. Don't you remember?" The truth unleashed, Harriet went to her lover's side and held her hand. "And no one cooperated."

"Could it be one of them?" That lady who lived next to Gabi projected enough hostility to start a border skirmish; she might be holding a grudge. I bit the gingersnap. Hard and stale, it made a loud crunch as a chunk broke into my mouth. An absence of dental insurance reminded me to suck on the piece rather than lose any teeth over the spicy sweet.

"We thought of that," said Harriet.

"Did they leave any kind of explosive like at Gabi's place?"

"No, nothing to link it to her problems." Judy joined me at the table. Harriet stood behind her, gnarled hands resting on her partner's shoulders. "Neither of us believes our neighbors could have done it, but their kids could've."

"Anyone in particular?"

"A couple of possibilities, but nothing definite."

"You're not going to give me names, are you?" Why would they protect someone who'd done such a hurtful thing?

"We told the police about our suspicions and nothing came of it," Judy said. "We don't want you to go hot-dogging around and making trouble for us. Or your niece." She reached for a cookie, sniffed, and put it down. "I hope you don't take offense, Ms. Solomon, but we've lived our entire lives with people making wrong assumptions about us. It's unpleasant and we don't like to rock the boat, as they say. You're not exactly subtle."

Oh, and *they* modeled tact incarnate.

Harriet came over to me and patted my head. Why did everyone treat me like a puppy? I half expected her to get a bone from the cupboard, a little good-bye treat. "It's all right, dear, we were just as bad at your age."

I wanted to swat her hand away, but it wouldn't have been *subtle*. "Well, I appreciate you telling me as much as you did." Standing up, I laid the rest of the cookie back on the plate. "I'd better get going."

"It's been nice seeing you again, dear," said Harriet, donning a hostess's smarmy but dismissive persona. Amazing how she switched, a social chameleon. "Tell Gabi we miss her."

Escorted by Judy, I stepped outside, but left one foot in the door. "Do you remember when your house was vandalized?"

Judy looked back toward the kitchen, as if searching for Harriet's permission, or cue, before answering. "Why does that matter?"

"I'm just curious about whether it was before or after Gabi moved into the neighborhood. I mean . . . did she know about what happened to you?"

"She sure did," said Judy. "She's the one who called the police in the first place."

34

Sometimes the people we think we're protecting need our help less than we do. Had I gone too far trying to shield Gabi? This and other charming thoughts screwed their way into my certainty. Mothers, at least most of them, knew how to handle kids. Not me. So why was I taking on that role?

At the police station, the receptionist's eyes reflected remembered resentment and her sloth-slow response to my request for the detective asserted her power over me—her ability to inconvenience my life. She needed that victory and I did, too. Without it, she might sabotage future attempts to contact Sanchez, crucial ones.

After an era, the policeman came to the crumpled lobby and led me back to his postage-stamp work area, its cluttered tables and chairs stacked with mounds of paper.

"Why did you go to Professor Wahl's cabin?" Sanchez cleared a place for me to sit.

"Gabi asked me to."

"Why?"

"She thought he might be there. This was right after her miscarriage. She wanted to tell him, to have his support. It was a natural reaction." The narrow room gave me claustrophobia. I started to sweat and worried that my makeup would waterfall down my cheeks, off my chin into a muddy lake on my lap.

"What else did you do?"

"When? At his place?" With the back of my hand, I tried to subtly—

Judy would have been so proud—sop up the forming perspiration on my face. "You've got it all there."

Sanchez smacked his lips a couple of times with the crinkled nose of an acid reflux sufferer who'd eaten habañero stew. Sure, it could have been simple indigestion. The more likely alternative was that I'd become a bad taste.

"You want everything? The trip to the VLA, the cranky salesclerk, Magdalena, the Kelly Mine? Everyone I talked with?"

"I'd like to corroborate your whereabouts."

"You can't believe I have something to do with this."

"Please, Ms. Solomon, just tell me." He rubbed his forehead.

It behooved me to cooperate. Better to appease him than a late-night visitor from one of those humorless federal agencies he'd mentioned. Obligingly, I added as many details about yesterday's events as memory allowed, and I dared to include people, conversations, and even what I ate at Evett's. I finished the recitation and escaped feeling like I'd barely missed a land mine.

He'd let me leave too easily, but speculation could only worsen my mood.

Once outside, I dialed Bailey's number for the second time that morning.

"Hayes," she said. I heard the staccato of fingers racing on a keypad.

"Why didn't you call me back?"

"I'm on deadline and haven't checked my messages." She spoke with the sincerity of an inept trial lawyer. Her duplicitous response kiboshed my urge to share the info about CiCi Wahl and the bomb squad guy.

"Oh, well, I won't keep you then."

The typing ceased. "Is there something I can do for you, Sasha?"

I turned onto California Street. There was a convenience store on the right. I decided to get a cup of coffee to slay the stale gingersnap flavor coating my tongue. "Since you're so busy with a deadline and all, do you think you could give me the number for that bomb squad guy? I'd be glad to call him myself."

"He's even busier than I am, Sasha. Why don't you tell me what you want and I'll ask him the next time we interview." Sure, her words had the sheen of honesty, but they slithered with subterfuge. Okay, so did mine. But I felt a nasty jab of discomfort in the ease of her diversion. Could she be involved in Gabi's problems more than I realized? Had she concocted the bombing with the bomb squad guy for a story? Heaven help me. How could I even think such a thing? It rang of lousy fiction, freshman plots, B movies.

"No, that's okay. I don't want to be any trouble." My hands transformed to talons grasping the steering wheel.

"I'd be glad to do it," she said.

"Never mind." Breathing irregularly, I hit the accelerator and headed out of town. Bailey couldn't be involved. Could she?

35

The diamond morning gave way to hazy midday granite. I shoved the doubts about Bailey into a protected vault of denial, the conspiracy paranoia too absurd to believe and just plausible enough not to dismiss. Gunning the Subaru south, I took the San Antonio exit and caught Highway 1. With that turn, the trip toward the bosque made me miss Peter anew. Why did he have to go?

Gabi's predicament fueled my melancholy and confusion further. Judy and Harriet's revelation made me uneasy. Why hadn't my niece mentioned the vandalism at her neighbors' home? Duh. Probably because she didn't know about what had happened at hers. And why was that? Because I'd been so intent on protecting her that I'd marred our communication. If she'd been told right away, maybe I'd have a clue about how to proceed in finding her attacker.

The blue highway made an elongated curve near the railroad tracks at the edge of the Bosque del Apache's marshland sea of dried grasses waving in the wind. A roadrunner, tail feathers pointed in a perpendicular line, streaked in front of the car and disappeared into the dormant undergrowth.

A few minutes more and the road became a roller coaster of ruts and hills. The lonely horizon hinted at what it must have looked like centuries before with sapphire mountains in the distance, hard and unforgiving ground underfoot. The earliest Spaniards to claim this land, clutching water-filled animal skins, must have cried out to God in despair. Merciless sunlight, scant food, poisonous snakes, prickly cacti. "Socorro" means "help" or "succor" in Spanish. The Picuris Indians, near what is now the county's namesake, helped these parched, miserable travelers when they were close to death. Little did the kindhearted indigenous people know they'd abetted their own conquerors.

At mile marker 28, the turnoff to Ft. Craig lured me off the main road and a few miles down a dirt one to an empty parking lot. A golden New Mexico flag, with its red Zia symbol, buffeted and clanked on a pole alongside its bigger red, white, and blue brother.

Wind cuffed my ears and blanched strength from my bones. Desolate. At one time, more than 4,000 soldiers, not including officers' families and the traders who helped keep the place running, had been stationed here. It was difficult to believe that these stacks of rocks—remnants of storage rooms, a sally port, a hospital—had once been one of the largest forts in the West. Battles had been fought here against "Indians." A huge Confederate campaign in the Civil War had been squashed.

In less than 200 years, most of the buildings and clearings had been reclaimed by dirt and tenacious native plants. Even so, I could sense the presence of others and could almost see the prisoner shivering in his earthen room, a single blanket for warmth on a snowy day. Beyond the air's whoosh, phantom rifles banged and boys screamed, their cries coloring this land with dreams destroyed before they'd had the chance to become men. The chill that enveloped me had nothing to do with the wind. It was the reality of war, of death, of impermanence.

Though only a shell of what it once was, Ft. Craig spoke with an austere eloquence that needed to be heard. It deserved a larger audience beyond the dedicated volunteers who cleared and cleaned, or the Civil War buffs who re-enacted battles here.

At the car door, my nose rouged from the martial wind, I paused to bow to the souls who'd fallen here. "Please. May you all rest in peace."

What a bounty to be back on the paved highway, back in the present! An old brown pickup, its fenders round and gentle, approached from the other direction. We nodded in greeting. Still, I couldn't relinquish the sorrowful tugs of the unseen dead at the fort. I reached in my purse and extracted the bottle of tarry Chinese pills that had become less and less effective against my hallucinations, and swallowed four more than recommended.

Frigidity continued to seep though my feigned composure. What would Darnda have done out there at Ft. Craig? Stupid question. She would have communed with the ghosts and encouraged me to do the same. The image of my plump friend brought much-needed relief, then a laugh, and released me from the fingers of that icy arena.

Since my purse was open anyway, I decided to give Darnda a buzz. The phone's low battery had another idea. No wonder the trip had been so peaceful.

A large sculpture came into view, standing out against the mesa's flat top. Its flanks, the color of dark chocolate, reached upward to a central fan of turquoise. Named *Camino de Sueños*, the Road of Dreams, it indicated the junction to the El Camino Real International Cultural Heritage Center. I hoped the lengthy moniker would be the only awkward thing about it.

Another drive down another isolated road, though this one was in better condition than Ft. Craig's. To the left of the gravel parking lot hunched a house. Though small, it'd be more convenient for staff than having to commute every day.

Before me, perched high on the butte in the middle of absolutely nowhere, the main building looked like it was made of construction paper. At its front, five flags swished on tall poles. The two that interested me most hailed from Mexico and Spain.

The overall effect, especially the view, astonished me. I had to brace myself against the car for a moment to take it all in. Regaining my equilibrium, I walked the narrow plank of an entrance into a bright, new space of glass and music, white walls and polished floors. My high heels ticked an uneven beat in the empty hallway.

"Hello?" The lack of people amplified my soft voice.

Isabel Apodaca came out of an office area to my left. "Ms. Solomon? What a nice surprise." She wore a sensible gray suit that matched the color of her unruly hair. Though overweight, she gave the impression of being solid rather than chunky and radiated a presence that was all business, no time for pomp. I flipped back to school days, when I'd first learned about sex and had spent the better part of three months trying to imagine my teachers in bed. Even those images couldn't rival the one of Isabel and her ex, Sam Turin, flitting in my head now.

Shaking the off-kilter porn scene from my mind, I said, "I've heard such good things about this place, I had to come see it for myself."

She looked at her watch. "May I give you a little tour?"

"Don't trouble yourself."

"It'd be an honor." Her smile brightened into cherubic beauty, banishing my first impression of her as being dour, mirthless. Happy with the change, I stopped analyzing the person in favor of paying attention to the building itself.

The structure's architecture intentionally evoked a ship sailing to the New World. Walking its clean floors mimicked a voyage. Beyond the vertical wall exhibits, blankets hung from the ceiling, a wooden cart that could have been used for the trip up the camino dominated a passageway, and an interior fountain gurgled. This multi-layered use of space created a fuller experience, one that affected the entire body.

"You'll notice we don't have a lot of artifacts here," my guide said. "We're an interpretive center. We explain and interpret history rather than provide a museum filled with gold coins and ancient pots."

Actually, I hadn't noticed. There was enough here to fascinate. "Why did you make that decision?"

"A lot of reasons. A big one was security. We're too far from law enforcement." We paused in front of a bas-relief of a mission church. "Of course, that wouldn't have been insurmountable if one of our biggest donors hadn't reneged on her pledge a few months before we opened."

We resumed our ascent up a ramp that even someone in a manual wheelchair wouldn't have found too challenging. "Anyone I know?"

"It's impolitic to say." Isabel pointed out a map delineating the route from Mexico City to Santa Fe. "Your boss wouldn't be happy to have the information floating around."

"Michaela?"

"No."

"Papi?"

"Let's go outside." It took all of her considerable strength to open the glass door against the wind.

Outside, sleeping gardens promised an education all their own. The first contained plants Native Americans would have grown centuries ago. Another boasted medicinal herbs, those *curanderas* (healers) used to combat gout, ease childbirth, and clear phlegm. I tried to envision the flowers, the smells.

The director's hair blew across her forehead. The bottom of her jacket flicked up, showing the strained buttons on her blouse and the large silver cross studded with malachite she wore on a heavy chain. The jewelry shone in the sunlight. "It wasn't Papi," she said.

"Then, who?"

"It was catty. I shouldn't have mentioned it."

"If it's someone I have to work with, I'd appreciate a heads-up. I promise to keep it confidential."

To the east, a lonely plateau rose toward the Rio Grande. It displayed nary a trace of human touch. This, even more than the informative exhibits within the building, was the true strength of the center. A person could see, could sense, what those many tired travelers along El Camino Real had experienced years before the Pilgrims had spotted Plymouth Rock.

"Have you met his daughter?" said Isabel, pulling me back into this decade.

"CiCi?" The thorn piercing the bottom of too many people's feet. She nodded.

"What a doll," I said, taking the chance that Isabel shared my revulsion.

"Indeed." Another quick glance at her watch and Isabel motioned us back toward the door. "I'd rather share a room with a rabid dog."

"She's that bad?" I said.

"She's worse."

36

On Christmas Day 1887, Conrad Hilton first opened his itty-bitty eyes in San Antonio, New Mexico. In my mythic version of that moment, the future founder of the mega-hotel chain squiggled at his mother's breast and smelled red chiles in the winter air. That's all his minutes-old brain needed to understand that the keys to true happiness lie in comfort and great food. That might also explain why the little town of his birth, with a current population of a small high school, has two of the best burger joints in the United States.

Across the street from the older, world-famous Owl Café is a pip-squeak of a restaurant named Manny's Buckhorn Tavern and Grill. Its green chile cheeseburgers have garnered international praise and often rank in travel magazines' top choices for good eats.

I'd often dine at the Owl, settling into its dark booths and decades-old atmosphere. But today, the smaller venue attracted me. I was in the mood for kitsch. Manny's tavern used to be Manny's *house*. How can you not love that? He raised a passel of children there, serving take-out burgers from his family's kitchen window. In fact, a bathtub still sits in the bathroom, though if you pull back the shower curtain, you'll see it's used for storage now.

Lunch ordered, I pondered my next move. In Albuquerque, saintly Paul faced a flood of estrogen gurgling from the traumatized seas of my sister and her progeny. It wouldn't be fair to let him handle these torrents on his own. He had enough work to do taking care of Mother's appointments with specialists; home visits from physical, occupational, and speech therapists; the complaining. So, I *should* go to her house right after lunch.

The aroma of roasted green chile chortled up my nose before the plate hit the table. I closed my eyes and breathed deeply, my lips twitching with anticipated gratification, my hands reaching for the bun. What I really *wanted* to do was to go back to the hotel, whip out the laptop, and work until the wee hours of the morning. An online investigation of everyone's favorite little rich girl might be useful, too. Instead, I picked up the burger and bit.

The waitress came back to the table with my drink and laughed. "Did you know you just moaned out loud?"

I would have said something but my mouth was full again. You couldn't duplicate the smoky heat, the flavor of New Mexico's proudest fruit. That was another big reason why Peter would have to move to Maryland by himself. I pitied his loss as much as I felt sorry for my fellow countrymen who'd never experienced this bliss.

Too soon, my plate surrendered its prize and sat forlorn, the dot of catsup mourning its loss of fries.

Next door, the Pentimento Gallery offered fine artwork to mull while drinking a decent latte. Good coffee always requires chocolate. Catty-corner to Manny's, on the same side of the street as the Owl, the San Antonio General Store beckoned. The business's exterior still embraced its former incarnation as a gas station, but no greasy rags or pungent smells waited inside. Before me, in a clear glass case rested seven different trays of homemade fudge, from brown and white rocky road to an orange Amaretto.

Of course, I had to sample several flavors, *just doing my job, mind you*, before deciding on a half pound of the most traditional of the choices. While I stood salivating, a white-aproned woman came out of the kitchen with a yard-long sheet of magic-rock fudge, as yet unset, but almost enough to keep me glued to my place for a few more hours.

In a rare display of self-control, I left and headed back to Socorro. Too bad the fudge didn't last the twenty-some miles. At the hotel, the phone's message light blinked spasmodically. Licking the wax paper from the candy box, I punched the button to listen to the missives.

"Sasha, call me." Eva's grim voice sounded tinny, insubstantial. If she was at Mom's, why hadn't she used the landline? And why hadn't she called me on the cell phone? Oh, yeah. I pulled out the charger and plugged it in.

On the bed, I kicked off my shoes and popped on the television. The thick, drawn drapes brought a nocturnal gloominess to the room, though it was only four o'clock. After I returned Eva's call, a little snooze might be just the thing to relax me enough to go home. Alas, that duty took undeniable priority over everything else right now. Well, even nightmares would be nicer in my own bed with Leo curled next to me, purring. Snuggling under the hotel bedspread, I flexed and pointed my bare toes, finding the right position. It had been days since I'd felt this cozy. Maybe I could hide from the world a few more hours. . . .

The phone's ring ratcheted my heart into hyperdrive. Light from the television cast a bluish hue. I fumbled to axe the nerve-wracking jingling and knocked a glass of water off the bedside table, nearly taking out the clock radio with it.

"Hello?" My chest felt constrained by layers of tight adhesive tape. Was I having a heart attack? Oh, God!

"Sasha? Why didn't you call me?" Eva's panic made the fingers on my left hand tingle.

"I must've fallen asleep."

"Turn on Channel 8."

"Why?"

"Just do it and then call me back."

I found the remote and then the station. Bailey stood outside a brick building. "According to a source close to the investigation, Professor Wahl's reputation for seducing his students is legion."

"Dammit!" I yelled, shoving off the bedspread and turning on the light. If she tied this to Gabi, we'd be screwed.

To my utter horror, Davielle appeared on-screen. Her wig gleamed as if she'd just washed it. How had Bailey flattered her into this interview?

"My sister has always been very secretive about her work," Davielle said. "You've got to wonder."

"Great sound bite, you idiot," I said, pacing in front of the television.

"The police and FBI have refused to comment on Dr. Wahl's continued absence," Bailey said. "But sources near the investigation confirm he and Gabriela Shofet had a fight shortly before his disappearance. Ms. Shofet, an Iranian-American graduate student at New Mexico Tech, worked very closely with the professor on campus and, according to witnesses, at the secret lab on his property. The same lab that burned yesterday, endangering several homes in the area. Stay tuned for details at ten."

For the first time in my life, I understood what it meant to see red. I blinked and the bright color remained. Davielle had just forfeited any respect or courtesy I'd ever considered extending her.

The phone rang again.

"What the hell was Davielle thinking?" I said.

"That's not the point," Eva said. "I'm worried about Gabi's evasiveness. What else hasn't she told us? She's practically begging for Homeland Security to question her."

"That *is* the point. If Davielle hadn't opened her big mouth, the story wouldn't have had any teeth. Now it's got tusks." Sweat ran down my face and sides, an internal sauna. Early menopause? "Does your darling realize what she just did? Let me spell it out for you. She confirmed the affair *and* she made Gabi look like a terrorist." I punched the mattress and screamed, bending my wrist back at a bad angle.

"Sasha? Are you all right?"

"Is she there? Is Davielle there?"

"Why?"

"Because I want to kill her . . . please." Who did I know that had a gun?

"She's not here right now."

"Yeah, you *would* say that. Well, you can tell her we're going to have a little tête-à-tête when I get there."

"Sasha, calm down." Eva's matronly command infuriated me further.

"Davielle's not going to get away with this. She's got to make it right."

"Sasha, no one can make right what is so terribly wrong."

"Stop sounding like a Jewish Yoda." I turned off the television. "You're siding with *her* against Gabi?"

"Davielle's devastated. And she's got a right to be." Eva put her hand over the receiver and said something, then returned to me. "The truth has a way of coming out. Affairs always have collateral damage."

I pulled aside a drape and stared into the dreary, drippy night. Cars made their way up and down I-25, their headlight beams illuminating the wet asphalt. Our family crisis meant nothing to the drivers on their way north and south. "You talk about affairs with too much knowledge, Big Sister."

"When Zach finds out what his baby has done, Gabi will be as dead to him." She'd jumped too easily to thoughts of her husband.

"Talk about a double standard," I said, convinced my brother-in-law had strayed, the lousy philanderer. "What? It's all right for a man to have an affair?"

"That subject is closed."

"You can forgive your husband but not your own daughter?" Fueled by disbelief, I reached for the packet of free hotel coffee and bent to pick up my overnight bag. I couldn't remain in Socorro, not tonight, not when I had a niece to kill. How much did a bazooka cost? Or a nice little rocket launcher?

"Gabi knew it was wrong," Eva said. "It goes against everything we brought her up to do and believe."

"She's a kid, Eva. Kids blow it sometimes." Age really had nothing to do with it. We all made mistakes. Some of us just did so more readily than others. Guilt and more guilt. "Does Mom know what's going on?"

"Not yet."

"Are you planning to tell her?"

"Who are you talking to?" Mom's muffled voice pierced our conversation; she had to have sensed our disquiet. The receiver made a bumping sound. I wasn't done with Eva, but my mother had usurped the phone. "Sasha? Where are you?"

"I'm—"

"Paul and Davielle are finally getting some use out of that fancy kitchen of his. They're making dinner and bringing it here." Gossipy glee colored her next comment. "You know his wife kept kosher all those years? In Albuquerque? Can you believe it?"

"That's nice."

Her giddy laugh ushered in a dull headache. "You're coming, aren't you?"

The last thing I wanted to do was eat dinner there, to act as if everything was hunky-dory. But my absence could do more harm. At least in Albuquerque, I could muzzle Davielle. "Yes, I'll be there. Can I talk to Gabi?"

"She's taking a bath. It's terrible what happened to her, falling off of a bike like that."

They'd lied to Mom? Stupid move. Though her short-term memory had shattered, Mom remained astute. I'd bet a pound of tiramisu that she knew something was up.

"Let me talk to Eva," I said.

Another bump of the phone.

"Hi," said my sister.

"Who told Mom Gabi fell off a bicycle?"

"She came up with that herself."

"Wonderful," I said. "Did you know about Davielle talking to the reporter? Is that why you left me the message?"

"No."

"Is Mom still in the room?"

"Yes."

"Tell me why you called, Eva. I don't have time for twenty questions."

"Someone has been leaving me a lot of messages."

"Who?" With a tug, I ripped open the bag of coffee, licked a finger, and dunked it in. Maybe I'd choke to death before she could tell me.

"Mom, would you mind checking up on Gabi?" Eva waited and my mind whirled with horrid possibilities. After too long, she whispered, "It was the FBI."

"Oh, crap. I *told* you not to answer the phone."

"Sasha, if Gabi has done something against the law, we need to know. *I* need to know."

Had she gone mad? "What are you talking about?"

"The explosives, Sasha. What were they doing hiding their work? Why would they do that if it was aboveboard?"

"Oh, honey," I said, wanting to cry. "You've got to believe better of your daughter. You just have to."

"I believed she was a good girl. But this? And an affair? I don't know my own child anymore." No wonder she'd sounded so fragile a moment ago.

"Have you talked to Gabi about it? Asked her?"

"She's hiding in our old bathroom." Eva's resolve gained power. "I'm going to get to the bottom of this. I'm going to find out what Gabi is doing with that professor, what they're working on. And if it's illegal, I'll handcuff her myself."

37

Wouldn't it be great if whipped cream could save the world? Giant cans of sweet fluff deployed to political hotspots. The white stuff, enriched with protein and nutrients, sent to feed the starving, heal the sick. I indulged in the fantasy while taking another toke on the can, the speedometer in my car hitting levels hitherto unknown to the manufacturer, an open candy bar in my lap.

The frivolity passed, leaving a scum of worry. The schism in my sister's family threatened to cleave us all apart. Gabi's reputation teetered on ruin. If only I could fix it all. Right now, it'd be easier to turn New Mexico into a tropical paradise or keep New Orleans from ever flooding again. There were too many holes in this dike and not enough fingers.

Though murderous thoughts about Davielle brought a perverse pleasure, they only served as a diversion from what I really had to do—find who'd hurt Gabi. With that knowledge, I could change the current media tack to benefit my *good* niece. What were Bailey's exact words? She'd referred to an argument between Gabi and Wahl. Where had that come from? One person knew for sure and I planned to ask her what else she'd omitted. As to that *source close to the investigation*, if Sanchez turned out to be the blabbermouth, my instincts about him had been wrong. But who else could it be?

At the "Big I," the confluence of two large interstates, my steering wheel automatically veered to the left toward Leo and my house. Instead, with a yank, the recalcitrant vehicle traveled in the other direction. Minutes later, I parked in front of Mom's house. Before going to the large brass doors, I filled my mouth a final time with whipped cream, swallowed, and forced myself to repeat the mantra: "I will *not* cause a scene. I will *not* cause a scene."

Inside, two televisions blared a cacophony of commercials. Water gushed in one of the bathrooms. Voices carried to the front hall from the kitchen. I bellowed my greeting and walked toward the smell of sautéed onions and grilled bell peppers. Davielle's bombastic laughter slapped me, a hard hand of audacity against my raw nerves. How dare she be happy when she'd trashed her sister's life?

Assaying a disinterested gait, I gritted a smile and forced my feet forward.

"Sasha!" Mom said, joy alight in her eyes before it embered into remembered flaws.

Eva blew me a kiss and resumed setting the table. I didn't recognize any of the dishes or silverware. They had to be from Paul's kitchen; at least the kosher problem had been resolved. Paul hugged me like a father should and nearly broke the emotional firewall I'd erected. Davielle had enough sense to keep her back to me, as she continued to parse the dinner onto plates.

The only person missing from this Rockwell scene was Gabi.

"I need to freshen up," I said, knowing where to find her.

The sound of running water intensified with each step across the wide entryway, my bare toes digging into the plush antique silk rug. The only light in this part of the house shone from under the guest bathroom door. Could Gabi still be bathing? She'd be one of those wrinkled Japanese salt plums by now.

I knocked. "Gabi, it's Aunt Sasha."

"Go away."

"Sorry. No can do." Groaning with the descent, my cracking knees could scare a small rodent. I sat on the polished brick floor and leaned against the cool wood. "You're going to have to let me in or I'll just hang out here and blather until you do. I don't think you want the others involved in our conversation, do you?"

"What's the use? I'm done talking anyway." She had so many legitimate reasons to feel sorry for herself right now. Alas, self-pity consumed too much time.

"Kiddo, listen to me. Somebody stole your home computer and

messed things up pretty badly in your house. I need to talk to you about it before the police do."

Gabi opened the door. Steam coated the mirrors in the bathroom, but my niece wore stretch pants and a loose top. From the grunge on her bandages, including dried yellow ooze, she'd have a hard time convincing anyone she'd taken a bath today. The tub, filled with hot water, testified to waste in the name of self-preservation. New Mexico's drought conditions this winter proved less compelling than Gabi's need for privacy.

"What have you been doing in here?" I hoisted myself onto a counter glistening with pearls of condensation.

She pointed to the tub. "I needed to think."

Smart kid. I'd used the same technique in this house to escape Mom's constant chiseling at my sense of self-worth. Now, my omissions imperiled Gabi's. "I haven't been completely honest with you."

"Join the club." She sat on the closed toilet seat, her jaw squared, body tighter than a new pair of control-top hose.

"I bet you're feeling like it's you against the world right now." My therapist's tone, learned in grad school, caused her to recoil further.

"No kidding." The petulance ill fit her, but I liked that she was responding rather than hiding behind stoicism or erupting in yet another cascade of tears.

"The other day when you asked me to go to your house, well, I kept some information from you, deliberately x-ed it out. I thought I was protecting you."

She sighed. "Just tell me."

Her exasperation revealed my attempts to do it again. I'd been nudging the edges of honesty. She wanted, needed, the blunt truth.

"Your house was vandalized in a horrible way, Gabi." The misty mirror provided an excuse not to look at her. With my index finger, I drew one Chinese character, then another, buying time. "I don't want to go into every gory detail, but the thing that upset me most was that they painted 'Arab Whore' . . . on your front door. Can you imagine?"

Her head jerked back as if she'd just relived the pipe bombing.

"I called the police. Detective Sanchez came out." Lacking any good fingernails, I nibbled at a cuticle. "Then today, when I met the cleaning crew, there was this big mess inside. Your papers and clothes were thrown all over the floor. It had to have happened since the other time because I went into your house then, too." I pulled at a flap of flesh with my teeth and the finger started to bleed. The sink's cold water helped diminish the self-inflicted pain. "That's how I know someone stole your computer."

"Why doesn't anyone tell me anything? I'm not a baby."

"What can I say? It was a stupid decision. I thought I was protecting you." Might as well give her the rest. "You know that picture of you sitting in your advisor's lap?"

Gabi nodded.

"Whoever messed up your house broke the frame and ripped the photograph into pieces."

"Oh, hell." She gripped the side of the toilet seat with a white-knuckled hand, her other one useless on her thigh.

I slid off the counter and kneeled at her feet. The hard floor hurt my bony knees. Water soaked through my pants up toward my hips. "Gabi, we need to find out who planted the pipe bomb, who did this vandalism. We need to find the person who painted that ethnic slur, did the robbery, all of it." I pulled her clawed hand from its straining grasp and held it. "When I spoke with Judy and Harriet today, they said you might have some ideas."

With her good hand, Gabi picked at a scab under her chin. The motherly reprimand spiking my tongue tasted bitter but had to be swallowed. Even the smallest criticism could annihilate this tenuous conversation.

She cleared her throat and swallowed hard enough for me to notice the strain of it. "I do have my theories."

"Why don't you tell me?" I said.

"Why should I?" Her face reddened. "Why should I tell anyone anything? All anyone has done is lie to me and I'm sick of it."

Anger and pity waged an ugly battle. "The only person I know who has lied here is—"

"Go on, say it."

"You." I unbent griping knees and stood. "Listen, you and I . . . we're more similar than you think. I love you and want to help you, and I'll do it, if I can, without judgment or rules or moralizing."

Hushed footsteps made sneaky sounds outside the door. A loud breath exhaled through the wood. Gabi's widened eyes belied our mutual concerns. How much had the eavesdropper heard?

"Gabi? Sasha?" Mom's voice paralyzed us both. "Dinner's ready."

"Okay." I held a finger to my mouth, imploring my niece's silence. "We'll be there in a minute." After the rubbery steps squeaked away, I reached for Gabi's good hand and pulled her to my side. "Sweetie, you need to tell me because I'm all you've got."

38

Tension ping-ponged around the table. If Eva said more than three words, I'd wear a chastity belt. Mom searched our faces for the rules to this edgy game. Paul soldiered away, telling story after vaguely amusing story, though his previous attempts floundered at his feet. Davielle's couscous remained in a mound on my plate.

After the unsuccessful meal, I kissed Mom on the cheek, her rice-paper skin dry but warm. I left the table and dishes for others to clean. This wasn't my mess. None of it was. Davielle might have been surprised that no one else offered to help tidy up. Still, it gave her an excuse to avoid me, and that suited both of us.

I paused in the front entryway, my hand searching for the damn car keys. Gabi passed me on the way to my old bedroom. I followed her and flicked on the overhead light. The guest room, cluttered with modern paintings and clunky maple furniture, brought too many pit-in-the-stomach memories. Or maybe I was hungry. My gaze stumbled from emotional trigger to emotional trigger and landed on my niece's little bag of clothing, lying in a pitiful lump on a large, unfriendly chair.

Within seconds, Eva and Davielle rushed down the hallway outside the room, their conversation keeping pace.

"The past is past," said my sister.

"She takes after him, Mama," Davielle hissed. "Do *something*."

I held up a finger to warn Gabi to keep quiet, but they'd already gone into another room and closed the door.

"Do you ever feel like a stranger in your own life?" I said, feeling my long-ago adolescent alienation grabbing hard at my ankles.

"All the time." Gabi flung herself onto my old bed, an action re-enacted so often in my youth that seeing it now reminded me of the coolness of the bouncy surface against my cheek. Her sense of dejection intensified in this room where I'd cried so many times, sure that no one loved me.

Oh, hell. I couldn't let her stay here, not in this room, not with Davielle urging Eva to turn against her. "Would you like to spend the night at my house?"

"Really? You'd do that?"

"I'll even give you my bed."

At the front door, cowardice overtook my bravado and I yelled, "Gabi and I are going. Bye." We didn't stick around long enough to hear objections.

The sky muddied to a dismal brownish black and spat an icy rain. The sound of the drops hitting my windshield resembled a cellophane wrapper being removed from a piece of hard candy.

The farther we drove from Mom's house, the lower Gabi's shoulders settled. I punched on the radio and its accordion-laden song blared with a chorus that named different cities in New Mexico. Gabi moved her head to the beat, a light smile on her face. For a moment, all seemed right with the world.

Leo ran in front of the car, his eyes phosphorescent pools. I slowed in the driveway to avoid hitting him. He shook the moisture off his coat and raised each paw in a finicky gesture of disgust at the puddle accumulating on my small porch. At the door, he wrapped his body around my legs and then Gabi's, yowling and complaining.

Inside, my casita smelled stale. I couldn't believe it had been only days since I'd gotten the phone call from Socorro, the harbinger of this mess. Leo looked at Gabi and jumped onto the armoire, ready to impress a new food source with his trick. I made the clicking noise and he launched himself off, a furry torpedo, landing in my arms with claws extended. We'd have to work on that detail. Gabi laughed like a little girl and I would have tried to get him to do it again, but she'd already gone into the kitchen. Without raisins for a reward, Leo struggled out of my hold and followed her.

In a cabinet, behind two packages of linguine, I found the container of dried fruit and gave him his due. Gabi laughed about that, too, her joy unleashed by the relief of normalcy. She inspected the place and smiled, picking up this and that, and I realized that she'd never been to my home before. A naked feeling crawled underneath my skin, my inner workings there for her to see. The same kind of discomfort had accompanied Peter's first all-nighters here. Maybe it only happened with people who mattered to me.

Leaving Gabi to commune with my traitor of a cat, I went into the front room to pour myself a drink. Just seeing that bottle of Glenlivet brought solace. If Peter had been around, I might have felt guilty for the Pavlovian response, but not now. I'd earned a drink. Even though the half-used bottle from last night had made the trip to Albuquerque in the trunk of the car, it wouldn't have made me nearly as happy to go out in the bad weather to get it. This bottle symbolized something else, though I couldn't articulate it.

Ah, wonderful. The second taste opened the cells in my mouth and glided unimpeded down my throat.

"May I have some?" Gabi sprawled on the couch with Leo splayed across her chest. She cradled him with a single arm. His purr thundered to where I stood.

"Sure," I said reluctantly, and poured her a less generous shot. "So, basically, you've pretty much rejected your entire upbringing."

Gabi sniffed the drink, a disturbing glint in her eyes. "Not the love of God, or the belief that it's up to each person to make the world a better place." She licked the inside of the glass. "I just don't buy most of the man-made rules. God is divine. People suck."

"That's a succinct philosophy."

"You'd feel the same way if you'd lived through the last few days." She was too absorbed in her own drama to remember that I had.

Rather than push her buttons with my own shrill martyrdom, I looked at the cat clock suspended above the kitchen door. Its pendulum tail eased the passing of time. Now, it ticked ever closer to 10:00 p.m. "The news will be on in a minute. If you want to enjoy your scotch, this might be a good time to leave the room."

Gabi acceded without protest. *Wise girl.* I turned down the television's volume and reclined on the rug to hear every puerile word. A fire in a popular restaurant shoved *The Gabi Show* into a less important slot. I'd never thought of arson as a useful tool in my PR bag of tricks, but the possibility held a certain appeal. A couple of well-placed accelerants might knock the interest in Gabi's life right out of the public's consciousness.

Not tonight, though. The anchor used my niece to tease viewers into sticking around after the first spate of commercials. Insomnia, erectile dysfunction, acid reflux. If I didn't feel sick before, just watching them could do it. Another scotch helped my mood. Food would do wonders for the heartburn. Nada in the fridge. But, behind a dusty can of ravioli in the pasta cabinet where I'd found the dried fruit, peeked an old square of baking chocolate from a distant attempt to make Peter a cake from scratch. I brought it with me to dip into the alcohol. Not a culinary victory, but not an entire defeat either.

After the second break, Bailey came on, wearing a mauve jacket over a light beige blouse. It became her in a preppy way, but she shivered when she introduced the piece.

"Good. Maybe you'll catch pneumonia," I said. My ersatz friend stood before a building at New Mexico Tech, presumably where Wahl had his office. This late-night rendition used most of the same footage spliced into the snippet on the six o'clock broadcast, including Davielle's damning footage. Only at 10:00, the most-watched time of night for the news, the segment lasted a lifetime longer. I downed my drink and muttered nasties under my breath until Bailey's face had been replaced by cute kids running a holiday food drive. *How sweet.* Why couldn't they be the butts of Bailey's scandal-mongering?

"Sources close to the investigation." Plural. Bailey mentioned them twice. I could draw only one conclusion. People had been leaking details to her. One of the most obvious sources had to be Detective Sanchez, who had specifically warned me to leave the media relations to him. What could he possibly gain by compromising the investigation himself?

Gabi shuffled in, wearing my only pair of slippers, her glass of scotch no emptier. Two things were wrong with this picture. She'd been going through my closet *and* neglecting to appreciate my expensive liquor. Before I could chastise her, she said, "How bad was it?"

"On a scale of zero to ten, I'd give it a nine." Leo wandered in and cuddled against my stomach. "Don't get too comfortable," I said, stroking his fur and hoping to get the same motor-loud purring he'd granted my niece earlier.

Gabi sat on the couch behind me. "What should I do, Aunt Sasha?"

"What part of this are we talking about?" I rolled over and balanced my head on one hand to look at her.

"Everything."

The chocolate had melted in my hand. I poured a tiny bit of scotch onto my palm and licked it, thinking. "Let's start with the vandalism. Who do you think might have done it?"

"It's only a hunch."

"That's better than nothing."

"Do you remember Ralph at the hospital?"

I nodded.

"He and his brother, Marcel—you met him, too—used to run around with a bunch of punks. A gang. That's who I immediately thought of when it happened to Harriet and Judy because Ralph's mom lives next door to me and she's such a nosy bitch. One word from her and I bet her boys would jump." Gabi drank the scotch in one gulp.

I winced.

"How else could anyone do that in the middle of the day without people seeing something? It had to be someone from the neighborhood."

"Okay, so it was Ralph."

"No, not him. His friends . . . or Marcel's." She scootched forward. "Here's how it happened: one of them told a friend who told a friend and, *bang*, you know how it goes." Her voice scurried up the scale at the end of the sentence and she stared at the ceiling as if it held answers.

"What?"

"I've kind've been wondering about Heather, too. You remember her?"

Boy, did I. My first impression of Gabi's friend had picked up on a profound latent anger. "It's quite a coincidence the two of them just happened to be at the hospital the morning you got hurt."

"You sound like they planned it." She called for Leo, and Benedict Arnold, with his tail held high, left the crook of my stomach and trotted over to her. "They both work at the hospital, but they couldn't have known I'd be there that morning."

Not unless they had something to do with the pipe bomb. "You were saying something about Heather?"

"I don't remember this too clearly because of the drugs they gave me that morning, but when I first saw her, she seemed almost too upset. You know?"

I played with a fiber that had loosened from the rug, hoping not to dam the flow of her words.

"Of course, she and Marcel have been dating for a couple of months," said Gabi. "So, if she thought his old buddies did the stuff on my porch, that might explain it."

"I hear it's hard to get out of a gang."

Gabi shrugged.

A late-night talk show came on and I didn't have the heart to listen to any pseudo-funny monologues. I leaned forward and turned off the TV. Could Gabi really be that deluded? She'd just given me more than enough reason to check out her "friends."

"What about the pipe bomb?"

"I have no idea."

"Oh, come on. If your buddies know who messed up the porch, they've got to know about the bomb, too."

"There's no way."

If I could have shaken her without causing further injury, I would have. But that, and the fact she'd closed down so many times before, kept me focused on getting as much information as possible before it happened again. "What about CiCi Wahl?"

"What about her?"

"Did she know about the affair?" My glass must've had a leak; it was already empty again. I held it up, searching for possible chinks.

"No. We were very discreet."

"Right. Aaron Wahl, a professor known for seducing students, was discreet."

"I'm done talking." Her face flushed to a dangerous scarlet.

"Ah, but I'm not."

"Just leave me alone!" She stiffened. Leo jumped off the couch and ran into the kitchen.

"If you leave this room, you can kiss my help good-bye." I wanted to throw her out of the house, douse her with freezing rainwater, wake her up. "Is that really what you want to do, Gabi? Or do you want to sit down, calm down, and talk to me?"

After a few long minutes, my niece returned to the couch, and, after pouring myself another scotch, I perched on the small coffee table in front of her. "Who do you think took your computer and ripped up that photo?"

She considered the questions. "The computer sounds like Marcel. He's been trying to get the specifics about our project since I got there." She crossed her legs and leaned back. "But Aaron is his advisor, too. I can't see Marcel tearing up the photo. It doesn't make any sense."

"Is he gay?"

"I told you, Marcel's dating Heather." She said it with such vehemence, her denial sizzled in the quiet night.

"Let's focus on the computer."

Leo peeked out of the other room.

I snapped my fingers to get his attention, but he ignored me. "You don't seem particularly upset. I thought you'd be frantic."

"Why? I back everything up." She went to the armoire. Without asking, she helped herself to another drink, too. If it had been anyone else, at any other time. . . . "I've passworded it all. Plus, we put the really critical files in a safe-deposit box. No one's going to find out anything we don't want them to find out." Gabi's naïveté stunned me. Had she no idea how ruthless people could be? My stomach became a cauldron of acidic compounds.

"You *do* know the FBI is looking into your advisor's disappearance and what you were doing in that lab?" I'd thought the news would squash her optimism, but she didn't miss a beat.

"So?"

"*So*, we're talking about the FBI here. They probably know about that safety-deposit box already."

Was that amusement on her face? A dismissive smirk, as if *I* were the Pollyanna in this scene? "Aunt Sasha, they wouldn't do that. They have no reason to include me in their investigation. That's just ridiculous."

Flabbergasted at her innocence, I spluttered my mouthful of scotch, wetting my arm. "Where have you been since 9/11?"

"You're being way too paranoid. I'm a U.S. citizen and I've done nothing illegal. Neither has Aaron."

"Then why keep it such a secret?"

"This again? I've already explained everything." Gabi slumped in front of me. "Look. Without context, sure, our work could be misinterpreted."

She drank the whole glass in one gulp again. I almost slapped her. "We wanted to be absolutely positive before we published. It's not the kind of thing you brag about until you're absolutely sure."

"Gabi, listen to me. Find your computer, and, if you can, get the contents of that little safety-deposit box and ship both of them to the other side of the world."

Any other time, my niece's laughter would have made the angels sing. Tonight, however, they frowned at how readily she tempted fate.

39

Night chased the morning's tail and slammed it against a wall. Insomnia had become my constant companion. Before sunrise, I gave up and got up. There wasn't enough coffee for a full pot. I brewed a strong batch of Earl Grey. The unflattering image of Detective Sanchez intruded into each thought of Gabi. Could he be a crooked cop? I'd heard of such things but always assumed they happened elsewhere, in big cities like New York or L.A. What was so special about little ol' Socorro? Why couldn't it happen there?

Soon enough, the sun would nudge the final darkness away. Who could I call to find out if my suspicions about the good detective were on target? With a slap on the table that made my tea splash out of its mug, I remembered someone I truly trusted. And I had his home phone number.

Last spring, when tiny lambs entered the world bleating and baby birds ate their first regurgitated worms, I'd met another detective. Chalk it up to the season, a weakened faith in the world, and the kind of attraction that's embarrassing in retrospect, but Henry LaSalle had parked himself in my heart and remained there today. It had happened on the outermost notches of the Bible Belt in Clovis, New Mexico.

From religious beliefs to movie choices, from music to food, we had nothing in common. Henry had had the good sense to end things before they got serious. Would you believe we'd never even consummated our relationship? He'd proven much stronger in that regard than I would have been. Still, every time I thought of him, a subcutaneous shiver traveled the length of my spine.

Henry kept weird hours and I'd learned that it didn't matter when I called. If he was conscious, he'd answer. He'd also been a policeman for a long time in New Mexico and knew a lot of people in law enforcement around the state.

My rolodex, the old-fashioned kind with index cards, balanced on top of a massive oak desk. With impatient fingers, I punched in Henry's number and waited.

"LaSalle." Sleep had lowered his voice to a goose-bumpy sensuality.

"Hi there."

"Well, I'll be."

I remembered his warm breath on my neck.

"Sasha. You just made my good dream better."

Did I mention the man had a way of making me feel appreciated? Another long-distance relationship doomed to failure. The thought honed the upcoming reality with Peter into sharp perspective. Who was I kidding? We'd never make it work.

"I'm sorry to call you so late," I said.

"It's early, Honeydew." He emitted a lion's rumble. "Now, what do you need?"

"Is it that obvious?"

"Yes." He yawned. "I'm a policeman, remember?"

"That's what I wanted to talk to you about." A bit more preamble might have been nice, if for nothing other than to fuel the memories of his arms around me. But it was five in the morning and I didn't want to waste his time. "I'm working on a project in Socorro."

"I like Socorro."

"I do, too."

"But, what?"

"Do you know a detective there by the name of Sanchez?"

"Which one? I know two or three in the area."

"I don't know."

"Sheriff's department or police?"

"Police. He's about my age, maybe a little older, thinning black hair, always dresses the part of the western lawman—you know—blue jeans, cowboy hat, boots, fancy belts with big buckles."

"It's probably Vincent. Nice guy, right? Honest."

"That's what I wanted to ask you about."

"What's going on, Sasha? Are you playing detective again?" Why did everyone assume this was some kind of game?

"You know that pipe bombing that happened there? In Socorro? It was my niece. And that professor who disappeared is her advisor."

"I heard about that."

"So, no, I'm not playing detective, Henry. I'm trying to get at the truth and people around here are being mighty squirrelly." I curbed the bleating before it repelled Henry further.

"I see."

"Don't patronize me," I said with more force. "Tell me if you know Vincent Sanchez enough to vouch for his honesty. That's what I need to know."

"I don't like the sound of this already." He cleared his throat. "Do you have information to the contrary?"

"Only a hunch. He's lied to me a couple of times, but I want to trust him." I took the phone with me into the kitchen, along with the mug of lukewarm tea, and sat at the table. "And when he's not lying, he's not telling me the whole truth."

"He doesn't have to."

"I know." I wanted to avoid that particular lecture, one of Henry's favorites. "Only now, I think he might be leaking information to the media, stuff that could really hurt my niece's reputation." Leo followed me in and jumped onto my lap, his paws on my chest, his nose touching mine. "If he is, then I can't confide in him, and I definitely can't give him the stuff I'm finding out."

Henry's silence made me wonder if he'd fallen asleep. I'd've worried but his breathing didn't sound calm enough. Leo purred and rubbed his head against my cheek. I stroked his fat belly, glad for the company.

"I don't know what to tell you, Sasha. I trust him from what I've seen and heard. He's not running for office, so I can't imagine he'd be in love with any reporters." Henry fell quiet again for a minute. "I think he's on the up-and-up, but I'm not you."

"So, what do I do?"

He yawned, apologized for it, and then said, "I think he's honest. I'd trust him, if I were you."

"'Kay," I said, unconvinced. Sanchez still worried me. Was he covering up for one of his relatives? CiCi, for example? And who was Bailey's other source?

"If I hear anything else, I'll call."

"Thank you."

Leo nestled in the bowl of my crossed legs, his ears twitching with dreams of slow mice. I contemplated other prey.

40

After nearly an hour of reading the canticles of St. CiCi, I had to take a break. Wellesley? Who would've believed that Cecilia Sanchez graduated with a major in philosophy from that fine women's college? I sipped the tea then shook my head. She was also on seven dozen nonprofit boards of directors and had been given more than one award for philanthropy. Had any of these reporters ever met the woman? Their smarmy articles dripped with honeyed praise.

I needed a dose of reality and left the house in search of spicy, honest food. The Flying Star restaurant on Rio Grande wasn't too busy yet and the two green chile and cheese muffins filled with scrambled eggs would be a good breakfast. Add hash browns to the mix and life looked better. The food's sharp, yummy smells filled my car. As long as green chile grew and chickens laid eggs, hope remained in my heart.

Back home, I parked in the driveway and ate pieces of potato that had broken free from their packaging. It was time to lay the snare. My fully charged cell phone in my lap, I dialed Detective Sanchez's number with greasy fingers. His voice mail picked up and I left a cryptic message, one that might entice him more than usual.

The bag of food made too much noise, crinkling and crackling when I removed my key from the front door and made my way to the kitchen. Leo yowled, a furry band of supplication at my heels, ready for his part of the booty. Unwrapping one of the sandwiches, I tossed a few pieces of scrambled egg on the floor and went to the pantry to get him his own meal. My phone chirped and I answered it quickly before Gabi awoke.

"Ms. Solomon, this is Detective Sanchez." Behind his voice, I could hear a car honking.

"Detective, thank you for calling me back."

"You mentioned new information?"

I wanted to confront him, to demand to know why he'd talked to Bailey. With a hard bite to my hand, I smothered that impulse lest it come out in my voice. "My niece told me about the other case of vandalism in her neighborhood."

"Yes." A guarded response.

What the hell was I doing, trying to con a cop? The room seemed too dark, sinister. I left the food on the table and rushed to the window to open the blinds and let the pure light of morning cleanse my conniving soul.

"Ms. Solomon?"

"Did you ever talk to Gabi? Really question her about it?" Leo now pawed at the paper covering the muffins. I pushed him off the table.

"Speaking of your niece, where is she?"

"Gabi gave me the names of some people who might have been involved in both crimes, and who might know what happened to her computer." Without waiting for a response, I told him most of what I knew, including the piece about Marcel trying to get the details about her proprietary research and my theory about CiCi's involvement and probable jealousy.

"That's all very interesting, Ms. Solomon, but I need to find your niece."

"So you can make her look even worse?"

"What are you talking about?" His tone trivialized my anger, and, like a brushfire that rushes up a tree and crowns the dry canopy, this conversation flared dangerous for us both.

"Did you watch Channel 8 last night?"

"I did."

"I wonder where Bailey Hayes got the information to assassinate my niece's character. Don't you?"

"I thought it was pretty obvious. Her own sister."

"What about those *sources close to the investigation*, Detective? Do you have any idea who they might be?" This was a good example of why

I never should have agreed to help Gabi. I couldn't investigate anything without jamming a gargantuan foot into my mighty mouth.

The silence that met my outburst caused frost crystals to form under my fingertips. I paced the kitchen floor before expanding the trip to and from the living room. Sanchez coughed but didn't speak. I couldn't hang up without risking further animosity. There was no return now. I might as well stop all my questioning and buy my niece a ticket to Katmandu until this blew over.

"Ms. Solomon, several people are looking for your niece," he said without the faintest clue of what he might be thinking or feeling.

But, hell! He hadn't denied it. "I'll let her know."

"Do you understand what I just said?"

"Yes." I took a bite out of one of the muffins.

"I don't think you do. Let me rephrase it. If you know where your niece is and we don't, you'll be in trouble, too." He coughed. "Do you understand now?"

"I do, sir. I'll have her call your office as soon as I see her again." The lie stuck to the roof of my mouth. "So, do you think you'll check out those people I mentioned? It's interesting that all of them—except CiCi, of course—made such a point of visiting Gabi in the hospital the day she was injured. Maybe they were really scoping out how long she'd be out of commission before going back to her place to search for that proprietary information."

"I'll be in touch, Ms. Solomon."

His blatant disregard for my idea made me push harder. "Or, maybe they had guilty consciences about what they'd done."

"Please make sure your niece gets my message." He gave no hint that he'd even heard what I'd said. "The sooner she gets in touch, the sooner she'll be able to carry on with her life."

"Like hell."

He disconnected abruptly.

I stared at my cell phone, wondering what had just happened. Why hadn't he denied my accusation? Who could I go to from here? Who makes sure the police are clean in a small town? Oh, I hated this with all of my heart.

Gabi wandered into the kitchen, her nose tilted up in the air, her pink tongue exposed between dry lips. "That smells great. What is it?"

With regret, I pushed one of the muffins toward her.

"Wow. Thank you." Her rust-colored hair no longer startled against alabaster cheeks; they'd pinkened during the night. The swelling in her face had gone down, too. I liked that her eyes didn't seem so tired, though the bruises surrounding them would take much longer to subside. Still, she'd begun to heal, at least physically, and that was enough for this morning.

At 7:00 on the dot, my landline rang.

"Sasha?" Eva's weariness colored the single word in gray.

"Are you all right?"

"One of Mom's friends pulled some strings and got us an appointment for Gabi at a plastic surgeon at eight. I'll pick her up within the next half hour."

"That's good news." You know how some things hit you a minute after the fact? Well, Eva wasn't speaking in her normal voice. There was a dirty subtext to it.

Sure enough, she said, "And then I'm taking her to the FBI."

"You can't!" I put down the food. "You can't just feed her to the wolves."

Gabi came to see why I'd shouted. She mouthed a question. I slashed it down with an angry hand.

My sister's sigh sounded like she had a third lung. "Stop being melodramatic. This has to happen sometime."

"Not yet. Not until we have a plan. You haven't thought this through."

"That's all I've been doing for hours. Gabi has to talk to them. She can't hide. And, if she doesn't show this morning, they'll come knocking at *your* door. Do you want that?"

"You *didn't*."

"I certainly did. This is a matter of national secur—"

"Bull."

"What's done is done, Sasha. I'm Gabi's mother and this is going to happen today. End of story."

"I can't believe you'd—"

"I'll be by in a few minutes."

41

The sourness of surrender permeated my kitchen, its stink worse than any meal I'd ever tried to cook. Our easy breakfast palled into a slogging funereal rhythm, the minutes attenuating into hours. I tried to lighten things up with gallows humor, breaking into a chorus of that classic childhood ditty, "Pray for the dead and the dead'll pray for you." But my niece couldn't muster the shadow of a smile.

Eva knocked on the door with the strength of a Spartan army and found two somber women, one dressed for an execution, the other seething mutely. Before Gabi left, I gave her the manila envelope with the pieces of photo that had once testified to a happier time. Maybe it would give her strength for the upcoming onslaught of accusatory questions. She nodded a thank-you and put it in her duffel bag, a weary frown fixed upon a mouth that was too young for such an expression. Then Eva wrapped a proprietary arm around her daughter's shoulders and escorted her to the door. I was too angry to say good-bye.

Once alone, I wandered from room to room in my casita, muttering and kicking furniture. My unfortunate feet protested with spiky pains skidding above each big toe. Finally, with my heart resembling a nuclear disaster, I sat at the desk and sought, once again, to lose myself in the refuge of work.

Pros and cons, lists and diagrams. I toiled at a frantic rate, forcing any thoughts of family back into the muck of my mind. After a solid two hours, I had dozens of strong reasons why each of the approaches, the state fair and the overarching concept, made good sense. Maybe I'd cop out and offer both arguments for the foundation board to choose. Or perhaps I could give them to Papi. He made more decisions in his sleep than I did awake, and probably hit on the money every time.

The trouble with rising early is that even if you're productive, you still have most of the day left. Only fifteen more hours to go before I'd try sleep again. My promiscuous brain butterflied from thoughts of Gabi at the doctor to Gabi with faceless FBI agents, from Zach betraying Eva back to Gabi sitting in prison. I toyed with the idea of going to Mom's and confronting Davielle, but nixed that thought. If I angered her too much, she might call the major networks.

Seeking comfort, I dialed Darnda's number, knowing she rarely answered the phone. By leaving a message, I'd provide myself something to look forward to today.

"I was just thinking about you," she said, picking up before it rang. "What are you doing right this minute?"

"Devising ways to pull myself out of depression. You're far better than a pill."

Darnda's laughter brightened the day by 50 percent. She invited me to an early lunch, thank goodness. That still left too much of the morning to stew.

I went to Whiting Coffee and bought six pounds of mocha java beans. They also had a great selection of marmalades. I picked up two containers of bitter orange and a jar of corn and black bean salsa. With that purchase, I'd have fruits and vegetables in the house. Peter would be so proud.

At home again, fixing a pot of coffee, I shifted through the coulds and couldn'ts of helping Gabi. Without all the pieces, the results of her interviews with the government folks, creating strategies became an exercise in ifs and maybes. Also, two new challenges had mushroomed into the equation. Chances were that Eva would try to limit my access to Gabi now. My sister had made it clear that she thought Auntie Sasha was a bad influence. I understood the desire to blame and suspected Eva didn't have a clue about her youngest daughter's rejection of so many of the rules of her upbringing. And then there was Bailey. I'd viewed her as a good information source, if handled correctly. Now, I'd have to be a virtuoso to get what I wanted without kindling her inquisitiveness.

My head hurt. I poured another mug of coffee and went into the bathroom to find something for the pain. Gabi's scotch glass sat empty on my front table and it made me sad to think of her in a room somewhere cornered by government interrogators who couldn't care less for the girl they confronted. Thrusting away that image, I pushed myself to try to find a foothold to help her. There had to be something I could do.

CiCi looked like Mother Teresa on paper, but I knew she and her philandering hubby Aaron would never gain admission at the pearly gates. It seemed awfully convenient that my niece's advisor disappeared right after the pipe bomb. A cynical person might think he'd set the thing himself. Or that he'd decided to skip town to leave my niece to take the fall for his nefarious behavior. Had he really been kidnapped? If so, those *sources close to the investigation* were keeping mum on that account.

Why was the FBI so interested in Gabi in the first place? Bombs, that's why. From her explanations, her secret research was hardly the stuff of terrorism unless, maybe, it got into the wrong hands. I knew my niece well enough to have faith that she would never apply the technology to harm people. The good professor, on the other hand, lied easily. What if he merely used my niece and her dazzling intellect to supply the bad guys with an even more powerful weapon?

I had to get a sense of him, of who he really was beyond the glowing descriptions and canned press releases. I wanted hearsay, tittle-tattle. Back to the Internet. Too many hits on news sources, just the kind of thing I didn't want. Then came references to articles he'd written, papers he'd delivered at conferences around the world. Did Zach know him? Eva would never tell me now.

I clicked on a few academic abstracts and found six names unique enough to research further. After that, I keyed in each name. Two came up with recent references in departments at prestigious universities. Sharada Ranga. Was she affair material? She chaired the chemistry department at UC Berkeley. And, blessed be, Amiram de Gammo worked as a professor right here at the University of New Mexico.

Next stop: the online white pages. Home numbers appeared. All hail to the wonders of an electronic world. Ranga and de Gammo didn't know it yet, but they'd been selected as my interviewees. I tackled the long-distance call first. This would be the week to contact both professors, that brief period of accessibility before Thanksgiving rolled in and ended the semester, creating a communications moratorium in most colleges. I dialed the California phone number. After two rings, an

Indian-accented female voice came on the line and said Sharada, Smita, and Kri weren't available right now. They'd return my call as soon as possible. Wonderful.

Emboldened by my first success, I called the University of New Mexico operator and asked for Professor de Gammo's office number. She gave it to me. Easy as that. Hah! Who needed a license for this detective stuff? I dialed and a man answered.

"Yes?" His accent put him in, or close to, Israel.

Suddenly, I didn't know what I wanted to say. If he watched the news, it was possible he would have already condemned my niece. Hell, if he was Israeli, he'd have no sympathy for any kind of person who might be a terrorist, who'd have a secret laboratory. Oh, it just sounded so Frankensteinesque.

"Hello, my name is Sasha Solomon. I'm writing an article about the chemistry department and wondered if you'd have a few minutes for a short interview in the next day or two?" Someone in my neighborhood was playing the drum loudly, a consistent, irritating banging.

"Solomon?" The thick breathing on the other end of the line made me wonder if he had a respiratory problem. "Sasha Solomon?"

"Yes, sir."

"Who did you say you were with?"

"*The Weekly Alibi.*" I hoped the hip free paper had a different demographic than Israeli chemistry professors.

"How long will this take?"

"Ten, fifteen minutes at most."

In the seconds of his pause, I heard papers rustling. "I have time before my eight o'clock class tomorrow. Shall we meet in my office?"

"That would be wonderful. Thank you so much."

When we disconnected, I looked at the clock. Ten thirty. When had I started to emulate a pathological liar? Easy. When someone had rigged a bomb in my young niece's mailbox. No one—not my family, police, media, her own boyfriend—seemed to give a damn what happened to her now. That left me. With a foolhardy faith in her innocence, I'd jumped into the vacuum created by their hardheartedness.

Beyond that, I wanted to save the Shofets, large and small, though they might never thank me for it. The rancid truth was that no matter how upstanding my sister, brother-in-law, and their children might be, if this story exploded into national news, none of their reputations would be safe. Without a counterpoint effort, the devastating trajectory of ruin would begin with the destruction of Gabi's career and evolve into charges of impropriety in Eva and Zach's lives. It didn't take a Cassandra to see my sister rejected by her own community in Pikesville, losing her job at Johns Hopkins on some trumped-up mischief. Zach's Iranian heritage could blast him back to the country his family had left so long ago. The whole Shofet clan could be smeared because of a vain and selfish professor's mammoth ego and unbridled libido.

My phone rang. "Hello?"

"Is this Sasha Solomon?" The woman's accent lilted with saffron rice and yogurt lassi.

"It is. Is this Dr. Ranga?"

"Yes. Do I know you?" Curiosity laced her response with a tentative trill.

"No, you don't, but thank you for calling me back."

"I haven't much time."

I wanted to build rapport, but she'd truncated that impulse. "I understand you worked with Dr. Aaron Wahl at MIT?"

"Yes? Why?"

I'd already lied once this morning. Did I want the bad karma of doing it twice? "Have you heard what happened to him?"

"No." The monosyllable belied her caution.

"Oh." I paused. "Well. He's disappeared."

"How very sad," she said with the concern of a chunk of lead. "What has that to do with me?"

"Dr. Wahl is my niece's advisor at New Mexico Tech."

"I think this conversation is over."

The about-face stunned me. "Please, I need your help. My niece and Dr. Wahl have been involved in a—"

"How did you get my name?" The reserve in her voice warned she was poised seconds away from disconnecting.

"Please, Dr. Ranga. I found your name on the Internet, from when you published papers with Dr. Wahl. My niece is in trouble because of this man."

"I don't see how I can help you."

Hope grew in each moment she stayed on the line. "Doctor, I love my niece. I know she couldn't be involved in anything wrong. Please. I just want to know two things. Did Dr. Wahl have a reputation for infidelity when you knew him? Would he ever be careless enough to blow up his own lab? And, would he be capable of working with terrorists?"

"That's three things, Ms. Solomon." I detected a teacher's amusement. Thank God.

"I'm sorry."

"Hold a minute, will you?" I heard a child say something in a language I couldn't identify. Dr. Ranga responded in kind. Then there was a sound like an uncorking and she came back on the line. "Ms. Solomon, I understand your distress for your niece. Dr. Wahl most certainly had a reputation for seducing his students. Anyone who didn't respond to his attentions found her career sidelined. Lucky for me, only my mind attracted him." Her words flowed without a hitch; she wanted to get this out in a single torrent. "As soon as I could, I found a job on the West Coast, as far away from that man as possible." Even her sneeze sounded feminine. "Now, was that sexual predator capable of working for terrorists? I don't know. Certainly his ego and insecurities needed constant feeding." The young voice I'd heard before whined in the background. Dr. Ranga grunted but didn't put the phone down. "The one thing I can tell you with absolute assurance is that he would never endanger his life, or anyone else's, when it came to explosives. He was the single most vigilant researcher I've ever known."

I rushed to speak before she disconnected. "Just one more thing. Did you ever hear of anyone stealing Dr. Wahl's ideas or research?"

"That's preposterous. If anyone was doing the stealing, it was Aaron." This time, the child in the background cried for her attention. "I really must go."

"Thank you so much for your time."

"Please, Miss, do not call me again."

I hung up the phone and stared at the Chinese poster on the wall opposite my couch. I'd picked it up in Hong Kong years ago and had given it to Mom. She'd stashed it in one of her many closets, an unwanted gift. I'd found and reclaimed it for myself during one of her stays in the rehab hospital. The picture had those wild mountains, the fjords of Gwei Lin, the ones recently submerged in the name of progress and hydroelectric power. Today, those irregular peaks brought thoughts of buried beauty and secrets.

How many lives had Aaron Wahl destroyed?

Would he take Gabi down as well?

42

"It meant *love*," said Darnda, abstaining from her customary Hells Angels garb for something even odder today. I'd just shown her the motion my late-night ghost had repeated in the hotel room. "You know, *love*. What you feel for your cat . . . and chocolate."

"I think it was Gabi's advisor." I broke a piece of broccoli into smaller ones and dipped them in the ranch dressing. "Does this mean he's dead?"

"Not necessarily. He could have been dreaming, or having an out-of-body experience. I really have no idea." My friend wore a full-head, bulky multicolored knit hat that made me sniff for ganja, though I knew Darnda didn't smoke marijuana. A single corkscrew of hair sproinged from its rainbow-hued prison. A faux snakeskin belt girded her plump waist. The rest of her clothes ranged from dark black to blacker black, down to the pointy boots on incongruously dainty feet. The whole thing had a kind of psychedelic Goth look . . . I think.

"You practicing to be a zombie from Jamaica, mon?" I pointed from her head to her chest. We'd met at one of those big salad bar chains because my friend, and biggest client, wanted to lose weight before going to L.A. I hadn't told her to do it; weight didn't matter as much as her choice of clothes. And, frankly, given the way she dressed, no one would notice anything else.

"Oh, this?" She pushed a shred of carrot to the side of her plate. "No, I was just in the mood for something different. Plus, it really annoys my grandkids." She had at least eight—biological or adopted—I knew about, all of whom were in high school.

I continued my tale of woe and watched her expression move from playfulness to concern. Her face, never clogged by makeup, housed a red nose and showed every capillary that had burst during her years as a fervent drunk. From what she'd told me, she'd spent a cool decade trying to suppress her gift through self-medication, self-destruction. I didn't know her then and was glad of it.

"Why didn't you call sooner?" Darnda shuddered, loosening another spiral of hair.

"I didn't want to go into it." Finished with the green vegetables, I moved on to the purple cabbage and jicama. Using a spoon, I dabbed them with dressing and munched.

Through her mouthful of pasta, she said, "Do you remember Tammy's husband Jeff?"

Tammy was one of the many children who called my friend "Mom." Darnda had two kids on her own and had also married into several other families, or taken in waifs informally off the street. I could never keep any of them straight, certainly not their spouses and offspring.

"Nope." The chunk of garlic bread tasted good with the dressing, too. Better than the broccoli. Fries would have been nice.

"Well, Jeff works for the FBI." Darnda got up. "I need more of this mouse food to fill me up." From what I'd seen, the ratio of raw food to cooked on her plate fell entirely on the processed side. In the short time we'd been talking, she'd consumed a baked potato with sour cream, bacon, and scallions, as well as two kinds of pasta with cheesy sauces, a bowl of clam chowder, and four microscopic pieces of iceberg lettuce.

I hadn't fared much better. Raw vegetables didn't go with tragedy, and my recounting of Gabi's story merited several banana splits. A single strip of green bell pepper lay on the plate. I formed it into a heart and then an oval while watching passersby. Why did skinny people always seem to eat the best? Stupid question. That's why they were skinny.

"Jeff might be able to help you figure out what's going on, in a general way," said Darnda, scrunching back into the booth. She'd crafted a sundae with crushed toffee bits and chocolate sauce on top. "Isn't this great? The soft-serve is completely sugar free. No fat, either." She took a bite, her gaze focused on nowhere but the sweet sensation in her mouth. "I love these places."

"They don't work if you don't eat right."

"What are you talking about? I had more veggies today than I've had in a month." She wiggled her fingers. "Give me your cell phone." A minute later, she was talking with Tammy and asking about the kids' Tae Kwon Do classes, their last nosebleeds.

I abandoned her in search of succor and my own parfait. After all, it was impolite to let someone eat by herself.

"It's settled. Tammy'll make sure Jeff calls you today." Darnda handed the phone back to me and it rang. "See, there he is now."

"Sasha Solomon," I said, expecting an unfamiliar voice. Instead it was one I knew all too well.

"Have you given any thought to what we spoke about this morning?" said Detective Sanchez.

"The vandalism?"

"No. Your niece."

A thunderclap of fury pounded in an already stormy psyche. How dare he call to rub it in? I slammed down my spoon, prepared to lambaste him with every scrap of blame swirling in the hurricane of my helplessness.

"You—" Without meaning to, I looked up.

"Breathe," mouthed Darnda.

Wise advice. I exhaled bilious responses and filled my lungs with the restaurant's mac-and-cheese aroma. Perhaps Eva had changed her mind after the doctor's appointment. Maybe she'd declined to let the Feds skewer her daughter. Unlikely.

"You should talk to your buddies in the FBI," I said to him.

His silence satisfied me in a perverse way. I liked the idea of him feeling out of the loop.

"Tell me, are you here in Socorro?" The man sounded almost human. I wasn't going to fall for it. Too late. I remembered how kind he'd been to me at the hospital, how hard he'd tried to get Gabi to tell him the truth.

"No, I'm in Albuquerque."

"Thank you." He disconnected without rancor.

"That was your policeman, wasn't it?" Darnda said, using her index finger to clean the last drops of melted ice cream out of her bowl. "You don't need to worry about him, you know. He's all right."

"Oh, come on, Darnda. How do you know that?" I'd told her about Bailey's snitches.

"Your aura, baby girl. You trust him."

The rest of the lunch passed in planning the trip to L.A. Hard to believe that by this time next week, I'd be done with the first phase of the San-Socorro project. God willing, all of the business with Gabi would have died down by then, too.

My phone rang again.

A grin lit Darnda's face. "That's Jeff. I'll bet a brownie on it."

"You're on."

Sure enough, the voice on the other end claimed to be Jeff Smith. He was on his way to lunch and offered to meet while he ate.

"Is his name really Jeff Smith?" I said to Darnda when we walked out of the restaurant. She'd volunteered to come since I had no idea what the guy looked like.

"Is that what he told you? 'Smith'?" She slapped her thigh and guffawed.

We drove in separate cars so that my friend could leave for a regular Wednesday afternoon reading. In the new parking lot, Darnda looked at me and said, "Smith. That's rich."

Decorated in 1970s vinyl with a blue-haired waitress to match, the Country Kettle was located across the street from the Cracker Barrel. Guess which one had the most customers? Darnda headed straight to a plastic-molded booth where a youngish man sat drinking coffee and reading the newspaper.

He stood, a Sears Tower next to Darnda, and gave her a warm hug. "Great to see you, Mom."

"Nice to see you, too, Mr. *Smith*," she said. "This is Sasha *Smith*. She's good people, so don't play games with her." Darnda tugged me down onto the bench seat. "She'll try to return the favor."

I could feel Jeff assessing me. His brown eyes and hair matched exactly, both a rich walnut hue. Clipped nails topped clean hands, unlike my own. If he worked outside in a garden, or on covert stake-outs, he'd been religious with sunscreen.

Our waitress broke the silence with a plain BLT, chips, and a thin slice of pickle on a plate that had once been white.

"What kind of pie do you have?" Darnda said.

"You've got to be kidding," I blurted.

"I need to be grounded to talk to spirits." She glanced at her watch.

The server went through a list from memory. She wore a black and white uniform with thick-soled shoes, the kind meant for long hours on one's feet. Deep lines dug around her lips and spoke to the penance of bad choices.

"Sasha?" Darnda nudged me back and ordered the pecan à la mode.

"Yes? Uh, I'll have cherry."

Jeff had already finished half of his sandwich. He ordered the lemon meringue for dessert. The waitress padded away, her beige stockings rubbing together and making a dull, mushy sound with each step. We drank water and waited for our baked sweets. One of the other tables emptied and our server cashed them out.

"So . . ." said Darnda into the uncomfortable quiet. "Why don't you tell Jeff what you told me?"

"I'm sure he already knows everything anyway." My petulant voice embarrassed us all. Less than twenty yards from the freeway, the restaurant's windows opened onto that gray ribbon of hopes and destroyed lives. Criminals and celebrities had taken it. Maybe Aaron Wahl had, too.

"It's not my case," said Jeff, picking up the pickle. "But I know people who're working on it and if you've got information I can pass it on."

"Pardon me for saying so, but the FBI doesn't have a sterling reputation for guarding people's civil liberties," I said. The chip on my shoulder had grown into a heap of suspicion. "I don't want to contribute to my niece's troubles when she hasn't done anything wrong in the first place."

"Sasha, what's gotten into you? I wouldn't have set up this meeting if I didn't think Jeff wanted to help," said Darnda.

"You've got to trust someone. Mom, here, says you're all right, so I'm extending my hand. Are you going to take it?" Unflustered, Jeff polished off the rest of his meal and moved the paper away from his sweating water glass.

My face flushed. I wanted to walk out.

"Why are you so angry?" he said.

"She's got issues." Darnda winked at us both, diffusing the tension for the duration of her smile.

Jeff held up his coffee mug so that the waitress could refill it. She came with the three plates balanced on one arm and the pot in her other hand. Neat trick. She must've practiced it for years.

"I feel like my niece has already been convicted."

"She hasn't, you know. That's not how we work."

"From where I'm sitting, it looks as if she's been convicted because of her surname."

Laughter erupted from behind the double doors to the kitchen. The waitress came out a minute later with two large bowls, their contents steaming. When she'd served the people at the other table, she began bussing dirty dishes and sponging down booths. Each time she bent over, a small strip of her yellowed slip became visible.

"Mom told me about your bad experience with Agent Frenth in Clovis," said Jeff, scraping up a last speck of meringue.

"Hah! That's an understatement," said Darnda.

"That's not what this is about." I stabbed a sour cherry and dipped it in red goop.

"It's a shame you don't trust the Bureau." He pushed away his empty plate. "You talk about not wanting to be judged unfairly. Well, I'm asking you to give me, give us, the same courtesy."

He had a point, though I didn't like it. "Okay. Tell me how to help my niece."

"I'll only know when you give me everything you've got. I need to know it all."

That was asking too much. "Once I do that, you'll shut me out and I won't have any recourse."

"You know my Mom." He glanced at Darnda. "That's recourse enough."

"I'll spank him if he's a bad boy, Sasha."

Jeff reached into his back pocket to get his wallet. "Let me ask you something. What's your real goal here? To play detective or save your niece?"

Not again.

In the end, I did the info dump. It didn't lighten my load, but it made me feel a little less alone. We all said our good-byes under the gloomy midafternoon sky. Though brownish, the clouds lacked heft. We'd have no snow today.

In spite of Eva's probable interference, I'd hoped to hear from Gabi by now. But my chatterbox of a cell phone remained inert. A swath of unplanned hours opened before me, oppressive and bleak. What to do? Every option dead-ended after a minute or two.

My bad mood couldn't get much worse. What a perfect time to visit CiCi.

43

Aaron Wahl's house apexed a large hill overlooking New Mexico Tech's winter-brown golf course. I wound up the street, marveling at the general eccentricity and lack of cohesion among the faculty homes. You could find just about any architect's wet dream in these five or six blocks of large buildings, everything from classic adobe to ultra mod, seasoned wood to butt-ugly concrete.

Though it boasted beige and red brick, the structure that most interested me evinced less personality than a splinter. Had the good professor and his wife built it to spec? If so, their souls were even more bankrupt than I'd assumed. A black Hummer sat in the driveway. Strike two.

I parked on the street and walked up the fake flagstone path between the xeric landscaping. Shades of gray, pink, and ochre gravel created designs that, together, reminded me of a checkerboard someone on drugs might appreciate. Here and there a tuft of dried grass broke through the ground, a shriveled cactus waited for warmth, and a bush shivered in the wind. The mousy ring of the doorbell sounded in the darkened house. If anyone was home, they must be conserving energy.

The unmistakable percussion of high heels headed toward me. Could I be this lucky? Could CiCi really be home?

"You're early," she said, opening the door. "I told you to be here at—"

I don't know whose face fell first.

"You." She wore a lime green pantsuit that worked somehow.

Maybe it was the matching shoes. Her hair had been teased into a thin confection of curls, caramelized cotton candy. The makeup on her face could supply an entire beauty pageant.

"Mrs. Wahl?" All I could think of were the myriad nasty comments about Papi's daughter from respected people like Marta in Magdalena, Isabel at the Camino Real, the librarian, Gabi's rancor. Slack-jawed, I stared at her.

She recovered first. "What do you want?"

"I'm sorry to bother you. I promise it won't take much time." Had I struck the right tone of flattery? Servility?

"I have nothing to say to you." She prepared to close the door.

A look at those long, pointy nails made me relinquish the idea of rushing her. If scientists sought the original source of flesh-eating bacteria, she'd be a good bet. "I might have some information about your husband."

A worried wife's eyes might have widened at my words, or she might have gasped. Not CiCi. With a blandness rivaling uncooked tofu, Aaron Wahl's supposed soul mate said, "How do you know my husband?"

"May I come in?"

"No." CiCi moved dead center in the doorway, so that I'd have to overpower her to enter. Perhaps she thought she could block my view, but even with heels on, she only came up to the middle of my nose. "Say what you have to say, or leave. I don't care. I have an appointment."

Since this entire visit was ad-lib, this might have been a good time to turn tail. Only thing was, Cecilia Sanchez annoyed the hell out of me. My sympathy tilted toward her husband right now. No wonder he'd had affairs. Just imagine sleeping next to *that* at night. She'd curdle any sensuality into cottage cheese before the ink dried on the marriage certificate.

"CiCi!" called a man's voice. Would this be a repeat of the scene at Papi's? I didn't have the stomach for it.

She didn't turn around, but yelled, "Not now. I have company."

Inside, footsteps padded toward us. A second later, Marcel stood behind her.

"Hi there," I said, extrapolating a thousand unsavory reasons why he'd be at her house, his unshod feet in navy blue socks, his shirt wrinkled. "Does Heather know you're here?"

"Sure," he said, before turning around and leaving us standing there.

"So, what do you want?" CiCi closed the door all but two inches.

"Okay, here's the deal," I said, deciding that Marcel didn't merit attention for now. "Your husband has been missing since his advisee, my niece, was hurt by that pipe bomb. Since I don't believe in coincidences, he has to be involved in that crime in some way. But I can't ask him, you see. I also can't ask him about the secret work he was doing in his lab in Hop Canyon."

"You're no policeman. This is none of your beeswax."

Beeswax? That was rich. "It's awfully convenient that your husband just disappeared. Even more interesting is that you'd bother to call the police when he's probably stayed away from home, without telling you, many times before. Why did you happen to call this time? What was different?"

"I don't know what you're driving at. My husband was kidnapped."

"Bull. No one believes that phony ransom note."

"How dare you."

"I think you know where he is and you're both playing it so that my niece takes all the blame."

"Are you crazy?" She stepped back, an expression of absolute disbelief pinching her praying mantis features. "I don't need Aaron. He needs me."

"Why do you stay married to him? What do you get from all the aggravation?"

"Who the hell are you to ask me these questions?"

"Come on. With your money and looks, men must be breaking down the doors to get you. That guy from the bomb squad sure seemed interested."

"I'm sure I don't know what you're talking about." I'd hit a nerve; she'd responded too quickly.

"Oh, stop playing naïve, lady. You can't be serious."

"You can watch the press conference tomorrow and see just how serious I am." She looked beyond me. "I'm going to offer a reward for information leading to Aaron's return. And if you keep bothering me, I might just slip and mention something about your slutty little niece."

Oh, for a vial of acid to etch that smirk off her face! "You wouldn't dare drag her into this."

Her lips pooched into a pout. When she spoke again, she'd shed her snottiness in favor of gamine. "I can always tell Daddy Dear how you came to my house and accused me of all kinds of horrible things." She smiled to make her point. "It'd be such a shame to have him take you off his pet project. Why, it might even kill him."

Behind us, a car pulled into the driveway, its beams illuminating the darkening front of the house. I turned to see who it was. CiCi slammed the front door and a warm breeze parted the hair on the back of my head. I stood my ground, waiting to see who'd emerge from the light-colored Prius.

My favorite bomb squad cop stepped out, a bouquet in his hand.

"I know you," I said, in the dusky light.

He considered me for a moment, shook his head. "I don't think so."

"You used to date Bailey Hayes. She set me up with one of your friends." The one that looked like a toad. "A couple of years ago, maybe less."

"Ms. Hayes?"

"The woman who interviewed you on television the other day. Pretty, blonde like CiCi, only much better looking." He had to be Bailey's "*sources* close to the investigation." Right. Reporters had been known to fudge a number or two over the years. The plural in this case sounded so much more impressive.

"I was interviewed by several reporters. Now, please, would you mind stepping out of my way?" His composure waffled not a bit. Maybe I was wrong. No. I couldn't be that off.

How wonderfully wicked. Bailey wanted to jump to a national market and had planted a source right in the middle of the story. Sure, the theory had problems and holes you could fit blue whales through. He was a policeman, for one thing. They didn't normally work undercover for reporters. *And* he was boinging CiCi. That seemed a bit above and beyond the call of duty.

44

Paranoia trolled the slime of my overactive imagination and dragged my doubts beneath its oily surface. Given the drive back to Albuquerque, I had plenty of time to pervert even the purest motive. Had Bailey engineered this entire thing? Ludicrous. There was no guarantee it would work, that the story would be picked up by the national media in the first place. My phone rang. Rather than pull off the freeway, I ignored it. If someone wanted me badly enough, she could call back. Swirling angst interfered with my concentration. At this rate, Bailey would have another angle to pursue. *In a tragic turn of events . . . Sasha Solomon . . . dead aunt.*

The phone rang again when I pulled into the driveway.

"Sasha," said Bailey. Strained cheerfulness tinged the greeting. "How are you?"

"What a coincidence. I was just thinking about you." I decided to remain in the car until my knees strengthened. Could she have some kind of spying device, a camera, a GPS tracking doohickey, attached to my vehicle? Oh, hell, I was totally losing it. "How's it going?"

"I just had the most interesting conversation with your niece."

"Really?" Leo leapt onto the hood of the car. He popped down again quickly. It must have been too hot. I unlocked the car's door and held it open so that he could sit on my lap.

"Indeed."

I stroked the cat and considered my next words with the care of a mother using a fine-toothed comb on a toddler's matted hair. Could Gabi really have been stupid enough to talk to Bailey, despite my warnings?

"Are you still there?" Bailey's inquiry came with a dozen barbs.

"Yes."

"What's with the tone, Sasha? Are we playing a game here?"

"Yes."

She laughed, then the merriment stalled. "Why didn't you tell me Gabriela was having an affair with Dr. Wahl?"

"Did she tell you that?"

"Yes." Bailey's split-second hesitation screamed of a trap. I'd missed many chances and had failed in one hundred ways during the last few days, but my friend wasn't going to catch me this time.

"If you want the truth, you should talk to Gabi rather than depend on Davielle for your facts. She's got her own envious agenda." So what if I besmirched my oldest niece's credibility? It felt good, a small inkling of the revenge I'd wanted. Bailey didn't need her for a bosom buddy anyway. My legs regained their fortitude with the assertion. Leo in my arms, I went into the house and threw my coat on the neglected NordicTrack. I bet Bailey had a personal trainer, someone to help her keep that figure svelte and those abs taut. Well, I had a cat.

"That's why I'm calling." She geared up for the pitch. "Get your niece to talk with me. Convince her it's for her own good." Her about-face was impressive.

"From what I saw last night, you're more concerned about breaking into a new market than about what happens to Gabi." I went to the armoire and got a drink. For all my resolve to cut down on the scotch, this didn't seem like the time to deprive myself. At least I'd managed to avoid driving while drunk. That had to count for something.

"She needs to tell her side of the story—"

A knock on the door. Gabi stood there, her arm newly wrapped, her face pale. I let her in and went outside to see who'd dropped her off. No car in sight. I drew the front drapes against the spies I imagined lurking just out of view.

Gabi headed straight for my bar and poured too much scotch into a glass. I sighed. If she stayed much longer, I'd have to instruct her on the proper way to drink my liquor. It was my duty as an older, wiser woman. Plus, each bottle of Glenlivet nearly broke my bank account.

"We strive for objectivity in our reporting, Sasha. You know that." Bailey's delivery sounded so smooth, so seductive. She'd probably used the same words to coerce interviews a thousand times before. Only this evening, I had even less reason to trust her.

"Hey, Bailey, I have a question for you. When and where is Cecilia Sanchez holding her press conference?"

"At three thirty, on the plaza." She swatted the answer out, a gnat of distraction. "Now, what do you say about talking to your niece for me?"

I could have pretended to be on the road, that the connection had failed. Instead, I hung up, unwilling to talk with her anymore. She made my head hurt.

The phone rang again.

"Aren't you going to get that?" Gabi looked at me.

"It's the reporter from Channel 8. Do *you* want to answer it?"

Gabi put her glass on the table fronting my couch before flopping onto the futon. "She's already talked to Mom and Davielle. You'll be happy to know Aaron has now entered the national consciousness."

"What makes you say that?"

"That lady, Tracy Ingalls, from that show . . . what is it called? Oh, I know, *Now: 24/7*. She called Grandma's house while Mom and I were at the doctor." Gabi sniffed in disgust. "When we got back, Grandma was so excited she practically peed in her pants."

Damn. "So, did you talk with the famous Ms. Ingalls?"

"No way."

"Did anyone from the family?"

"I don't think so, but I'm not sure. Davielle was avoiding me."

"Bailey wants your side of the story about the affair."

"Oh, I'm like so sure." Gabi snorted. "Why can't they all leave me alone?"

If you hadn't had the affair in the first place, you wouldn't be in this mess. "Does Davielle know about it?"

"Mom told her. It's like she's already disowned me." Gabi's hot anger had made a full recovery. Good thing. She'd need it until several people either forgot her name or put her file in a large, locked cabinet.

"Give her some time to adjust. The rules she lives by are pretty rigid."

"Hah! You're telling me!"

The phone rang again. I turned it off and put it back into my purse.

I also unplugged the landline. When I returned, Gabi was on her second drink. I could tell; the glass held more than it had before.

"Guess who's holding a press conference tomorrow to talk about her hubby?" I joined her on the couch, kicking off my shoes and trying to tempt Leo to jump up.

"You're kidding. Cecilia is actually going to pretend to care?"

"She's going to offer a reward for useful information."

"Probably so she can finish the job herself."

I drank down the Glenlivet. "You think she has something to do with his disappearance?"

"She probably killed him."

"Waitaminute. What makes you think he's dead?"

"If he weren't, he would have contacted me by now." Tears formed in her eyes. Gabi had deluded herself into thinking Aaron Wahl was Prince Charming. I let it pass. In my heart of hearts, I knew he wasn't dead. No. He was sitting on a beach somewhere, drinking a frozen daiquiri, a plate of pineapple and mango within reach.

"Hey, I've got an idea. Why don't we go to the press conference? Since it's in a public place, we can make faces at Cecilia from the back row."

Gabi swiped at her face, unwilling to cry. "I'd like that."

"What did the doctor say about your hand?"

Gabi's hollow amusement worried me. "She said I was lucky. Pretty ironic, huh?"

Thank God for small miracles. "How did it go with the FBI?"

"They think Aaron is working with terrorists. Not the homegrown variety; no, they have visions of international intrigue." She shook her head and covered her eyes with her hand. "They kept asking me where he got his supplies, why he had so *much* of everything. And then *where* did he get it? Again and again and again, like an endless loop." She straightened, rigid, and gasped. Her hand found the front of her mouth. "Oh my God!"

I didn't dare speak.

"There must've been a weird taggant on something. That has to be it!"

"A what?"

"A taggant. It's a kind of microtag on certain materials so that you can trace where they've come from. They use them on all kinds of things like ingredients for explosives, equipment, and dangerous stuff like those anthrax samples from laboratories." Gabi stretched out, her legs on top of my thighs. Leo wandered toward the kitchen with a faint meow. "It's possible Aaron got something from a bad source. I can see it happening, maybe, but to think that he was up to something illegal is just stupid."

"Well, that might explain why the FBI is involved in the first place." It made sense. What I didn't say to Gabi was that if her lover had resorted to purchasing illegal materials, he might resort to other illegal activities as well.

"Did you know they've seized everything?" she said. "All the work papers in his office, his business, everything."

Again, silence seemed best. Gabi's uninterrupted monologue yielded more tangible information than I'd been able to glean on my own. I looked down rather than halt her words with eye contact. "I think you're right about them finding the safe-deposit box, too."

I couldn't keep quiet anymore. "What will you do if they seize your research? Can you still do your work? Can you complete your master's somewhere else?"

She thought about that for a long time. "I think I'm going to have to."

45

The snow-dusted Sandia Mountains strove to reach an aquatic sky that stretched over the frigid city too early the next morning. I chose to pay for visitor's parking on the University of New Mexico's main campus. Dressed in heels and a nice suit for my meeting back in Socorro, I pressed the button in the structure's elevator. The temperature hovered in the forties and you would have thought it was summer by the number of students sporting shorts and T-shirts. You could feel the end-of-term energy in the air, a quickening and gravity combined. Next week, after Thanksgiving, coursework would sprint toward final exams and term papers.

Faculty and students bustled across the wide sidewalks and walkways. Striding among them reminded me of my own college days. Those were good times, except for the boyfriends, especially in grad school. The University of Michigan had had so much money, so many resources. I thought the entire world consisted of exciting, endless possibility. Oh, to have that glorious naïveté again. Oh, to be like Gabi before any of this had happened.

I entered the heart of UNM and passed the offices of the university's student newspaper, *The Daily Lobo*. My path continued next to the biology building with its steamy-windowed greenhouses. The *Homage to Mother Earth* sculpture, its monoliths carved with symbols of grains and vegetables reaching upward, rendered the sky even bluer. A quick turn to the west and I could see Clark Hall, the chemistry building. Its bland planes and angles taunted future architects to transform it into something interesting.

Up the dirty stairway and to the left, I went to meet Amiram de Gammo. He sat in a typical college professor's office that was small, cramped, crowded with books. His wrestler's body was covered with a lowland gorilla's complexion, and about as much fur. Steel-wool hair shot out in a fuzzy arch atop his head with its flat nose and two blunt lines for a mouth. When he looked up, only his humorless eyes moved. The tome in his hands snapped closed.

"Dr. de Gammo, I'm Sasha Solomon."

"Sit down." Though light shined through the blinds, Amiram de Gammo's presence inhaled it. I'd never met such a guarded man in my life.

"Sir, I don't want to take too much of your time."

"Well, then perhaps you'll tell me why you lied on the phone. You're no reporter."

I held up my hands. "I'm busted. Sorry."

He put the book on his desk and leaned back in his chair. "You've got one minute to tell me why I should speak with you."

This wasn't going the way I wanted, not at all. My confidence as a crack investigator, a clever private eye, dwindled to a string bean. *Wait one damn minute!* I'd helped solve two murders in less than a year. I could do this. I could. Really.

"Fifty seconds, Ms. Solomon. Either you tell me the truth or you go." It may have been a bluff, but I didn't want to call him on it.

"I'm here to find out what you think about Aaron Wahl. I know you worked with him at one time."

"And what is your interest in this?"

"If you saw the news, you know. My niece is in trouble because of him. I don't want her career destroyed before it even starts because of something he did, or didn't do."

"For whom are you working?"

"On this?" I scratched my forehead. "Myself. I'm just trying to find out about this guy and to help my niece any way I can."

"You may ask me a few questions."

Gosh, thanks. What an imperious creep. I didn't like him. He didn't like me. At least we both knew where we stood. "Were you friends with Dr. Wahl?"

"We were never friends."

"So, your paths haven't crossed recently?"

"I'm afraid I can't tell you about that." Somehow, his eyes darkened.

"Okay, then, would you give me some of your impressions of the man?"

"He's a class-A bastard." De Gammo looked at a square clock on his desk. "Ambitious, calculating, and totally ego-absorbed. He's never cared who he steps on to get where he wants to go."

On the professor's wall hung a framed photograph of three children, their smiles standing out against dark skin. Could he be married? I pitied his wife.

"I have the feeling when people talk about how horrible he is, they're thinking of specific incidents, particular students."

The professor picked up a raku-glazed mug and sipped. With his free hand, he played with a shoelace on his hiking boot, an incongruously childish action from this stern man. "Your niece's father is Zachariah Shofet, right?"

"Yes."

"He's a good man. Smart." De Gammo put the mug down and wiped his bottom lip with a finger. "That's what confuses me here. Why don't you ask your brother-in-law about Aaron? Why come to a stranger?"

"He's still in Italy." It was better than trying to explain why I'd avoided talking with Zach privately. I was afraid I'd murder him for having an affair, no matter how long ago.

"Your niece is well-known, too." De Gammo sat back farther, crossing his short legs at the ankles. With a huff, he shifted his position in the chair again. "At MIT, Aaron drew distinctions between his male and female students. The males had to massage his ego and avoid flirting with his latest conquests. Ah, but if they were too smart, had ideas of their own, or were too handsome, he'd happily smash them into paste."

Everyone painted their complaints about Aaron with the same vague strokes. Where were the damning details? "Please give me something more than that. An example. A name. Someone or something I can work with."

"You realize it's been years since we worked in the same institution?"

"I do, but I need something. Please."

He stood, gathering a handful of papers and a notebook. No! He wasn't going to leave me hanging. How could I ever get a true picture of the man? I didn't budge.

The professor regarded me with a frown. "One of my classmates at MIT was brilliant. Everyone knew that he'd be the one to discover a new compound, develop a world-changing technology. His name was James Padilla and he was from right here in New Mexico. His undergraduate years were marvelous. But in graduate school, within two months of attracting Aaron's attention, Jimmy dropped out." De Gammo rubbed his forehead with a chubby hand. "This was a crime. A student so broken he couldn't continue his studies."

"What happened?"

"All I know is that he committed suicide soon afterward."

"How awful."

"One more thing, Ms. Solomon. Those of us who work in explosives technology, we're a small community. We may not like each other, but we do know each other." The professor opened a battered satchel and put the notebook and papers into it. "I decided to meet you for your niece's sake, and Zach's sake, despite your dishonesty." He moved closer to the door. "Here's a bit of free advice. Don't lie to anyone else in this community. You'll attract the wrong kind of attention to you and those you love."

I still hadn't gotten up.

"I have class in a few minutes." The professor turned off the light and pointed at me. "Leave. Now."

46

Zach's phone went straight to an automatic messaging system. "Call me," I said, leaving the number and pulling onto I-25. My prediction about the weather confirmed my moronic psychic abilities anew. Snowflakes as big as quarters heaved themselves against the windshield. My wipers struggled, their ragged strips squeaking on the glass.

"Why don't you replace them?" said Gabi.

"I like the view."

Gabi's head remained turned, watching the world go by from the passenger's seat. I didn't begrudge her the small ease of being chauffeured. Too soon she'd have to take responsibility for traveling her own road.

Though I'd offered my home for as long as she needed, my niece didn't plan to make the return trip with me after the press conference. She had decided to stay in Socorro, to bring order to the disarray of her life and figure out her next few steps. From what I could tell, she hadn't even tried to say good-bye to her sister or mother.

The snow came down harder once we left the city limits. I fantasized that the icy feathers fell from a ripped cosmic pillow. An appropriate image for what had happened in our family, too, though without the gentling whiteness before me. We seemed to be taking sides, Eva and Davielle versus Gabi and me. Did it have to be so polarized?

Billboards lined the freeway, some clutter, some art. My favorite declared, "Deming, New Mexico: Pure Water and Fast Ducks." I loved the sheer silliness of that. Other signs earnestly urged people to visit the places I'd seen during the last few days. Slogans enticed with clever puns. "Whoop it up!" Can you guess? Yep, that was for the Bosque del Apache.

Slush formed and squished out from under the tires, but it didn't impede us. Soon we took the exit and headed down the small ramp of a road past the earthen, tiled sign welcoming us to Socorro. On California Street, a makeshift poster advertising a Civil War re-enactment clung to a telephone pole. The inclement weather curled the paper, making the ink run in red, black, and blue. Just beyond Bobbie's Bobbin Sewing Center, we took a right onto Manzanares Street.

"You could have turned on Bullock," said Gabi, breaking almost an hour of silence.

"I coulda, but I didn't wanna," I said. "I drive for beauty."

"You won't find much here."

"That's not fair." In spite of CiCi, I'd come to like the town and its sprawling county very much.

White-topped dead grass surrounded the plaza, giving it a post-card touch. Soon the city would dress up its town center with pine wreaths and Christmas lights. Would luminarias—those paper bag, sand, and candle combos that every New Mexican adored—line the gazebo? I decelerated, imagining the square in its holiday finery and the changes that would come with the visitors' center. I quietly prayed that the project's designers and masterminds would retain a traditional New Mexican feel. It'd be wonderful to be part of a project that truly improved the regional economy.

I smacked my lips and sighed.

"What?" Gabi's question launched porcupine quills of hostility.

"I'm just thinking."

"I'm not your responsibility, Aunt Sasha. I can take care of myself."

My foot poised above the brake, hands tense around the steering wheel, I spoke with admirable control. "I'm glad to hear it, Gabi. Because my entire existence isn't centered on you."

That shut her up again, but I didn't mind. The slick streets required attention anyway. When we arrived at her house, I waited until she waved from the open door. A dishonorable relief enveloped me when she disappeared from view. Living with contradiction, my world flourished in paired emotions.

Not exactly on the way to my meeting at the foundation, I stopped at the Pump 'n' Snak for a quick cup of coffee and an emergency ration of chocolate. Four candy bars didn't feel excessive, especially when they'd be parsed over several hours. Plus, I'd have to drive back to Albuquerque after the press conference . . . in the dark . . . maybe I needed five.

Standing in the parking lot to open the first sweet, a thought: they might move the conference to a warmer local; I'd have to hunt that info down, too. My cell phone sounded and I reached into my purse to answer it while unlocking the car door.

"Sasha?" Zach's confusion was natural. I rarely called him. Now I had to figure out what to say.

"Hi. Have you talked with Eva?" Should I ask him about the affair? About Aaron Wahl?

"We've been playing phone tag. How's Gabi?"

"You'd better ask her yourself." I started the car and cranked up the heater. Where was he right now? In the United States? Still gallivanting around Italy? Professor de Gammo's charm and basic homeliness found an echo in my sister's husband. While *they* deserved each other, Eva didn't.

"I need to get to a meeting. Did you have a reason for calling me?" My brother-in-law's impatience made me want to stall, to run up his long-distance minutes.

"How well do you know Aaron Wahl?"

"Why?"

"Did you know Jimmy Padilla?"

"Why are you bringing up these names, Sasha? What's going on?"

What I noticed was that he wasn't answering my questions. "When did you have the affair, Zach?"

"What are you talking about? You have no right to ask me that."

Unable to face his deflections, and even more unwilling to hear his honest answers, I disconnected. Within a breath, the phone rang again. "What?"

"Sasha." Eva's icy worry blasted through the mike, freezing the edges of my ear. Zach hadn't had time to call her, had he? "Where are you?"

"In Socorro. Why?"

"I'm at your house. I keep knocking, but no one comes to the door. Is Gabi with you?"

"Why do you want to know? So you can force her to talk to someone else?" I noticed I'd answered her question with my own. Could I be the bigger person here, the one to ask forgiveness? Not yet.

"I'm worried about her."

"You should have thought of that before hauling her down to the FBI." My anger had a steely whiteness to it, the kind that made a clean cut through flesh.

Eva coughed. "Sasha, I have no fight with you. I need to talk to Gabi. Do you know where she is?" She sniffled. "Please?"

My urge to punish her, to make her pay for Gabi's bad decisions, evaporated. I propped the phone between my head and shoulder and unwrapped another bar, regretting the snack almost as enthusiastically as I ate it. "I brought her down with me. There's a press conference this afternoon about her advisor."

"They're going to interview her?" Panic strangled each word.

"No. His lovely wife has called it."

"What time?"

I automatically looked at my watch. "Three thirty."

"I'm coming."

That was the last thing I'd expected her to say. "Don't. We're planning to hide in the back and throw stale popcorn."

"I should be with Gabi."

"Really, Eva. There's no need." A chunk of caramel stuck to my hand. I sucked it off but discovered a piece had fallen between my thighs. I retrieved *that* while parking the car in front of the Val Verde.

"Have you ever heard of *yetzer hara*?" Eva had switched into lecture mode.

I found yet another clump of chocolate on my knees. It would have been better to get my dependable standby; whipped cream wasn't so messy. "It sounds like Hebrew."

A shaft of sunlight split through the cloud cover. I watched its slash of gold transform a leafless bush into a gem.

"Good job, Sashala." Was this my sister's way of apologizing? "*Yetzer hara* is man's evil inclination and *yetzer tov* is the inclination for good."

"So?" The lesson in Judaica could've put me to sleep as readily as the rabbi's talks at Shabbat services on those rare occasions when Mom took us to the synagogue.

"Soooo, all of us struggle with both sides. Both are necessary, Sasha. Without the evil inclination, people wouldn't succeed in business. They wouldn't push forward. Even though their motivations may stem from evil, they can always turn them to good." She sounded like she'd changed locations, from outside to in. "Gabi's struggle and my struggle and your struggles are all part of a conflict that has waged in people's hearts since Adam lusted for Eve."

I dropped another piece of the bar and reacted too strongly. "Dammit!"

"Are you still listening, Sasha?"

"Yes, professor."

"Enough of your silliness," Eva said. "*Yetzer tov.* That's why I have to be with her."

I didn't buy it. "Have you forgiven her, Eva? Or are you going to rub in your disappointment and judgment the entire time you're here?" My displaced fury leaked out like too much mayo on a sandwich.

"My struggles are my own, Sasha. But a mother's love for her child is unassailable, through grief, through adversity, through everything good and bad. Gabi needs me. She needs her mother."

Maybe, I thought. *Maybe not.*

47

Adorned with spots of smeared chocolate on the bottom of my shirt, I arrived at the San-Socorro Foundation desperate for the balm of work. Michaela met me at the door with an unanticipated hug.

On the way to the conference room, my shoe made scratchy sounds until I stopped and removed a piece of candy wrapper that had adhered to the bottom. Even if I was being good, sugar plagued me.

Olivia Okino already presided at the large table. Beside her, a woman spoke on an impossibly small cell phone. Another tapped on a sleek laptop that made mine look clunkier than a bass violin. The room's light effervesced on the expensive material of the two unknown visitors' suit jackets. I felt as classy as a cockroach.

"Sasha, you know already know Olivia." Michaela pulled out a chair for me. With an open hand, she indicated the woman to her left. "This is Bonnie Markham, the public information officer for New Mexico Tech."

"Hello," I said, covering my smudged slacks with my purse.

Gaunt with baby fuzz brown hair, she rose to shake my hand. I bowed into her hello and noticed the dullness of her skin, a sallow pastiness. An odor of decay drifted from her shadow-swaddled body. I hoped I was hallucinating. Otherwise, she must be terribly ill.

Michaela, playing the hostess well, introduced me to the second woman. "And this is Lupe Jonson, our primary architect."

The young woman's waist-length, blue-black braid sparkled with hints of glitter. Octagonal eyeglass frames, with triple rainbows of blues, pinks, greens, and yellows, accented her curiosity. Good thing she wore solid-colored clothes. Otherwise, it would have been impossible to look her in the face. While we shared hellos, four more people came in. I recognized them from our first meeting.

Without preamble, we got down to business. I elucidated my initial ideas and the problems determining which plan would work best for the center. After the presentation, I proposed that we leave the final decision to Papi and the board of the San-Socorro Foundation; they'd be paying for it anyway.

"Sasha, please, make a firm proposal," said Michaela. "Commit. Believe me, it'll be better for all concerned." This was the most directive she'd been with me and I didn't exactly like it, but I refrained from public comment.

For two hours, the group sledgehammered through this idea and that, leaving the rubble for me to reassemble. At our first break, I cornered my boss. It appeared my assignment had changed without discussion of the new terms. "I thought I was supposed to narrow the parameters, not finalize them," I said, the mug of coffee shielding my face from the others.

"Why don't we talk about this in my office?" Michaela excused us. I followed her, curious and, frankly, a little put out. This wasn't the first time a client had altered requirements midstream. I just didn't want to adjust to something new in the middle of a family crisis.

"Have a seat," she said.

The chair exhaled in protest, a gassy, embarrassing sound, when I plunked into it. "Is something going on that I need to know about?"

She took an audible breath, lips parted, face as expressionless as a newly Botoxed matron. "Some of the board members are having a problem with this project."

"Oh, jeez." I could see the entire thing unraveling. "It's Cecilia, isn't it? She wants me fired as revenge against my niece."

"Well, I don't know about that. But, believe me, if she wanted you fired, that'd only make you more attractive to the rest of them." Michaela picked up a filigreed letter opener and twirled it in one hand. Its dagger shape made me want to grab it from her, lest she cut herself. "You've got no idea how many people are involved on this board. Papi's brother and one sister, all of his children, cousins, an ex-wife. It's a nightmare. At first everyone agreed. Now that we're making real progress, people are starting to watch out for their petty interests. Papi thinks we've got to break ground so that the project is a fait accompli." She looked out the window. When she faced me again, her eyes shone with moisture. "In case you didn't know, it's a bit of a race for time here. Papi is old, Sasha. And he's got cancer. The prognosis is good, but if something were to happen . . ." Two teardrops fell down her cheek before she wiped her face with a tissue. "If he dies, I don't know what'll happen."

"This is awful. I had no idea."

"Thank you." She'd already banished the display with her usual calm. "CiCi's problems aren't helping either."

"And what's *her* agenda?" I said. Above Michaela's head hung a santo of a man in a monk's robes with birds on his shoulders. A deer ate from his hand. What would Saint Cecilia be known for? Patroness of infidelity, pettiness, and Chihuahua snouts?

Michaela glanced at the clock on the wall behind me and sat straighter in an attempt to staunch her emotions. "We'd better get back. The others will be wondering."

Photographs, many of them black and white, lined the hallway on both walls. "Are these Papi's family?"

Michaela turned to see what I was looking at. "Yes. His brothers, sister, and the various kids and grandkids." She pointed to a large color photo. "These are Papi's children. Luis, Mario, Tony, Angel, and Cecilia."

His sons had dark hair and eyes, with gazes so intense you knew they had to be intelligent, no-nonsense people. CiCi looked so out of place, as if she'd been born a teacup dog, prized for pedigree rather than personality. Funny how I always thought of her in terms of female dogs.

"I heard CiCi has a brother. Which one is he?"

"He wasn't here for this picture." Michaela pointed to another one near the door to the conference room. A light-haired boy posed in a baseball uniform with a bat raised as if ready to slam a home run. He had to have been in high school at the time.

"What's he doing now?"

Michaela stopped. "He's trying to put his life back together. A long time ago, he accidentally killed a classmate, a black boy, and being the ignorant, cocky kid he was, José bragged about it. Long story short, he was old enough to be tried as an adult and the jury was only too happy to throw the book at him . . . and his father. It was a bad time." She began to walk again. "He got out of jail a few weeks ago and has been staying with Papi until he figures out what to do."

I hurried into the room after her, intrigued by the sadness in her voice. She'd be about José's age. Had they been friends? There was no time to pursue it now. The group around the table had coalesced in our absence. Olivia had been elected spokeswoman.

"Sasha, we've been talking. All of us prefer what you call the 'state fair' approach." She paused to look at each of the others, as if to confirm her statement before continuing. "We think it would be easier for tourists to understand." When she finished, she folded her arms in front of her chest, a blood-and-flesh shield against my probable protests.

Wrongo. Their work meant less for me. "Great. Consider it done. I'll come up with a final by next Tuesday."

My rapid agreement must have surprised her. "You're sure?"

"This is wonderful. It makes my job easier. Thank you." Finally, some forward motion in my life. I couldn't have been happier. Well, except . . . I wanted lunch. "Is there a good restaurant near here? It needs to be quick and easy." I put on my coat. "If anyone wants to join me, I'd be happy to have you."

"If you go to Pasadita's, I'll come," said the architect. "I haven't been there in ages."

Bonnie from New Mexico Tech decided to join us, too.

We drove in separate cars, a bad decision considering the cramped, crowded parking lot. That should have been an indicator of the happenings within. This was an old-time establishment, the kind that bred generations of loyal customers. Inside the door, the smell of red chile and *carne adovada* cuddled up to our salivary glands. Could there even be twelve tables in the entire restaurant? None seated more than six people comfortably. Only one waitress darted from person to person, but customers helped her, getting their own water, bussing dishes. Laughter fizzed and conversation buzzed. I loved every second of it.

We picked the only seats available in the second room. Our little table, hunched in a corner, was covered with a plastic red and white checkered cloth. The plump waitress, her hair pulled back in a negligent ponytail, gave us menus and water at the same time. We ordered variations on enchilada platters. Mine had two cheese and one chicken smothered "Christmas" style with both red and green chile.

When we'd been served, Bonnie cut into her lunch and with a frown said, "I can hardly taste anything anymore. It's awful."

"Why?" Lupe dumped ten ounces of honey on her meal. Most of us who liked that hot, sweet flavor faked it by putting honey on a sopaipilla (a bready, deep-fried piece of heaven) and then surreptitiously letting the liquid fall upon our other food as if the result was a pleasant accident. I'd never seen anyone quite so brazen about the combination before.

"The chemo has affected my taste buds. But, hey, I'm here. It's a small price to pay." Bonnie took another bite. "Oh, well. Consider the alternative."

What was the proper etiquette here? She'd brought up the cancer. Did she want us to ask about it? At least knowing about her illness brought a kind of confirmation of my earlier hallucination. That was the problem, though. I was right just often enough to make it difficult to know when to trust my intuition and when to throw it out with a scream. Call me selfish, but I couldn't hear about this woman's struggles, couldn't own her suffering too. Not when Gabi's troubles, and my nightmares, offered so much room for unhappiness already.

"Lupe, are you from here?" I said.

"I was born in El Paso but spent most of my life in New York."

"So, how did you end up in New Mexico?" With the recklessness of someone who knows she won't see most of the people who surround her ever again, I dumped honey on my own plate. What liberation!

"All good roads lead to Papi Sanchez." She opened another sopaipilla. "I just *love* these."

"What do you mean about Papi?" said Bonnie.

Lupe held up her hands and made quotation marks with her fingers. "Young, dirt poor Hispanic girl makes good." She shrugged. "You can probably still find articles about me online. I was quite the success story a decade ago. Suffice it to say, Papi paid for every scrap of my education—*paid* for it, mind you, not *loaned*—from my first year of high school on. He's never asked for anything in return until this project." She loaded her fork with dripping food.

Lupe's answer pleaded for more questions, but Bonnie, the PR pro from New Mexico Tech, addressed me instead. "Have you had a chance to visit our campus?"

"Not yet. I'm going to try to drive around for a while after we finish here. Then I have to go to a press conference."

"Are you talking about CiCi's upcoming performance?"

What an amusing way to put it. I nodded.

"I bet half the town will be there," she said. "Aaron isn't well liked, but he's almost as famous as his lovely wife. It's bound to be a zoo. I'm glad I'm not running it."

"Do you know CiCi personally?" I hoped Bonnie would be a good source of dirt. Perhaps our ties in PR would unlatch the reluctance to badmouth a community icon.

She picked up the honey bear and said, "That woman could turn this into acid."

Heh heh heh. "Have you known her long?"

"Years. Papi's foundation has been very important to Tech since forever. So, I've seen the family at various functions over the years. Even when CiCi and Aaron were living in Boston, she'd jet in for events. She had to keep her fingers in it all." Bonnie put her plate, at least two-thirds of the food uneaten, on a table that had emptied next to us and opened her purse. "I think she makes it her business to be the fly in everyone's soup. It's a power trip."

"Has she ever messed with your funding?"

Bonnie laughed. "No, she doesn't have *that* much power. She just likes to pretend she does. In a way it's good. It keeps us all on our toes, waiting for the health inspector, spraying insecticide." She removed a handful of pills from a plastic container and swallowed them with two gulps of water.

Lupe eyed Bonnie's plate while finishing her last enchilada, but our tablemate didn't appear to take the hint.

"I haven't met her husband yet," I said, wanting as much info as possible before Bonnie realized how gossipy she was being. "Are they a good couple?"

Her face turned scarlet. I jumped up, prepared to perform the Heimlich maneuver on her. She waved me down to my seat again and finished her glass of water. "I'm sorry to scare you." Her face remained bright and her eyes gleamed with enjoyment. "Yes. I really do think they deserve each other."

"Why is that so funny?" I sopped up a final bite of chile and stuck it into my mouth with a flourish.

"I can't believe I'm being so catty." Bonnie picked up her rejected lunch and separated the food her fork had touched from the rest. She scooped the remainder onto Lupe's plate, receiving unabashed delight in return. "Aaron is brilliant and has lent prestige to our school, but he's one of the most egotistical people I've ever met. CiCi is even worse. A perfect match."

"I don't follow."

"She's the only person who has the gall and wherewithal to pull him off of his pedestal."

"How?"

"I'm not sure about her innate intelligence, but her money is far more abundant than Aaron's. She can keep him on a very short leash, if she wants to."

I thought about that for a minute. If CiCi had such control over her husband, why did he endanger his comfort with affairs? It smacked of recklessness, of self-destruction. Perhaps even self-loathing.

Over the years, I'd had enough windbag clients to know that the largest outward ego usually had the puniest one within.

48

Plaid-garbed fanatics knocked their frozen little balls around New Mexico Tech's snow-whitened golf course. With the way I was feeling about former boyfriends, Aaron and Peter, it might have been nice to see a few of them sink into those sand traps headfirst, their pom-pom socks and cleated shoes sticking out like gaudy lollipops.

My hostility found no further kindling during the drive around the loop of road encircling the university. The splendid new Student Activities Building testified to the administration's understanding that without its base, it couldn't exist. One of the reasons Socorro had so much going for it stood to my left. Each year enthusiastic audiences enjoyed operas, mariachi galas, and Broadway plays at the Macy Center. It was the star of the school's cultural life. Across the street, the mineral museum tempted with its specimens dug and blasted out of the mountains nearby.

Acronyms ruled here, byproducts of tekkie sensibilities. The campus air had a frisson of precision, cleanliness, that made me feel smarter by association. This would be a great place for a scientifically minded Goldilocks, or one Gabriela Shofet, to spend her postgraduate years. New Mexico Tech felt *just right*.

After my short tour, I headed to my niece's house to pick her up early. With half of the town intending to watch CiCi's histrionics, finding a good place to blow raspberries would be challenging. The black exclamation mark of Eva's rental car hunkered in Gabi's driveway. My hand reached for the door, but Gabi met it with her own, her face wet with new tears. At the rate our family was going, we'd single-handedly reduce a drought to nil.

"Why didn't you tell me she was coming?" Gabi whispered, her breath scorching my cheek. Barefoot, dressed in pajama bottoms and a fuzzy sweater, she'd never convince any reporter she was competition for her lover's wife. I'd have to remember the outfit in case we needed it for an interview.

"I was in a meeting for hours." I put a hand on her thin shoulder. "If you want, I can ask her to leave."

"I don't need you to fight my battles."

"A bit testy, aren't we?" I went inside, thinking she'd better recant if she wanted my continued help. "You'd better get a move on. We've got to find a good place and this'll probably be Socorro's media event of the century."

Gabi's face contorted into such a look of hatred, I stepped back to protect myself. "Why is that bitch getting so much attention?"

"Such language!" Eva's scandalized comment glided in the air like ash, light but formed from heat.

"Because she happens to be a member of the town's most famous family. And your Prince Charming is internationally known," I said. "And because Mr. Perfect may have been working with terrorists."

"He wasn't!"

"Do you really know that?"

"Please, let's have a little peace here." Eva stroked her long skirt, banishing imaginary wrinkles into hand-ironed straightness. Shoes fit for a schoolmarm peered from under the thick material. With a little head covering, she could have passed for a Mennonite.

I walked into the kitchen. A teakettle steamed on the stovetop. In the sink, a cast-iron pot soaked beneath the bubbles of dishwashing liquid and steaming water, a rim of burnt egg visible. Her fridge's interior hadn't been filled and no ice cream graced the freezer. With nothing to divert me, I returned to the front room, wanting a shot of scotch or two. This scene would test anyone's resolve to be a better person. "Why don't I come back when you're ready?"

"Just give me a few minutes." Gabi exited to where I'd just been, banged around for a minute, and returned with a mug. "Here, have some tea."

The steaming liquid had twigs floating in it—an unpleasant reminder of the Chinese brew my acupuncturist exhorted me to drink, the one that took five hours to make and stunk up the entire house. He claimed the latest batch would free me from all otherworldly hallucinations. Hey, if I were a spirit and smelled that stuff, I wouldn't stick around either.

Still, I accepted Gabi's proffered peace offering and took my place at the desk, letting mother and daughter resume their discussion. Apparently it was the noiseless kind, big on furtive looks and low on words. Or maybe they were practicing for a mime performance. Whole civilizations emerged, prospered, and declined while we sat there. I had time to inspect every micron of Gabi's newly restored front room, her face, Eva's face, and the specks of dust residing on two windowsills.

"You got it back?" I put the mug down and tapped the computer.

"Yes."

"Was the house this clean when you got here?" I said, wondering if Detective Sanchez had arranged a second visit from Spot Off.

"Yes."

If only Gabi's place had a clocked that ticked, the sound might break the tension. "Well, this is fun," I said.

"Sasha," said Eva, warning me to behave.

"At least you're talking," I said. "You do a great imitation of a rock. Have you thought about taking it on the road?"

"I can do without your sarcasm." Eva pursed her lips, her gaze traveling sideways to my niece. "We've made our peace."

Gabi actually huffed before walking out of the room again.

"Yeah, I can see that." I crossed my legs. "What on earth did you say to her, Eva? She was on the mend and now you've put her back a couple of centuries. Was it worth it? Did it feel good to be so self-righteous?"

"You should know. You did the same thing to Zach."

"He deserves it." This time I wasn't backing down. "What did you say to her?"

"Only that she's not going to stay here. Or, if she is, she's going to have to pay for it herself. Zach and I think she needs to be closer to us."

"In Israel?" My shoes dripped on Gabi's floor, minute muddy puddles from the wet dirt in her front yard. "Israel is safer?"

"At least they won't be killing us because we're Jews."

"You can't be serious." I stood up. "I suppose those restaurant and bus bombings are because *they* love us." I left Eva contemplating my verbal scud and went in search of Gabi.

Dressed in dark slacks and an understated shirt, she huddled on the closed toilet seat, head on her knees, hair nearly sweeping the floor. "I don't have a lot of money, Gabi, but I can help you stay here if that's what you want. We'll find a way," I said, perching on the ledge of the bathtub.

Her dry eyes evinced such tragedy I wished she were crying instead. "You don't understand, Aunt Sasha."

"Have you thought about asking Grandma Hannah for help?" Between inheritances and divorce settlements, Mom had more than enough money for round-the-clock healthcare, round-the-world trips, and graduate tuition for one very deserving grandchild.

Gabi tried on the concept. Why mention that Mom's gifts always came with ropey strings? "Do you think she would? That she could?"

"Two things, Gabi. I have power of attorney for her finances, so I can help there. And if you put the request in terms of your parents being unsupportive about your nonobservant lifestyle, I think she'd positively sing." Mom adored the idea of sticking it to any authority but her own.

A blue, unsteady spark of optimism sputtered, gaining strength on Gabi's face. I'd provide the reality check later. Mom might as easily refuse our entreaties. But this would give me something tangible to work on, a way to really help my niece since my investigative powers seemed to be so ineffective.

I looked at my watch. "We'd better get going."

49

A city's worth of cars beat us to our destination. They lined the plaza and side streets like abandoned hopes. Television vans with their bright, canned slogans dotted the square, too. We had to park far away, the long walk giving us more time to be uncomfortable with each other. The weather, in typical New Mexico fashion, had changed yet again and a blue sky spread over us. The sun's weak rays and wisps of clouds reminded me of torn gauze.

CiCi, in her mauve coat, commanded attention. She stood, a colorful slip of a thing, flanked stoically by several tall, clean-cut men in dark suits. They'd amassed in the middle of the gazebo like actors on the set of an action movie, just before the assassination attempt. Detective Sanchez shrunk behind the somber display, his cowboy hat preventing him from disappearing completely. What struck me most were the obvious absences. Papi wasn't up there lending visible support to his daughter. Neither were any of CiCi's brothers.

"Sasha!" Bailey flounced from across the street, her smile as wide and welcoming as a slow river. "And this must be Gabi. I've wanted to meet you for so long. Would you have time for a couple of short questions?"

I pushed Gabi and Eva behind me to interrupt my friend's efforts. "Go find us a good place to hang out."

"This will only take a minute," said Bailey.

"It'll take even less than that." I shoved my transfixed relatives into motion. Eva stumbled a little before taking Gabi's arm and urging her away.

When Bailey started to follow, I grabbed her camel hair coat in a death grip. "No. You're not going to bother them right now."

"You can't do this, Sasha. Remember the free press?" She tried to yank away.

"I'd think you'd want the information I've got about that lady up there." I pointed at Cici. "I'd think you'd want that more than just about anything else right now." I shrugged. "Maybe I'm wrong."

It worked. Bailey hesitated.

"You know that bomb squad guy I wanted to talk with? Well, I finally placed him. You two used to date. Right?"

"So?" She stepped closer. I had her now.

"Guess whose fuse he's lighting now?" Pardon the pun, but bombs were on my mind.

Bailey made a wee choking sound, a cross between a gurgle and a suppressed scream. I guess she wasn't quite over him yet. "You've got to be kidding. Are you sure?"

I nodded. "As sure as I know my name. I saw them playing hide-and-go-seek at her daddy's house a few days ago. It grossed me out even before I knew who she was, or who she was married to." My friend's appalled expression elicited pity, but with Gabi in my life, I had none to spare. "Oh my God! You're not still dating him, are you?"

In a small voice she said, "No. We broke up ages ago. It's just so weird to think of him and her." She couldn't have looked more disgusted if she'd just discovered maggots in her rice cake.

"Are you all right?"

Bailey moved her head side to side to regain her composure. "I've got to get ready. I'll see you after the conference."

"Be sure to ask CiCi the *tough* questions." I grinned, but the reporter had left.

Up front, the microphone squawked, and an obnoxious, high-pitched reverb squealed until the man at the sound console fixed the problem. People in the audience removed their gloved and mittened hands from protecting frosty ears, and shuffled, waiting. Eva and Gabi had found a good spot on the southeast corner of the plaza, away from the majority of the assembled crowd. Back in the peanut gallery, a few others loitered, as unofficial as we were. I passed a man in black sweats, large sunglasses. His down coat was an unattractive gray. We nodded a conspiratorial greeting.

One of the suits next to CiCi, our MC for the day, announced the ground rules with an appropriate air of menace and solemnity. His tone made me search the audience for men with those weird earphones that secret service folks wore, with the curly wires halfway hidden behind enormous necks. According to our host, CiCi would make a short statement, after which the lead investigators would answer what questions they deemed fitting. CiCi would be available for two-minute individual interviews after the half-hour conference. Gee, what fun.

Mrs. Aaron Wahl stepped up to the mike and tapped it twice. "Can y'all hear me?"

"Oh, brother. When did she get that cute little Texan *thang* going on?" I said, feeling a gleeful snarkiness. It would have been more fun to have someone smile in response.

"Be quiet, Aunt Sasha. I want to hear." Gabi's eyebrows met in a dark line. She faced forward again, her chin pointier than I remembered.

The sunlight dwindled behind a bank of clouds, its frail luminescence echoing CiCi's tremulous words. "As many of you know, my husband, Dr. Aaron Wahl . . ." Here, she held a lace hanky to an eye. Excellent acting. "My husband Aaron disappeared three days ago. Since then . . ." She stopped again to look to her right and left. "Everyone has been *so* good to me." One of the men put a steadying hand on her shoulder.

"What a load of crap," said Gabi.

"Hush." I'd noticed the bomb squad guy standing next to Detective Sanchez. Where was Bailey? Did she see him? I squinted and stood on tiptoes to get a better view of the reporters busy scribbling on their pads in the front row.

"With the investigators' permission, I've decided to offer a seventy-five-thousand-dollar reward for information that helps find my husband."

People murmured surprise. Some couldn't help but exclaim shock at the award amount. Too much? Too little? I didn't know. It sure was a far cry from the millions demanded in that phony ransom note.

Overhead, waves of birds made their way back to the bosque. As one, we watched the Canadian geese, their raucous honks drowning out CiCi's next words for a moment.

"Please," she pleaded, "if anyone knows what happened to Aaron, tell us. I need to know he's all right."

The eerie cries of a group of sandhill cranes embodied all of CiCi's sorrow and gave it a more poignant voice. Head bent far back, I searched for the thin lines of their wings in the scant upper atmosphere. There they were, dozens of them, nearly gossamer against the ever-darkening sky.

"Bullshit." Gabi had spoken a little too loudly. People turned to look at her. "What a crock of bullshit." This time, her comment carried farther.

"Gabriela! This isn't the place," Eva said.

The ripple of Gabi's words rolled forward. Someone in the gazebo put his hand to his forehead and searched the crowd. He pointed our way. CiCi's crying stilled. She craned her neck and that formerly soft jaw hardened into titanium. A snap of energy crackled and an enormous static charge arced searingly toward us. CiCi pointed a finger at Gabi. "Whore!"

Everyone goggled, following the plane of her hand to our corner. Eva and I tried to obscure my niece with our bodies, an impossible task since she had a good six inches on either one of us.

"You! Arab whore!" Venom erupted from CiCi's mouth in a putrid, greenish stream. I knew no one else saw it, and I wished I'd been spared the vision of poison penetrating Gabi's chest.

Time stopped long enough for me to take action.

"We should go. Now," I said, shoving her backward. *Arab whore.* I hoped Detective Sanchez had taken note. If not, I'd make sure he did, or would press the point with Bailey. One way or another, we'd nail CiCi for that vandalism at Gabi's house.

In response, my niece's fury burned bright. Mouth opening, she prepared to let loose with something that'd she'd regret for years as it was played and replayed on local and—if raucous enough—national news. Hell, it would be picked up by late-night talk show hosts, comedians. It would flow through the Internet, get millions of hits on YouTube, if she didn't watch out. In the split second of silence, I clapped one hand over her face. No way would I let her ruin her life for the likes of CiCi. My other hand dug into her traumatized wrist while I distracted her enough to save her from herself.

"Ow!"

"We're going right now, Gabi. And you'll keep your mouth shut or I'll break your bad arm all over again," I said. The look of utter horror on her face nearly stopped me. Eva, sensing the trouble, joined me in pushing her daughter away from the square.

Snap. The moment sprang to life again. Reporters began to turn around, their cameras glinting toward us.

"Whore! How dare you come here?" CiCi's cries riveted the media in her direction again, center frame, full focus. This would be far better footage than the award announcement. I hoped spit flecked her lips and gathered in white strands at the edges of her mouth. The more rabid she seemed, the better for Gabi. "Filthy whore!"

Then, somewhere in the front, Papi Sanchez's quiet voice slapped his daughter silent. "Enough."

In the waning light, CiCi's eyes held a diamond madness. She could have put the pipe bomb in Gabi's mailbox. She'd lived with someone who knew the ins and outs of explosives. They'd been married for years, enough time to pick up some of her husband's expertise. At the very least, she'd know where to find the supplies.

In the gazebo, the law enforcement types had stepped away from her as if disassociating themselves from a repugnant smell. Perhaps they were reassessing her story, reconfiguring the information she'd given them. *One could only hope.* Face the color of a stewed tomato, her rapid breaths emitting spurts of steam, CiCi brought to mind a wild horse after a lengthy fight.

Below his daughter, standing on the grass in front of her drama, Papi put on a black hat that matched the thick cloth coat he wore. I recognized two of his sons as they held him steady at each elbow. Between them he resembled a burned pine tree, thin, blackened, and lifeless. Such gloom surrounded him, his well-defined features had acquired a filmy blur.

For eighty-five years, he'd struggled to do good in this world. As the sun lost its battle with the horizon, I feared CiCi's outburst was only the beginning of Papi's personal twilight.

50

Thank goodness Eva and Gabi had left by the time the television cameras searched the crowd for the object of CiCi's continued wrath. Bailey moved through the audience, heading my way. Before she could call my name, I'd begun to run.

I caught up with my sister and her charge quickly, feeling oddly pleased. CiCi had just protected Gabi. Her tirade made for better news.

Anger ramrodded my niece's spine, causing her gait to be stiffer than her physical injuries merited. Her face twisted with fury and embarrassment. Good thing no camera had caught this response. Still, I insisted we zigzag through several neighborhoods to avoid enterprising news crews.

"What a disgrace," said my sister.

"Yes, that was quite a show," I said.

"I think I'm going to be sick." Gabi stopped and bent so that she wouldn't hit the pavement. Then she threw up.

This, Eva understood. She held her daughter's hair back from her face, for the second time in as many days, and murmured encouragement. "Everything is going to be all right. We're going to take you away from here. It'll be good. You'll see."

Gabi broke free from her mother's reassurances. For a moment, her hands bracketed her head. She let them fall. "Oh, for God's sake, Mother! You're blind if you think everything is going to be fine."

Eva grimaced at her daughter's language as much as the rebuke behind it.

"Part of healing is believing you *can* heal," I said.

"And you, with your platitudes." She faced me. "I don't see how things have worked out so great in *your* life."

"I'm exactly where I want to be."

"Right." Gabi spat at the ground. I couldn't tell if she'd done it to get rid of a bad taste or to scoff at me. "Living check to check, having a miserable love life, manipulating people every day in the name of your work. Yeah, I'm sure that's exactly what you hoped for when you were my age."

"When I was your age, all I thought about was sex."

She'd started walking again, faster, with purpose.

"You're more book smart, and further along than I ever was, Gabi. But you're just as stupid," I said.

She wheeled on me with a speed I wouldn't have thought possible, given that she'd so recently been in the hospital. "Oh, *that's* the pot calling the kettle black, isn't it?"

In spite of myself, I laughed.

"What's so funny?"

"Did you really think you'd live happily ever after with Aaron Wahl? Was that your master plan, to be the wife of a man thirty-plus years older than you? Did you think any of it through, Gabi? Or did you just take a one-way trip to fantasyland?" She opened her mouth to respond but I didn't want to hear her excuses. "No. You didn't think any of it through. Not with that wonderful, analytical mind of yours. You threw all your objectivity right in the garbage disposal and pressed the button." I pushed past her and turned around, blocking her path so that she couldn't make a quick getaway. Only a few cars were on this street. I wasn't quite sure where we were. "Even if you'd gotten married, Gabi, how long do you think it would have been before he found another mistress? Or did you think you'd change him with your love? I can't believe how stupid you've been."

"Enough with the *stupid*," said Eva, catching up to us. "Both of you, stop it. Can't we have some peace here?"

Gabi hugged herself. I couldn't see her face well now but imagined the betrayal she felt. How could I have been so callous?

Ashamed, I ran ahead to heat an unbearable coldness of heart. The two of them didn't bother to keep pace. Eva murmured words to Gabi that couldn't possibly bring comfort. The sound of her voice, accompanied by revving cars and the occasional ambulance, carried the loneliness of lives unfulfilled. I held on to an image of Peter next to me in bed, his unblemished arms around me, his breathing soft and regular on my face. But the happy picture disintegrated as thoroughly as a gale-blown spider web, replaced by a shivery sort of feeling. I closed my eyes, using the discomfort as an excuse for Gabi and Eva to catch up. When they didn't, I looked. They'd stalled down the road.

Convinced our lives skirted a calamity, I headed back. My attention landed beyond where they stood, on a shadowy van. Its sides were painted with flames that seemed to swirl and bend as if real. "What the hell?" I strained to get a better look. The vehicle trawled the street, windows open with the driver looking for something. "What's he doing?"

"Who?" Both Gabi and Eva searched for what I watched.

"The guy in that van. There's something wrong with it." And, in an instant, I knew that the car wasn't the problem. "Run!"

Without thinking, I grabbed them. Gabi screamed in pain. My hand clutched her injured arm again. Hoping to cover their bodies with mine, my violent tugs pulled them with me to the left. The van sped up and headed straight at us. Eva realized what was happening and ran on her own. I dragged Gabi. Her cries punctured my resolve, slowing us down. No, we couldn't stop!

"This way." I panted, yanking them toward the side yard of one of the modest homes that defined the street. We moved farther in, seeking somewhere to protect ourselves, to get away before the vehicle rammed into us. Our footsteps crunched over dried leaves. A loud crash. The van hit a mailbox before it backed up with a grind and a screech and drove off into the night. I couldn't read the license plate from this distance, didn't have the presence of mind to get more than a cursory description of the vehicle. God willing, Eva or Gabi had done better.

Outside lights now brightened the evening. Two front doors opened in unison.

"What's going on here?" said a woman, her hair wet, a black bra visible through an open robe. We emerged from our hiding place on the side of her house. "Who are you?"

"Jeanne, are you all right?" said a man crossing our path and scaling the steps to her door. "Look what they did to your poor mailbox."

"Oh, no!" She ran to inspect it. "What happened?" she said more gently this time.

Relief weakening my knees, I fell to the ground and kissed it. Eva sang a prayer of gratitude in Hebrew. Gabi didn't move. A manic laugh escaped my mouth, then tears robbed my breath and I put my face down again and cried into the winter grass. Maybe, if I wished hard enough, I'd wake up.

The two homeowners stood near us, their confusion and concern apparent in clucks and tsk-tsks. In a delayed response to the trauma, my body wrestled control from my mind and my breaths morphed into gasps. Somersaulting heartbeats. With both arms, I pushed up into a cross-legged position and tried to orient myself. Eva mumbled and swayed in prayer. Gabi had shut down, unresponsive to the strangers' questions. The hapless witnesses of this odd scene consulted privately, their voices just loud enough for me to hear over the roaring in my ears.

The man motioned to the woman's open door and said, "You should call the police."

I think I said, "Please do."

51

Wisps of color also rose from Eva and Gabi like steam on a hot road after a rainstorm. Porch lamps flickered, each shudder a rainbow. No amount of icky Chinese tea or slender acupuncture needles could ever halt my hallucinations now. Even with eyes firmly shut, the visions penetrated my defenses and poleaxed my faith in reality.

Pain pulled my fractured focus to a throbbing howl in my left shoulder. I'd jammed it while shoving my family out of the way. With a moan, I flopped sideways, letting my other shoulder lead me down to the blessed ground, my cheek touching the welcome stillness of frozen earth.

Time had a wavy quality, distorted and fluid. It could have been minutes, or seconds, before the sound of a siren drew to a near-deafening pitch. Tires crunched on the street. I opened one eye. Detective Sanchez glowed gold with compassion when he stepped out of the squad car, accompanied by an unfamiliar officer. I blinked away the new color show as best I could.

Other cars converged on the scene. Television crews vied for turf in front of us, reporters launching into their intros. "In another odd twist to an already strange case . . ." and "Controversy continues to surround the missing Dr. Aaron Wahl as his graduate student and her family were nearly run down . . ."

"Ms. Solomon?" Detective Sanchez knelt next to me. "Are you all right?"

"I don't know."

He offered his hand. I reached for it and yelped. He turned to the other policeman and said, "Jim, call a bus. I think we have some injuries here."

"No, not an ambulance. Please." I worked my way up on the uninjured arm, spit out pieces of dried grass, and rose on quivering legs. Sanchez put a helpful arm around my waist and escorted me to the porch. There, still bolstering me, he interviewed Gabi. Eva sat on a wooden swing, her legs pushing slowly, a cup of steaming liquid in her pale hand.

"Would you like some hot chocolate?" said the woman whose yard had been torn up in the attack. "It's decaffeinated."

As if I'd ever sleep again. "Yes, thank you."

She went into the house and I took my place next to my sister. The swing's back-and-forth motion soothed my frayed nerves. Eva slanted into my side, just so, and the warmth of her presence shielded me from the world. It had always done so, from the time we were young children and Mom's furious outbursts made me wet my pants with fear.

"If Aunt Sasha hadn't pushed us out of the way, we'd be dead for sure," said Gabi, coming to life with a vengeance.

"She's right, you know. I saw it all," said the man from next door. "That girl saved their lives." He inflated my actions, his chest as round and proud as a fat robin's, as if he'd coached me himself. "Got the first three letters of the license plate, too."

Gabi continued her story and I listened when I could. The pain in my shoulder became hot stabs. Not a good sign. Beyond the porch, spots of light demarked where the reporters did their business, little circles of sensationalism. They sidled their way toward us like insects, pushing past the other policeman, buzzing and encroaching on my once peaceful life. Against all my best attempts, my family had become breaking news—again.

One woman surged forward, a wave of hungry energy. A cameraman followed, holding his machine as steady as possible given his quick pace. *Bailey.* Our eyes met and she must've mistaken my recognition for permission because she began to mount the steps. When a policeman moved to stop her, she said, "It's all right. I know them."

I blinked, unable to respond.

She reached out, holding the mike an inch from my mouth. "Did someone try to kill you, Sasha?"

"I . . . don't know. I . . . think so." When had I ever stuttered before?

"Who do you think it was?"

My mouth opened, but I had no words in my throat. Instead, I drank a sip of the hot chocolate and shivered. "I . . . I think someone was aiming for us."

"Did you recognize the driver?"

"Get her out of here." Detective Sanchez pushed her away. "Jim!" The policeman who'd driven him to the house bounded the stairs in one leap. "Get these reporters out of here."

"Ma'am, you'll have to leave." Though polite, the officer's tone hinted at jail time. Joined by her cameraman, Bailey stepped back. He continued, without laying a hand on either one, to force them off the porch. "Ladies and gentlemen, this is a crime scene." At those words, the other policemen jumped into action and began to rope off the area with yellow tape. "You'll need to relocate down the block. We'll let you know when we're done here. Thank you."

Protests mingled with the air, but the reporters obliged. A squawk from one of the squad cars cut through their grumbling. Detective Sanchez listened for a moment before speaking. "Ms. Solomon, do you mind waiting a minute? I need to listen to this."

"I'm not going anywhere."

Though Gabi had the most serious injuries before the attack, she now seemed the most animated. She flitted in front of us, descriptions flooding the porch in torrents of meaninglessness. Maybe it was nervous energy. "Aunt Sasha, I'm so sorry for everything I said to you. God, I didn't mean it. I was just so upset, you know? I don't know what I was thinking. . . ." On it went, dousing my disorientation in the chaos of familiarity.

Eva's body moved in tiny jerks. I pulled back to see her face. The prayers that brought so much consolation to her before had frozen on the wrong side of her clenched teeth.

"Sweetie," I said, putting a hand around her back. "We're alive. That's all that matters right now." It sounded hollow.

A tear rolled down her cheek but she refused to comment. Her complete despair seemed to plumb far deeper than this single incident.

When Detective Sanchez returned to the porch, he came directly to me, his pad ready. "Tell me what happened."

"Haven't you gotten that from everyone else?"

"I've gotten their versions. Now I need yours."

"A kind of Rashomon thing, huh?" I giggled inappropriately, my hands simulating earthquakes.

"What?"

"Never mind." Should I tell him about the feeling of impending tragedy that compelled me to take action? Darnda would've understood, but Sanchez didn't strike me as the kind of man who'd embrace anything other than the here and now. Too late. My self-censoring must've broken in the fall. "Here's how it is. I think the lovely and insane CiCi Sanchez Wahl hired someone to kill us."

"What makes you say that? Did you see something specific?" he said.

"Yeah, I saw CiCi at the press conference. You were there. She was acting like a lunatic."

"Indeed."

"She looked like she wanted to kill Gabi." I sat on one of my hands to still it.

"She certainly did."

52

Exhaustion compelled Eva and Gabi to stay in Socorro that night. Detective Sanchez put a policeman outside their hotel room door, just in case. Me? I headed home. Though each turn of the steering wheel seared my angry shoulder, crossing into Albuquerque's city limits did the rest of me good.

Seconds after the ignition rumbled to a stop, my cell phone rang. Rather than juggle possessions with a rotten shoulder, I answered before leaving the car.

"Sasha?" Darnda's voice worked its liniment into my tattered psyche.

"Hi." More words would burst the dam of my self-control.

"Are you all right? I got this really bad hit about three hours ago. Why didn't you answer your phone?"

"Can I call you back?"

"No, I don't think so," she said. "Start talking."

"Fine." I closed the car door with my butt. Leo greeted me on the porch, exuding sheepishness.

"Hey, I thought you were trying to keep your niece away from national attention," Darnda said.

"That's the plan." With the key in the lock, I tried to hold the phone between injured shoulder and ear. Too much pain. I dropped my purse and leaned against the outside of the house.

"Your friend Bailey has been touting a segment on *Now: 24/7* since the noon news. She's acting too happy about it."

"No one told me about that." I must've still been a bit slow from the day's events, because the full import of Darnda's words took a while to hit. "Dammit!"

"Sasha?"

Now: 24/7 had a mega-audience, the kind that penetrated across age and wealth demographics, the kind that would slam Gabi's reputation to straight to hell. "Darnda, I need to make a call."

"Don't do anything stupid, Sasha."

"Of course not." I hung up.

Home, sweet cat-sprayed home. The smell hit like eucalyptus in a sauna. I guess Leo didn't like me being away so much. Now, he rubbed my legs and purred loudly. I couldn't stay mad at him. My anger had a better target, anyway.

"Ah, sweetie cat. Come on. Come to Mommy. Yes, that's a big boy." I spoke in the baby voice reserved only for him, even as I dialed Bailey's phone number. Leo looked at me and opened his mouth. I thought for a minute he might say something witty. The way things were going today, I wouldn't have been surprised. Instead he yowled with a half meow, half purr and began his figure eight weaving between my ankles again. Mercenary cat. He loved me for my tuna; I had no delusions.

The phone rang on the other end. No answer. Could Bailey still be in Socorro? Shoot! With time to kill, I cranked the thermostat to eighty degrees and took a hot shower. At the back of the medicine cabinet, I found painkillers from my last hospital visit. I swallowed two and prepared to be dismayed.

At a little before nine o'clock, Albuquerque's prime time, I poured a modest amount of scotch and sat on my couch, resting my arm on a large pillow. Oh, goodie. Aaron Wahl ranked the first piece in the program. On the upside, it'd be over first, too. Other stories might crowd the limited space in viewers' memories. No one with any real discernment could possibly believe that the smoke, mirrors, and innuendo filling these minutes could pass for news.

At least Bailey hadn't made the jump to the national market yet. Now that I was feeling a little more rational, I realized that my friend had more integrity than that. The reporter who came on-screen had a perfectly stenciled evenness and spoke in front of a pristine house in Maine, Aaron's birthplace. He prattled about the professor's *brilliant* career.

"If I hear that word one more time I'm gonna spit." I tried to find a better position for my arm, one that would allow me to forget my shoulder.

The on-air blathering continued.

"Yeah, yeah. If Aaron Wahl was so damn brilliant, why couldn't he keep his pants on?" I said to Leo. "And I've seen his idea of interior decorating, too. Definitely *not* brilliant."

Viewers couldn't help but empathize with the pained reporter, his laser-calibrated frown deserving a Tony Award, now speaking about Wahl's darker side. "A side no one could have predicted."

"Oh, put a lid on the melodrama. This is supposed to be news." I finished the drink and contemplated another when, from a studio in Phoenix, shone the under-powdered nose and overeager eyes of Davielle Cohen. "You idiot!"

Leo sprang out of the room.

Davielle's waterworks sprayed droplets of anguish about Gabi rejecting her good upbringing for a life of sin. Her delivery had a rehearsed, shrewish ring, the kind of performance I'd expect from a television preacher whose tactics rested heavily on fire and brimstone. My eldest niece showed a promising aptitude for a career on an evangelical show. I'd have to suggest it. After I killed her.

The piece segued into a juicy peach dribbling half-truths about Wahl's infidelity and possible connections to a homegrown terrorist organization. The allegations had the substance of dandelion down. How could people believe this crap? One, two, three, and here came the commercial break, a gaggle of nothing ads topped with Bailey's teaser, including footage of me and my relatives, zombie blanched and disheveled in the porch's pallid light.

I didn't see the rest because the phone rang, making me jump.

"Sasha, are you all right?" Henry LaSalle's concern made various parts of my body stand on end.

"How do you know something happened?" I steadied my breathing, belatedly grateful that Mom wasn't on the line.

"I just saw you on TV."

"Oh."

"Oh? You looked awful, and that's not just because you've lost weight."

"Bless you." Desperation tumbled out of my meager laugh and

unleashed a summary of the day's events in a flashflood of jumbled details and topsy-turvy chronology. Henry listened without interruption. I calmed down in the aura of his supportive silence. "I've got a hypothetical question for you."

"I'm all ears," he said.

"Say I wanted to find out about someone who works in a specialized unit of a police force without tipping him or her, or anyone else, off. How would I do it?"

"Who are you talking about?"

"It's hypothetical."

"No, it isn't."

In my mind's eye, I could see his military-buzzed hair and stingray eyes. His face acquired a lacy pink flush whenever he was irritated.

"I think someone might be up to something," I said.

"That's nice and vague." He waited for me to bite. I didn't. "Is this still about Detective Sanchez? I thought we put that to bed."

"It's someone else."

"You contact Internal Affairs."

"I don't want to cause trouble if I'm wrong."

He sighed. "Be honest with me, Sasha. Come clean. Then I can give you real advice."

"I know you've been keeping track of the Aaron Wahl thing. Well, I think the bomb squad guy who's investigating the case is dirty. I know for a fact that he's having an affair with Wahl's wife."

"That's quite an accusation."

Disbelief in a friend is particularly repugnant. I almost hung up.

"I saw it with my own eyes." I went to the liquor cabinet and pulled out the last of the scotch. "Everyone who's in the field, who knows about explosives and knows Dr. Wahl, says he's extremely careful. There's no way he could have accidentally blown up his own lab." Rather than pour a drink, I consumed it straight from the bottle. "So, instead of second-guessing all of these people, I'm going with the idea that maybe they're right. Maybe, just maybe, someone set up Aaron Wahl. How hard would it be for someone who knows explosives and has access to them to place a bit of wrong evidence at the scene? Of all the kinds of people who could deliberately blow things up and cast suspicion, a bomb squad investigator would be a natural."

"Are you done?"

"Don't patronize me, Henry."

He, of all people, knew my outlandish ideas could be right. Now, I wanted him to say more, to tell me how reasonable I'd been, how rational, practical, and *brilliant*.

"Let me think."

"So, what do I do?" I watched Leo hop onto the top of the armoire and prepare to jump. With a bum shoulder and too much on my mind, I went into the bedroom to discourage him. The night wind knocked branches of the decades-old cottonwood in my backyard against the window with thumps and scratches, the only noise on my dead-end street. I peeked through the curtain at an orange, cloud-heavy sky, lit by light pollution.

"You don't do a thing," Henry finally said. "You sit there and come up with theories and, just like in Clovis, you call me and I do something about them."

"Like what?" I exhaled onto the window, making a palette of condensation to draw Chinese characters. Even though I could only remember a few of them, their graceful forms and the process of drawing them brought satisfaction.

"Like make discreet—that's a word you need to learn—*discreet* inquiries about the man."

"And then what?"

"And then nothing. Except if you notice anything else like this, you call me and I'll contact the right people to check it out."

"At least you're taking me seriously this time."

"My dear, I always take you seriously."

I didn't like it. He'd work behind the scenes and none of my family would get any resolution. "Henry, I'm not telling you this stuff so that you can set slow wheels in motion and I never hear about it. In case you can't figure it out, I'm trying to help my niece here. She's been caught in the middle of something that's not her doing and I want to help her get out of it, very publicly."

"It seems to me your niece brought quite a bit of this onto herself."

"Look, let's not debate Gabi's morals. She was pregnant and miscarried as a result of the pipe bomb in her mailbox. Her advisor and lover is missing. Her career may be ruined. I think she's paid a heavy enough price."

"Sasha—"

"Last time I came up with these theories, it was for a friend. This time it's my own family. You saw the TV. We're all involved this time. I need your help, Henry, as a friend. Can't you give it to me?"

"I'll do my best."

"Thank you."

"Hey? Isn't your birthday some time around here?"

I'd been so involved in my family's drama that I'd forgotten my own. "Yeah, it's tomorrow. Thanks *so* much for reminding me."

"Now why do you say that? You know older women are far more beautiful—"

"Than who?"

"You're too quick to take offense, my friend. I was going to say, 'Than anyone else in the world.'" His long-distance goodnight kiss landed gently on my cheek. "I'll call you soon."

Before turning off phones and the answering machine, I made one call myself. When Paul answered, I implored him to keep Mom away from the television, period. He promised to do it. With that reassurance, I watched the ten o'clock news and Bailey's treatment of CiCi's press conference and our subsequent misadventure. She did well enough, painting Gabi as the sufferer rather than the hussy. *Thank you, my friend.*

In bed that night, I dreamed I sat on a gray chair in a gray room. No one came in or out. At least I got sleep.

53

I thought about pouting, about going to a spa and eating nothing but chocolate for the day, but practicality conquered my self-indulgent brain by the time I'd put skim milk in my coffee. So much for birthdays. For now, Gabi needed to do an interview; the public needed to see her. Even though I'd take down my video camera and rehearse her until she hated me, in the end it wouldn't matter much what she said on camera. Her face, bruised in an abstract painting of sharp colors, along with that pale skin and innocent youth, would be enough to remind viewers over thirty of each imbecilic misstep they'd ever taken in love, and would uncork their yearning to be forgiven still.

Gabi's focus had to be on the Aaron Wahl she knew and loved, the gifted researcher who'd never make a mistake like blowing himself up, the scientist who strove to save our country against terrorists. We'd create an inverted sympathy pattern. The more we painted CiCi as a shrew, the better Aaron looked. I doubted my niece would have a problem with that. The challenge would be to get her to stick to a script. For this to work, Gabi would have to emphasize the fact that Aaron wanted a baby more than anything else, but that his wife refused to bear children because of vanity. *We could do innuendo, too.* If Gabi played up her innocence, which shouldn't be too much of an effort, she'd win hearts and minds.

"You mean it? An exclusive?" said Bailey.

"Just one little thing . . . I plan to be right there filming the entire interview, too."

"Sasha, you know my news director won't go for that."

"If you don't do anything to mislead or impugn my niece, we shouldn't have a problem."

"I won't have total control over the editing, Sasha. What happens if you don't like how the piece is put together?" She sighed. "This is going to be a hard sell."

"I know the realities of your newsroom, Bailey. I know you're not out to screw us. But, you must understand how bad this has been so far."

"This is very close to blackmail."

"It's insurance, Bailey." I blew on the coffee. "I'm not offering this to anyone else, unless you all refuse. Tell that to your news director."

Bailey hung up with a promise to call back as soon as she'd cleared it with upper management at the station. True to her word, the phone rang less than twenty minutes later. We worked out the details: an interview to be taped in Socorro at Gabi's house at noon today, to be broadcast at 10:00 that night.

"By the way, Bailey, did you ever track down your old boyfriend? I've still got a couple of questions for him."

"Oh, I completely forgot." If we'd been speaking face-to-face, she might have raised a wan hand to her forehead for dramatic emphasis. Another lie.

"Maybe I can find him through my buddy at APD's public information office." Why hadn't I thought of that before? Blame it on too much stress, I guess.

"His name is Mark Padilla," she said, throwing me a scrap and then negating the gesture with another immediate lie. "I'll get you his number."

"Padilla, huh?" The pieces began to make an interesting pattern.

Next I called my unsuspecting niece.

"It'll ruin my career," Gabi said.

"It'll ruin your career not to." I refilled my mug with strong coffee. "We need to get your side of the story out, and you're the best person to do it. I'm the best PR consultant you can have to do it right. I'm coming down early to rehearse you a couple of times, so you're not surprised by any of her questions."

"We're doing it here?"

"Yes, indeedy." I liked that she didn't continue to object; she'd already begun to prepare. "Let me talk to your mom."

"She's on her way back to Grandma's."

"What happened? I thought she was going to stay with you for a few days."

"There's been a change in plans."

Rather than sticking my hand into that beehive, I let it pass. There'd be an entire lifetime to repair their familial bonds. Right now, the next few hours could be better used to help Gabi conquer the interview. Since I'd be in Socorro anyway, I called Michaela and suggested an early dinner with anyone who wanted a last say in the project. She told me she'd put out the invitation right away.

A minute later, my cell phone rang and I checked the number. Darnda. She'd probably sussed out my plans in the ether and was calling to say something sensible and throw my tactics into disarray. She could be calling with happy birthday tidings. Either way, I couldn't spare the time—or emotion—to talk. After a few rings, she left a message. The phone rang again. Another New Mexico number this time. Could she have two phones? If she was that determined, and that connected to the spirit world, she'd know I was avoiding her and that would make her feel bad. I picked up.

"Happy birthday," said Henry.

"Yeah, well . . ."

"Look. I don't have much time; I'm at work. But I need you to listen to me very closely." No problem there. His voice lost so many decibels I checked the battery on my phone. "Do I have your full attention?"

"And more." Was he about to break out in a chorus of the traditional song? I guess I could bear it.

"Good." His pause had the quality of a stage whisper. "You need to stay away from that man you mentioned to me."

"Which one? The bomb squad guy or Detective Sanchez?"

"Mark Padilla. Stay away from him."

"Why?"

"As a matter of fact, I want you to stay away from the entire police department down there. Give them a chance to do their job. Can you do that for me?" Now he sounded patronizing again and I wanted to irk him.

"What if one of them calls *me*?"

"If it's Detective Sanchez, answer his questions. If it's Mark Padilla, tell me or Detective Sanchez about the conversation."

"So, I was right. He's crooked."

"I'm not saying that, Sasha." I heard his beeper go off, a noise that had made my heart sink when we'd first started seeing each other. "I'm just saying to be careful."

That should be my motto: Be careful.

Thoroughly jittery, I stuck close to home. My desire not to think about Henry's warning produced excellent results for both the San-Socorro project and Gabi's preliminary talking points. Maybe Henry deserved a thank-you note.

Showered and dressed, I went to the store and bought two cans of air deodorizer, strong enough for funeral homes, to neutralize Leo's nasty present. I cast him out of the house and locked the cat door so he couldn't slink back in. Shirt over my mouth, my last act before leaving was to spray both cans empty in the front room and pray for a miracle.

Emerging into the wintry day, I caught Leo watching me with narrowed eyes from above the doorway. His tongue stuck out of his mouth and one ear cocked menacingly to the left.

"Sorry," I said, missing our conversations, or the odd insanity that led me to think they were real. "You've done enough damage and I want Peter to spend the night at least once more before he leaves."

In less time than it takes to peel a peck of roasted green chiles, I'd arrived in Socorro. Gabi stood at the screen door of her porch. Her long-sleeved T-shirt and striped leggings gave her an anorexic air that would play well on camera. The world-weary look, one that shouldn't touch anyone under eighty, worried me. Marks spotted her face with the remnants of trauma and added a good abused patina; if anything, I regretted they didn't look worse. The stitches would move even the most recalcitrant heart. No brush should touch her scraggly hair until after Bailey left.

"Do you know what you want to wear yet?" A couple of dresses and a pair of pants draped her couch. A backpack lay there, too. "Is that your missing backpack from the day of the bombing?"

Gabi nodded, unaware that she sat on her clothes. "Detective Sanchez brought it to me himself." Her hand landed on a dress and she looked down at it before shifting her position. "Do you really think this is such a good idea?"

"It's the best one I've got." I pulled out the desk chair. "I think we can nip the potential for more negative media with a really good showing today. I'm not sure it'll get picked up nationally, given that piece on *Now: 24/7* last night, but it can definitely affect statewide opinion and you can use all the goodwill you can get."

Gabi's knees and legs still had enough bruises to make a statement. The scrapes and cuts had begun to scar over. They looked crusty and horrible, too. "Go with a dress and no stockings."

"It's cold."

"We're aiming for maximum pity here."

In response, her face gained too much healthy red. "What's that supposed to mean, Aunt Sasha? That I was victimized? That Aaron seduced me without my consent? You know, I'm not going to lie for you or anyone else."

"Oh, Gabi, get off it. I'm not the enemy here. Someone tried to blow you up. Ka-boom. Remember?" While I liked her defiance as evidence of her healing, it'd make her less likeable on camera. A bit of the victim would be nice, but if she couldn't muster that, we'd go for naïve sincerity. "Tell your truth about Aaron. How much you loved him, how he was so excited about the baby." I picked up a piece of paper and an orange felt-tipped marker and began to doodle, wanting to distract her from the anger. "Hey, I've got a question. Did you spend many nights with Aaron?"

"Of course not. He had to go home." She'd put on the first dress.

"So, where *did* you spend your time together?"

"Here and there." She regarded herself in the mirror. Her first choice hovered at about two inches above the knee. Black with fuchsia accents, it made her look very pale. Wonderful.

"Let's see what the other one looks like."

"You know I never wear these things, not unless I'm at a conference or something."

"Did you and Aaron stay together at conferences?"

"Never. We had to be careful. People would talk." She let the dress fall in a little circle at her feet and stepped beyond it to try on the second one. "Of course, we did pretend to go to a conference or two, and then went somewhere else." She smiled. "We had so much fun, but we could only do that a few times."

Gabi's lithe, almost-nude body brought back memories of when I hadn't been concerned about thunder thighs or cellulite, when I'd had the same nonchalance reflected in her every movement. I'd never have that secure feeling of beauty again.

Celibacy began to look better by the minute, if only I didn't have to give up sex to do it.

"What do you remember about the other night? About when the pipe bomb went off? That's the kind of thing Bailey is certain to ask," I said.

My niece shook her head and tried to zip dress number two. I helped her and then sat down again to judge its merits. Brown with reddish highlights, this dress picked up her hair color and complemented it. She looked good. Too good.

"Go with the other one."

"But it makes me look like death warmed over."

"That's the idea," I said, writing RIP on the tombstone I'd unconsciously drawn.

54

Bailey showed up at noon with as much joie de vivre as a felled tree. Though she feigned pleasure at seeing me, I could tell by her petroleum smile that my insistence on staying, and filming, rankled.

"Are you all right?" I said to her.

"Let's just do this. I've got to get back as soon as I can."

Watching her suck up to Gabi, I realized we could use this interview in an even better way. Sure, the main goal would be to improve my niece's collateral in the court of public opinion. To that end, I'd made Gabi rehearse talking points until the second the reporter knocked on the door. And, yes, I wanted to observe Bailey in action, to read her motivation, to see if she was really capable of the horrible things I'd begun to suspect.

But what if Bailey wasn't involved?

We could still lay a trap. My niece's willingness to do the latter hinged on her desire to save her rep as well as Aaron's. I walked to where Gabi sat on the couch and whispered in her ear, "While you talk about Aaron's scrupulous safety habits, I want you to hint that someone else maybe set the fire, that they may have planted evidence to make him look like a terrorist."

"What?" The volume of Gabi's voice made me cringe. I didn't want to draw Bailey's attention to our tête-à-tête.

Bailey's ursine cameraman came up and removed a piece of hair from my niece's unadorned lips. Shock lent sharper angles to Gabi's cheeks, deepening the shadows they created. If only we could produce it on cue for future television use. It held just the right combination of horror and incredulity.

"You can't think that's true," she said.

Bailey regarded us both, her eyebrows raised above the compact and her nose tilted for a last caress from the powder brush.

"I believe it with all of my heart." I retreated to my former position, dislodged the video camera from its cloth cover, and trained it on the scene. Scanning through the little monitor, I fantasized about a different career, maybe one in the movie industry.

Gabi looked as if I'd clubbed a baby seal to death. "Oh my God. Who?"

"What's this about, Sasha?" Bailey held her microphone and tested it. "Three . . . two . . . one . . ."

"Nothing," I said.

"Well, let's start. If we finish in time, I might be able to get it on the early broadcast, too." She nodded to the cameraman.

Watching her work, I realized how much better it was to be out of the public's view. Everywhere in New Mexico Bailey went, someone would recognize her. Real power lay behind the scenes with the puppeteer rather than the puppet.

The reporter began with a neutral comment, one that would surely be cut in editing. "I understand you want to set the record straight about Dr. Aaron Wahl."

Gabi responded without further prompting. "Thank you." Her nervousness played well, but because she maintained eye contact, she didn't come off as shifty.

Bailey didn't speak but nodded her head so emphatically I thought it might fall off. She must've been hamming it up for the camera. Maybe her goals lay less with the news than infotainment. She could supplant Tracy Ingalls; New Mexico girl makes good.

I cleared my throat, surprised at the hostility I felt toward my friend. Bailey's head remained pointed forward, but her eyes shot anger. The cameraman shook his head. Why did she make me feel so bitchy right now? Sure, some of it was her irksome beauty, but professionally, she'd treated the story last night with amazing evenness. So what if she lied about her former boyfriend? I'd had many opportunities to remember awful relationships myself. And, if she still felt for the guy, her reaction may have had more to do with jealousy about his latest bedbug.

"Aaron was an exceptional scientist and researcher caught in a love-less marriage." Gabi twiddled with a piece of fabric. Normally I would have groused, but the lowering of her gaze created a kind of humility, hitting pitch perfect on my monitor. "The night before I was injured with the pipe bomb, he told me that he'd filed for divorce and as soon as that was finalized, he'd marry me. Our baby . . . I lost our baby because of the pipe bomb."

Oh, no. She'd abandoned our agreed-upon messages. I held my breath, praying she'd only skipped a temporary groove.

"Really?" Bailey's reaction showed the greed of a cat spying a wounded bird.

"Who knew that within two days, I'd be in the hospital and Aaron would be missing?"

Bingo. A great sound bite. Gabi was a natural.

Tears filled my niece's eyes. I knew she wasn't doing this for show, but it pulled heartstrings nonetheless. I regretted my decision to give Bailey the exclusive. This should be available to every network in the world.

"Two things upset me terribly," Gabi said, wiping her face with a tissue. "The implication that Aaron could be working with terror-ists. All of our efforts are *anti*terrorist. We've been trying to come up with the exact formula for a particular kind of explosive, one that our country needs to understand and be aware of in order to protect itself from fanatics." She took a breath and stared straight at the camera. "If someone found evidence of illegal activity, it had to be planted."

Bailey actually gasped. I loved when that happened. A bombshell dropped, a reporter stunned. It made for a great story.

Gabi inclined her head back less than an inch and went in for the next volley. "And, the idea that Aaron could accidentally blow up his lab is preposterous. The only way that could have happened is if someone else did it." Gabi's forthright stare sealed the comment with resounding credibility. "I'd stake my life on it."

I focused my camera on Bailey. She'd lost color through the makeup.

The phone rang.

The cameraman said, "Dammit."

Where the hell was her phone? I jumped up and headed for the kitchen and, in the process, banged my bad shoulder on the door frame and shouted, "Ouch!"

Wrong number. By the time I came back into the room, the cameraman had packed his equipment.

"Why did you put that away?" I said, wanting Gabi to hit the points we'd practiced.

"We've got enough. Believe me," Bailey said.

Gabi remained where she sat, her face cadaverous.

"You poor thing." Bailey put a smooth-skinned hand, her fingernails blunted at their pearly ends, on my niece's leg. "You really think it was all a setup?"

"I do." Gabi's eyes became circles of extreme sorrow. "With all my heart."

55

Gabi's bravery descended into mild catatonia in the aftermath of the interview.

I would have axed my meeting at the foundation if it had been practical, or if my presence at her house did anything to help. She needed to be alone. I left with the promise to return in a few hours and had ample time on the way to the Val Verde Hotel to question my motives in insisting on that televised encounter.

In the foundation's lobby, two leather chairs faced a functioning fireplace burning piñon wood. After a quick hello to the receptionist, I flopped into one of the seats, exhausted. The adrenaline rush of setting a trap transformed into futility and depression. I dialed the Socorro police department's general number, identified myself, and asked for Detective Sanchez.

"I tried his phone but no one answered," said the operator. "Do you want to leave a message?"

"No, I'll call later." I disconnected and looked at my watch. Oh, well. I walked down the hall to Michaela's office.

"How *are* you?" She stood up to greet me.

"All right," I lied, hoping she wouldn't mention the attack on my family the night before.

She had the courtesy not to. On the way to the conference room, we talked about what we hoped to accomplish during this last dinner.

"I'll step in if anyone gives you trouble," she said.

The two of us sat at the head of the table waiting for the others to arrive. They entered with the spring of dying Mexican jumping beans, the pathetic ones that disappoint too many children. By the time every-one arrived, it was already close to six o'clock. Perhaps I could duck out early and go to a bar to watch the news. Nah, that'd be bad for business.

Would Eva be sitting in front of a television at Mom's? How would my sister react to the segment? Gabi's affair must have rubbed Zach's peccadilloes into her sensitive wounds with super-citrus bitterness. No wonder she'd given such mixed signals to her daughter.

Oh, no. How would Mother react?

Olivia Okino stood in front of me at the buffet. She put reasonable amounts of food on her plate. I opted for more. El Sombrero Restaurant had catered the dinner with authentic Mexican food. The tender meat in the *mole* sauce, the seafood enchiladas. Ah, this was how food was supposed to taste.

While the others ate, I stood. "I know all of you want to get back home, so this won't take long. I just wanted to run some new thoughts by you and to get your feedback before finalizing my work over the weekend." I took a sip of water and said, "Okay, here goes."

It took nearly twenty minutes to summarize my ideas about the state fair approach. Each locale would need a brochure or info sheet with a strong call to action. I'd also come up with suggestions for self-sustaining funding possibilities to keep the center updated and thriving, even if Papi's money went bye-bye because of internal politics.

Some of the eyes trained on me had the glossy luster of boredom. When I opened the discussion for comment, few people offered input. Once they knew they were going to get a piece of the pie, they'd stopped worrying about the flavor.

Bonnie asked about the size of each participant's area, and if all of them would be equal.

"I honestly don't know," I said. "That will depend on what the archi-tect and foundation decide."

Sam Turin objected because, if he didn't, we might like him.

"Wow," I said to Michaela while the others gathered their coats and began to pack up their briefcases. "I must be really good."

"That's why we hired you."

"Or I could have stunned them into a stupor."

"They heard you. And it covers me when they come next week

complaining about something. I don't have to listen if they didn't bother to respond tonight. The meeting was worth it just for that. Thank you." She cut her cold enchilada into small pieces and scooped up sauce with a new bite. "We need to set up another group think before you go."

"Why?"

"So you can help with the PR side of things when we start to build, to get regional and national attention."

"I'm going to do that?"

She smiled. "You will if Papi and I have anything to do with it."

"I thought you said he was sick."

"It's not as serious as the doctors had originally thought." She ripped off a piece of corn tortilla. "I think he's more sick at heart at this point. Cecilia did him no good yesterday, but he'll see his way through it."

How would Gabi's interview affect Papi? I considered mentioning it to Michaela, but she'd already turned away from me, tapping her water glass with a spoon.

"Everybody? May I have your attention?" she said. "Let's reconvene after the holidays. How about the same time in exactly three months? Will that work?" A few heads nodded. Sam mumbled something that no one bothered to ask him to repeat.

"Okay, and one other thing. Sasha talked about those brochures. Why don't all of you give it a shot before then? Let's see what kind of ideas you come up with. I'll distribute them for comment." She put a hand on my shoulder. "I'll make sure Sasha has copies of everything so that she can help bring cohesion to the entire effort."

Thus concluded the meeting.

Michaela and I chatted until the room cleared. A little after 7:30, I excused myself. It'd take time to convince Gabi to return to Albuquerque with me, and I wasn't going to let her stay in Socorro tonight to watch that interview alone.

It was dark outside. *My kingdom for summer's long days.* Still, it was early and I didn't worry about walking to the car by myself; I'd parked close enough. Hands full—my laptop, sheets of loose-leaf paper, an overlarge purse—and my shoulder bugging me too much, I balanced against the hood and concentrated on rearranging my load. That's when I noticed the missing notebook. Dammit. I'd left it at the foundation.

Turning, a mutter under my breath, I ran into someone walking quickly in the other direction.

He didn't make room for me to pass. Instead, he grabbed me so fast I didn't have time to brace myself. He held on to my coat and forced me toward the side of the building. No one was on the street, no one to hear me scream.

"Help!" I kicked at him and yelled, then I dropped my things and raised my hand to land a fist in his face. The muffled thump brought such satisfaction, I did it again and yelled louder this time.

His features had a blurry quality. Oh. He was wearing a dark ski mask. I tried to pull it off to see who'd be doing this to me, but gave up quickly. He was too big for me to take on from the front. I had to break free from his hard grip. The important thing now was to get the hell away from him.

A familiar van huddled in the alley, its front fender bent, a headlight crushed. My assailant kneed me in the stomach and continued to drag me toward it. In a life-saving moment, all the advice I'd ever heard from policemen, from all of those public service announcements, came back in a flood. *Never let him get you in the van. Never. Fight!*

I punched and kicked with every atom in my body. My screams earned a slap across the mouth, but it just made them louder. I tried to kick him in the crotch and missed, but my hand found a chain around the man's neck. I twisted it tight, hoping to cut off his breathing, but hurt myself in the process. Okay, fine. If that's what it took. It'd be a clue if someone ever realized I was missing. With my fury and fear at their peak, just before the crest and fall of hope, I grabbed as hard as I could and the chain broke, clinking to the ground.

New footsteps cuffed on the unforgiving pavement. Michaela called, "Sasha?"

The man shoved me down and ran. I hit hard, my shoulder bellowing with the exertion of the struggle and a new injury. A door slammed and the van started. Michaela shrieked, thrusting me up against the wall of the hotel a second before the vehicle barreled past us.

"He tried to run you over." She pushed buttons on her cell phone so hard I could hear them click, shook her head, and redialed.

"I know."

"Who was it?"

"I have no idea."

Beyond us, a motorcycle revved on California Street, its bursting noise violent against raw nerves. There was a breeze on the night air, the smell of car exhaust and old garbage. I feared I might wet my pants and tried to lower myself to the ground, but Michaela held me up and talked into her phone at the same time.

After she disconnected, she shook her head several times more, her eyes wide with disbelief. "You left your notebook. I thought I could catch you."

"Thank God."

"Are you sure you're all right?"

"No, but I will be." I glanced at my watch. It was almost 8:00. "I have to go."

"You can't. The police are coming." She surveyed the alley where I'd been attacked. "What's that?" After making certain I could stand by myself, she walked into the darkness, stopped, and stooped to pick something up.

I heard a siren and knew that if I stayed to make a report, it'd take at least another hour or more. I had to get Gabi. We had to be back in Albuquerque in time for the ten o'clock news. "Listen, Michaela, I've got to go."

"What are you talking about? You need to talk to the police. They need to know what happened." She came back to me.

"Give them my cell number. Please. I'll talk to them on the road, I promise." We walked to my car, just feet from the alley's treacherous mouth.

"And I'll give them this." Michaela opened her hand. In it lay a fine gold chain.

56

Gabi's profanities skittered out of her opened door on black scorpion legs. The Furies would have been more gracious. A half-empty bottle of Dewar's sat on her desk. Her computer hummed, casting the only light in the room.

"Where the hell have you been? I've been waiting for at least two hours." She picked up the bottle and took a swig. Putting it down with a thump, she pivoted to jet out more irritation. Her aggression short-circuited with a closer look at me. "What happened to you?"

I could feel the blood cold on my cheek from where it had met the pavement. Other than that, my goal was to avoid a mirror for the next few weeks. From recent experience, I could tell the bruises and rips on my flesh would evoke embarrassed pity from strangers, as if I were an abused housewife rather than a superhero fighting crime. Maybe I ought to wear tights and a cape with a big S and I on the front: *Super Idiot.*

"Aunt Sasha?"

"I'm fine." I hustled her to the door. "Let's go. We need to move if we're going to get to Albuquerque in time to see the news."

"Who said anything about leaving?"

"Gabi, don't give me any grief," I said, on the edge of slugging her. "Whoever did this to me might be looking for you, too."

Without another word, she shut the power on her computer and closed up the house. We sped north to the freeway. Switching gears hurt, my shoulder searing at each jolt. "I should've gotten an automatic."

"Why? What's the matter?"

"I'm in pain. You know what that is, don't you?" My ability to self-censor crumbled with each molten jab.

She turned full-face on me, mouth open. I glared her into continued silence. The drone of the car's heater was noise enough. Above the straight stretch of highway, stars prickled through the darkness like abandoned bits of cosmic glitter. After checking for police, I pressed the accelerator harder. Relief washed over me when we rounded the corner near Isleta Pueblo's casino, its sign flashing names of big winners, celebrity shows, and ticket info.

It was after ten o'clock when we took the exit off University Boulevard. My cell phone rang and Gabi opened my purse to answer it. "Yes?" She handed it to me. "It's for you."

"I can't take it. My shoulder hurts too much."

"She's busy. Can she call you back?" Gabi could have been any corporate secretary. She grinned and held the phone away from her ear. A man shouted on the other end. It sounded like Detective Sanchez.

I took it, looked at the number, and turned off the power. "Oh, well. We must have gotten disconnected."

My niece laughed, an emotional rope in the midst of my turmoil and fear.

Mom's street had a discarded air to it tonight. Only the tall ponderosa pines in her yard bothered to acknowledge our arrival. In the silence, I remembered my birthday and felt sorry for myself, for the fact that my mother's unpredictable awareness meant *she* probably wouldn't remember it. The realization made me feel small, a disappointed child. I parked behind Eva's car. Gabi held my purse so that I could search for the house key. The security light blasted on and the second of Mom's nighttime caretakers opened the door.

"It's a good thing you're here. Mrs. Solomon saw the news. She's pretty upset." The young woman did a double take. "What happened to you? You need a doctor."

I waved her off. Maybe it was a perverse desire to get sympathy that prevented me from going to the bathroom to wash first. Instead, Gabi and I went to where Mom sat in the kitchen, a plate of homemade cookies on the table and a steaming cup of herbal tea in her hand. The weatherman on the news predicted blue skies and a cold front for the seven-day forecast. Eva rose to hug her daughter.

Done with that greeting, my sister turned to me. "Happy birt—" Eva stood. "Oh, Sasha! What happened?"

"Hi," I said, planting a kiss on her cheek and heading over to Mom to do the same.

Gabi tried to follow, her lips ready to kiss, but Mom jerked away from the loving gesture. At times like these, I wished my mother's short-term memory loss was a little more effective. It would have been nice if she instantaneously forgot what she'd just seen. But the pips of resentment found fertile soil in her brain far easier than any kind of happy seeds.

"You didn't bother to tell me?" Mom remained seated.

Paul came in singing, "Happy birthday to you." He carried a cake with at least one hundred candles bright and merry. But the joy lasted only a moment. His open distress, the rush to look at my face with his mouth open and his hands at his cheeks, upset me more than Mom's words. "What happened to you, Sashala?"

"It's nothing."

"It has rocks in it." He put the cake on the table and went to the counter. Still staring at me, he tore off a handful of paper towels hanging beside the sink and wetted them with warm water. "At least clean it out a little before it scars over."

"I'm all right." I blew out a few of the flames.

With visions of African women, their intentionally scored skin symbols of beauty, I held the towel against my face and felt the bumps of pebbles. It wasn't vanity, or the shock of bringing some of the Socorro alley back with me, that wrestled with my composure; it was his concern.

"Such goings-on. Tonight . . . what I saw." Mom glowered at Gabi. "I had to learn that you were pregnant on television? That you were breaking up a marriage to be with a terrorist? What has this family come to?" She'd acquired an accent from the shtetl, a mirror of my sister's, and it sounded silly in her irreligious home.

"I'm sorry," I said, dabbing my cut. My contrition cowered in a tiny corner, the only space left by my potent self-pity. "I've been a little busy."

"He *isn't* a terrorist," said Gabi. "That was the reason I did the interview in the first place, if you'd bothered to listen."

Marvelous, Gabi. That's just the tone to entice your grandmother to shell out thousands of dollars for the rest of your education.

"Hannah, I thought the point tonight was to tell what a good man this Aaron Wahl is," said Paul, always calming Mom, always making sure she heard the truth. "Come on. Let's celebrate Sasha's birthday."

"You couldn't have let me know? You didn't trust me enough to tell?" Mom's insistence on carrying resentments to their crescendos caused her to miss the everyday joys that sustain most of us. I suspected that much anger helped her strokes along too.

Eva stared ahead, probably reviewing all the reasons she spent most of her life as far from Albuquerque as she could. A picture of a football game flashed on the television screen indicating the sports section of the news. The program would be over in a few minutes. Gabi helped herself to a cookie, unaware that each bite dropped crumbs onto the floor. A typical American family on a weekday night. Meanwhile, the candles burned down so that wax now began to mess up the cake. I didn't want it anyway.

Then Paul put his hand on top of Mom's and stroked it with pure, giving love. The beauty of that gesture made me grab the back of one of the chairs to keep myself upright.

"Mom, I'm sorry," I said. "You shouldn't have learned about it this way. It was my fault and nobody else's." Relieved by the apology, I went to a cabinet and brought out mugs for the rest of us. Without asking, I filled a pot with already warm water and turned on the stove. "If you want to be mad, be mad at me."

Bubbles of irritation tried to displace my good intentions. How dare Mom feel entitled to any of our secrets? She'd never been a person in whom Eva or I could have confided. In childhood, if we brought her something that disturbed us, she'd always take the other person's side. Why should Gabi trust her open heart with such an undependable receptacle?

"Family is worry. Where's Zachariah?" Mom reached for a cookie and put it on a napkin, oblivious of the arrow she'd shot at Eva. "You're not the only ones with secrets."

She was baiting us or had skipped a track. Either way, none of us had the energy to comment. I poured the boiling water into a ceramic teapot and put in two bags of decaf green, the kind with roasted rice. Everyone watched me, so I blew out the rest of the candles. No one clapped. A headache pressed up from the top of my spine, spreading with the curling fluidity of food coloring in water.

"I'll be right back," I said.

In the grand entryway, the large silk oriental rugs no longer moved under my feet; they were tacked to the floor so that Mom wouldn't trip. In my old bathroom, I flicked on the light. The mirrors, no longer covered in Gabi's steam, lined the wall behind the double sinks from counter to ceiling. A three-quarter-inch flap of skin folded over a line of pebbles. I removed them gingerly with a Q-tip. Using a washcloth, I tried to get at other chunks of dirt and small rocks on my legs through the tears in my pants. This wasn't going to work. Some of the debris was in too deep for my squeamish hands to remove. "Damn, damn, damn."

Raised voices carried from the kitchen all the way to my private fears of infection and permanent disfigurement. Vanity couldn't be denied its due, given the length of the cut. Going into the hallway, I got my cell phone, turned it on, and dialed Peter's number.

"Where've you been? I've been trying to reach you forever," he said by way of a hello.

"Don't make me apologize. Please. I can't do any more of this. Just meet me at my house when you get off work? I'll tell you the whole story, no commercials or breaks."

"A midnight rendezvous? It sounds kinky." The promise of love-making, tonight, almost tempted me to recant my plea. "Should I bring some sparkling cider?"

"Actually, could you bring a first-aid kit?" I said.

"Why?" The heat on the other end of the line plummeted fifty degrees.

"I have a couple of little cuts here and there."

"I'll bring it."

More than thirty messages showed on my phone's minute screen. They could wait. None would be good. In the hallway, I sat on one of the Chinese k'angs, a kind of daybed made out of rosewood, and listened. Whatever was going on in the kitchen hadn't settled and I had no desire to be part of it. Instead, I went in the opposite direction to Mom's bedroom in search of a non-narcotic painkiller in her medicine cabinet.

Two pairs of wet men's socks hung on a towel over the second shower in her bathroom. Yes, that's right. Mom's restroom could house a family of six. Curious now, I peeked into the walk-in closet. In place of some of Mom's clothes, Paul's suit jackets and shirts, his silk slacks and sweatpants, hung in tidy, well-organized groups. The two of them were shacking up. I grinned in spite of everything. Paul, a Jewish man almost as observant as my sister, living in sin? I smiled more broadly. Finally some good news in this family.

With a lighter step now, I walked back to the kitchen to bid everyone adios.

"Sasha, where's a good hotel near here?" said Eva.

"You don't have to go," said Mom.

"I do and I will."

"No," I said, seeing the trap and refusing to be put in the middle of it.

"Good. Then that's settled," said Paul.

"Okay. I'll stay at your house." Eva inched her way to the edge of the kitchen, to stand next to me.

"No again. I've got other plans." I reached for the mug someone else had poured for me and sipped the lukewarm tea.

"Aunt Sasha, we need to go somewhere else. Grandma has made it clear she doesn't want us here." Gabi's pout hit my nerves with the spikes of a barrelful of mature thistles.

"Oh, pish," I said, surprising myself with the word. "She just said you didn't need to leave. Paul wants you to stay, too."

"She won't stop denigrating Gabi," said Eva.

"She won't stop insulting Aaron."

"Why don't you just can it?" Suddenly, I'd had it. A tsunami of exhaustion ripped my composure. "All I've done for the past few days is worry about you and your damn problems."

"You weren't thinking one minute about me," said Mom.

"The hell I wasn't. I was trying to figure out a way to talk with you about all of this without you going off the deep end. I was trying to make sure no one would interview you and put you in an awkward position. I was taking care of Gabi, comforting Eva, dealing with Davielle, and on and on and on." I put down the mug so hard the handle broke off. Liquid sloshed onto the table. "Well, I deserve one night for me and I'm taking it. Eva, suck it up. Gabi, I don't want to hear another word about Aaron the Saint. He's having an affair with you, for heaven's sake. He's destroyed lives with his monumental ego. He isn't perfect, no matter what you think." I looked at Paul. "You're the only one who hasn't asked me for a thing and I thank you for that from the bottom of my heart." I blew him a kiss, shook my head, and blew kisses at them all. "Go on. Knock yourselves out. I'll be here tomorrow morning around ten. I hope to God you've all grown up by then."

57

Some birthday.

The heat-seeking missile, targeted at my family with such vehemence, had felt good in the moment. Too bad the liberation loosed grains of regret by the time I'd hit the grocery store's parking lot for a new can of whipped cream and a bunch of other birthday supplies.

At the cash register I realized the emotional truce I'd negotiated with Mom, one of which she wasn't aware, depended on my composed behavior. Lashing out at everyone, when all of them craved assurance, hadn't been a *brilliant* move. Poor Paul. He'd be the mediator. It was bound to be a bad night.

Not for me. Freed from their needs for a few hours, my spirits shed their remorse and proceeded to Mount Olympus. Peter's upcoming visit buoyed my mood as well. I'd get my celebration after all. The only thing really wrong with my world at that moment centered on pain. My shoulder screamed, the scrape on my face throbbed, and the holes in my pants air-conditioned the sensitive cuts on my shins.

"You stayed there all day and sulked?" I said to Leo, peering down at me from the roof. His tail swished haughtily, but he had a change of heart once the key had gone into the lock. In an instant, he reprised his mercenary meowing, weaving routine. Déjà vu all over again. Only this time, I didn't mind.

I turned on the porch light for Peter and upped the thermostat. Crude oil and natural gas prices couldn't keep me from indulgence. Wanton consumption's allure wrapped me in its sensual embrace. In the hallway, the answering machine's rapid blinking threatened to send it into convulsions. It was the old variety with aging microcassettes. Lately, anyone who left a message sounded like Marlon Brando in *The Godfather*, all gravel and no diction. This amused me and served as a disincentive to update the equipment. I opened the can of whipped cream and took a hit.

Watching the blinking light for a minute more, I said, "Go to hell."

In response to my challenge, the universe answered with a ringing phone. My message began its spin on the tape heads and I turned up the volume.

The caller spoke. "Ms. Solomon, this is Detective Sanchez."

I might as well get this over with. I called him back on my cell. "Hello?"

"You were right."

"Of course I was. About what?"

"The people who vandalized your niece's home."

"Marcel?"

"He was one of them. Along with Heather."

"Which time?"

"Both."

I suppose I should have been happier, but knowing that people Gabi trusted had done this to her made me incredibly sad. "Well, thank you."

"That's it?"

"Okay. Why did they do it?" Getting into flannel pajamas took work, especially one-handed. Maybe Peter could put my shoulder in a sling. Maybe I didn't want him to know more than he needed to about my broken body. If we made love tonight, I'd be sure to turn off the lights. Who knows? He might misinterpret my screams for the better.

"We don't know yet."

"Well, like I said, thank you."

"You don't sound like you want to talk," said the detective. Tonight, he wanted to chat? "I saw your niece's interview on the news. Whose idea was it to imply that someone set up Dr. Wahl? Frankly, I'd put conspiracy theories in your ballpark rather than hers."

"We exchanged ideas. Gabi's certain he'd never be careless enough to accidentally start a fire near explosives. That, and what I've heard from other people who know him, convinced me she was right. The conclusion was self-evident." I went into the kitchen and unpacked the baguette, bars of dark chocolate, sweet butter, and Australian Shiraz. Tonight, Peter and I could pretend we were in France. "How's the kidnapping coming?"

"No one said anything about kidnapping."

"I did, Detective."

"You jump to too many conclusions."

"You just said I was right about Marcel and Heather, didn't you?" I put the bag of flour tortillas on the table and eyed it, hungry. Leo inspected the new container of raisins and urged me to open it. I put a few in my pocket for later; we'd show Peter Leo's trick. Turning on the gas stove, I placed a tortilla directly on the burner to toast over the flame. "What about the lovely CiCi? Was she involved?"

"We don't know yet. I thought you'd be pleased with what I *do* have."

I bit open a bag of mini–chocolate chips and spread them on the warm tortilla and then put the entire thing in the microwave. "She's involved, Detective."

"You have proof?"

"The 'Arab whore' at her press conference did it for me."

"Interesting. Hold on," he said, his distraction evident. "We can discuss this the next time you come down to Socorro."

Dismissed. How tidy. All the vandalism committed by two people and solved in a matter of days. But what about the big crimes, the ones that could've killed Gabi twice? Or *me* twice?

With the snack in one hand and the whipped cream can clutched to my chest, I lay down on the couch and forced those questions out of my mind. It was time to reclaim my home, to wrestle back my life from family concerns. What mattered now was that the chocolate was sweet and Peter was on his way.

The doorbell rang and I stuffed the last of the tortilla into my mouth. He'd made good time. Opening it with a bow, I was surprised to see a stranger standing before me. For a moment, before he pushed his way in, I noticed something wrong with his shoe-polish black hair and magic-marker eyebrows. They matched his clothing too perfectly.

"I need to speak to Gabi." He balanced on the arms of the couch. "Sit."

His command brought me down into the chair across from him before I realized I'd complied. God willing, Peter would show up soon. At least that way it would be two against one. "I don't know where she is."

"I think you do."

God, he was handsome, but as I watched him, he aged. The wrinkles around his brown eyes and aristocratic mouth belonged to an older man. Even so, if he attacked me, there was no way I could win with this lousy shoulder.

Then it hit me. The color of his eyes was wrong, his hair completely off, but this had to be him. "Professor Wahl?" I squinted to get a better look.

"Stay."

Motionless, I stared at him, remembering the other times our eyes had met—at the hospital; outside the foundation when he'd sat in that van; at the edge of the plaza in the wake of CiCi's thermal blast. Where else had he followed me? Us? "It's you, isn't it?"

"Where's Gabi?"

"Wouldn't you like to know?" I didn't need to be afraid of him, not really. A well-placed knee to the groin and he'd be out of commission. Plus, I'd be doing all womankind a favor. "You prick. How could you let her deal with this alone?"

"Where is she?"

"You think I'm going to tell you anything?" If I dialed 911 and left the phone off the hook, the cavalry would come, sirens blaring into my neighborhood for the umpteenth time.

"Sit down."

"Why should I?" I stood.

He was up with the speed of a fighter jet, shoving me down, his strong hand digging into the bad shoulder. I bit back the yelp of agony. Showing weakness could only make him feel more dominant. Was it possible to run into the kitchen and grab a butcher knife? No. His gun's metallic shades of black forbade that option.

He used it to point to the chair. "Now, sit down."

"What's wrong with you anyway?"

"Where is she?"

"Go ahead and shoot me, then you'll never know." Could I be more stupid? I might as well take his gun and suck on it myself. Holy crap.

Didn't I have any sense at all? Where was Peter? I stared at the door, then at my captor. Screw my shoulder. There had to be a way to overpower this egomaniac.

"Gabi. Tell me where she is." He sat down and tilted the weapon in my direction. "I don't want to hurt you, but believe me, I will if I need to." To emphasize his point, he shot at the wall above my head.

We both jumped. His eyes widened broader than mine. His forehead glistened with the sweat of surprise. Obviously, the man wasn't used to firearms. That made me smile since he knew so much about explosives.

"You can't hurt me," I said with momentary confidence. Maybe he could be bullied into abandoning it.

"You know I can." His response carried enough true threat to nix the next snotty retort coiling on my lips.

I looked down at my feet.

"Do you know how it feels to be shot? Bit by bit? A bullet to each of your knees, a foot, your shoulder?"

"No," I whispered.

Leo slinked into the room, a furry caterpillar. I'd forgotten to give him dinner. Only his gluttony could move him to be anywhere near this scene. Still, he must've sensed the tension, something wrong, because he stayed close to the wall, legs bent, stomach low to the ground. He leapt onto the couch. Wahl hadn't expected the motion and jerked, squeezing the trigger by mistake and shooting a bullet into my floor.

"Jesus! What are you doing?" I'd moved off the chair, an automatic response, trying to protect my cat.

"Sit down!" Wahl took aim at me until I did as commanded. "Damn cat." He pointed the gun at Leo who, amazingly, had scrambled to the top of the armoire.

"Don't!"

"Shut up." He stood up and looked at Leo, his profile to me, the gun still trained on my best friend. "Where's your niece?"

"If you cared, you would have come forward. You wouldn't have made her suffer like this." I took off my slippers and pressed my feet against the brick floor. "Did you know she lost your baby? Huh? Did you know that?"

"Shut up!"

"She's been suffering night and day for you. For what? You're a worm." This was yet another example of why I'd never make it as a professional investigator. At this rate, I wouldn't live long enough to download the licensing information from the state Web site.

Gravel crunched under the weight of Peter's car in the driveway.

The professor turned around. "Who's that?"

I didn't want to answer.

"Tell me or I'll shoot your damn cat!"

What could he want with Gabi now? To sweep her away? To kill her? Every possibility slalomed through my mind, leaving a trail of unpleasant questions. I couldn't understand this man and would never want to. "That's my boyfriend. He knows I'm home."

Wahl shook his head. "Could this get any worse?"

"Why don't you put the gun down? We can talk. Maybe I can help you." Maybe flattery would work, if I could find anything nice to say.

"Shut up." Wahl eyed the door. "Let me think."

He didn't seem particularly *brilliant* to me. But I'd been doing some thinking of my own.

58

Peter slammed his car door shut and knocked. The optimism in its playfulness made me sick to my stomach. "Sasha? Come on, I'm cold."

Wahl motioned with his gun for me to answer the door. "Don't do anything stupid."

Hey, I was *all about* stupid.

"Hold on a minute, Peter." My hand on the lock, I twisted the key, stalling as if it were giving me trouble. At the same time, I made a kissing sound, the kind that caught a cat's attention, that hinted at tuna, smoked oysters . . . or raisins.

As if he had wings, Leo launched himself off the wardrobe toward me. Peter, wonderful, impatient Peter, pushed the door open and, confused, noticed the gun. Leo, his legs flailing as he realized he couldn't reach me, propelled himself toward the nearest logical runway and landed, with all his claws extended, on Aaron Wahl. The professor batted at the cat. Leo yowled and hung on for dear life. God bless him.

The gun went off again, this time busting my living room window. I threw myself onto Wahl and thrust my right elbow into his chest. His head hit the corner of my coffee table when we both went down. Leo let go and ran out of the room. I saw Wahl clench the gun's trigger.

"Watch out!" I yelled to Peter, who ducked. A bullet whizzed into the painting above my desk. "Shit!" I bounced all my weight on the man and heard him exhale roughly. He tried to buck me off, but I held on to the table and, in extreme pain, the bottom of my futon couch. We weren't going anywhere.

From my place on the floor, I couldn't see Peter or Leo. Wahl continued to struggle against me. I picked up the leg of the coffee table and slammed it into his wrist, the one with the hand holding the gun. The weapon went off again, a bullet thumping on the other side of the room.

"Would you stop that?" I bounced on him for emphasis and then slammed the leg on his wrist once more. "Drop the gun and I'll get off of you."

Wahl stopped moving. I didn't trust the lull, but in the quiet of the moment, I heard Peter outside my front window, giving my address to someone. The professor reared with all of his might, knocking me onto my back and sending shooting pains from my shoulder to the depths of hell.

I screamed in agony. From out of nowhere, Leo ran in front of my tormentor, tripping him on his way out the door. I heard a thud, a moan, and the glorious sound of a siren cutting through the sleepy night.

Hours later, Leo got my last can of smoked oysters. Watching him eat took my mind off the antiseptic Peter applied to the scrape on my face and a hitherto unexplored one on my scalp. He cleaned my legs, too, while harping on and on about my shoulder. "If you've torn your rotator cuff, you'll need surgery. Let me take you to the hospital."

"Not on my birthday," I whimpered. "If the pain gets worse, we can go."

We cuddled in my bed all night until Peter got up to go to work. I joined him in the front room, my arm around his waist. In the dark early morning, we said good-bye. Cold seeped through the window. Careful not to step on any shards, I went to the kitchen and retrieved a large bar of dark chocolate and took it back to bed with me.

Friday morning, weary and sad, I dressed in the oldest, fuzziest clothes in my closet before picking up Gabi to take her back to Socorro. A different caretaker answered Mom's door with a dishtowel and a smile. My family watched television around the dining room table. Apparently, the early morning news had been full of Aaron Wahl and me. Eva's hug brought so many lashes of pain that Paul and Gabi didn't even try to embrace me. Mom clucked but said little. Gabi resembled roadkill.

In the car, I said, "What are you going to do now?"

"I need to see him."

"I'm not sure they'll let you, Gabi." Tears plopped into her lap. "Are you sure you want to go home? I can turn around."

Beethoven's "Ode to Joy" chimed from her cell phone. How inappropriate. She answered it in a tremulous voice, then shifted away from me, the tears flowing more freely now. Was it Heather? Did I have the heart to tell her about her friend's betrayal?

My thoughts found a cesspool of shame. Could I ever face Bailey again? The things I'd thought she was capable of, my horrendous and unmerited suspicions, embarrassed me. What about Mark Padilla from the bomb squad? I'd actually thought he'd planted evidence at a scene to avenge his brother. I even considered the possibility that he'd rigged the pipe bomb in Gabi's mailbox. How had I become so indiscriminately mistrustful?

We were all the way to San Acacia, a bucolic meadow area about fifteen miles outside of Socorro, before Gabi spoke again. "Aunt Sasha, I haven't been honest with you."

This felt soul-important, a truth coming that in its utterance would change everything.

"Aaron never wanted the baby. That's what we fought about. He wanted me to have an abortion. I told him I couldn't, that it would be murder." She rubbed her forehead and eyes. "You might find it hard to believe, because I've given up so many of my parents' rules. But not that."

My mind roiled with hot notions, half-formed ideas, too many to consider the full implications of Gabi's newest revelation. I'd need space to think that through. "Who were you talking to just now?"

"Detective Sanchez." She wiped away tears and put her phone in her pack. "He's pretty sure Aaron set the pipe bomb as a message, to scare me. He wants to talk when I get to Socorro."

"Do you want me to be there?"

"No." She turned to face me. "Like you said, it's time I grew up."

We arrived in Socorro without fanfare. No one noticed. No one seemed to care. All the television crews were gone now, chasing new stories and angles. I dropped Gabi off at home and decided to get a cup of good coffee, and maybe some gelato, for the road. Past the plaza, I glanced at a person framed by a large window in the Manzanares Street Coffeehouse. Blonde. Pretty. Desolate.

The parking lot had few cars and the clean, dark blue Beemer confirmed my sighting. I had to make things right or our friendship would become uncomfortable purely because of me. It'd fade like so many others I'd let slough over the years.

"Bailey?" I said, watching her write on a yellow legal pad, an empty demitasse of espresso with a lemon twist on her right.

"Sasha. My God. I didn't expect to see you here."

I pulled out the seat across from her and said, "It must be kismet, because I've got an awful confession to make. I've been such an idiot. I'm so, so sorry."

Bailey listened to all of it, her face blanching, her hands holding the pad on both sides. "Why didn't you just ask me?"

"You seemed so hungry and so evasive. Every time I asked you about Mark Padilla, you came up with some excuse not to connect us. I know I was being ridiculous, but that's what paranoia did to me. Anything seemed plausible, even doubting you." I couldn't meet her eyes; humiliation shrank me into a wad of insecurity.

"Well, I'll let you in on a little secret. When I found out about your niece's affair, and Mark's with CiCi, I went into my own tailspin. Mark should've taken himself off the case the minute he found out about the Wahl connection." She let go of the pad and reached over to lift my lowered chin. "You see, I knew about his brother and how Dr. Wahl destroyed him. That'd be a plenty good reason for revenge. I thought he might have been planting evidence too."

Three people came into the café, stomped their feet against the cold, and laughed loudly. Dressed in cloth coats and shod in leather, they could have been professors at New Mexico Tech. I sighed.

"I can see how you might've gotten the wrong impression," said Bailey. "I'd started to investigate Mark on the sly and didn't want anyone tipping him off. If you'd talked to him, you might've mentioned my name and he might've figured out what I was up to." She waved at someone across the room. "You don't have a corner on mistrust, Sasha."

Our conversation wandered in other directions. We grasped at its normalcy, using mundane comments as affirmations that our friendship would survive. Rather than hug, we shook hands good-bye with a date for drinks already in both of our calendars.

I didn't have the heart to drive back to Albuquerque. Instead, I got a room at the Holiday Inn Express again. Twenty-four hours. That's what I wanted, what I needed to regroup. Out of habit, I'd put the laptop in the trunk this morning, so I could even work on the San-Socorro job if I wanted.

Before considering any kind of work, I stripped and took a long, hot bath, trying to suds away my melancholy. Too many lives had been hurt by Aaron Wahl. I hoped he'd rot in prison for his selfishness, his astounding arrogance.

Gabi's admission about the baby cinched another piece into position in this convoluted puzzle. The pattern's main components relinquished their blurriness. Something had kept Aaron Wahl in Socorro through the circus of Gabi's injuries and his purported disappearance. It hadn't been love. He wouldn't have let her suffer so if he'd felt any shred of kindness toward her.

No, he'd been planning his disappearance and the fight with Gabi provided the opportunity to stage it. Had he intentionally set her up? I thought so. Maybe the theory about his working with terrorists was right. I hoped someone would unravel that part and let us all know, especially Gabi, poor innocent and deluded Gabi.

What on earth had Wahl been thinking to take such chances, to disguise himself and watch the drama play out? It had to be ego. He believed what everyone else said about his brilliance. He thought he could trick us all. What a rush it must have been for him to disappear in the very place where everyone knew him, where they searched for him.

Gabi's interview, her mention of arson and planted evidence, must've hit too close to home and made him careless.

Alas, the hotel didn't have room service. After the bath, I wrapped a towel around myself and worked for several hours. When lunchtime rolled around, I dressed and ate at the El Camino. A few locals there recognized me, their conversations halting midsentence to gawk. Others didn't. No one spoke to me, though. I felt more like a pariah than a hero.

By late afternoon, the completed proposal lacked only a final proofread. I'd do that later this weekend. I started a pot of coffee, its familiar smell comforting, but not enough. With time to think, a sad loneliness stung my eyes. My call to the San-Socorro Foundation stemmed purely from the desire to hear a friendly, but not too close, voice.

"I was so worried," said Michaela. "I must've called you twenty times."

"I'm sorry." Another apology. Could there ever be enough to make me feel better?

After our conversation, I decided to listen to all the messages on the cell phone. Apparently, Michaela hadn't exaggerated. Bailey wanted to talk with me as soon as possible. Detective Sanchez requested the same thing. Peter had called twice. The person from Carlsbad wanted to remind me of his earlier call to talk about a possible job. Carlsbad? A city at the bottom of the state. The drive might be nice. . . . Darnda. Darnda again. A whole passel of people cared about whether I lived or died.

I cried for a while after that.

"Ms. Solomon?" The male voice and knocks on the door jerked me into an alert tension. No one knew I was here. No one but Michaela and Bailey. I peeked through the peephole.

"Detective," I said. "How did you find me?"

"I asked around."

"Ah." I stepped out of the way and he walked through.

"How are you?" He took off his coat and folded it over his arm.

"How do you think?" I sat down on the bed and picked up the Styrofoam coffee cup.

He nodded his head in acknowledgment and went to the desk chair. "You must have a million questions. Here's what I know." He leaned forward, elbows on his knees. "A few days before the bombing, your niece told Heather about the pregnancy. Heather told her boyfriend Marcel, and he told his cousin CiCi. She acted devastated. I say 'acted' because this was just the thing she'd been waiting for to finally divorce him. It'd be about the only reason Papi could understand."

"Oh. So she wasn't involved?"

The policeman held up his hand. "Let me get through this. It seems that Marcel has a bit of a crush on his cousin. He thought he'd earn points with her by hurting your niece, and, in the process, he'd hurt Dr. Wahl too. Or some such nonsense."

"So he vandalized Gabi's house? That seems pretty tame in retrospect." I could have easily come up with dozens of ways to cause more damage, more pain. Good thing vengeance took so much energy.

"I didn't say any of this made sense. They're just kids, Ms. Solomon. They didn't think anything through, not really."

"What about the door? Why paint that on there?"

"Heather heard your niece complain about subtle forms of racism ever since 9/11 and decided to use that to throw us off track."

"I guess I was the only one it did."

"You're not a policeman." He shrugged. "Remember the other night when you were talking about hunches, intuition? None of this felt like a hate crime to me. It felt more like smoke, a distraction. I can't tell you why."

"What about the computer? Did Marcel take it?"

"I don't think so."

"Aaron again? Why?"

The detective sighed. "Maybe he needed her notes, especially if he'd destroyed his own in the fire. I don't know. This is all conjecture."

"So, Aaron faked his kidnapping?"

Sanchez nodded. "He knows a little Farsi. That's when we started to suspect him, though. Like your sister said, any expert could see the note wasn't written by a native speaker."

"And it was Aaron Wahl who tried to kill us? To run us over?"

"It looks that way." Sanchez scratched his wrist. "We're still trying to figure it all out, and no one is being very cooperative at this point."

A car alarm went off outside and the detective tensed, listening. When silence blessed us once more, he refocused on his current task. "What was I saying?"

"You were going to tell me about the professor. Was he trying to kill Gabi or just set her up? Was he working with terrorists?"

"No. I wasn't going to talk about that. I can't." He stood, put on his coat, and buttoned it. His hands seemed older today, hinting of arthritis. "But I've got a feeling he won't get sympathy from any quarter. He's certainly lost all of mine."

I went to the door. "I don't understand why Aaron didn't just . . . I hate to say this, but, why didn't he just kill Gabi with the pipe bomb in the first place? He knew how."

"Maybe he loved her a little bit after all."

59

Between the fountain-floods of my unmanageable emotions, good things happened. Josie, my landlady, called. The window had been repaired and she promised someone would come on Monday to fix up the holes in my floor and walls. She'd also taken it upon herself to buy Leo a case of premium cat food, a reward for his valor. Her generosity and spunky conversation spurred me to take more action, to seek companionship, to affirm life. I wasn't up to having a heart-to-heart with Mom or Eva, but immersing my soul in friend-ship held tremendous appeal.

Even though I'd paid for the night, I checked out of the hotel a few hours after Sanchez left. The bright orange-pink sunset hurt my eyes. They'd shed too many confused tears.

Darnda cheered the dinner invitation with brazen glee. Peter promised to come over for the night. Even if my shoulder precluded physical activity, I suspected we could come up with something to while away the hours.

Once in Albuquerque, I headed straight for the Japanese Kitchen for sushi with my best *human* friend. Darnda had already claimed a booth. She looked beautiful to me, her hair tied back with a scarf, her bust escaping the confines of a too-tight bra and the too-low V-neck of her purple wool sweater.

"How can that possibly keep you warm?" I said, gliding into the seat across from her.

"It doesn't. But this does." She poured sake into a small cup and handed it to me. "How are you?"

"I thought you didn't drink."

"You do, sweetie."

With the first sip, the rice wine soothed me. "I can't have too much of this. I've got to drive."

"If you get drunk, I'll take you home. Now, enjoy." She pulled apart her bamboo chopsticks. "You haven't answered my question."

"Darnda, I can't talk about it yet. But I want to be with you. I need to be with you. Is that okay?"

"Just don't let it fester," she said.

"I won't." I drank some ice water to slow my urge to chug the sake. "Do you remember when I asked you about that ghost?"

She nodded.

"I have a theory that it was Aaron Wahl's conscience, his good side. That's why it was all green and confused. I think that whatever he was doing, he had to completely close off every good bit of himself to do it." I leaned back. "But even that wasn't pure enough to be white light."

"You might be right." Darnda shrugged and picked up a miniature pencil to mark the sushi order pad with our choices. "I can't say for sure because I wasn't there, but it sounds possible to me. And your intuition, when you care to listen to it, is usually a good guide."

"Yeah, well, I'm not so sure about that." I abandoned my moderation and drank the rest of the wine before it got cold.

We selected enough food to feed a Japanese baseball team and ate it all anyway. I didn't bother with more sake; Peter could medicate me tonight with his lovin'. After dinner, we walked to the car and Darnda planted a kiss on my cheek.

"I was pretty worried there, Sasha. Don't do that to me again," she said.

I put my hand over my heart. "I'll try my best."

Darnda's last appeal had an unforeseen effect. It activated my *yetzer tov*, my good inclination. With her love enveloping me in an invincible shield of gold strength, I decided to face family and try to smooth over the wreckage of my outburst. The traffic to Mom's house was lighter than I wanted it to be.

Yet again, everyone sat watching television. This time, they'd moved to the den. Eva and Paul had a Scrabble board out, their game well under way. Mom had been playing solitaire before she got up to give me a hug, my explosion already forgotten. I winced but didn't let pain spoil the moment. The others pretended nothing had happened. Still, I apologized, and for the first time in a long while, the action felt good.

A few hours later, Leo didn't greet me in the driveway and I felt a moment's panic until I opened the door and found him sacked out on the couch, a half-eaten bowl of raisins on the table. Josie must've decided to remunerate him further.

"Oh my God," I said, imagining what that much dried fruit could do to his itty bitty kitty intestines. I'd be cleaning after him for a month.

He opened an eye, found my face, and closed it again.

I ran to his box and changed out the litter. Then, because I expected the worst, I found another large box, lined it with a plastic garbage bag, and filled that with litter, too. In the middle of these efforts, Peter arrived. Before I had a chance to offer him a drink, he'd undone five of the buttons on my shirt. In spite of the subsequent workout, I forgot the pain in my shoulder. But when the phone rang before sunrise, I bolted upright and screamed with a new slice of misery, the horrid premonition of another family emergency a breath away.

"Go back to sleep," said Peter. He broke our spooned embrace and tiptoed out of the room. I heard his low voice asking questions and the silence of him listening to the responses. With Peter's place open, Leo leapt onto the bed and nuzzled me until I lifted the covers so he could curl up next to my chest.

"I have to go," Peter said. "We're shorthanded at work."

Without turning on the light, he gathered his clothes and tiptoed from the room. A few minutes later, I heard the front door close. Alone, I stroked Leo and massaged my nose into the back of his furry head. His loud, languid purr brought an unadulterated sense of peace, well-being.

"Oh, Leo, I'm so glad you're in my life," I mumbled, skating on the outer edges of sleep once more.

"Yeah," he said. "Me, too."

Acknowledgments

Several people, a dog, and a cat lent me their names for this book; all exhibited great courage. My gratitude to each one.

Thanks to the *anonymice* for their prods and to readers who sent frequent nudges to remind me that an audience awaited this new work. A special nod goes to B. G. Ritts for her generous enthusiasm and efforts on my behalf.

Call me paranoid, but some of the research topics for this project made me nervous. Luckily, many wise experts came to my aid. Richard Saul, bomb technician for the Albuquerque Police Department; Dr. Cathy Aimone-Martin from New Mexico Tech University; and Drs. Courtney and Meghan Vallejo helped me understand far more than I would have from books or Web sites. Dick Knipfing, news anchor extraordinaire from KRQE-13, also graciously endured frequent questions. Any mistakes I've made regarding chemistry, explosives, bomb squads, or an ambitious television reporter's goals are entirely my own.

I wrote this book twice. Thank you to Joshua for having the patience to wait out my confusion. Thanks to the marvelous people at the University of New Mexico Press for continuing to have faith in Sasha and her ability to present a unique picture of our state.

As always, friends and family listened to my whining and celebrated my victories with equal dedication. I could not have written this book without their love, compassion, and astounding senses of humor.

Peter, Hope, and Lily—you remind me daily that my life is truly blessed.

Discussion Questions

1) What are your first impressions of Sasha? Does she seem strong-willed or flexible; content with her life or searching for more; involved with current affairs or unconcerned; tolerant or not?

2) Sasha embarks upon a PR project to boost Socorro County tourism. Why does she think that public awareness is so important to nonprofit organizations like the one she's working for?

3) We see the conflicting personalities in Sasha's family. How does being around her mother, sister, and nieces make Sasha feel about herself?

4) How is sister Eva "more Jewish" than Sasha? Are there places where their beliefs intersect? Do the lifestyle rules found in more conservative Judaism and other religions restrict people, as Sasha believes, or provide freedom, as Eva asserts?

5) In Chapter 28, does Eva's eloquence about her faith surprise you with its seemingly contradictory beliefs?

6) Is the conflict between Sasha and Eva because of religious beliefs or their distinctive personalities?

7) Do you believe, like Eva, that human beings have both *yetzer hara* (evil tendencies) and *yetzer tov* (the inclination for doing good)?

8) Is Eva justified in questioning whether Gabi's Jewish heritage played a role in the bombing? Do you think law enforcement considers religious or cultural background in violent crimes?

9) Gabi is Jewish, with an Iranian father, yet she is pegged as an "Arab." Do you think it's common for people to stereotype others? Do people confuse nationality, religious practices, and cultural heritage?

10) Why is Detective Sanchez hesitant to share information or his opinions with Sasha?

11) Why is journalist Bailey Hayes so eager to break the story of Gabi and the pipe bomb? How does Sasha use the media to achieve her own goals?

12) Does public opinion shape media coverage or does media coverage shape public opinion? Do you think the media is growing more or less sensationalist?

13) What is the role of "spin" in this case, and in the news in general?

14) How do Sasha's public relations skills shape her investigation?

15) Do Sasha's personality quirks help or hinder her investigation?

16) What defines a hate crime?